The Goodguys, The Beginning

Thomas Woods

Published by Thomas Woods, 2025.

THE GOODGUYS, THE BEGINNING

First edition. April 28, 2025.

Copyright © 2025 Thomas Woods.

ISBN: 979-8218659936

Written by Thomas Woods.

THE GOODGUYS
the beginning

CHAPTER ONE

"Have you lost all love for our Empress?!" Azarelia said, trying to keep ahead of me as we walked. Her white silk dress flowed across the marble floor while tears streaked down her light brown face. "Have you lost all respect for the Land of Effulgence?!"

Symbols of ethereal flashed across my mind. The massive double ironwood doors slowly swung open. My twelve Red Immortals, all dressed in red robes with hoods completely covering their faces in unnatural darkness, followed behind me in rank and file. Four Conduits clothed in translucent white energy led the way before me. The silhouette of feminine bodies was all that was left of them. Their minds were trapped in eternal bliss while their souls fueled my insatiable power.

"You defile all that is good with her presence."

"Oh Azarelia, it is not I whole defiles all that is good, but rather you who defiles all that is evil," Scarlet said. A long and elegant yet revealing dress of pure blood hugged her body tightly. "Now prostrate yourself before your empress, for today, my father gives me the kingdom."

"Begone from this place, you foul daemon," Azarelia said with a scowl.

"Azarelia," I whispered. The pain in her green eyes was deep.

"Ooo, temper temper," Scarlet said, flipping her long dark red hair over her exposed shoulders. "She's a feisty one father. May I take a bite out of her now?"

"But you will do as you will." Composing herself, Azarelia curtsied before me. "Now, how may we serve?"

A grand throne room with white marble pillars, arches, and diamond chandeliers lay before me. Standing all alone as if expecting us was a girl no older in appearance than sixteen. She had long blonde hair, deep blue eyes, and flawless white skin. A strapless white gown gently hugged her body while a diamond-studded golden tiara sat atop her head. There was sadness written across her face.

"Oh, Father, thank you so very much!" Scarlet said, approaching the Empress. "She looks so-delicious."

"You will not lay a finger upon her. I forbid it," Azarelia said.

"For your age, you are quite naive." Scarlet ran the back of her hand across the Empress's cheek. "I have waited eons for this very moment, and soon I will devour your soul and drink your blood as if it were a fine wine to be savored," Scarlet whispered, turning her gaze towards Azarelia. "I will crush her bones into a fine powder. A spice that I will sprinkle over her flesh." Scarlet bit her lower lip. "And as for you, you will be my slave for all eternity. Your tears of sorrow will forever pleasure me with the memories of today."

Azarelia's straight black hair was draped over her shoulders while tears fell to the floor. "Thank you again, Father, for giving me the kingdom." I pulled out a tiny vial and handed it to her. "A gift for my accession?"

Scarlet opened the vial and tilted her head back. A single tear drop from the Empress splashed across her tongue. Clenching her fist and closing her eyes in what appeared to be a moment of pure ecstasy, Scarlet exhaled slowly. "Oh, the pleasure! The sorrow! I-I can taste it, Father."

Mouthing the words of Ethereal, I drew my katana with power surging through my veins. In an instant, my Red Immortals and Conduits dissipated into nothingness, leaving only their red robes on the floor. Their souls were absorbed into my katana's wispy black translucent blade.

Scarlet's eyes got wide. "Father?!"

Forgive me, my daughter, but in this manifold of time, your purification will be painful. With a blur of motion, my blade passed effortlessly through Scarlet's neck. Not a moment later, all that was her was drawn into my sword. The small glass vial shattered upon hitting the floor.

"Forgive me, my Empress," I said, my blade still out to my side.

Tears streaked down the Empress's cheeks. "There is nothing left to forgive," she said.

"May I have but one last favor?" I said.

"Anything you desire."

"Comfort my wife in her hour of mourning. And teach my son to know justice and to do good."

Azarelia gasped, covering her mouth. She was sobbing.

I ran my blade through my heart. A small black rift tore through the marble floor at my feet. This is where it will all end, where the flux of time will converge.

My vision went dark.

I woke up breathing heavily and shivering from a cold sweat. My chest ached. It was five forty, a few minutes before I had to wake up for school. After taking a long shower, I combed my wavy brown hair to perfection, threw on some blue jeans, a black T-shirt, and brown work boots, and headed for the kitchen.

"Good morning." I sat down at the breakfast table and began eating the cereal already made for me.

"Good morning, honey," my Mom said. "Did you get a good night's sleep?"

"Yeah, until I woke up from another nightmare."

Mom rubbed my back. "Was it about your father?"

"No, just the same dream I've had for years. As real as it's always felt."

"I'm sorry to hear that, love. So, are you going to be school president again?" she said.

"We vote on it today, but probably."

"That's good."

"No, not really."

Mom laughed. "Oh, sweetie."

"What?! You don't understand. These kids are ruthless!"

I finished my bowl of cereal and put it in the dishwasher. Slinging my brown leather jacket over my shoulders, I kissed my mom on the cheek and headed for the door. "Be prepared to pull me down from the flagpole."

It was another warm and sunny day with a gentle breeze blowing. Up ahead at the end of the block was a group of kids waiting for the school bus, and with them was Karen, the long brown-haired junior who was always looking for an excuse to laugh. She's full of life and has been a good friend of mine since we were little.

"Hello, Browny," Karen said.

"Morning, Karen. You're looking good today."

"Wish I could say the same, but I can't," Karen said. "I mean, look at you. You're wearing the same old jeans and worn-out jacket you wore last year."

"And?" I said.

She rolled her eyes. "Don't you think leather is out of style? Besides, it's a new year and time for some new clothes."

"Thanks for the vote of confidence, Kari Berry."

"It's Karen, Browny. And by the way, you're welcome."

The jacket once belonged to my father, and since I've been wearing it, people have been calling me Browny. Honestly, I liked it.

It was a little past seven when the bus dropped us off at the school. Kids were scrambling and milling about everywhere; as expected, it was chaotic.

"Hey, Browny." a familiar voice yelled. "Over here, my man."

Looking around, I saw Matt standing by a wooden bench in the grass. He was one of my best friends, standing five feet and nine inches tall and weighing around one hundred sixty-five pounds. He had brown eyes and short, parted black hair and was wearing black jeans and an untucked, crisp red dress shirt.

He smiled at me with one hand in his pocket and his backpack slung over one shoulder, looking as cool as he always does.

"It's great to see you again," I said. We embraced in a quick hug.

"You too, and today it's a new party, and we've been invited," Matt said.

"We certainly have, so where's Nathan?" I said. "School starts in ten minutes."

"He's getting off the bus right now," Matt said, pointing to where he was.

It didn't take long for Nathan to make his way through the crowds of kids and find us by the bench. With blue eyes and short spiked black hair, he's just as tall and heavy as Matt is. In comparison, I'm the tallest by an inch and the heaviest at one hundred and seventy pounds. We're all seventeen and play on the football, baseball, and wrestling teams for Janestown High School, which is located in Janestown, Arizona, but our passion is fighting. We all train under Xavier, Monday through Friday, from four to six pm in the school's gym, and we've been training together for six years since the academy first opened up.

I'm the most experienced fighter in the class, having earned black belts in both Muay Thai and jujitsu, while Matt and Nathan are only black belts in Muay Thai.

"So what's up, guys? You all ready for a new year?" Nathan said. "We're seniors, baby. Only one more year of this crap, and then we're off to college."

Keep dreaming, Nathan. You know your parents have no money to send you to college," Matt said, "It was all used to fix your face."

Nathan rolled his eyes.

I burst into laughter. Last week, Nathan was technically knocked out during a live exhibition match. It shocked us all because none of us had ever lost.

"So, who do you have for the first period, Browny?" Matt said.

"Mrs. Winston, English," I said.

"That sucks, man; I hate English," Matt said, making a disgusted face. "I won't have her until the third period."

"Hey. Same here," Nathan said.

We headed into the school toward our lockers, which were right next to each other.

"Hey guys, what's up?" Johnathan said.

Johnathan was another one of my friends who had short brown hair and was about my size. He was wearing black cargo jeans, a white T-shirt, and skater shoes.

"Nothing much, man, just living the life here in little ol' Janestown," Matt said.

"No, you're not, loser!" a girl said, walking past us.

"That's gotta sting," Johnathan said.

"Ooo, not a good start to the school year, buddy," Nathan said.

"She'll come around," Matt said.

"So, how are you today, Johnathan?" I said.

"A whole lot better than Nathan, that's for sure," Johnathan said. We all laughed.

Three girls walked up to me, including Michelle, who was last year's volleyball captain. She had long, straight black hair and light brown skin. "Good morning, Scott," she said.

"Hello," another girl said in almost a whisper.

"Morning, ladies."

Matt nodded. "What's up, girls?" he said.

One of the girls put her hand in his face. "Not talking to you," she said.

Matt put his hands in his pockets and looked down at the ground. "Dang, it's like that today, uh?"

"I just wanted to let you know we're all voting for you this morning. You did a wonderful job for us last year, and I appreciate that." Michelle said, running her hand through my hair.

I glanced over at my buddies. "Uh, thanks?" I said. This had to be a setup.

The girls smiled. "Now, don't screw it up, and oh yeah, we want new uniforms this year, and you're going to get them for us," Michelle said.

The girls walked away. "So much for the new football jerseys," I said.

"I don't know how you put up with it, Browny," Nathan said.

"I'm a sucker for pain, I suppose."

After a few more minutes of small talk, we all said goodbye and headed to class, but before I could make it in, I was stopped by arguably the most beautiful girl in school, Jessica Woods. She was Johnathan's younger sister by a year and had long light brown hair, green eyes, and a pretty smile. She was wearing a knee-long white dress that gently hugged her body and white sandals.

"Good morning, Browny," she said. "I heard about your tap-out win last week. Congratulations. And sorry that I couldn't make it."

"Hey Jessica, thanks, and don't worry about it," I said.

"So, anything new going on?" Jessica said. Her voice was like an angel's, so soft and soothing. I liked her and always have, but not in that way. She's more like a sister to me.

"Nothing new," I said. "And are those new earrings?" My heart was fluttering.

"You noticed-" The bell rang. "Well, I'll talk to you at lunch, okay?" Smiling warmly, she headed off to class.

The school day seemed to fly by, and before I knew it, it was time for football practice. And like I expected, I was again, for the fourth year in a row, voted school president.

I met up with Matt and Nathan in the locker room, where we changed into shorts and cleats. Everyone who had played last year was here again, along with some freshmen tryouts.

After reacquainting with my teammates, we headed to the football field, where our coaches waited. To our left sideline was the soccer field where the girls were getting their practice underway, and beyond that was the baseball field. A thick forest surrounds the school and fields and is fenced off to prevent anyone from wandering off because, over the years, many kids have gone missing. Rumor has it there is a chasm only a few hundred yards east of the school near the plateau, the plateau that jutted over a hundred yards into the air, but no one has ever come back alive to confirm it.

"So what's up guys?" I said. "Did you score any freshmen?"

"I've already got a girl, Browny," Matt said.

"Nope, not yet." Nathan took off his shirt. "But once they see me running around with my shirt off, I will."

"Ahh, Nathan, my man. I thought we already discussed this," Matt said. "Yes, you're gunned in with abs of steel, but you've got a face only your mother can love. Though after last week's beating, I doubt even she loves it now."

Matt's rip on Nathan had everyone laughing, even some of the freshmen.

"What did I miss?" Johnathan said, walking up to us. "Who's getting roasted?"

"You're not missing much. Nathan's ego is taking a lashing, that's all," I said.

Nathan just stood there nodding his head with a half-cocked grin.

With it being a new season, it was again time to prove our varsity status. I've been our team's starting fullback and linebacker for three years now, and hopefully, I'll earn the same positions again. Matt was our running back, safety, and special teams returner, while Nathan was our star receiver and cornerback. Last year, we won seven games and lost three. It was a heartbreaker when we lost in the second round of the single A playoffs, but crap happens.

"You guys ready for this?" I whispered.

"You betcha, man," Aaron said.

"Let's rock their world," Johnathan said.

The girls were just finishing their practice and making their way to the watering hoses along our sideline.

"What's going on, Scott?" a freshman said.

"You just follow my lead and don't let any of them get away, got it?" I said.

"Yeah."

"You guys ready?"

"This is what I live for," Matt said, rubbing his hands together like he was pretending to be cold.

"Let's do this shit," a senior said.

Everyone followed me to the watering hoses. It was hot outside, and we were sweating like animals. The girls, however, were not, and tradition called.

As the girls drank from the PVC pipes with holes drilled in them, two of my players began to unscrew the hoses from the pipes.

"What's going on boys?" Laura, the soccer captain, said.

"Oh, nothing much. Some of the boys are just a little hot, that's all," I said, trying to hold back my laughter.

"Scott, you better not be lying to me because if this is what I think-" Laura said.

"Get 'em!" I yelled. Quickly, the entire football team encircled the soccer girls and began hosing them down with cold water. The girls screamed and tried to run, but we boxed them in, forming a human chain.

"Scott, you're gonna pay for this, you asshole!" Laura screamed as Aarron held her down to the ground. Nathan was spraying her.

"Such a potty mouth for such a beautiful girl," Matt said.

"Let us go, Browny, please!" Karen cried.

I laughed at her and shrugged my shoulders. "Sorry Kare Bear."

By now, most of the girls were sitting in the muddy field, waiting to be drenched. Some cried out in protest while others silently accepted their punishment, and Jessica was one of them. She was sitting on the wet ground with her knees held tightly to her chest, shivering as Aaron poured water all over her head. I couldn't help but laugh. It was times like these that made me feel so alive, and I wished it would never end. But our coaches put a stop to it. We'd pay for this with extra sprints and such, but it was worth it and has been every year.

After a quick shower, the four of us headed for the gym, where Xavier was waiting. He was a Japanese man around fifty years old with a bald head and a strange green dragon tattoo on his left forearm.

"How was your first day, guys?" he asked with a slight Japanese accent. No one answered. "Okay, grab your sparing partners and get to work."

"That was one heck of an armbar you rolled that guy into," Johnathan said.

"Yeah, I guess," I said. We began to trade lazy punches. "But you kicked the crap out of your opponent."

"Always do," he said. I gently took him down and fell in between his legs in his guard. "So, are you going to get any formal weapons training?"

I pushed down his left knee and climbed onto his side in side control. "I don't know, maybe."

"When I turn eighteen this April, I'll be joining the Sukagi Weapons Academy," he said. "I can't wait to kick some ass with some weapons."

"Like who, your sister?"

Johnathan shook his head. "Ha ha."

A few hours later, after more basic techniques and drills, Xavier called an end to our session, and we walked home. "So, did you have a good first day or what?" I said.

"I sure did, and you know, I'm really starting to take a liking to Karen," he said. She's funny, and well, you saw her running around in her little soccer uniform." Johnathan looked at the ground with a smirk on his face. "She's really smart and personable."

I chuckled softly. He is so full of it. Karen is the cheer captain, and the last thing that he was interested in was her personality. "That's great, my man. It sounds like you're maturing."

He shot me a look. "I've been mature for a long time now, and you know it. I think I'm going to ask her out tomorrow; take her out to the city in my junk of a truck."

"Yeah, I think you two would be great for each other," I said. Karen was so out of his league. "Have a nice night, and say hi to Jessica for me, would you?"

He waved to me and continued down the street. "I will."

"Good morning, Scott," Laura said. Five other girls surrounded me in the hallway.

"Oh, hi, girls," I said. "what's up?" My eyes darted from girl to girl.

One of the girls slammed me up against my locker. "If you ever hose us down like that again, Scott, we're going to mess you and your football team up," she said.

A smile crept across my face. "Bring it."

Another girl pressed herself against me, forcing me harder against the locker. "We'll make sure that you're not prom king this year."

I sighed. "Okay, now you're talking, girls," I said. "What do you want?"

"Keep your dogs off us," Laura said.

"And don't pull the 'I'm not the team captain' crap either. Just do it." one said.

"You girls drive a-"

"And take me to the prom with you," another said.

"That's eight months away, I mean-"

"Ladies, Scott," Principal Norwall said. "How are we doing today?" His arms were crossed.

The girls quickly backed away from me. "Oh, nothing much, Sir," Laura said, wiping her hand across my shoulders, pretending to dust me off. "We're just ensuring that the school president does what we've elected him to do."

"Carry on then. Just make sure that Scott can at least speak by the time you're done with him."

"Principal Norwal?!" I said, sighing.

The girls closed back in on me as he walked away. "Now, where were we girls?" Laura said.

"Heading off to class if you know what's good for you," Johnathan said.

"Tell Lassie here to back the hell off, Scott," a girl said.

I looked over at Johnathan. "I can't do that, I'm sorry."

"Let's go, girls," Laura said. "Scott's smart, he'll do the right thing."

"He'd better hope so," one said, flicking me on the nose. The girls walked off.

"So what the heck was that about?" Jonathan said.

"School president issues, the prom, and the tradition."

"What?! The girls didn't like their annual hosing?" Johnathan said.

"Not at all, and they threatened not to vote me prom king again."

"I wish that I could be king for a day."

"You'll have your moment. We all do."

"Not in this lifetime."

With the ringing of the third-period bell, everyone hurried out of class and into the chow hall. It was my second favorite time of the day after my MMA training.

"So, what did your mom pack you for lunch today?" I said.

"Same old," Jonathan said.

"Have you asked her out yet?"

"No, not yet."

"You can't go around being scared your whole life, Johnathan. Live a little," I said. Now, come on, now is your chance." I made my way over to Karen's table, sat across from her, and waved at her frantically. Her girlfriends giggled. "Hey Karen, how are you?"

Johnathan slinked behind me.

"I'm great, Browny, and you?" She traded looks with her friends.

"Can you girls do me a favor, please?" I said.

Johnathan sighed and stared at the floor. He was blushing.

"Like what, be your girlfriend?" a girl said. I smiled at her.

"Jessica is a really nice girl, and I was wondering if you guys could talk to your friends and vote for her homecoming queen."

"You're sweet on her," a girl said.

I laughed hesitantly. "It would mean the world to her-please."

"Oh, he's so cute when he begs," one said.

The girls laughed. "For you, Browny, sure," Karen said.

"Thanks, Karen, and you girls are the best," I waved goodbye.

"Homecoming queen, eh? She's going to love that," Johnathan said.

"But don't tell her, though. I want this to be a surprise. And why didn't you ask Karen out?"

"Really?!" he said. "Come on, man. In front of her friends?!"

CHAPTER TWO

Weeks passed by, and the memories of each day seemed to blur into one. It was a scorching hot Saturday the day before Halloween, and Matt and I were lying in his front yard, letting the sprinkler spray us with water. It was refreshing but not very exciting.

"Hey, do you want to go downtown and get something cool to eat?" I said.

"Heck yeah. Let's get some ice cream or pop or something," Matt said.

"You have any money. I didn't bring any," I stood up and brushed myself clean of the grass that had clung to my wet body. "I'll pay you back later."

"Sure do. I just made fifty bucks busting my butt mowing some lawns, and I've got more coming, too," A few moments later, he came back outside with money in his hand. He looked agitated. "Here's eight, man. Do you want to hit the lake after we're done gorging?"

"Why didn't we think of that earlier?" I said. "But yeah, there's probably some girls down there that we can play around with."

Our bike ride through the neighborhood streets and into town took only five minutes, the same time it took us to polish off our ice cream.

"So, what are you going to do after school?" Matt said.

"Maybe college. I don't know; that's what my mom is pushing me towards," I said. "You?"

"I'm moving out ASAP; that's all I know," he said. "My future looks pretty bleak, man."

"What are you talking about?" I said.

"Nathan's the only one with money to go to college, and he's got the grades for it, too. Hell, if he tries to get a wrestling scholarship, then he won't have to pay."

"That could be any one of us, man," I said.

"Yeah, right."

He was clearly upset about something, and it bothered me. "What's wrong, man? You know that I know you better than you know yourself."

"I know he's stealing from me. I had fifty dollars, and when I checked, I only had twenty," Matt said. "He's taking it when he searches my room. I know he is."

"Again, huh?"

"Yeah, it's nothing really, a few bucks here and there," he said. "But you know, I get these lectures from him telling me not to do drugs and stuff, but there he is in the bar, twenty-four-seven," He took a drink from his soda. "Does he even know me? I'd never mess myself up with that crap."

"Don't let it get you down, man; we have an awesome time at the beach ahead of us," I said. "Besides, I'll pay you back."

"Don't worry about it. My money is your money. You know that."

It took us about ten minutes to bike to Lake Caldell, which is less than half a mile north of where we live. It's a small freshwater lake with low, rocky cliffs to the side along the traffic-less highway and trees along the other. It's a lovely lake, and it's nearly crystal clear.

"Hey, there's Jessica and Nathan," I said.

"It's one o'clock," Matt said. "That leaves me with five hours to party." Throwing his bike down, he ran and dove headfirst into the water.

"You guys trying to beat the heat, too?" Jessica said as she grabbed one of my pops. She was wearing a long gray T-shirt and yellow swimming shorts.

"Yeah, and it looks like a lot of people are," I said. "What is it out here? Ninety-five degrees?"

"Hi, Scott," a girl said from behind me.

"Oh, hi, Chandler, how are you doing?" I said.

"Fine," she said. "My mom wanted me to thank you for watching me earlier."

"You're welcome, sweetie," I said. "What do you think we should do tomorrow?"

"Can we play in the park?" she said.

"Anything you want, Chandler."

"Thank you, Scott," she said. "You're so nice." After hugging me, she ran off and jumped into the water.

"I didn't know that you babysat," Jessica said.

"Yeah, all the time now."

"Are you why Mrs. Morgan said she already found someone?"

I looked at the ground and tried to contain my laughter."

"Ugh, you jerk," she said. "How much are you charging? And it better not be less than I do."

"Actually, I don't charge anything at all."

She punched me in the shoulder and scowled. "Quit, I need that money, you jerk!"

I laughed again. "Is that all you got?

"Are you going to flirt all day, or are you going to help me beat these guys at some water volleyball!" Matt yelled.

"Yeah, yeah, I'm coming," I said. Jessica just looked at me with her pretty green eyes, drinking my pop. "What?!"

"I didn't say anything," she said. "Now give me a bite of that." She grabbed the candy bar from my hand and took a bite.

"Wow, you sure are demanding today," I said. "But on a more serious note, what are you going to wear for Halloween?"

She smiled. "You'll just have to wait and see."

The afternoon just melted away, and before I knew it, Matt had to go home. Unlike my mom, who was quite relaxed when it came to my curfew, Matt's parents are strict. He has to be in by six every night, including the weekends.

After Matt went on his way, I decided to lie in the sand and soak up the last rays of sunshine. By this time, everyone had already left. There was just me and some other guy fishing on the lake's far side. A few hours must have gone by because when I woke up, the sun was beginning to set. The sky was burning a beautiful reddish-orange color. It was calm and peaceful listening to the lull of the lake and the gentle rustling of the leaves. I wanted to stay a while longer, but I had no idea how late it was or whether or not I had already missed dinner. Reluctantly, I hopped on my bike and headed home.

It was five in the morning on a Friday when my alarm woke me up. Normally, I wake up at six, but today is Halloween, and I need the extra time to get ready. Everyone at school was going to be looking their best, and being the most popular guy in school, it was mandatory that I look top-notch.

"Oh my Scott, you look horrible," my mom said.

"That's what I'm going for."

"You're not going to wear that all day, are you?"

"Of course, Mom, It's Halloween," I said. "Don't tell me you've forgotten your good old days of dressing up."

"Oh, I do. It just wasn't this extravagant, though. So, how late are you going to stay out?"

"Well, it depends on the guys, maybe twelve or one o'clock. Is that all right?"

"That's fine, sweetie, but bring some extra fruit. I don't want you eating just sugar all night long."

"Thanks, Mom." Once I had finished my breakfast, I grabbed my lunch and extra fruit and hugged her goodbye. It was going to be a perfect day for trick or treating, cool and overcast.

"That's a nice look for you, Browny. It suits you well." Johnathan said. He was standing on the sidewalk in front of my house.

"Thanks. What are you? A soldier?" I said.

He was wearing forest green fatigues with black steel-toed boots. His brown hair was even shorter now, spiked and dyed black.

We began walking towards the bus stop. "No, not really."

"That's pretty cool what you've done with your eyes." He was wearing black contacts.

"Yeah, it's the coolest thing about my costume," he said. "So, who's going to be your first victim? Who are you going to kill and eat?"

"Your girl, Karen, now watch this!" I stumbled up to Karen, who was looking at me with disgust. "I want to eat you, Karen, your brains. Brains!" I grabbed her shoulder and tried to bite her, but she wasn't having any of it. She shoved me backward, but just as she did, I squeezed a hand pump that squirted out some fake blood from a hole in my cheek. I got her good across her chest, staining her pink shirt. My whole face was covered with a prosthetic mask that was covered with cuts, bruises, and even loose bits of flesh. I even wore clothes that were torn and bloody. I looked awesome.

"Damn it, Scott!" Karen yelled. "I'm not in the mood!" She pulled her shirt away and stared at the bloodstains with disbelief. "Now, look at what you've done!"

My smile quickly faded. "I'm sorry, Karen," I didn't know it would upset her that much. "I'm sorry."

A sly smile crept across her face. "I'm a psycho, Browny-see?" She showed me a medical bracelet on her left wrist. Everyone started laughing at me. "You're too gullible, Browny, and great costume though." She patted me on the shoulder.

"Your costume hits a little close to home, don't you think?" I said.

Karen's smile faded into a glaring look.

Once at school, I eagerly looked for Matt and Nathan, curious to see what they were wearing. Almost everyone had dressed up, which made it difficult to find them, but sure enough, I found them by their lockers.

"Is that you, Nathan, under that hideous sheet?" Johnathan said. He lifted up the sheet to reveal the embarrassed look on Nathan's face. "It is you!"

"Yeah," Nathan mumbled.

We all laughed at him.

"Ugh, this is not acceptable, man," I said. "Even Karen has a better costume, and all she's wearing is a bracelet with disheveled hair as if she just crawled out of bed."

Nathan's plain white ghost sheet covered the length of his body and had two eye holes. That was it. Pitiful. Matt, on the other hand, was dressed up like a sophisticated vampire. He was wearing a black tuxedo with a red tie and black dress shoes. His face was painted pale white, and his black hair was slicked straight back. Even his fangs looked real.

"I think it would be best, Nathan, if you sat by yourself today at lunch," Matt said. "I can't be seen around this, guys. I've got a rep to uphold."

"Yeah, this is pretty bad, Nathan," I said.

"What happened to the goblin costume that you wore last year?" Matt said.

"Donated it," Nathan said.

"What a shame," I said.

"Yeah, for sure," Johnathan said.

"So, guys, could you do me a huge favor?" I said.

"How huge?" Johnathan said.

"I need you guys to convince everyone you can to vote for Jessica as homecoming queen," I said. "Can you guys do that?"

"Sure thing, but what do I get out of it?" Nathan said.

"Name your price," I said.

"Respect," Nathan said. I looked him up and down while he shrugged. "I had to try."

"I'll see what I can do," Matt said.

"You sure are pushing this queen thing," Johnathan said.

"What can I say? She deserves it," I said.

Waltzing up beside me was Jessica. She was wearing a tight knee, long white dress, white open-toed high heels, and a yellow halo above her head. She was looking good.

"Hey guys, is an angel allowed to hang out with vampires and zombies?" Jessica said.

"You wore that dress last week. Now beat it before I beat you," Johnathan said, shaking his fist at her.

Jessica's smile quickly faded into a look of shock. "I like this dress, you jerk!" She stormed down the hall.

"You can hang out with us, Jessica. I think you look stunning!" I shouted.

She kept walking.

"You love her, dude," Nathan said.

"That was harsh, don't you think, soldier boy?" Matt said.

"She knows I was joking," Johnathan said.

We stared at him.

"Okay, okay, I'll go and apologize to my little sis. I was slightly out of line there," Johnathan said. "Oh, and Browny, I'll be sure to ask her out for you."

Now, everyone was staring at me. "Come on, guys, it's not like that," I said. "She's more like a sitter to me-really."

"Whatever helps you sleep at night, Browny," Matt said. "And the longer you fight it, the more it hurts in the end."

"All right, fellas, it's a little past six, and we have about two hours until the trick or treating and the kiddie scaring begins," Nathan said. He had removed his ghost sheet and tied it to his belt loop so it could drag along the street. We've been walking aimlessly around the neighborhood for hours now. "So what are we going to do in the meantime cause I'm getting bored."

"You're such a mess, Nathan," Johnathan said.

"Stare and beware, 'cause I don't care," Nathan said.

Matt shook his head. "Ugh, that was gross. Do not ever say that again."

Johnathan and I laughed. The humor between those two always cracks me up.

"So what are we going to do, because he's right. This is boring," I said.

"I know. You guys want some real adventure?" Johnathan said.

"Adventure, dude?" Matt said.

"Yeah, what do you say we check out the Dark Woods," Jonathon said. "I've heard of people seeing ghosts and weird monsters and stuff in there."

By now, the overcast sky had grown darker, with thick black clouds and an ominous sign of rain.

"I heard that, too," Matt said.

"And I've heard that there's nothing," Nathan said. "Now come on guys, you don't really believe in ghosts, do you?"

"No, not at all," I said.

"No one has ever come out of those woods alive, so you tell me," Johnathan said.

"They probably fell down the chasm back there," Nathan said.

"Speaking of things that don't exist," Matt said.

"That's right, so let's go and check it out," Johnathan said. "Seriously, what are you guys afraid of?"

"Nothing, man. I'm just saying that we are not going to find anything," Nathan said.

"Browny, you want to go?" Johnathan said.

"I don't know, man. It's getting dark out and its too dangerous out there," I said.

"Are you, the big bad Browny, afraid of the dark?" Johnathan said. "Do you need me to hold your hand? Will that put you at ease?"

"Don't be a wuss, Browny," Matt said.

"Alright. Fine. I'll go," I said. I really didn't want to go and, for obvious reasons. The last thing I wanted to do was trounce around in the woods messing up my costume, but if it made them happy, then hey, why not?

We were only a few blocks away from the school, and with the plateau to guide us, we cut through a few yards and a large grassy field until we stood at the edge of the Dark Woods. A fence with a red warning sign barred our entrance, but we easily climbed over it and began to make our way through the dense shrubbery.

The forest's canopy was a thick, tangled mess of branches and leaves, which blocked out most of the light. This is why they called it the Dark Woods.

"This place is creepier than it looks," Nathan said.

"Yeah, creepy," Matt said, rapping his fist on one of the trees. "I've never seen trees like this before. So hollow and charred."

I agreed with both of them. Every tree was dead or burnt from the inside.

With a snap, the tree that Matt was pushing on fell over. Nathan scurried to avoid the falling branches, shielding his head with his arms. "Hey, man, careful with that crap. You almost hit me," Nathan said.

Johnathan laughed. "What's wrong with you guys? This place is awesome."

"Sure it is," I said.

"I've never been this far in these woods before, and they're so weird," Johnathan said. "But I like it."

We must have traveled some distance into the woods because up ahead and to the right, I could vaguely make out the plateau, and something else I had never noticed until now. There was a large tower of rock jutting up about a hundred feet above the plateau's surface near its edge. The remaining light was fading fast, and the wind overhead was beginning to pick up. A cold shiver raced down my spine as goose bumps formed along my arms.

Nathan pointed to his watch. "Hey, it's seven o'clock already," he said. "Shouldn't we be heading back?"

"We're just getting started out here, bro. Besides, now that we have carved a path, it will only take a minute or so to get back," Johnathan said.

I began to tear the bark of a dead tree. "Hey guys, take a look at this," I said. "I'm not aware of any fire being able to do this." The core of the dead tree was charred black, but its bark wasn't.

"That is strange," Johnathan said as he tore out a chunk of its core. It crumbled in his hands. "It's almost like pure ash."

"Holy-" Nathan cried out. "Did you see that?" He was holding his switchblade and pointing it about frantically. "It's over there! Over there!"

"What is it, man?" I said, looking in the direction he pointed.

"Something is out there, guys, and I mean it! Something is out there!" Nathan said. He was breathing heavily.

"Calm down, dude, and put that thing away," Johnathan said.

Matt picked up a large stick. "It was probably a bear or something-"

Johnathan cupped his hand over Matt's mouth. "Shhh, everyone, quiet," he whispered.

Everyone quieted down. The leaves rustled in the wind, and then something brushed my back. My blood turned to ice, and before I knew it, I was racing through the woods with reckless abandon toward safety. Low tree branches struck me in the face, and occasionally, I stumbled over some bushes, but I kept running.

Soon, I found myself standing all alone in the middle of the large grassy field with my hands interlocked behind my head, catching my breath.

Matt climbed over the fence and made his way towards me, breathing heavily. "What the hell was that back there, man?!"

"I don't know. I just had to get the heck out of there," I said. "So where are the other two?"

"I'm right here," Nathan said, appearing out of the woods. "I followed you, Matt, but Johnathan, I don't know where he went."

"Should we look for him?" I said.

"No, he'll be fine," Matt said.

"Or at least wait for him?" I said.

"You don't want to be late for the scare fest, do you?" Matt said. "Besides, this was his idea, and this is what he gets."

"Johnathan!" I yelled towards the woods. "Head this way!"

"Yeah, let's go, guys," Nathan said, glancing back at the woods. "He'll be alright."

"Guys-" I said.

"Should I ask him out for you, Browny?" Matt said. "Now come on."

Twenty minutes later, after stuffing our faces with pizza at Nathan's house, we grabbed some pillowcases for the candy and headed into the night. The neighborhood streets were no longer empty but filled with costumed kids trick or treating. It was going to be a great night.

"So what did you really see back there, Nathan?" Matt said.

"Nothing, man. I saw nothing at all. I was just trying to find a way to get us out of there so we could trick or treat." We crouched low behind a car.

"Then why were you trembling?" I said.

"And with your switchblade?" Matt said.

"It was all part of the act," Nathan said. "All part of the act."

"Uh-huh," Matt said.

"Shhh-here they come," I whispered. Three young kids were walking down the sidewalk towards us. They were laughing and eating some candy from their bags, blissfully ignorant of the terror that was about to befall them. "On my mark."

Once the kids were closer, we jumped out from behind the car and yelled, waving our hands frantically. The children screamed and ran off crying, spilling some candy. We all laughed and began to pick up the spilled candy.

"This is so unbelievably fun," Matt said. "Why didn't we do this last year?"

"It is fun," I said. "But so messed up."

"And in more ways than one," Nathan said, picking up some spilled candy.

"Oh great. I think we've been made," Matt said.

I stopped laughing. Jessica and Karen were storming towards us, and they didn't look happy.

"Oh my gosh. You guys are such jerks," Jessica said. Her arms were crossed over her chest, and the frown on her face meant she wasn't playing around.

"Did you guys really think that you were going to get away with this?" Karen said.

Matt threw out his hands in protest. "What do you gals mean?"

"Yeah, we're not doing anything wrong," I said, slinking behind Matt and Nathan. "We're just giving them the complete Halloween experience, that's all."

"You're not doing anything wrong?" Jessica said sternly. "Taking candy from kids isn't wrong?"

I snickered quietly.

"Wait a sec here, by 'take their candy,' do you mean they dropped it on the ground while running away screaming?" Matt said. "Because if so, then no. It's finders keepers, ladies."

I tried holding back my laughter, but it was just too funny. I burst out laughing. Nathan was cracking up, too.

"You guys are bullies, and I'm going to see to it that you return that candy to those poor kids," Jessica said. Karen put one hand on her hip.

Jessica continued to scowl at us with her arms still folded across her chest. She's so cute when she's angry.

"Look here, sweethearts, we'll give you each ten percent of our candy, but only if you keep quiet about this, okay?" I said.

Jessica gasped. "I am truly insulted that you think I can be bought, Scott," Jessica said. "Now apologize to those kids and return their candy, and tonight!"

Karen looked over at Jessica and then at me. "Deal, ten percent," she said.

Jessica's mouth dropped open. "Karen!" she said.

"Excellent. Now, hold out your bag. I'll pay you now," Matt said.

"Awesome." Karen held out her candy bag.

Matt then ripped the bag from her hands and took off down the street. "Run!" he yelled, throwing a fistful of candy onto the pavement. "Here's your ten percent!"

Nathan and I wasted no time and ran away with him, leaving the girls in our dust. Karen yelled something, and I'm pretty sure she swore at us, but I was too busy laughing and running to pay much attention.

"Did you see the look on Karen's face?!" Nathan said. "She was ticked off!"

"She sounded ticked," Matt said.

"Yeah," I said. "And she had the nerve to say that I was gullible."

"Ahh, this is so awesome," Nathan said through laughter.

"Oh yeah," I said.

"So, you guys ready for more kiddie scaring?" Matt said, grinning from ear to ear.

"Heck yeah," Nathan said.

"Then let's make it a night to remember," Matt said.

Our night of terror seemed to fly by, and before I knew it, we were saying our goodbyes and heading our separate ways. It was just past one am, and the streets were empty. The night air was brisk, and the wind howled. I was tired from walking and running around, but my bed was of no comfort to me. For hours on end, I tossed and turned, occasionally falling asleep, but only to wake up a few minutes later in a cold sweat. And whatever sleep I did get was plagued by vivid and terrifying dreams. I kept falling and falling and falling.

For the next two days, the three of us stayed low. The neighborhood was looking for the 'hoodlums' that scared and robbed their little ones of their candy. And if they found out that it was the mature and responsible ones of the community, then there goes our good reputation.

So, on top of lying to everyone, which only made me feel worse, we had to beg and plead with Karen not to turn us in. She agreed, but we had to give back her loot and then some, as well as obey her every command until the following Friday. She had us good, but my real concern was Jessica. Luckily for us, she and her brother were up in Colorado visiting some relatives for the weekend. We weren't going to have to deal with her until Monday, and hopefully, by then, all of this will have died down.

It was a quarter past seven on Monday when Jessica approached me at my locker. I had two days to prepare for this moment, and now it was time to put that practice to use.

"Jessica, I'm terribly sorry for what I did. It was wrong and-"

"Browny, I don't care about that right now," Jessica said. "Have you seen my brother anywhere?"

"No."

She frowned. "You haven't seen him all weekend?"

"No. I thought he went to Colorado with you."

"No," Jessica said. "Look, I'll talk to you later." She hurried down the hall.

I was confused. The last time I saw Johnathan was in the woods. That was the last time Matt and Nathan saw him, too, but I was pretty sure he was okay. He probably just didn't want to visit his cousins, that's all. But none of that stopped me from worrying for the next two and a half hours about where he was and if he was okay, especially with Jessica so distraught.

"Johnathan!" I cried out, standing up in class. I began walking towards him, but after hearing some snickers, I decided to sit down before embarrassing myself further. After handing the teacher a pink tardy slip, Jonathan took his seat next to me. "I'm sorry for ditching you in the woods, man," I said.

"No big deal," He said.

"So, where the heck have you been?" There were minor cuts and scrapes along his arms and face, and he was still wearing his Halloween costume.

"Up visiting my cousins. Why?"

"That's not what Jessica said."

"She's lying, man," Jonathan said. "And whoa, man, you sound truly concerned."

I breathed a sigh of relief and slouched back down in my chair. Something deep inside me didn't feel right. Jessica wouldn't lie about something like this, but then again, no one would ever suspect the three of us of doing what we did to those kids on Halloween. I guess she's no different.

During lunch, Matt, Nathan, and I sat with the rest of the jocks like usual. Johnathan, however, was sitting two tables ahead of us with Karen and the cheerleaders. He was all cleaned up and was holding Karen's hand.

"What's up with Johnathan?" Nathan said.

"I think they're going out now," Matt said. "At least that's what I heard."

"That's the rumor," Aaron said.

"Dudes, we have to make fun of him," a jock said.

"Heck yeah, man," another said.

"Hold on, guys, not yet," I said. "Let me go confirm this first." The guys could barely contain their laughter as I made my way over to Karen's table. "Hey, Jonathan and Karen, how are you two doing?" They both stared at me with suspicion written across their faces. "I wanted to know if you two were going out, and if so, congratulations." I tried hard not to laugh. They knew what I was really here for.

"Are you going out with anyone, Scott?" Anna, the sophomore, said. She, along with the other cheerleaders, giggled.

"I saw you at last Saturday's football game, Scott," another said. "You were looking good."

"Uh, thank you?" I said. The girls laughed some more.

Karen smiled. "Yes, we're going out now, Browny."

With their love for each other confirmed, I gave my buddies the thumbs up, and that's when the hooting and hollering began. The sudden surge of attention caused Karen's cheeks to turn pink.

"You two enjoy your lunch now." After patting Johnathan on the back, I rejoined my friends at the table. Karen then stood up and made her way towards us.

"Browny," Karen said, leaning over the table across from me.

"Ooo, Scott's in big trouble now," Aaron said.

"Do I need to remind you of your place?" Karen said. With a quick shake of her head, she flipped her long brown hair out of her face. "And call me by my proper name-understand?"

"Oh no, Scott, don't take this from her!" one of my buddies said. "Don't take this from her."

Everyone at our table was laughing, but everyone else in the chow hall was silent.

"Come on, guys, it's not that serious," I said.

"Browny," Karen said with raised eyebrows.

I sighed heavily and looked down at the table. "No, Ms. Brey, you do not need to remind me of my place."

"No, you didn't, Scott! No, you didn't!" Aaron said. The guys at the table laughed even harder.

"Matt, Nathan, come over here," Karen said. "You too, Browny."

"You two are in trouble too?" Aaron said. "This just keeps getting better and better." By now, everyone in the chow hall was staring at us.

"Come on, Karen, this is pushing it pretty far," Matt said.

"Oh, is it? Are you really willing to find out what will happen to you if I tell?" Karen said. "Besides, this will be the last day that you have to obey me if you do as I say, okay?"

"I don't know about this," Matt said, looking back at me.

"Yeah, you owe us until Friday, and it's only Monday," Nathan said. "So what's up with that?"

"Yeah, but I think it's worth it," She pointed to the ground. "Now, guys, drop to your knees and kiss my feet." Gasps echoed the chow hall.

"I'll take my chances with the principal, honey," Matt said. "There's no way that I'm going to be remembered in the yearbook for this." He sat back down.

"Way to show her whose boss, Matt," Aaron said.

I slowly let out my breath. "Alright, Ms. Brey." Dropping to my knees, I prostrated myself before her and kissed her sneakers, and that's when the entire lunchroom burst into laughter. Karen was laughing so hard that she was crying, and with my utter humiliation complete, I quickly scurried over to my seat, burying my head in my arms. I had never been more embarrassed in all my life, but truthfully, I really didn't mind. Karen was a good friend, and if she asked me to do it again, I probably would.

Nathan quickly bowed down and kissed her feet, too, but the entire lunchroom was in such an uproar that I don't think anyone noticed.

For the rest of the day, up until we went home, we were the butt end of everyone's joke. Even the teachers who heard what happened had a laugh at us. After all, it's not often that the three most popular guys in school get put in their place by a junior. Like I said, she had us good, but the alternative was worse.

"Excuse me. Do you mind if I sit with you?" a girl's voice said.

I opened my eyes and sat up, and standing to my left was a long, brown-haired, blue-eyed, tanned girl wearing only a pink bikini top and white swimming shorts.

She looked down at me with a shy smile, digging her toes into the sand.

"Sure."

My name is Mary, Mary Jane," she said, sitting next to me and offering to shake my hand. "What's yours?"

I didn't know what it was, but something about her made my heart pound. The hairs on my arms stood on end.

"Scott," I shook her hand. "But everyone calls me Browny."

"Why do they call you that, if you don't mind me asking?"

"Oh, it's just a nickname that everyone calls me because I always wear a brown leather jacket," I said. "I think it's a pretty cool name."

"I think it's funny, Scott. It reminds me of the Girl Scouts when I was a Brownie scout."

I laughed. "Oh sweet, I'm a girl scout."

She playfully pushed me over. "I didn't mean it like that-Browny scout."

The beach was packed with screaming kids running around and playing in the water, but I was so absorbed in Mary's sparkling blue eyes and soft voice that it seemed like we were the only ones there. "So, are you new in town? I've never seen you before."

"Yes, I am. I just moved here from Indiana with my mom."

"Indiana, huh?" I said. "Well, this is a pretty small town where everyone knows everybody. So, I think you'll like it here," She smiled at me. "So, how old are you?"

"Believe it or not, I just turned eighteen today."

"Wow, then happy birthday Mary Jane," I said. "Here's a birthday hug." I wrapped my arms around her and patted her back. The smell of her lavender hair enveloped my senses. A shiver passed down my spine.

"Thank you," She said, drawing half a heart in the sand. For a brief moment, our eyes met, and a warm feeling overcame me. I finished the other half of the heart. "I'd really like it if you came to my birthday party, Scott." She put her hand over mine.

"I'd love to Mary Jane." I leaned over and kissed her softly on the cheek. She blushed and smiled, a smile that I will never forget.

We ended up walking around the lake for hours on end, talking about everything under the sun. It was as if we had known each other forever, and that night, while celebrating her birthday, I knew that I could spend the rest of my life with her, my sweet Mary Jane.

CHAPTER THREE

It was homecoming Friday on the twelfth of November, 1993, and as expected, I was again elected homecoming king. My hard work paid off, and everyone voted for Jessica as Queen. The look on her face when they announced it over the intercom on Wednesday was all the thanks I needed. Finally, the town's sweetheart was queen.

The school day started like normal, except at the end of the fourth period, when we were all excused to join the parade. For over an hour, Jessica and I were driven around the neighborhood on a football field float while the band played and the town cheered for us. Tonight, she and I would share the customary first dance at the homecoming party at the school, and I couldn't wait.

"So, is black the new you?" I said.

"You can say that," Jonathan said.

All he'd been wearing for the past two weeks since Halloween was black. Even his hair was black, short, and spiked. "So she's finally going to be yours, Browny. Are you excited?"

"No, man, Mary Jane is my girl," I kicked a rock down the street. "But don't get me wrong, I like Jessica, and everyone knows that, but not in that way. I mean-"

"Mary Jane, uh? I still can't believe you got her so quickly," Jonathan said. "She hadn't even finished unpacking by the time you put the moves on her!"

"Well, it was really her that-"

"No need to explain yourself, man," He patted me on the back. "This dance with Jessica is really your way of testing the waters to see if she likes you as much as you love her."

"Jessica is just-"

"Shhh, I know you're in love with my sister, and so does everyone else," Jonathan said. "I'll see you tonight." He ran off down the street and into his house.

"Yeah."

It was just past six when I got home, meaning I only had an hour to prepare for the dance. So, after taking another quick shower, I put on a black tuxedo and dress shoes and made my way into the living room.

"Oh, you look so handsome, Scott," my Mom said. "If only your father was still here to see you," She kissed me on the cheek and straightened out my tux. "You'd make him so proud."

"Mom, I have to go."

"Alright, sweetie, but remember that this is her night, not yours," she said. "Now make her feel special."

"I will, Mom," I hugged and kissed her." And I love you, and I'll be home around eleven."

After picking up Mary at her house and driving to the school, we headed to the gym, where everyone gathered.

The walls and ceiling of the gym were ornately decorated with streamers, banners, and hundreds of balloons. On the far end, where the wrestling mats would normally be, was a large stage with a DJ and all his stereo equipment. There was table after table of commissary goods just waiting to be devoured along the walls. The lighting was dim, and the music loud. It was going to be another awesome school party.

"Thank you again for the flowers, Browny," Mary Jane said.

"You're welcome, my little honeybee," I whispered into her ear.

Mary was wearing a tight red dress with spaghetti string straps and red high heels, and her brown hair was wrapped in a bun atop her head. She was looking gorgeous.

"Hey, it's my king," Matt said. "You look sharp, you really do."

"Thanks, so do you," I said. "But what's up with the tie?"

He was wearing a black tuxedo like mine, but instead of the traditional bow tie, he had on a bright red full-length tie.

"Ah, you know, I have to keep it original," Matt said. "And who's this lovely thing?" He took hold of Mary's hand and kissed it.

"Good evening, Matt," Mary said.

"Hey Nathan, what's going on?" I said. "And Erin, how about you?" Erin was a junior, and they have been dating for about a month now. They're a pretty cute couple, but I doubt they'll last. Nathan can't seem to keep a girl for the life of him.

"I'm great, Scott, thanks," Erin said.

"Same as always, Browny, and you know that I'm only here for the cake," Nathan said.

"Uh hum!" Erin nudged him in the ribs with her elbow.

"Oh, and to dance with Erin," Nathan said.

Principal Norwall waved me towards the stage. "Well, guys, they're calling me upfront to get this party started."

"Now, don't hold her too tightly when you dance with her," Mary said. "You just remember who you're going out with."

"I love you too, Mary."

She smiled coyly and gave me a quick kiss on the lips.

"Yes, Principal Norwall," I said.

"You have always set a good example for these students to follow Scott, and I'm proud of you for that," he said. "You're going to be a strong leader one day, and I can't wait to see what becomes of your life."

"Thank you, sir, but I'm no angel."

"Well, tonight you are," Principal Norwall said. "Now, step into the hallway. You know the drill from there." Patting me on the back, he led me to the door next to the stage and opened it.

Standing all alone in the dimly lit hallway was Jessica. She was wearing an elegant white gown and white open-toed heels. Her light brown hair was hanging freely down her bare back while her bangs draped across the sides of her face, but most stunning of all was how her green eyes sparkled in the dim lighting.

"Jessica, words cannot describe how beautiful you are." I brushed her bangs behind her ears and kissed her softly on the cheek.

"Thank you for doing this for me, Scott; thank you so much," she said, her voice almost a whisper.

"Anything to make you happy, my angel."

Jessica blushed and looked down at the floor.

A moment later, our school's vice president congratulated our football team and our new homecoming queen.

It was again Jessica's time to shine, and when she walked out on stage, waving, the crowd erupted in thunderous applause. I couldn't help but smile ear to ear.

"Johnathan?" I said. He was leaning against the lockers, dressed in his usual black clothes. "What are you doing back here?"

A sly smile crept across his face. "She's hot, isn't she?"

"What?" I said. "She's your sister?!"

"Yes, she is, but that doesn't change anything now, does it?" He turned around and began to walk down the hall. "You ever imagine what she looks like under that dress? I don't."

Did he really just say that?! I mean, he's never spoken about Jessica like that before. In fact, he's beaten up people for saying less.

"...and you're homecoming king-Scott!" our vice president announced.

I was still in shock over what Johnathan had just said that I didn't know what to do. I wanted to smash him out, but then again, he was my friend. It was also Jessica's night, and I refused to ruin it for her. But did he really say that?!

I walked onto the stage to the cheering of the crowd and took hold of the mic. Johnathan's words were still echoing in the back of my mind.

"Good evening, ladies and gentlemen of Janestown High. Are you ready to get the greatest homecoming dance ever started?" The crowd cheered enthusiastically. "But before we kick it off, I have a few things to say. First, I want to thank each and every one of you for voting me king again. I'm honored to have earned your respect and admiration over these past four years, and I'll do my best to lead Janestown Killer Bees to victory tomorrow." Again, the crowd cheered.

"We love you, Scott," a girl yelled.

"I love you too," I pointed at her. "And second, there is a woman whom you all know I care for dearly. A woman who is so sweet and tender-hearted that she deserves more than our respect. She deserves to be our queen-Jessica."

Jessica wiped the tears from her eyes and hugged me tight while the crowd cheered.

"Thank you," she whispered in my ear.

After a quick bow, I led Jessica by the arm towards the middle of the dance floor. She was glowing like an angel and smiling at me so warmly. That's when I knew this meant the world to her, and it was all worth it.

Hugging her close to me with one arm around her waist, her hand in mine, we began to dance to the slow music. Her skin was soft, and her perfume soothingly intoxicating.

We held each other closely for nearly four minutes and danced as if we were all alone under the moonlight. I didn't want this moment to ever end, but like all great things in life, it did. So that's why I've always believed in enjoying the life you live because you'll never know when it will all come crashing down.

At the end of our dance, I hugged her one last time and joined Mary, who was still clapping for me.

"You did a very nice thing for her, Scott," Mary said. "Now come here, my little Browny Scout. You're all mine now." Grabbing and pulling me tightly to herself, Mary Jane kissed me with passion. She tasted good, like strawberries.

"You looked like a true professional out there, Browny," Nathan said.

"Yeah, only I could have looked better, my man," Matt said.

"Yeah, yeah, thanks, guys," I said. "Now, let's enjoy the rest of the night because tomorrow is the big game. Six o'clock, it's show time!"

"Hell yeah!" Aaron said.

"That's right. We're going to be champions tomorrow!" Matt shouted.

"Oh yeah!" Nathan yelled, pumping his fist in the air.

My feet ached, and my stomach was about to burst by the end of the dance at eleven. With a final farewell to my friends, Mary Jane and I left the school.

"Karen?" I said. She was sitting on the grass near a wooden bench with her hands covering her face. She was crying, and a small trickle of blood was running down her chin.

Mary gasped. "Oh my gosh, Scott."

"Come here, Karen," I knelt next to her and embraced her in my arms. "Everything is going to be alright. We're here for you, and we won't leave you." I pulled out a napkin from my breast pocket and wiped the blood off her chin and lips.

"H-how could he d-do this to me?" Karen said. "He hit me, Scott. H-He hit me be-because I wouldn't...I wouldn't..." She started to cry again.

Michelle was standing by the school doors with her hands covering her mouth. Several other people were gathering around.

"I know Karen, I know," I helped her to her feet. "Now, let's get you home. I'll walk with you."

"I'll catch a ride with someone else, Browny," Mary said, rubbing Karen's back.

"I'll take you home, Mary Jane," Michelle said.

"Thank you, Michelle, and you'll be alright, Karen. Scott will take care of you, sweetheart." Mary hugged Karen, blew me a kiss, and walked back inside the school with Michelle.

Slinging my leather jacket over Karen's shoulders, I led her by the hand down the poorly lit street. The night air was cool and crisp.

"He thinks that I'm not worth loving. Like I'm worthless as a person. Like I'm-"

"Stop right there, Karen. That's nonsense."

"Maybe I am stuck up, or nothing." Karen stopped walking and again broke down into tears.

I faced her and put my hands on her shoulders. "No, Karen, you're not," I said. "You're a strong and beautiful young woman who has a long and wonderful life ahead of her."

"Everything was fine in the beginning, but then he changed. He started yelling and calling me names, and when-"

"No one who loves you will ever treat you like that, ever," I said, trying to conceal the anger in my voice. I was going to mess him up. "Now listen to me, Karen, you are one of the most bubbly and cheery friends that I have ever had the pleasure of knowing, and that's saying a lot. Especially for a girl."

She laughed tentatively.

I brushed her hair out of her eyes. "Is that a smile under there?"

"Quit it."

"There's the girl I know,"

Sniffling, she wiped the tears from her eyes.

"I know times like these hurt Karen, but you can't dwell on them. There's more to life than misery, especially for a girl like you."

"Thank you, Scott."

"I'm always going to be here for you, Karen. Always," I said. "Now get your beauty sleep. You have a long day of cheerleading tomorrow." After hugging her tightly, I waited for her to go inside her house, but she just stood in the middle of her driveway, staring at me with a wounded smile.

"You're a good person, Scott. This is why everyone loves you. So don't you ever change, don't you ever." A few more tears rolled down her cheeks.

"Don't you start this again," I said. "It took me nearly half an hour to get a laugh out of you, so save these tears for something like when you get married."

With a short laugh, she again wiped the tears from her eyes and gave me a quick wave of goodnight.

My walk back to the school was cold, and the drive home was lonely. I tried not to think about the events that surrounded Karen that night, but I couldn't believe that one of my good friends would do that to her, to anyone, really. I guess we were all changing for better or for worse.

The following morning, while our football team was waiting for the buses in the school parking lot, I confronted Johnathan. I didn't care if I missed the championship game or got suspended for fighting. I wanted to let him know, and everyone else, that if you beat up a girl, I'd piece you in, especially if she's my friend.

"So, is this the new you, too?" I said with a raised voice. "Beating up your girlfriend, Johnathan?" People started to gather around.

"What's going on, Scott?" Aaron said.

Johnathan turned around and smiled at me. It was the same sick smile he gave me in the hallway last night. "You can say that."

I removed my leather jacket, dropped it to the ground, and shouted, "Everyone get out of the way! How about I put you on the ground like you did Karen, you bastard!"

Everyone started to clear out and quiet down.

"What did he do, Scott?" someone said.

Karen pushed her way through the crowd. "Browny!" she yelled.

"What's going on, Browny," Nathan said.

"He hit Karen in the face last night," I said. "And now he has two choices. Beg her for forgiveness or swallow his frickin' teeth."

Karen stood behind me and wrapped her arms around me. "You don't have to do this, Scott. He's not worth it." She scowled at Johnathan. "Are you a jerk?"

Matt looked shocked. "You hit Karen, dude?!"

"That's super low, man," Aaron said.

"So what's it going to be?" I said. "She's right here. So make your choice."

Nathan glared at Johnathan. "I have your back, Browny. I'll help beat him down."

Johnathan looked at the ground and sighed heavily. "I'm sorry, Karen."

I looked around at everyone. "Is that it? Is that all you can say after what you did? Why don't you drop to your knees and apologize? She at least deserves that."

Johnathan took off his letterman's coat and knelt on the pavement. Some of the football players and cheerleaders laughed, but not me. I was dumbfounded.

"I will not wrap my apology in excuses, though I have many. Instead, I will say what I can to alleviate the pain I've caused you," Johnathan said. "I am sorry for everything hurtful that I have said to you, and I'm truly sorry for hitting you. If I cannot convince you through words of how sorry I am, then perhaps in the future, you will let me prove to you in deed, my sorrow," He stood up and grabbed his coat. "I'm very sorry, Karen, and I promise to make this up to you in a big way." Johnathan walked off and headed down the street.

We beat the Wildcats twenty-eight to twenty, and for the first time in our school's history, we were the single A state football champions.

CHAPTER FOUR

"Hey girls, how are you?" I said as I took a seat at the lunch table next to Mary. Putting my arm around her, I gave her a quick kiss on the lips. "Hello, my love."

"Hi, Browny," Mary said

"Hey, Scott," a girl said.

I smiled at her. "Well, Mary Jane, I was thinking that it would be best to embarrass you now in front of your friends rather than in private." Reaching into my pocket, I pulled out a small felt-covered box and opened it. "So, as an early Christmas present, I got you this."

Mary gasped. "Oh my gosh, Scott! It's beautiful."

"Wow, Browny and you two have been dating for only how long now?!" Jessica said.

I took the silver heart locket from the box and clasped it around Mary's neck. "I know this isn't much, but wait, there's more." With a wave of my hand, Aaron strolled over and handed Mary a huge stuffed teddy bear and a bouquet of wildflowers. The other girls at the table oo'd and ahh'd.

Blushing, Mary wrapped her arms around me and kissed me relentlessly. "Oh, you're such a sweetheart, my little Browny scout. Thank you so very much!"

"I want a sparkly new silver necklace for Christmas," a girl said.

"There's a picture of me inside, so I'll always be with you."

"Where's my present, Browny?" Jessica said.

"Yeah, where's our presents, Scott?" another girl said.

"Never mind them. Just kiss me," Mary said.

After a pleasant lunch with the girls, I headed to my locker.

"Hey, Browny," Karen said.

"Oh hey, Karen. What's up?" I said.

"Um, I never really thanked you for what you did for me at homecoming."

"Sure you did. You didn't tell on me for scaring those kids on Halloween."

"That was before this, and besides, you bowed down and kissed my feet, remember?

"Yeah, that was humiliating."

"I'm sorry for that," Karen took hold of my hands with hers. "What you did really meant a lot to me, Scott. Thank you." She leaned forward, kissed me on the cheek, and hurried down the hallway.

Finally, it was the day that every kid dreams of. Christmas. It's also a favorite of my mother's because it's one of the few days of the year when my grandparents can visit.

"How are you doing at school, Scott?" Grandma said. We were all sitting at the table eating a traditional turkey dinner that she and Mom spent all day preparing. And like usual, it was delicious.

"I'm doing alright, grandma."

"Don't let him fool you. He has a 3.8 G.P.A.," Mom said.

Grandma shot me that look out of the corner of her eye. I smiled back.

"How's sports going for you?" Grandpa said.

"We beat the Wildcats last month, so now we're the single A state football champions. But now it's wrestling season, and I'm already two, and oh."

"Well, good. Did you score any touchdowns or make any spectacular plays?" Grandpa said.

"No, but Matt and Nathan did," I said, passing the dinner rolls to my Mom. "And really, we won because of them."

"Speaking of your friends, how are they?" Grandma said. "Oh, and are you dating anyone?" She nudged me with her elbow. "Do you have a special someone? A girly friend?"

I saw where this was going, and I wasn't having it. "They're doing fine," I said. "So, what have you guys been up to?"

"They should be doing wonderful now," Mom said. "Before you came over this morning, he stopped by each of his friend's houses and gave them all a present. He even gave his girlfriend Mary Jane a silver heart locket last week."

"A girlfriend, uh," Grandpa said.

"She's a really beautiful, polite young woman," Mom said. "He's in love with her."

"Mom, you're embarrassing me," I mumbled.

But it was already too late. From that moment on, until everyone was done eating, they only wanted to talk about how she and I were doing. Do I like her? Where have I taken her? Is she the one? It was thoroughly embarrassing.

"May I be excused, please?" I said.

"Certainly, Scott," Mom said.

"Can I take any of your plates?" I said, standing up.

"Yes, thank you, Scott," Grandma said. I picked up her plate and put it in the dishwasher. "He's becoming quite the gentleman, isn't he?"

"And he's a fighter, too." Mom said.

"How's that going for you?" Grandpa said. "Have you won any more tournaments?"

"It's going great, actually, and yeah, I have," I said. "Just last week, I won by submission."

"That's really impressive. You're getting quite good," Grandpa said.

"He's really a good kid, but he's something else in the cage." Mom said.

The month of January didn't seem to last very long. I was just too busy to notice the days flying by. Our wrestling season was now in full swing, and we've had eight team matches so far. I was still undefeated, and so was Matt, Nathan, and Johnathan. It's expected that the four of us will defend our championship titles again this year, but we'll see.

The cold was numbing, and dark gray clouds loomed overhead. It was a Saturday afternoon in January, five days before Jessica's birthday party, and we were all outside having a giant snowball fight with some of the other kids from the neighborhood.

It rarely snows here in Janestown, but when it does, no one misses the chance to play in it, and today was a record in snowfall. We got about twelve inches over the past few days, which covered everything, but unfortunately, school wasn't canceled. Everyone lives so close together in this small town that we could just walk there. There's really no need for the buses; that's why I love it here in Janestown.

"Eat this, Michael!" Matt yelled, flinging a snowball at his chest. His shot missed but tore a huge chunk off the top of their snow fort.

"Alright, guys, take cover!" I yelled. "They're hitting us pretty hard, so we're going to need a new strategy if we're going to win." Everyone hunkered down behind our wall.

"And how do you suppose we do that general?" Karen said.

"First, we need to fortify our wall," I said. I could hear the soft thudding of snowballs slamming into it. "It's too thin and low. It needs to be thicker and higher, but we also need to build an extension of it angled slightly towards their position."

"That's a good idea, Browny," Nathan said.

"Now, second," The opposing side wasn't taking a break like we were and was lobbing snowballs over our wall. "Gosh darn it!" I just got hit. "Second, we take out their walls, and we need cover fire for our snow retrievers and wall builders. Aaron and Karen, that will be your responsibility. So cover us well."

"What about me?" Jessica said.

"Patience, honey. You and Mary Jane need to get some fresh snow for the firing squad," I said. "Matt and Nathan, we're going to build the wall. Now let's move it."

"You got it," Nathan said, clapping his hands.

Matt glanced at Nathan through the corners of his eyes. "What was that? he said.

"What?" Nathan said.

"That little clap thing."

"Oh, well, you know. It's what we do when we break the huddle in football. It's habit."

"Well, it's retarded, so quit it," Matt said.

"You're retarded," Nathan said, shooting him a scowl.

"Come on guys, really?!" I said.

Nathan threw up his hands in protest and looked at me like I was stupid.

Building the new wall and reinforcing the old one under fire was difficult. First, Matt and Nathan had to run around and pack snow into a huge rectangular bin. Then, they had to lay the snow block next to the existing wall so I could join the two sections together. That's when I took a lot of hits, even some to my face. When your side is only throwing two snowballs to the enemy's eight, you're bound to take some hard hits.

It took us about ten minutes to rebuild, and once we were done, it was time for us to administer the pain.

"The right side of their wall is crumbling!" Jessica yelled after one of her snowballs slammed into the enemy's fortress.

"Good shot, Jessica," Matt said. He hurled a snowball and struck a kid in the arm. "Focus all attacks on their wall!"

I hid behind our wall and watched Mary Jane run around. Her long brown hair fluttered every which way as she ducked and weaved to avoid the incoming snowballs. She was a tough competitor, yet so sweet, gentle, and beautiful. A snowball slammed into her face. I laughed.

She glared at me. "Are you really laughing at-" Another snowball struck her in the head.

"Get your head down, Mary!" Grabbing her by the jacket, I pulled her down on top of me. Brushing the snow out of her ears, she kissed me with her cold lips.

"I love you," she whispered.

"I love you too."

Out of the corner of my eye, I noticed that Johnathan was standing a few feet away. He was all decked out in a white snowsuit with a snowball in his hand.

"Hey, is it alright if I play with you guys?" he said. "It looks like you guys could use my help."

I looked over to Karen, and after a moment's hesitation, she nodded.

"Sure, man, now take some cover, and let's kick some butt."

I felt slightly uncomfortable with him being here, but only because I didn't know how Karen felt. This would be the first time since homecoming that they'd be this close. I had no idea how they'd get along. Really, this was the first time since anyone had hung out with him. I couldn't help but feel sorry for him. After all, I still thought of him as a friend.

"Alright, everyone, change your ammo to ice balls and target their walls!" Matt shouted. Torquing his arm back, he threw an ice ball into the enemy's fortress, which blew a gaping hole through it.

"Nice shot, Matt," Johnathan said.

"Take this," Jessica said, hurling an ice ball. A minute later, their walls came crashing down.

"Get 'em, guys!" Nathan yelled. Jumping over our wall, he raced up to the boundary line with a snowball in hand and buried it into the back of a fleeing kid. With no walls to take cover behind, we easily picked off our opponents, and after a good twenty more minutes of pain, they called it quits.

"Well, that was pretty fun, guys," I said.

"It certainly was, man," Aaron said. "But I think I'm gonna head home. I'm freezing." Brushing the snow off his cap, he waved goodbye and headed for his house.

"Yeah, I'm cold too," Jessica said. "Besides, it's almost our curfew. We'll see you guys tomorrow."

"I don't know what you're talking about, sis," Johnathan said. "I'm staying."

"No, you're not. Now let's go." Jessica tugged at his suit, but Johnathan quickly broke her grasp.

Unfortunately for him, none of us wanted to stay out. Matt had homework to catch up on while I had school committee proposals to read, and everyone else just wanted to warm up. So, after saying our goodbyes, we all went our separate ways except for Johnathan. I wanted to keep walking down the street and get home, but something didn't seem right with him. He was slowly wandering around the field where we had been playing, with his head hung low. He looked lost. Almost detached from reality. Nothing has been right with him since that night. He fell to his knees and began to cry.

"You alright, man?" I said, resting my hand on his shoulder. He wiped his eyes and stood up. "Do you want to talk about it?"

"You-" he mumbled. "You wouldn't understand."

"Maybe, maybe not," I said. "But I'm here for you."

"No one can," he said. "No one can understand."

"You don't know for certain. Besides many people-"

"I do, Scott, I do," he said sternly.

I sighed. It was clear that whatever was bothering him, he didn't want to talk about. "Well, then, I hope you'll be fine, Johnathan. I really do."

"Oh, I will," Patting me on the back, he walked away. "But will you?"

A few days later, it was again another ordinary day at school, but being the third of February, it was also Jessica's seventeenth birthday. Of course, I couldn't help but embarrass her, so during lunch, Matt, Nathan, and all our friends sang Happy Birthday to her. It was a song that she didn't want to hear again by the end of the day, and who could blame her? She had it sung

to her three times that day, with one more on the way.

Later that night, we were all sitting around in the Wood's living room, giving Jessica her presents. It was a small party, and only a few friends were invited, but it was still a blast.

"Thank you very much, Mary Jane," Jessica said, setting down her new CDs. "These are a much better gift than a twenty dollar gift card-Nathan." She grinned at him.

"Yeah, you've kind of been lacking in the creative side there, buddy," I said.

"I figured she could use the money, you know," Nathan said.

"Browny's right, man, you have definitely not been yourself recently," Matt said, putting his arm around Nathan's shoulders. "Is there something that you want to talk about, my man? Something that you want to get off your chest?"

Nathan brushed Matt's arm off and scooted further from him on the couch. "I'm good, guys. Really, I'm good."

"Whatever you say, dude," Matt said.

Sitting next to Jessica on the couch, Johnathan pulled out a small box and handed it to her. "Happy birthday, sis."

After tearing off the wrapping paper, Jessica opened the box and pulled out a silver necklace that had a small ruby pendant dangling from it. Everyone got quiet.

"Um, thank you?" Jessica said. She was looking around at everyone with a confused look on her face.

"You're welcome, sis. I thought it would spruce up your jewelry collection."

"Awkward," Matt chimed. Everyone laughed.

"Wow, Johnathan, it's like that between-" Nathan said.

"Who wants some cake?" Mrs. Woods said, standing up in a hurry.

"This guy," Matt said, pointing to himself.

A moment later, Mrs. Woods returned with a homemade chocolate and cherry cake from the kitchen. It had seventeen candles on it, and once Jessica had blown them out, we cheered for her. The cake was delicious, but like the rest of the evening, it didn't last long, and before I knew it, I was lying in my bed, falling asleep.

"Hey Browny?" Johnathan whispered, leaning over his desk behind me.

"What's up, man," I whispered back.

"I forgot my wrestling shoes at home, so could you tell the coach I'll be ten minutes late?" He said. "I had to wash them, and I think that I left them in the dryer."

"Johnathan, do you want to sit back in your seat and stop looking over Scott's shoulder?" Mrs. Morgan, our math teacher, said.

"Yes, Mrs. Morgan. I do," he said.

"No problem."

"Thanks, dude."

Fifteen minutes later, the one-fifty bell rang, and school was out. Standing by my locker, putting away my books, I saw Jessica walking down the hall.

"Hey, who's this beautiful thing?" I said, stepping in front of her.

"You're not supposed to be flirting with me, Browny," she said.

"I think that silver necklace looks good on you, especially with your dress."

"I'll tell Mary."

"What?!" I shrugged my shoulders and raised my hands with a stupid look. "I can't give a dear friend a compliment or two?" She chuckled, finally.

"You're so retarded," she said. "But thanks, today sucked."

"That's too bad."

"It was one of those days, you know."

"Yeah, I've been there."

"But at least I get to go home and relax."

"You certainly do, Jessica," I said. "And tell your brother to hurry it up."

"Hurry, what up?"

He forgot his wrestling shoes at home, so he's going back to get them."

"What an idiot. He should have to do extra laps or something for being stupid." She looked over my shoulder. "I have to catch the bus. I'll see you tomorrow, okay?"

"Alright, but no more of these bad days," I said. "You know I can't stand it when you're sad." She smiled and rolled her eyes. "Now, take care of yourself, sweetheart."

"I will, and thank you." Smiling warmly, she gave me a quick hug goodbye and left the school.

"Where the heck is Johnathan?" I said. "It's almost four."

"I have no idea. Maybe once he got home, he decided not to come," Matt said.

We were mopping the wrestling mats and setting up our MMA training equipment.

"He said he'd be ten minutes late, not two hours," I said.

"Oh well, his loss," Nathan said. "Now, let's get this equipment set up."

"Is everyone having a bad day?" I said.

Two hours later, our MMA training was over, and everyone went home, but not me. Johnathan never showed up.

The sun was warm to my skin, and the gentle breeze carried the smell of freshly cut grass. It was a lovely day with not a cloud to be seen. It's days like this, I wish I could be down at the lake relaxing and soaking up the sun on the beach.

Once at Jessica's house, I knocked on the front door and stepped back. One moment turned into two and then three, but no one answered. I knocked again. The door slowly swung open.

"Johnathan? Jessica?" I walked inside. All the curtains in the living room were closed, and the lights were off. It was oddly quiet. "Mr. And Mrs. Woods, are you guys home?" My heartbeat was all that answered me.

I walked down the hallway and opened up Johnathan's bedroom door. He wasn't there. Up ahead, I saw that Jessica's door was slightly ajar, so I pushed it open and walked inside.

"Jessica, there you are."

She was lying atop her bed, sleeping in her favorite knee-long white dress. I wanted to wake her, but she needed her beauty sleep. She had a long day ahead of her tomorrow.

I don't know how long I stood there watching her resting peacefully before the tears began to roll down my cheeks. A cold shiver coursed throughout my body, and I felt like throwing up. The light around me began to fade to black, and from that moment on, all I could remember was running, and for how long, I don't know, but when I got to where I was going, I fell down and let it all out.

She was so young and beautiful, so innocent. My angel.

Three days later, on the sixteenth of February, Jessica's funeral was held. Nearly four hundred people were in attendance, all showing their respect for the girl who meant so much to them and to me.

"Do you have any words that you would like to share in remembrance, Scott?" the pastor said.

Walking across the stage, I placed my speech atop the pulpit. Pausing, I exhaled slowly, my lips trembling. She was so peaceful. So beautiful. I just couldn't. I placed a red rose across her folded arms and collapsed to my knees before her, tears streaming down my face. My sobbing uncontrollable. Why?! She was so young. Sweet. Why? It was just too much.

The warmth of Mary's arms enveloped me as she held me close to her chest. Images of her slashed throat kept flashing before my mind.

The cops said there were no signs of forced entry or missing valuables, which ruled out a botched burglary. They also believed that Johnathan had been kidnapped. He's been missing since the murder, and none of his belongings were packed. There was no physical evidence linking Johnathan to the crime, and Mr. and Mrs. Woods were still at work, which also ruled them out as suspects. No one heard or saw anything. Nothing. Jessica was murdered, and

Johnathan was kidnapped. I lost two friends that day as well as a piece of my heart.

I love you, Jessica.

CHAPTER FIVE

The following weeks of my life seemed to drag on. The Woods immediately moved out, saying that they couldn't bear to live in the house that their daughter was murdered in, and who could blame them? I could hardly walk past Jessica's locker without struggling to hold back my tears. School just wasn't the same without her, and neither was I.

It was now Sunday, the fifteenth of March, the third and final day of the single A state wrestling championship. As expected, I advanced to the finals with an undefeated record. Both Matt and Nathan advanced as well, but they had already wrestled today and won the championship for their weight class.

"They'll be calling you out any minute now, Scott, and if you win, we'll take home the team trophy." the coach said. "Are you ready, 'cause that's a lot of pressure?"

"I'll pin him, coach," I said.

"That's what I want to hear, and remember to check in at the scoring table," he said.

"Do you see the guy warming up in the red and white singlet on the second mat from the left?" I said.

"There's eight mats and hundreds of wrestlers in this stadium, Browny. You're going to have to be a little more specific," Nathan said.

"He has blonde hair," I said.

"I see him," Matt pointed. "Is that the guy you're wrestling?"

"Yeah, he's a freestyle champion," I said. An announcer over the intercom called me to mat two.

"Freestyle, uh?" Matt said.

"Uh-huh," I said. "Let's see if his freestyle is any match for my jujitsu."

"Make me proud, Browny," Mary said.

"Good luck, Scott," Erin said.

"I see him now," Nathan said. I shook my head.

After checking in with the scoring table, I took my place in the center of the mat across from my opponent. He was slightly taller than me and weighed a good ten pounds heavier. Usually, I would wrestle in the one hundred and seventy-one weight class, but with Johnathan missing, I had to wrestle in the one hundred and eighty-nine weight class. With short, bleach-blonde hair, he struck me as the type of person who thought he was bad but really wasn't. I can't stand guys like that.

Once we shook hands, the referee blew his whistle, and our match began. Immediately, my opponent took a shot at my right leg. Kicking my leg back, I sprawled out on top of him, wrapping my arm under his neck in a front headlock. He squirmed and struggled to break free and wrap up my legs, but my defense was solid.

Throwing my legs underneath him, I wrapped them around his waist while switching my lock around his neck into a guillotine choke. It was illegal, but I didn't care.

The referee awarded my opponent two points for the takedown, but surprisingly, he didn't see him choking.

Hooking his left leg with my right and pushing off the mat with my left, I twisted my hips and swept him onto his back. I released the choke but kept the headlock. I then slowly pressed his shoulder blades to the mat while controlling his squirming body with my full mount.

The referee blew his whistle and stopped the match. My opponent was pinned, and I was now the one hundred and eighty-nine-pound state champion, my fourth state championship title in four years.

My friends and teammates cheered loudly for me, along with Karen and the cheerleaders, as my hand was raised in victory. Still, and for some reason, I felt empty inside, like something was missing.

"That was one heck of a move you pulled out there, Browny!" Matt said, giving me a high five.

"That's how you take the championships!" the coach yelled, hugging me. "Great win, Scott! That was a great win!"

"A thirty-nine-second pin?!" Nathan said. "You nearly tore his head off!"

I sat down on the bleachers and took a drink of water.

Mom hugged me tentatively, careful not to get too much sweat on her. "Congratulations, sweetie. You did really well out there." She was glowing proudly.

Mary sat on my lap, faced me, and draped her arms around my shoulders and kissed me. "I'm so proud of you."

"Let's go collect our trophies, guys." the coach said.

Once the tournament ended at eleven, all the state placers and champions were called to the award stand to receive their medals. Afterward, the highest-placing teams in the yearly point standings were awarded a team trophy. With three state champions and two placers, our team scored just enough points to take first place in our school division. It was an exciting way to end our wrestling season and one that I will never forget.

By the time I got home, it was nearly one in the morning. I was tired and ready for bed, but sleep evaded me. For hours, I tossed and turned, waking up several times from the same depressing dream.

I sat up and looked at the clock. It was three am. With my heart pounding, I climbed out of bed and put my clothes on. I felt uneasy, almost scared, and for some reason, I felt like I had to get out.

After climbing through my window, adrenaline pumping, I crept through my neighbor's backyard and wandered the empty neighborhood streets. The night air was brisk, and the moon bright. Despondent feelings plagued me while voices whispered in my ear. I wanted to scream and let it all out, but I couldn't, so I suffered in silence.

And then, standing before me as though I had been drawn to it all along was Jessica's house. The front door was slightly open, so I walked inside. White sheets covered all the furniture, and the air was stale. Stopping at Jessica's room, I hesitated to go inside. Fresh memories of that terrible day flooded my mind. Choking back tears, I opened her door.

White moonlight poured through the bedroom window, illuminating Jessica's perfectly made bed. I struggled to keep myself from crying, but memories of her blood-soaked pillow and lifeless body were too much to bear.

Kneeling by her bed, I let myself go. A feeling of peace washed over me.

"Don't cry for me," the voice of an angel said.

I wiped my tears away and looked up. Hovering off the floor, barefoot and in her favorite white dress, was Jessica. Her green eyes sparkled brightly in the moonlight while her long brown hair flowed as if blown by a gentle wind.

"W-What?"

"You have to be strong now," she whispered. "For them, you have to be strong."

I couldn't believe what I was seeing or even what I was hearing. I couldn't believe any of it. "B-But, you're..."

With a wounded smile, Jessica floated through the wall and down the street.

"Jessica-wait!" I cried out as I climbed through the window. I then chased after her from street to street and through yard after yard. Still, no matter how hard I ran, she always stayed a dim figure ahead of me. Before I knew it, she had disappeared into the Dark Woods, leaving me behind in the large grassy field, exhausted. Despair filled my heart.

"Jessica, please don't leave me." I strained to see her in the woods, but it was too dark. "Jessica."

Upon seeing her weaving gracefully between the trees, I again chased after her, but like before, she stayed one step ahead of me.

Her presence, though distant, was comforting, and I no longer feared the darkness. I then lost sight of her, and a feeling of dread washed over me again. I stopped and listened, looking around. The shadows of the trees moved in ways that I couldn't explain.

"Jessica-don't leave me," I whispered, trying not to wake the woods. "Jessica, please."

Off in the darkness, I caught a pair of beady black eyes staring at me. It's formless figure, like a shadow, shimmered in the faint light ahead. A coldness crept up my spine, and fear overcame me. I ran.

Trees and bushes flew past me, and I ducked and weaved to avoid them, but the poor lighting caused me to trip over a fallen branch. I hit the ground hard, breaking the fall with my arms.

Gritting my teeth, I rolled onto my back and waited for the pain to subside. Blood ran down my right forearm. Nothing was broken, though. It was just a flesh wound.

After regaining my senses, I looked around for the shadow, but it was gone. The early rays of dawn then burst over the eastern horizon, filling the sky with light. Breathing a sigh of relief, I stood up and glanced around.

Before me lay a large circular stretch of featureless desert with a small lake off in the distance. Jagged, but low mountains surrounded the desert on all sides except the small area behind me where the Dark Woods ended. To my right and only a few yards away stood the sheer-faced, three-hundred-foot-tall plateau, and to my horror, I had tripped only a few feet from what was rumored to exist, the chasm.

It extended over a football field in length with a width close to fifty feet at its widest point. The plateau overhung the entire chasm by about ten feet except for the tapered beginning that I stood dangerously close to.

Picking up a rock, I dropped it into the chasm and waited for the sound of it hitting something to echo back at me. Nothing. The chasm was a bottomless, black abyss.

"It's not polite to throw rocks at one's house, Browny," a familiar voice said.

Startled, I turned around, and standing before me, wearing forest green fatigues and black steel-toed boots, was Johnathan. His hair was black, short, and spiked, but there was something about him that was different. It was his piercing black eyes. They were real, not contacts. He was holding a small branch.

I took a step back, mindful of the chasm. "J-Johnathan?"

"How ironic is it that had you fallen another foot to your right, you'd have suffered the same fate as I?" Smirking, he tossed the branch at my feet.

I wanted to hug him, seeing that he was still alive, and ask him where he'd been all this time. But I was so confused. I mean, what the heck was wrong with me? First, I saw Jessica, and now I was seeing Johnathan?! Maybe I was dreaming peacefully asleep in my bed. Or maybe I was hallucinating, or perhaps it was all real. I didn't know, but then I saw Jessica's silver necklace and ruby pendant hanging around his neck.

"Johnathan?"

He smiled maliciously. "Now you see, don't you?" He held up Jessica's pendant. "We all have our price, Scott, and this-" He kissed her pendant. "This was mine."

His words stabbed me in the heart like a knife. It made sense now. All of it. "You fucking, bastard!"

Stepping forward, I threw a heavy right in the hopes of taking his head off. I wasn't going to piece him in for what he did. I was going to kill him.

Nimbly ducking away from my attack, he countered with a lightning-fast left into my exposed ribs. Incredible pain pulsed throughout my body, which brought me to a knee. The pain was nearly unbearable.

Getting up, I threw a few jabs that he somehow avoided, so I took a shot at his legs in an attempt to take him down. In a blur of motion, he side-stepped me without a hand of mine touching him and struck me in the side of my face. I fell to the ground and felt a small trickle of blood running down my cheek. I was dazed but still in it.

"You are no longer the superior fighter, Scott," His face was expressionless, and he was as calm as ever. He wasn't even breathing heavily. "And you can no longer protect them."

I climbed to my feet and wiped the blood off my face. Pressing forward in my traditional Muay Thai stance, I threw a jab followed by a hard right hook. Again, almost effortlessly, he avoided my attacks.

Before I could pull my fist back, he stepped into me and drove his elbow into my chin. My knees buckled, and I collapsed to the sandy ground. My head swam, and my vision doubled.

Kneeling on my chest and grabbing my hair, Johnathan ground the side of my face into the dirt with his elbow.

"I will spare your life, but only this once, and only so you may live with knowing that she will be my slave for the rest of eternity, as will everyone who you hold dear to your heart," He whispered into my ear. "For slowly but surely, I will steal them all from you, one by one."

When I had fully recovered, he was gone. I lay there on my back, staring at the cloudless blue sky. It was such a beautiful day.

For the next several hours, I wandered around the Dark Woods, trying to find my way home. Trying to answer the burning questions that I had, but I found neither. Instead, I found myself standing before a chain-linked fence and, on the other side, the football field.

After climbing the fence and crossing the field, I walked into school. It must have been between classes because the hallway was packed with kids.

"You alright, Scott?" some guy said.

"Yo Scott, do you need help, man?" asked another.

Everyone was staring at me. "I'll be fine, guys, thanks," I continued down the hall towards my locker.

"Are you sure, Scott? You look hurt," a girl said. "I'll get Mary Jane."

"No, don't. I'll be fine," I said. " I just need to clean up, that's all."

"Dude, Browny, where have you been, man?" Matt said.

I opened my locker. "Oh, just walking around. Thinking about things."

"I can tell, but man-" He looked at me intently. "Are you okay?"

"I fell down, that's all. So, how are you?"

"Fell down? Yeah, right, and I'm a rock star."

"Good morning, Browny; how are you?" Karen said, walking up from behind me and patting me on the back. I chuckled. If only she knew. "Ooo, you're cut, Browny."

"He's fine, Karen; he'll talk to you later," Matt led me by the arm into the bathroom. "We have got to get you cleaned up, my man." Wetting down some paper towels, he wiped the blood and dirt off my face and arms. "Did you get into a fight or something, Browny? You can tell me, man. You know that."

I smiled at him. "Please don't tell Mary. I don't want her to worry."

"Alright, I'll respect that, man," he said. "We've got an assembly today. Sixth period, so be ready, my president."

For the rest of the school day, all I could think about was everything that happened that morning, and before I knew it, I was standing in the middle of the gym with the whole school staring at me.

"Hey, Scott," Principal Norwall said, nudging me.

"Huh?" I muttered.

"Alright then, they're all yours," He handed me the mic. "Take them away."

"Um, how are you all?" The crowd cheered with some applause. I had no idea what was going on. The wrestling team was standing to my far left, while Karen and the other cheerleaders were standing to my right. She looked concerned. "Yeah, that's good."

Principal Norwall put his arm around my shoulder and took hold of the mic. "Scott, as the team captain and one hundred and eighty-nine-pound champion, do you have anything to say about this year's team performance?" He stepped back.

I took a deep breath and cleared my mind. "Yes, yes, I do. We had three state champions and two state placers this year, not to mention a first-place team trophy, which is a testament to everyone's hard work and dedication," I pointed at our coaches to my left. "Not to mention the expertise of our coaches. Thank you." The crowd cheered louder. "I also want to thank our lovely cheerleaders who cheered us to victory and to all of you for your support. Thank you all." The crowd again erupted into thunderous applause.

I raised my hand. "Alright, Killer Bees, alright. That is two trophies that our teams have won for you. What more do you want? A baseball championship?" The roaring of the crowd was deafening but uplifting to my spirit.

Strutting her way over, Karen took the microphone from my hand.

"Hey Karen, do you have something you want to say?"

"Yes, Browny, I do," Karen said into the mic. "Well, actually, it's a question for you."

"Ask away, lovely."

"Why did you forget my birthday last Saturday?" The crowd quieted down. I just stood there. "Yeah, I cheered for you on my birthday during the state championships, and you never said happy birthday to me."

Oos and ahhs filled the gym while the wrestling team and cheerleaders laughed at me. I could feel my face getting hot with embarrassment. I don't think I forgot about her birthday, did I?

I motioned to a wrestler to get a garbage can, which he quickly retrieved. "I've got a present for you, Karen. It's a garbage can!" The teachers standing off to the side shook their heads. "Now get over here, Karen!" I said, lunging for her.

Nimbly avoiding my grasp, Karen ran across the gym, laughing all the way, but she was no match for my speed. Catching her, I picked her up and slung her over my shoulder like a sack of potatoes. The crowd was cheering wildly.

"Please don't throw me in there," Karen said. "Please don't!"

"Do I can her?" I yelled. "Do I can this cute blue-eyed cheer captain?"

"Don't you do it, Scott!" a cheerleader yelled. "Because if you do, then we will never cheer for you or your boys!"

"Can her! Can her!" the crowd chanted. Surprisingly enough, even the teachers were yelling at me to can her.

"Please don't Browny! You'll ruin my uniform!" Karen yelled as she slapped me on the back repeatedly.

"Oh yes, you're going in, Kari Berry!" I unslung her off my shoulder and stuffed her in the garbage can. Only her kicking feet and flailing arms were visible. Laughter, hooting, and hollering filled the gym.

"Get me out of here!" Karen screamed.

"Okay, you asked me too." I pushed over the can with my foot and watched her tumble out with the rest of the trash.

"You're such a jerk, Scott!" she yelled. Standing up and brushing herself off, Karen stormed past me and rejoined her laughing cheerleaders.

"And yes, Killer Bees, your baseball team will try their best to bring another trophy to this great school."

After Principal Norwall's closing comments, we were all dismissed, and the entertaining school day was over. All that was left now was baseball practice and MMA training. Both of which I wanted to end. I just wanted to go home.

"Xavier?" I said.

"Yes, Scott. What can I do for you?"

"I want to take my training to the next level."

"Why? You're the best amateur fighter in the state, undefeated with sixteen wins. Is that not the best you can be?"

"You've already said it. I'm the best amateur. I want to be the best professional. I want to know everything there is to know about fighting, including martial weapons."

He placed a hand on my shoulder. "Are the cuts and bruises on your body why you seek this training?"

"Yes."

Xavier sighed. "In all of my eighteen years of martial arts instruction, I have never seen a student with as much potential to be the best as you are, and you know that I do not say that lightly. But I must say that only a few have found the path you wish to follow, and fewer still have succeeded," He picked up his black duffel bags and headed for the door. "Starting tomorrow, you will train with me from six p.m. until eight p.m. every weekday and every weekend from six a.m. to twelve p.m. This training takes precedence over all else. Do you understand?"

"Yes, sir."

"Defeat spurs many to greatness; few to perfection," he said. "Now go home and clear your mind."

That night, I again had trouble sleeping, so I just laid in my bed and stared at the ceiling while the hours passed by. Now, thinking about it, I did forget about Karen's birthday.

CHAPTER SIX

The third period had just begun when my science teacher called me to his desk. He handed me a pink hallway pass and told me to see counselor Catherine.

I had a pretty good idea of what she wanted to talk about, and if I was right, I didn't want to. What I did want to talk about, I knew no one would believe me. So what was the point? I mean, heck, I didn't even believe it myself.

"Good morning, Scott. Why don't you take a seat and make yourself comfortable." Catherine said. Closing the door, I sat in the chair across from her. "Do you want a mint?"

"No thanks."

"So how do you feel today?"

"Wonderful. How about you?"

She wrote something down. "That's great to hear, Scott, and I'm sure you are probably wondering why I called you in here. So, I'll get right to it. Some of your friends are worried about you, saying you haven't been quite acting like yourself recently. Do you know what they're talking about?"

"Yeah."

"Do you want to talk about it?"

"No."

"I know we've been through this before with your father, but I wanted to remind you that talking about your feelings is perfectly okay. You don't have to hide them."

"Yeah."

Again, she wrote something down. "You have great friends, Scott. I know they'll be there for you if you need them. You have to learn to trust them."

"Yeah."

"If you need anyone else to talk to, you know where I am.

"There you are, Browny. I've been looking all over for you." Mary said. I was milling around the baseball field, watching my teammates run through some basic in-field drills.

"Oh, hi, Mary."

"I feel like you've been avoiding me this past week. Is everything alright?"

"No, no. I just needed some time alone, that's all."

"I'm really worried about you, Scott, and so are your friends."

I put my arm around her and kissed her. "I'm alright, sweetheart."

She pulled away from me. "No, Scott. No, you're not," Her smile faded into a look of worry. "And yesterday at the assembly, you looked out of it. You looked out of it all day, and you're not doing much better today."

I sighed. I hated seeing her so worried, but what could I do?

"Is it Jessica? Because I know that she meant a lot to you," Mary said.

"It is, but I need to deal with it in my own time, Mary." I brushed her brown hair out of her eyes and kissed her forehead.

"I want you to trust me with your feelings, okay?"

I pulled her close to me again. "Okay, Mary Jane, what did you need me for so badly that you searched everywhere?"

"Tomorrow's Matt's birthday, and I wanted to go shopping for his present with you tonight."

"I can't honey. I have MMA training after baseball practice."

"You can't miss this one session to shop for your friend?" Mary tugged on my arms. "It's his birthday, Browny."

"I know, but I just started training professionally. It would look bad on me if I missed my first session."

"No girlfriends allowed on the field, Scott," the coach said.

"Sorry, coach." I picked Mary up in my arms and carried her across the baseball field. "But we can skip school tomorrow if you'd like."

"You'd skip school instead. I would never have thought."

"Sweetheart, I have a 3.4 GPA. I think I can miss a few classes to go shopping for my best friend." I laid her in the grass behind the school and sat on top of her, careful not to crush her slender body.

"Oh really? Training is more important than school?" She stroked the back of my neck with her fingers. "Well, does your training teach you how to do this?"

She pulled down my head and tried to get me into a headlock, but I was on to her and easily slipped out of her grasp. With her arms extended, I carefully rolled her into a loose arm bar. Mary laughed and giggled, tapping my leg. Releasing her, I let her crawl on top of me.

"Now you're pinned."

"Besides, I have to buy Karen some presents and-"

"You really forgot her birthday, didn't you?"

"And I want to make up Valentine's Day with you."

Her eyes lit up like saucers, and she kissed me firmly. The taste of strawberries filled my mouth while a lavender aroma filled my senses. She was beautiful, and I wanted to spend the rest of my life with her.

"I love you, Mary Jane, my little honeybee."

"I love you too, Scott," She kissed me again. "But please, tell me what you're feeling. I care for you, so don't be afraid to talk to me, okay?"

"I will, Mary. I will."

Before long, it was time for her to go and baseball practice to begin, and once that was over, my MMA training with the guys began. We rigorously conditioned with lightweights for an hour and a half and then spared full speed for thirty minutes with no breaks. It was physically exhausting.

Once everyone had gone home, my professional training with Xavier got underway, but it was anything but professional. All I did for the next two hours was condition and practice hand-eye coordination drills. I wasn't very happy about my 'professional' training, but maybe he was preparing me for something later. Who knows.

I woke up early to the singing of the birds. Sunlight streamed through my bedroom window, and I could tell that today was going to be another gorgeous day.

After taking a quick shower and putting on a pair of black jeans and a plain white T-shirt, I walked into the kitchen and made myself a bowl of cereal.

"Good morning, Sweetie, you look cheerier today," Mom said. "Are you feeling better?"

"Morning, and yeah, I'm much better. Is there anything you need while I'm out and about?"

"Yes, thank you. The list is on the refrigerator."

Sitting down next to me, Mom laid her hand on my arm. "Is this your way of making up Valentine's Day with Mary Jane?"

"Mom."

"What?"

"You know what."

Mom gave me a strange look. "Oh, before I forget again, Mrs. Engels called me to tell you to stop by her house sometime soon."

"Why?"

"She wants to pay you for doing her lawn."

"I was doing her a favor, but if she insists." I threw on my brown leather jacket and hugged Mom goodbye.

"You do too many favors for people, Scott."

"And yet I still somehow get paid for them," I said. "Besides, someone once told me that generosity is worth more than gold."

Smiling, she blew a kiss at me.

"Oh my. Would you take a look at you," I said.

Mary Jane was wearing a white halter top with a pink knee-long skirt and sandals. Her long brown hair hung freely down her back while her silver heart locket around her neck sparkled in the sunlight.

"And you too," Grinning, she wrapped her arms around my neck and kissed me. "So, are you ready, my love?"

"Yes, ma'am," I said, opening the car door for her.

It took us about forty-five minutes to drive from Janestown to Flagstaff, and once we got there, we wasted no time and began shopping for Matt's presents.

An hour later, we had bought him a few gifts and a ton of party supplies. We went a little overboard, spending nearly eighty dollars, but it wasn't as if he would get a lot from his thieving parents.

Mary exited the dressing room wearing a short, bright red skirt. "So, how about this? Is it me?" She twirled around. "Do I look good in it?"

"Of course, you look good, baby," some guy in forest green fatigues said. There were two others dressed just like him.

"You look real good," another said.

Mary brushed her hair behind her ears and looked at me. "Thank you?" The three guys walked away laughing.

"You always look good, Mary Jane. I think it compliments your toenail polish."

She wiggled her toes. "You noticed."

"I notice everything about you, Mary. Now, what do you say we get something to eat?"

"Sounds nice. Give me a minute to change."

After she dressed, we took a short jaunt across the street to Applebee's, where we ate lunch.

Mary was talking about something, but I wasn't paying attention. I was too busy staring at her, thinking about things. With a short wave of her hand, my trance was broken.

"Browny, you're staring at me."

"I'm sorry, honey," I said. "You're so amazing to look at, and I find it fascinating to watch you eat."

Blushing and with an embarrassed smile on her face, she looked down at her nearly empty plate. I had barely touched the food on mine.

"Watch me eat?! Am I not supposed to?"

"No, I just didn't know that women ate," I said. Mary laughed.

"You're funny sometimes," Mary said. "Hey, I just scored a ten-fifty on my SAT, and I was wondering if you were going to attend Northern Arizona University with me."

"That's the same college mom and I were talking about," I said. "I was going to apply there as soon as I took my SAT."

"So you're going with me?!"

"It sure looks like it."

She leaned across the table and kissed me. "So, where will you stay?"

"Probably with my Mom right here in Janestown."

"Same here," Mary said. "My mom doesn't have the money to pay for the dorm, and I don't want to live in an apartment."

"Yeah."

"I was also thinking that because the new quarter won't begin until September, we can take a trip to California," She said. Reaching across the table, I took hold of her hands and squeezed them gently. "I want to go to the beach and surf and-"

"I don't ever want to lose you."

Mary frowned. "What do you mean, Scott? I'm not going to leave you."

"I don't want to lose you-"

"You're not going to lose me."

"Like I lost Jessica."

For a long moment, Mary just stared at me. I could see the pain in her eyes. "How can you say that, Scott? How can you say that to me?"

"I'm sorry, Mary."

"She was murdered Scott."

"I'm sorry."

"Now I'm really starting to worry about you, Scott. I really am."

I sighed and looked down at the table. "Please don't."

Mary stood up and grabbed her purse. The saddened expression on her face said it all. "That's what people who love each other do. They care for one another," Tears swelled in her eyes. "I guess I haven't been a good girlfriend for you to trust me yet, and I'm sorry for that."

"No, Mary. It's not that."

She dried her eyes. "I hope, I hope that you'll let me in one day because I can't keep watching you do this to yourself."

"I'm sorry, Mary Jane. I'm sorry."

Mary didn't say a word to me on the drive home, and I couldn't blame her. Today was supposed to be our Valentine's, and I messed it up.

That night, on the eighteenth of March, we celebrated Matt's eighteenth birthday at my house. The sky was overcast and raining steadily, but that didn't stop us from throwing him an awesome party. I just wished that I didn't feel like what the weather looked like.

My room was quiet and peaceful, with only the sound of the rain striking my window to be heard. I couldn't stop thinking about Jessica and everything that happened in the Dark Woods. It was like a dream, but it felt so real. And it was tearing me up and my life.

"Browny, here you are," Nathan said. "What are you doing in here, all alone?"

"Oh, nothing really. I'm just watching the rain, that's all."

He patted me on the back. "Come on. Let's get you back to the party. Your mom is serving cake and ice cream right now, and she's wondering where you're at."

I had to get out of this town.

Over the next few weeks, things started to get better for me. Our baseball season was now in full swing, and my professional training with Xavier was going great. However, it only consisted of hand-eye coordination and strength drills.

I spoke with Mary and apologized for not being open about my feelings. I promised to change and be more open to her, no matter the problem.

"Hey, Karen," I said, walking up to Karen at her lunch table.

"You are not welcome at our table anymore, Scott." a cheerleader said.

"Karen, I'm really sorry for forgetting your birthday and-"

"She doesn't want to hear it. Now leave us alone," another girl said.

Karen was eating her lunch, trying hard to ignore me, but underneath her draping hair, I could see her smirking.

"Would this make you feel any better, Karen?" Reaching into my backpack, I pulled out a huge box of chocolates and set it in front of her.

"You're going to have to do better than that, Scott," Michelle said. "You canned her in front of the whole school, and it's gonna take a whole heck of a lot of 'I'm sorry' to make up for that."

"Oh, Browny, you're the best!" Karen cried out. Leaning over the table, she wrapped her hands around me in a tight hug.

"I know, and that's why I got you all a box of chocolates too."

Michelle took my backpack and rummaged through it. "Girls, we're eating chocolate!"

The girls jumped up and swarmed me, grabbing and pulling me in every direction as if I were their play toy. Karen continued to smother me in her arms.

"Uh, ladies, I have a girlfriend." Mary must have noticed the commotion because she was making her way towards me. "Oh, my goodness. Here she comes!"

Karen released me, but the girls continued to lavish me with their affection. "Can him, girls," Karen said.

Did she just say what I think she said because, if so, this isn't good? It's lunchtime, and there's a lot of food in those garbage cans.

Four girls, one for each limb, grabbed me and carried me toward the nearest garbage can while the others circled around laughing. Everyone in the chow hall was cheering and laughing at me. I could have broken free, but I'll let them have their revenge.

"I will totally decrease the percentage of commission sales for the soccer and cheerleading programs to zero!" I yelled. "No more money! None! I have the power!"

"You just go ahead and try, Mr. President!" a girl said.

"Mary Jane!" I yelled. "Mary, please help me!"

Everyone in the lunchroom was laughing. "Just don't mess up his face, please," Mary said.

"Ugh, Mary!" I couldn't believe she would let these animals who call themselves cheerleaders can me.

The girls held me over the garbage can. "Are you sorry, Scott?" Karen said.

"I'm sorry, Ms. Brey. Please forgive me!" I was trying to make this as comical yet believable as possible. It was the last few months of school and it's times like these you'll always remember.

"You're sorry?" Karen said.

"Yes, Karen. I'm sorry."

"Are you going to forget my birthday again?"

"No, ma'am."

"Then I forgive you," Karen said. "Let him down, girls." They set me on my feet and walked back to their table.

"Thank you for the late birthday present, Browny. It really means a lot to me." Karen leaned closer to me while placing her hands on my chest. "I know you're going through a lot right now, but if you need someone to talk to, please come to me," She whispered in my ear. "I'll always be here for you, always."

CHAPTER SEVEN

"**S**o you're moving out after school, uh?" I said.

"Yeah. One more month, and then I'm gone," Matt said.

It was sweltering out. Over one hundred degrees, and the only way to cool off aside from sitting in the house was to go swimming in the lake. It was twelve in the afternoon, and we were halfway there when Karen rolled up beside us on her bike.

"What's up, boys, heading off to the lake?" Karen said.

"We sure are Kare Bear," Nathan said. Karen shot him a look that could kill.

"Good one, Nathan," Matt said. "That was great. I think I'll start using that one."

"Yeah, it was, but I like Kari Berry myself," I said.

"It's Karen, guys. Now say it with me, Kar-en."

"We know Karen. We just don't respect you," Matt said. We all laughed at her.

"Jerk," she said, frowning.

"I'm sorry, Karen. I just couldn't help myself," Matt said.

"I sent a letter to the Phoenix Police Department asking them what I needed to do to become a police officer," Nathan said.

"A police officer, huh?" Karen said. "That's cool."

Reaching into the cooler I was carrying, I offered her a pop. "So that's what you're going to do with your life, huh?"

"I think so," Nathan said.

"Right on, man," Matt said.

"What's going on in your neck of the woods, Karen?" I said.

"Not a whole lot. I'm just looking for a date for the prom," she said.

"Aren't you getting a little ahead of yourself, Karen?" Matt said. "Proms three weeks away."

"No, not really. Almost everyone has a date already. Browny has Mary, Kyle has Alicia, and Aaron has Michelle. The pickings are getting pretty slim."

"How is it that the school's cheer captain is the only one without a date?!" Nathan said. "You're cheer captain, Karen!"

"I don't have a date," Matt said.

"That's because you're ugly," Nathan said. I chuckled.

Karen smiled at him. "You do now."

"Ah, great. I walked into that one," Matt said.

"You sure did, sucker," Nathan said.

"Hey, you're not my first choice, either," Karen said. "So don't give me that."

"Speaking of Mary, there she is, Browny." Nathan pointed to her.

"Yep, there she is," Matt said. "And judging by the looks of it, she's going to have many dates for the prom." Nathan chuckled.

Rushing out of the water as if the guys she was playing with didn't exist, she embraced me. Her wet body quickly soaked my shirt. "No. She's with me," I said.

"I went over to your house to get you, but your mom said you weren't there," Mary said. "I missed you, sweetie." She hugged me tighter.

"I'm sorry, I was training with Xavier all morning." Taking off my shirt, I picked her up in my arms. She immediately wrapped her bare legs around my waist and kissed me.

"Awkward," Matt chimed.

Karen was staring at me. "Yeah, you guys can quit kissing any moment now," she said.

"Come on, guys. Let's go have some fun in the sun," I said.

"Wanna play water volleyball?" Karen said.

"Certainly, if those guys don't mind," Nathan said.

"Oh, they won't. They like you guys," Mary said.

"Aren't they sophomores?" Matt said.

"Yeah, so what?" Karen said.

"Ah, you know," Matt said. "I just got to watch my rep. I can't be seen hanging around freshies, and sophies are pushing it."

Nathan chuckled. "What rep?" he mumbled.

We walked to the water's edge. "You guys don't mind if my friends play, do you?" Mary said.

"Hey, it's Scott, Matt, and Nathan," one of the guys said. "You guys are more than welcome."

"And you're the cheerleader that Scott stuffed in the garbage can, aren't you?" another said, pointing at Karen. His friends laughed.

"Yep, that was me," Karen said, rolling her eyes. She then lightly punched me in the shoulder.

"Alright, the teams are Mary, Matt, and you two versus me, Karen, Nathan, and you," I said.

"Why can't I play on your team?" Mary said.

"Because you'll just grope and kiss me all game long," I said. "Besides, I need something beautiful to look at."

"What?!" Matt threw his hands in the air. "I'm not good enough for you? After all these years we've been together, it's like that?"

Everyone laughed.

For a few hours, we all fought for the title of volleyball champion, and in the end, Matt's team won. Afterward, we all sat down in the sand and talked about the usual things until the people at the lake went home one by one.

"So, who wants some refreshments?" Nathan said.

Karen stood up and slapped Nathan's hand. "Tag, you're it!" she said enthusiastically. "But you have to give us sixty seconds to hide."

We all stared at each other. Was she serious? Hide and go seek? A moment passed, and then, all at once, we jumped up and took off into the woods. A minute later, Nathan came looking for us.

Keeping him in sight, I crept through the bushes and followed him. A few minutes later, he found Karen and began to stalk her.

"Run, Karen!" I yelled.

With his cover blown, he sprinted towards her. Karen ran for her life, and so did I.

Just a bit later, I saw Matt and Nathan chasing Karen along the beach. Tiring, Karen stopped and began to back away from them until she was touching the water's edge. If I had to guess by her hand gestures, I'd say she was pleading with them about something.

Seeing that the game was pretty much over, I came out from behind the bushes.

Nathan grabbed Karen and slung her over his shoulders.

"Don't do it, Nathan, don't!" Karen screamed. "The water is too cold!"

Once up to his waist, Nathan tossed her in, and that's what started our water fight. Thirty minutes or so later, we were tired and sat down on the sandy beach.

"It's getting kind of late for me, guys," Karen said, drying herself off with a towel.

"Yeah, it is almost eight-thirty, and I'm getting hungry," Nathan said.

"We also have school tomorrow," Karen said.

"Come on, guys, seriously? How often have we all stayed out this late past curfew?" Matt said. "Brown Stuffings, here's twenty bucks to get us some snacks and make it snappy."

It took me a moment to register what Matt had said. "Brown Stuffings?!" I said. We all looked at each other and burst into laughter. "Alright, what do you guys want?"

After taking mental notes of what everyone wanted, I jumped on Karen's bike and headed off to town. Fifteen minutes later, I returned to the lake with two sacks full of goodies.

The sun had already set, and Nathan was tending to the campfire, which was our only source of light and warmth. It was a lovely night, and the sparkling stars made it even lovelier.

"Here's the goodies, guys; now dig in and enjoy." I passed out the bags and sat next to Mary.

"You never told us what you're training extra hard for, Browny," Nathan said.

"To be honest, even I don't know," I said. "I just asked Xavier to help me go professional, and all he's doing is putting me through some strength and coordination drills."

"You're going professional, eh? That's good. I still don't know what I'm going to do when I graduate," Matt said.

"Did I tell you guys that Browny and I will be attending the same college?" Mary said.

"We sure are," I said.

"That's great guys. Where at?" Karen said.

"Northern Arizona University," I said. "And I received a full four-year wrestling scholarship."

"Wow. That's great," Nathan said. "So when did you plan on telling us about that?!" I shrugged my shoulders.

"A scholarship?!" Karen said with a look of astonishment. "Wow!"

"I really miss Johnathan and Jessica," Matt said.

The fire crackled in the chill of the evening.

"I know," Nathan said.

"I just don't know why anyone would want to murder her or Johnathan," Matt said.

"The cops said that he was kidnapped-right?" Karen said.

"They just haven't found his body yet," Nathan said. "That's just their way of giving the family some hope."

"Things like this will never make sense. But we'll get through it," Mary said.

"How are you doing, Scott? You going to be alright?" Matt said.

"I miss her a lot, but I'll be fine though," I said. My fight with Johnathan was replaying in my mind.

"Mmm, this is some good stuff," Nathan mumbled as he shoveled a sloppy s'more into his mouth.

"You have really soft hair, Mary Jane," I said.

She was resting her head in my lap, smiling at me while I combed my fingers through her hair.

"I love you, Browny," she said.

"I love you too." Leaning down, I kissed her.

"Come on, you two. Spare us that mushy crap," Nathan said.

"I think I want to be a nurse when I graduate," Karen said.

"Are we still talking about what we want to do with our lives?" Matt said. "Because I don't think we are."

I shook my head. "No, I don't think so."

"Yeah, so can it, Kare Bear," Nathan said.

We laughed at her while Karen folded her arms and frowned. "You guys can be real jerks sometimes."

"Toughen up, little lady," Matt said.

"S'more?" I said, offering her one.

"No, Brown Stuffings." Karen pushed my hand away.

"Do you want it, my little honeybee?"

Mary nodded her head, so I put the chocolate mess into her mouth and kissed her.

"Do you guys ever stop?" Nathan said.

"Hey man-" I looked up at him. "This is a romantic moment, and I'm going to savor it for the rest of my life," I said. "Do you have a problem with that?" Nathan recoiled. I couldn't hold my composure anymore and laughed at him. So did everyone else. He really thought I was serious!

"Are you two going to get married?" Karen said.

I looked down at Mary. "I'm going to love this woman for the rest of my life and never let her go."

"So, is that a yes?" Mary said.

"As soon as I turn eighteen, you're going to be my lovely wife, and I your loving husband."

Sitting up, Mary held me close and kissed me with slow passion. "I love you so much."

"And I love you too, my sweet little honey bee," I whispered in her ear.

It wasn't until eleven-thirty when the five of us decided to head home and call it a night.

I stretched my arms above my head while yawning. "Man, I'm tired."

"Me too, but last night was worth it," Matt said.

"Yeah, it certainly was."

"Scott, please come to my desk," Mrs. Carver said.

"Looks like I'm in trouble now." I walked to her desk. "Yes, Mrs. Carver?"

"The counselor wants to see you," she said.

I looked back at Matt and shook my head. He was silently laughing at me as I walked out of the classroom. What did she want to talk to me about this time?

Upon entering her office, I saw her sitting behind her desk. The Principal and the Sheriff were standing beside her.

"Good morning, Scott. Why don't you take a seat," counselor Catherine said.

I sat down. "Good morning."

"Before we get started, Scott, I want you to know that you're not in any kind of trouble. We just have a few questions to ask you about last night," Principal Norwall said.

"The fire was all Karen's idea," I said. "She has blue eyes, brown hair, stands about-"

"That's not what we're here to talk about," the Sheriff said.

I looked around at all of them

"About what time did you guys leave the lake last night?"

"Around eleven-thirty or so, sir."

"Who did you walk home with?" The Sheriff said.

"Everyone, sir."

"Who walked home with Karen?"

"Matt," I said. "But what's this all about? Is something wrong?"

The three of them traded looks. "Karen's mother called us earlier this morning," the Sheriff said. "Karen never came home last night."

A sickening feeling washed over me. Please, not Karen. Not her. Not again.

"We're looking for her right now, and if there's anything you know that might help, now would be the time to tell us."

My mind began to swim. "Scott, are you going to be alright?" Catherine said.

I stood up and walked out, closing the door behind me.

News of Karen's disappearance spread like wildfire, and three hours later, her lifeless body was found only a few hundred yards from where we had camped at the beach. School was immediately canceled, and the police questioned everyone, especially the four of us. Still, nobody knew anything, not even Matt, who was the last to see her. It was the sixteenth of May.

The last month of school dragged on forever. The murders of Jessica and Karen were still too fresh for me to enjoy the prom, and despite being elected prom king again, I refused to go. Instead, I had a romantic dinner with Mary Jane at a fancy restaurant in Phoenix.

Matt, out of all three of us, was the only one who went to prom, but only to honor his date with Karen. She was elected prom queen.

We graduated high school on the twelfth of June, class of '94. It was supposed to be a day of celebration, but like the prom, it was a day of mourning.

Nathan was our school's valedictorian and now attends the Phoenix Police Academy.

Matt, like he said, moved out after graduating and lives in an apartment in Phoenix. What he's doing now no one knows.

"It's kind of lonely now, isn't it?" Mary said.

The sun was warm, and a gentle breeze rustled the leaves of the trees around us.

"Yeah, it is," I said.

"I miss everyone."

"So do I, Mary. So do I." I reached across the wooden table and held her hands. "I love you, Mary Jane."

"Ohh, you're so sweet."

"I'm moving to Japan."

Mary's smile faded, and she pulled her hands away from mine. "What?!"

I walked around the table and hugged her from behind. "I am so sorry, Mary, but I have to train."

"Y-Your scholarship? You were g-going with me?"

"I turned it down. I'm sorry."

Gripping the sleeves of my t-shirt, Mary wet my chest with her tears. "Why do you do this to me, Scott?! You never tell me! You never tell me what you feel or what you think!"

"Mary."

Mary stood up, tears streaming down her face. "Jessica and Karen, they can't love you anymore," she said. "I can, but if you don't let me in, then I might as well be dead, too."

I sighed and looked at the ground. Her words cut me deep, but she was right. I wouldn't let her in. I couldn't. That night still haunted me, and something about this world didn't feel right. Nothing did.

Mary kissed me on the cheek. "I love you, Scott. I really do, but you make it so hard," she said. "Now you go train in Japan. I'll be waiting here for you."

CHAPTER EIGHT

O n the tenth of July, at two am, I packed my things and rode
with Xavier to the Phoenix Sky Harbor International Airport.
My heart was heavy, and I felt terrible for leaving Mary behind, but I
had to get out of there. Janestown was sucking the very life out of me,
and I couldn't bear the thought of losing any more of my friends. I
won't be able to take it.

I was never given any details concerning my training until we
were on the plane and in the air. For the next two and a half years,
I was going to train under the tutelage of Master Yusokagi, a grand
master of the ancient art of ninjutsu.

Honestly, I thought it was ridiculous. Ninjutsu?! Those were
the people that you read about in comic books and see in those
fake kung-fu movies. I was a real fighter, and there's nothing fake
about what I can do. However, when Xavier began to explain to me
what the martial art of ninjutsu consisted of, the fighting style, the
weapons training, and the combat tactics, I began to have second
thoughts. I also began to reconsider whether or not I wanted to go
through with this type of training. After all, I just wanted to become
a professional fighter. But then again, it was an opportunity of a
lifetime that only a few have ever had the chance to accept. So I did.

Twelve hours later, we arrived in Tokyo, Japan, and after a few
shorter flights and a boat ride, we finally arrived at a small remote
island near the islands of Osumi. It was partly cloudy, and the ground
was still wet from last night's rain. The smell of the ocean was new to

me and refreshing. Everything about Japan was refreshing, from the unfamiliar trees and bushes to the insects and the animals. I could already tell that I was going to love it here.

After a twenty-minute long hike along the trail through the woods from the dock, we arrived at a rather large, traditional-styled Japanese house. It had a sloped roof that overhung a spacious front deck and two open-air windows on either side of the double front doors. A stone staircase led up to the deck while four stone pillars supported the overhanging roof.

Standing on the deck was a short, stocky older man with a bald head and short black goatee. He was wearing a black robe with red bands along the cuffs of his sleeves and black leather sandals. A strange green dragon tattoo decorated his right forearm.

Xavier bowed deeply at the waist. "This is my student Scott, and I have trained him as you have required Master."

"It is great to finally meet the one who is so highly spoken of," Master Yusokagi said in English with a slight Japanese accent.

"The honor is all mine, sir," I said, offering to shake his hand. He just looked at me.

"You will call him Master and bow before him," Xavier whispered.

"I apologize, Master." I bowed at the waist with my hands by my sides.

"My plane back to the States leaves here in a few hours," Xavier said. "I will see you again once your training is complete."

"You're leaving already?!"

With a final bow, Xavier patted me on the back and headed down the dirt path.

"Come. I will show you to your room."

It was nearly three in the afternoon when I finished unpacking in the room that I'd be calling my own for the next two and a half years. It had one window, a simple closet, a dresser drawer, and a bamboo bed. There was no electricity, indoor toilet, or even running water. Worse yet, I had to clean my clothes in a nearby stream and hang dry them. It felt like I was living in a third-world country, and honestly, I didn't think that I was going to make it out here, especially without any toilet paper! I guess this is what I get for wanting to be a professional.

"Master Yusakagi?" I said, looking around. I couldn't find him anywhere.

A sword slashed down at me from around the corner and stopped a mere inch from my throat. Stumbling against the wall, my adrenaline pumping, I prepared to fight my attacker, but it was Master Yusokagi.

"Do you admit that had I carried through with my attack, you would be dead?" he said.

I took a few deep breaths and calmed down. "Yeah, of course."

"Why is this?"

"Because you surprised me."

"The art of infiltration is not an easy one to learn, but it is what makes us who we are," he said. "And when I'm done with you, you will never be seen; never be heard." Sheathing his sword, he led me out back, where an amazing assortment of training equipment stood. Some of it, I recognized, but most of it I didn't, like the giant jungle gym that stood several stories tall. It had oaken balance beams, horizontal ladders, ropes, swinging manikins, and target boards everywhere.

"Today, I will test you, and tomorrow, at dawn, I will train you. It will end at dusk."

For the next five hours, master Yusokagi put me through a variety of physical tests to gauge my overall athleticism, and by the end of it, I was hurting. Falling twelve feet off a balancing beam onto hard dirt and getting your hand whacked by a wooden stick because you weren't fast enough to move it out of the way doesn't feel too good.

Once back inside, Master Yusokagi made us some rice and fish served with tea. It wasn't bad, but I could tell that if this was all that we'd be eating, then I was going to get sick of it really fast.

All in all, it was a pretty fun day, and I couldn't wait to get the next one started, and for the first time in a long time, I got a good night's sleep.

It was still dark out when the master Yusakagi woke me early the next morning. I was eager to start training, so I jumped out of bed and changed into a loose black ghee. After combing my hair, I joined Master Yusokagi in the living room for a breakfast of oatmeal and eggs.

"Good morning, Master," I said.

He answered in Japanese.

"What?"

"You will learn to speak Japanese while you are here," he said.

"Yes, Master," I said. "So what am I going to learn?"

"What did Xavier teach you?"

"He taught me Muay Thai and jujitsu Master."

"No, you have it all wrong," he said. "He taught you how to fight. I will teach you how to kill."

Was he serious? Kill?!

"Now come, it is time to begin your training."

A few moments later, as we stood out back stretching, the early rays of dawn burst over the horizon. For a brief moment, I felt like I was still in Janestown before it changed forever.

"Attack me." Master Yusakagi said.

"What?"

"Attack me."

I shook my head. "Alright."

I raised my fists and prepared to fight while Master Yusokagi watched me. Hesitantly, I threw a few lazy jabs, but he slapped them away. I then kicked at his head, but in one fluid motion, he grabbed my leg, chopped me in the throat, and threw me to the ground. Stepping over my leg, he twisted it until I tapped.

Coughing and flexing my knee, I stood up. "Impressive."

"Your attack is all wrong," he said. "Now again."

Bouncing around to loosen myself up, I threw a hard right hook to his chin. Blocking my arm with his, master Yusokagi stepped into me and pushed me over his right leg that he'd planted behind mine. I fell to the ground but quickly scrambled to my feet.

Knowing that I couldn't win the fight on my feet, I decided to try and take the fight to the ground. After a few feints, I took a shot for his legs, but he under-hooked my arms and tossed me to the ground like a rag doll.

Standing up, I threw a straight kick at his chest. Grabbing my foot, he jerked me forward and onto my back. Stepping over my leg, master Yusokagi bent my knee backward over his and twisted. Again, I tapped.

I stood up and brushed myself off. "Enough," he said. In just under a minute, he put me down three times as if my seven years of MMA training were worthless.

"Do you see the difference in our styles?"

"Yeah, I'm beginning to."

"Good, then it is time you learned to kill with your hands."

For the next several hours, master Yusokagi instructed me in the basic techniques of judo and ninjutsu, and because of my previous training, picking up these new styles came naturally and quickly. Afterward, he went inside and returned with a handful of weapons.

"This is a katana, and it will be your primary weapon." He handed me a wooden sword. "But you will master the basics with that before touching this." He withdrew the katana, a single-edged blade over three feet long, from its sheath. It had a sharp angled point and a silk-laced handle. "In time, you will learn to use your ninjutsu and katana as one."

Sheathing his sword, he picked up a wooden sword and began instructing me. Two hours later, my body was covered in welts and bruises.

It was difficult learning how to sword fight, but even more so with the kusarigama, a long chain with a sharp sickle on one end and a steel ball on the other.

By the time the sun was low in the sky, I had learned how to use a plethora of weapons, from the katana, kusarigama, nunchaku, and the bo staff to knives and shuriken to the bow. I learned quickly, but I could tell that it was going to take me years to master them all.

That night, while I lay in bed waiting for sleep to overcome me, all I could think about was Mary Jane. I had only been gone for two days, and already I missed her. Her smile. Her playfulness. The taste of her lips and the smell of her hair. I missed it all, but now that we were so far apart, he wouldn't kill her.

Holding her picture in the moonlight, I kissed it and fell asleep with her in my hands.

"Pick up your katana and defend yourself," Master Yusakagi said.

"Yes, Master."

Deflecting his downward slash at my shoulder, I countered by chopping at his lead leg. Blocking my wooden katana, he struck me on the wrists, which disarmed me. I gritted my teeth and waited for the pain to subside.

"Hesitate, and you will die," he said.

Picking up my sword, I attacked before he could ready himself, or so I thought. Blocking my attack with amazing speed, he kicked my leg out from beneath me and slammed his sword into my ribs. More sharp pain pulsed throughout my body.

"Make a mistake, and you will die."

Thrusting his sword at me, I slapped it away and cut at his stomach. Deflecting my attack, master Yusokagi kicked high at my head, but I ducked under it. Lunging forward, I thrust at his chest, but again, he blocked my attack and chopped at my leg. I hobbled around on one leg, trying hard not to show the pain on my face.

"Enough," Master Yusokagi said. "You have much to learn, and if you do not want to sleep in pain, learn quickly."

"Yes, Master."

He picked up a wooden knife. "There are many vital areas on the human body that, if struck, will kill quickly." Using the knife, he slashed at my inner thighs, my diaphragm, my neck, and under my armpits. "Your training must become instinct, not thought, and instinct comes from repetition."

I spent the remainder of the day learning form after form of how to kill or disable someone with or without a weapon, but there were so many unique locks, chokes, and strikes that it was difficult to keep track of them all. I couldn't learn fast enough. I wanted to know everything.

After picking up and putting away the weapons, I joined Master Yusokagi in his study to practice my Japanese.

From dawn to dusk, I trained for sixteen hours every day, just like he said.

"It is cold out, isn't it?" master Yusokagi said.

"Y-yes M-Master."

The sun was setting, and I could see our breath in the air. I spent nearly all day learning how to sneak without making a noise and how to cover my tracks in the woods. I even learned to stealth swim, a technique that reduces visibility and splash in the water. That is why I was shivering. My clothes were still soaking wet.

"It is going to be difficult to concentrate, but that is why you train," he said. "Now control your body and attack the swinging targets."

Reaching up, I grabbed a hold of a wooden plank and hoisted myself up to the first level of the jungle gym. A target board on the third story began to swing, so I hastily climbed to the top and threw a knife into it. It wasn't a great hit, but at least I hit it.

Upon seeing a target swinging on the second floor, I leaped onto a narrow board ten feet below and away from me. I landed awkwardly and nearly fell, but I recovered quickly and hurled a knife into the swinging board fifteen feet away. I missed the bull's eye by only an inch.

"Well done."

Master Yusokagi climbed up the structure, joined me on the second level, and drew his staff. "We will finish the day with a final test," he said. "Defend yourself." He swung at my ankles.

Jumping back, I pulled my staff off my back and attacked with an upward swing. My staff connected with him in between his hands and nearly disarmed him.

I then chopped down at his head, but he easily deflected my attack and slammed the end of his staff into the meat of my shoulder. He could have struck me in the collarbone, which would have broken it and disabled me, but we were only sparring. Still, the strike hurt.

Returning his punishment, I struck him in the stomach with an upward swing and again thrust at him, but he grabbed my staff and yanked me forward while kicking my right leg from out beneath me.

I spun violently and fell hard on my back onto a walkway on the first floor.

Jumping down and landing gracefully on the walkway, master Yusokagi swung his staff at my head.

With my staff on the ground, I quickly drew my nun chucks and knocked away his attack. I flicked my nun chucks at his knee and kipped to my feet.

Dancing back to avoid my blow, he used his superior reach and swept me off my feet with his staff. I landed on my side, on the hard ground below. Master Yusokagi climbed down and approached me.

Staggering to my feet, I swung my nun chucks at his neck, but he blocked my attack.

He then tried to trip me by stepping behind my right leg with his and striking me in the chest with his staff.

Catching his staff with my free hand, I yanked him by it over my right leg. He tumbled to the ground, but I failed to disarm him, a critical mistake.

Rolling with my throw, he swept me off my feet with his staff and placed the point of it on my throat. I slammed my fist on the hard ground.

"You fought well; now come inside," he said, helping me to my feet. "We must talk."

"One more time, Master."

"Another time. Now come."

I was frustrated with all the mistakes I made and wanted to keep training until I reached perfection. I knew that I should have disarmed him while he had the reach advantage. But I guess I had plenty of time to learn from my mistakes.

After changing my clothes and drying off, I sat with him in the living room.

"The cold not only slows the body but the mind as well," he said. "Learn to control your mind, and you will control your body."

"Yes, master."

He took a sip from his tea. "I have enrolled you in a three-day tournament in Kagoshima. It begins tomorrow."

"Really?"

"There are no weight classes or rules except for no eye, throat, or groin strikes. So free yourself of the rules and restrictions that were placed on you during your previous fights."

"You really set this up for me?" I said. "Is this going to count as a professional fight?"

"Yes, but you will have many fights, not just one," he said. "You may even have to fight many times each day."

"Thank you, Master Yusokagi, thank you."

"There will be many people of importance watching you, Scott. Win this tournament, and you will fight for the most prominent league in the world, Pride."

"Pride Fighting Championship?!" I said. "You really think I'm ready for this?"

"You were ready since the first day I met you."

I had trouble falling asleep that night because I couldn't stop thinking about tomorrow's tournament. I was finally going to fight professionally.

CHAPTER NINE

I woke up the next morning around eight, put on my street clothes, and ate another bland breakfast of oatmeal and eggs. I couldn't wait to get to the city and be around people again, but more than anything, I couldn't wait to call my friends, especially Mary Jane. I haven't spoken to any of them since I left, which has been who knows how long, and I wasn't going to be able to until after the tournament. Master Yusokagi wanted me to focus on my fights.

After a long boat ride through Kagoshima Bay, we took a bus to the city until we reached the arena where the tournament would occur. It was the tenth of January 1995.

Once inside the arena, I checked in at the front desk, where I signed a medical release form along with a few other waivers. Afterward, I was given a quick physical by a doctor who cleared me to fight and led me downstairs to a large locker room. It seemed like Master Yusokagi was well known and respected because everyone bowed before him. I could even overhear people talking about me as his new student; at least, that's what I could pick up with my rudimentary Japanese.

There were over forty other fighters, mostly Japanese, who were stretching and preparing to fight, and honestly, I felt intimidated. I've never fought a man before, and certainly not a professional, but this is what I lived for, and I certainly wasn't going to back down now.

For the next several hours, I watched as fighter after fighter left the locker and returned bleeding and bruised until a referee informed me that I was fighting next.

My heart was pounding, and my adrenaline was flowing. It was finally time.

"Well, this is it, eh?" I said.

"Focus on your training and nothing else," Master Yusokagi said.

"Yes, Master."

The walk down the dimly lit hallway and into the arena was overwhelming. Lights flashed everywhere, and hundreds of spectators cheered from the stands while Japanese music played in the background. This was nothing like my amateur fights in the past, nothing at all.

After being inspected by a referee, I entered the ring and waited patiently in my corner to fight. A moment later, the announcer took center ring and introduced us to the crowd in Japanese. From what I could understand, my opponent weighed seventy-six kilograms and was a Muay Thai black belt with ten wins and four losses.

"And over in this corner, we have Scott, who stands one hundred and eighty centimeters tall and weighs eighty-one point six kilograms." the announcer said. "He is a Muay Thai and jujitsu black belt with this being his professional debut." The crowd was cheering loudly.

We touched gloves and went back to our corners. A moment later, the bell rang.

My opponent wasted no time and kicked at my head. Ducking under it, I lunged forward and took him down with a single-legged takedown.

He groaned loudly from the impact and wrapped his legs around my waist in full guard, but with a few vicious elbows to his head, he relaxed his guard, which allowed me to scramble past it and fully mount him.

I then began to rain leather down on his face, cutting him open, and with most of my shots landing cleanly, he reached up and tried to pull my head down, but he over-extended his arms.

Grabbing his right wrist, I threw my left leg over his neck and fell over to my left. With his body pinned to the mat by my legs, I arched my back and increased the pressure on his elbow. A second later, he tapped.

The crowd cheered with a loud uproar.

Standing up, I bowed before my defeated opponent and to the crowd. The referee took hold of my hand, raised it, and declared me the winner. But for a moment, I couldn't believe it. I had just tapped out my opponent in less than two minutes. I am a professional now.

Once back in the locker room, I sat on the bench and calmed down. I couldn't believe that it was already over or even that easy to beat my opponent.

"You exploited his weakness and defeated him quickly and cleanly," Master Yusokagi said. "Well done."

"Thank you, master."

"You will have one more fight, but it won't be until tonight. So rest your body and replenish it. Your next fight will be even tougher."

"Do you know who I'm fighting next?"

"No, now clear your mind and focus on the fight ahead."

It was a little past seven at night, three hours after my first fight, when another referee came searching for me.

"Are you Scott?" the referee said in Japanese.

"Yes, sir," I said in Japanese.

"You are fighting Takai next," he said. "You have five minutes."

The other fighters started to whisper amongst themselves.

"Takai is expected to win this tournament again," Master Yusokagi said. "He's undefeated with sixteen wins and a black belt in both judo and taekwondo."

I sighed. "Sounds like my work is cut out for me, uh?"

"Have confidence in your training, Scott, and remember what I've taught you."

"Yes, Master," I said. "You've been training me in Judo. What belt would I be considered?"

"Let the number of defeated opponents measure your progress, not belts."

A few minutes later, I was standing in the ring waiting to fight. Across from me was Takai. He was my height but twenty pounds heavier, and it showed by his bulging muscles.

The crowd was cheering wildly and chanting his name. Staring me down, he pointed at me. The bell rang.

Takai rushed into the center of the ring and kicked my left leg.

Raising my leg, I checked his kick and threw a few jabs to back him off.

He then kicked at my head, but I blocked it and countered it with a straight right that struck him cleanly on the chin. Stumbling backward, he covered for a brief moment. That's when I delivered a powerful kick into his exposed left side.

Cringing in obvious pain, he circled away from me, throwing a couple of stiff jabs, one of which caught me above my left eye. He then threw a heavy right hook, but I slapped it down while closing our distance and struck him in the face with my elbow. It was a vicious strike that broke his nose, but I was too close. He took a shot at my legs.

Under hooking his arms, I tossed him to the mat. Scrambling to his feet, his nose bleeding profusely, he kicked my left leg. Checking it, I threw a hard left hook that split him open under his right eye.

Without hesitation, he threw a straight kick at my chest, but I grabbed it, and with one clean motion, I jerked him forward and kicked his other leg out from beneath him.

Ripping his leg free of my grip, before I could step over it and submit him, he stood up and rushed me.

Unable to evade him, I clinched with him, pressed him up against the ropes, and drove my knees into his venerable ribs. He groaned loudly and lowered his arms to protect his sides. I then smashed my elbow into his temple and slipped in an uppercut, dropping him to his knees.

With his head still firm in my grasp, I drove my knee into his bloody face and again into his chin. He slumped to the mat unconscious.

Brushing my brown hair off my sweaty brow, I bowed before my defeated opponent. The crowd was silent, but my heart was not.

After the referee raised my hand, I bowed to the crowd and returned to the locker. I felt pretty good.

My upset win over Takai was the talk of the tournament, and after my third win the following day, some were saying that I would be the new champion, but I didn't believe them. There had to be someone more skilled than me; after all, I was just an eighteen-year-old kid.

On the twelfth of January, the third and final day of the tournament, I won my fourth professional win by knocking out a Muay Thai and Aikido black belt in forty-five seconds. I was now going to fight for the Kagoshima Championship trophy.

It was a little past seven at night, and I was sitting all alone in the locker room, waiting to fight. I've never been this excited in all my life, except for the day I met Mary Jane, but that was a little different.

"Scott, are you ready?" a referee said in Japanese.

"Yes," I said in Japanese.

"Let's go, you're being called out."

I sighed and looked over at Master Yusokagi. "You have made it this far. Now finish what you have started and show them why you are the best."

"Yes, Master."

The walk through the hallway and into the ring seemed longer this time. The strobe lights were flashing, and the music played like usual, but the atmosphere was somehow different. This was the championship fight, and all eyes were on me, Master Yusokagi's student.

After our introductions, my opponent and I touched gloves and waited in our corners until the bell rang.

Circling me, he threw a few jabs, which missed their mark, and kicked at my body. Grabbing his leg, I followed through with his momentum and hurled him to the mat. I practiced that move with Master Yusokagi more than I liked, but the practice paid off.

Scrambling to his feet, he threw fist after fist for my face, but I easily blocked or slapped them away. It was as if he was moving in slow motion as if I knew what he was going to do before he did it and how I'd counter it. I was finally reacting, not thinking, just like Master Yusokagi was training me to do.

Pressing forward, I threw a few jabs, one of which caught him cleanly on the chin. I then kicked high at his head, which he ducked away from, and using the same momentum, I spun around and drove the heel of my other foot into his kidney. It was a perfectly timed strike.

Groaning loudly, he stumbled backward, holding his side.

Feinting a high kick, which he covered up for, I hurled my leg into his exposed ribs with everything I had.

A sickening crack echoed throughout the arena. He doubled over, holding his left side, so I kicked him again, but this time, I struck him cleanly across the face, knocking him violently to the mat.

With blood pouring down his face, he tapped the mat and rolled onto his back. The referee stepped in between us, waving his arms frantically. The fight was over.

I bowed before my opponent and walked over to Master Yusokagi in my corner. "Thank you so much for training me, Master Yusokagi. Thank you."

"Do not thank me yet. You still have much to learn," he said. "Your victories are a testament to your ability to fight. Something you already knew how to do, not kill, something you have yet to do."

"Well, I've still learned a lot from you, and that's why I thank you."

He just smiled at me.

A few moments later, the referee raised my hand while the tournament sponsor declared me the champion and handed me a large glass trophy.

Hoisting it above my head, I walked around the ring to the crowd's cheering, smiling ear to ear. I bowed deeply and waved to them good night. I was now an MMA champion, even if it was only a small tournament.

Once back in the locker room, I sat on a bench and calmed down. There were no words to describe how I felt, and being a champion was everything I had dreamed of- well, almost everything.

After taking a quick shower and getting dressed, the tournament sponsor led me to an office where I met four Pride Fighting Championship representatives. They were impressed with my skills, and just as Master Yusokagi said, they wanted me to fight in their league.

I was so excited that this was happening that I didn't let them finish explaining all the formalities before I signed a two-year contract worth two thousand U.S. dollars per fight plus bonuses. I was now a true professional, fighting for the largest MMA organization in the world, and my first fight was scheduled for this April.

Later on that night, to top everything off, I got to call my friends and family. It's been over six months since the last time I spoke with them, since I left, which has felt like an eternity.

My mom was doing great and proud of my accomplishments, especially when I told her that I won five thousand dollars and signed a contract with Pride, but she missed me dearly and wanted me to visit her soon. I didn't tell her I'd be here for at least two more years.

Nathan graduated from the Phoenix Police Academy at the top of his class last December and was now a rookie police officer. He wants to be SWAT, but he won't be eligible for a few years to come. He still lives in an apartment but will be buying his first house soon. I was pretty happy for him.

Matt, on the other hand, was working as a bouncer at a bar named Double Duece. How legal that is, I don't know; after all, he's only eighteen. He says he's doing fine, but honestly, I was concerned for him. He traded in his apartment for a small trailer on the outskirts of Phoenix. He couldn't make the payments anymore.

After an hour of talking to my mom and friends, I called Mary Jane.

"Hello, Mary Jane?"

"Scott?" Mary said. "Oh my gosh, I can't believe it's you!"

The softness of her voice brought back so many memories, and the emptiness. "I-I've missed you so much, Mary." I struggled to hold back my tears. I've been so selfish. So afraid.

"I've missed you so much, too, Scott," she said. "Are you crying?"

"Um, no. I just got something in my eye, that's all."

"Ohh, my little Browny Scout," she said. "You know, If I were there, I'd wrap you up in my arms and smother you with kisses, right?"

"What I'd give to let you do that," I said. "So, how are you, my little honeybee?"

"I'm doing fine, but I'm just a little scared."

"Scared? Of what?" A million thoughts began to race through my mind. "Is someone trying to hurt you?"

"No, no. It's nothing like that," she said, her tone lowering. "It's just that Janestown isn't like it used to be. It's changed so much since you left."

"I know, Mary, but things-people change."

"Another girl was murdered. A very young girl," Mary said. "She was stabbed and drowned in a pond."

For a long moment, I hesitated to say anything, but again, what could I say? He was killing people again. "That's horrible, Mary. I'm so sorry."

"It keeps getting worse and worse over here, Scott, but I'm sure you don't want to hear about all of that, so I'll tell you what I've been doing up to now," she said, regaining the perkiness in her voice. "Well, I've decided to major in pediatrics, and currently, I'm working as a nursery worker in a daycare."

"So you want to work with kids?"

"Yep, I sure do."

"That's good to know that you're doing so well, Mary, it really is," I said. "So, does Matt and Nathan visit often?"

"All the time, and speaking of friends, your Mom finally showed me all your baby pictures."

"Oh great."

"You were such a cute little baby," she said.

"And that's why I don't show anyone those pictures," I said. "And speaking of doing well, I'm now a professional fighter, sweetheart."

"Oh my gosh, really?"

"I just signed a two-year contract to fight for Pride, and I'm also the new and undefeated Kagoshima tournament champion."

"You finally made it, Browny! That's so wonderful," she said. "So when's your next fight?"

"This April, and if you can't come, you can watch me on pay-per-view."

I could hear her gasp. "You're going to be on TV?! You're like a celebrity down there, aren't you?!"

"Well, almost," I said. "The Pride scouts were impressed with my fights and said they haven't seen a fighter like me in decades, which is really saying a lot."

"I'm so happy for you, honey, and I can't wait to see you again. I will try to come, but I can't promise anything. Midterms will be around then."

I took a moment to gather myself. "You know, I think of you every night, Mary Jane. And right before I go to bed, I'll kiss your picture and fall asleep with you in my arms. It's the only way to be close to you while you're so far away."

There was a long pause on the other end. "You're going to make me cry."

"I know, but I miss you so much, and I want to hold you again, my little honeybee."

"I miss you too, Scott, and I'll always be here for you. Waiting for you to come home and sweep me off my feet."

That night, I cried myself to sleep. I had run away from the secrets I held within, and in the process, I left behind the one who loved me so dearly, all alone and scared. I hated myself for being so selfish to her, but more than anything, I hated running. But at least she was safe. He wouldn't kill her if I was so far away.

CHAPTER TEN

Three months later, on the twenty-fifth of April, Master Yusokagi and I flew to Tokyo for my debut fight in Pride. I was already a star here in Japan, being known as the unknown American fighter who all of a sudden became an undefeated champion of a premier tournament. Apparently, the fighter I defeated for the trophy was a Pride fighter himself and was once the light heavyweight champion. To add to the hype surrounding me, I was only eighteen. And, of course, Master Yusokagi's student.

This earned me several endorsements from sports and energy drink companies, who agreed to sponsor me if I wore their logos in the ring. I even had a whole team of trainers, medical personnel, and even an attorney, not to mention a ton of money. This was more than I had ever dreamed of, but it was going to take some time to get used to all the attention, not to mention the burden of having to live up to the hype surrounding me.

Despite all this, I still trained alone with Master Yusokagi at his residence from dawn to dusk, day after day. My ninjutsu training came first and foremost.

"Your opponent is a Muay Thai and jujitsu black belt with a background in taekwondo," one of my trainers said in Japanese.

"He'll want to stand with you, and he just lost his championship belt, so he's going to get back on top by knocking you out," another trainer said. "This is the main event of the night, the fight everyone came to see. Now go out there and show everyone that you are the best."

"They're really stacking the cards, aren't they?" I said.

"Focus, Scott, and remember your training," Master Yusokagi said. "It is what makes us who we are."

"Yes, Master, and thank you for everything."

"Thank me when your training is complete," he said. "And only when you are tested will you know if I have trained you well."

The walk down the long white Pride ramp that led to the ring was overwhelming. Strobe lights flashed everywhere, and my theme music, Metallica's, 'Wherever I May Roam,' filled the arena. Thousands of screaming fans cheered for me while the TV cameras followed my every step. My heart was beating a thousand miles per hour, and the excitement showed on my face. I had finally made it big. Now, all I have to do is do what I do best: fight.

After my formal introduction, I returned to my corner and waited for the bell. A moment later, it rang.

Rushing out to meet me, my opponent threw a few jabs to distract me and followed with a hard kick that connected with the inside of my right leg. I could tell right away that he was a seasoned fighter, and after taking a few more kicks to my legs and a heavy right to the side of my head, I could also tell that his Muay Thai was superb.

Circling me, he again kicked at me, but this one was aimed at my head.

Lunging forward, I blocked his kick with my left arm and drove my heel into his supporting knee. With a loud pop, his leg buckled, and he collapsed to the mat. My timing was perfect, and my strike dead on.

The crowd moaned and groaned as if they were the ones that had been kicked. Knowing that my opponent was disabled, I stood at the ready. There was no need to hurt him further.

With my opponent rolling around and groaning loudly on the mat, his corner threw in the towel, so the referee called a stop to the fight. The crowd cheered loudly, and a moment later, they began to chant my name. Browny. A cold chill raced up my spine.

After bowing before my opponent and the crowd, the referee raised my hand. At the same time, the announcer declared me the winner by technical knockout. In just over thirty seconds, I defeated the ex-middle weight champion of the world for my sixth professional win. My name was added to the list of top-ranked fighters in the world, and my popularity soared to new heights.

Several months later, after my second win in Pride, I entered the Grand Prix open-weight tournament. It was one of the most prestigious tournaments in Japan, and there were over a hundred fighters from all over the world, all vying for the one belt.

I fought five times in ten days and went undefeated to claim the championship title. It was the first time in the Grand Prix history that someone of my professional experience and age won the tournament.

Six months later, in January of '96, I re-entered the Kagoshima tournament to defend my title. Five fights and three days later, I retained it.

I was the undefeated superstar of Japan, and with every victory, my popularity grew. I was on the front pages of newspapers and magazines and talked about on sports shows. I was hounded by photographers and endearing fans every time I fought, but despite my fame and all the money I had earned, the one thing that I didn't have was Mary Jane. I called her after every fight, and she watched me on pay-per-view whenever she could, but she was too bogged down with school to come and see me. Patiently, like the loving woman she is, she faithfully waits for me to come back home.

Upon entering the arena to my theme song, the crowd chanted my name. This was my first title fight in Pride, and I was a seven-to-one favorite despite my opponent being the three-time defending champion. My adrenaline was pumping, and I was overly excited, but outwardly, I remained calm with a blank expression on my face.

Once I climbed inside the ring, the crowd quieted down.

"Introducing the fighter to my right; standing one hundred and eighty centimeters tall and weighing eighty-three point seven kilograms, he is a Muay Thai and jujitsu black belt with a professional record of twenty-seven wins and no losses, all by way of knockout or submission within the first round, the challenger-Scott," the announcer yelled in Japanese. The crowd roared to life.

"The whole world is watching you, Scott. Now show no mercy and take his belt," Master Yusokagi said.

"Yes, Master."

With a bell ring, we touched gloves and began to circle each other.

Feinting to my right, I threw a left hook that caught him clearly across the temple. I then kicked at his head, but he blocked it and threw a right hook of his own.

Slapping it down, I lunged at him and slammed my right elbow into his nose. I felt it break, and before he could recover, I buried my left fist into his liver.

Cringing, with blood pouring down his face, he threw an arcing left to keep me at bay. Catching his arm under my left arm up against my body, I stepped back with my right leg and twisted my body in the same direction. The sudden and violent motion jerked him forward, forcing him to a knee. I then smashed my knee into his face and continued to apply pressure to his elbow and shoulder until he was lying face-first on the mat. It was a simple but very effective standing arm lock.

Waving his arms in the air, the referee called a stop to the fight. I didn't realize it, but my opponent was unconscious. The crowd was cheering and chanting my name with bellowing enthusiasm.

Like a surge of adrenaline, the excitement began to rush through me. Smiling proudly, I bowed before my opponent and raised my hands in victory. Rushing into the ring, my team hoisted me atop their shoulders. I was now the middleweight champion of the world, and it felt like nothing I could have ever imagined. It felt like a dream.

A few moments later, the owner of Pride Fighting wrapped the championship belt around my waist as the announcer declared me the winner by knockout. With the cameras flashing and the crowd chanting my name, I bowed before the owner and once to each corner of the crowd.

"Congratulations, Scott, congratulations," the announcer said. "You have proven yourself to be the champion above champions, and it all began at Kagoshima. Tell us, Scott, who is the middleweight champion of the world that Japan loves so dearly?"

I took a drink of water from a water bottle that my trainer had given me, and then I splashed some on my face. "My name is Browny. I was born and raised in Arizona but adopted by the humble and great people of Japan." I said in Japanese.

"Browny, eh?" he said. "I can only imagine what you're feeling right now as the champion. So, is there anything you want to say to your fans?"

"Yeah. I want to thank my Master and Xavier for their invaluable training because I would not be who I am today without them." I took a moment to catch my breath. "Thank you, guys. I also want to thank my team, who has helped me prepare for every fight, and you, the fans, for making the pain worth it. Thank you all." The crowd erupted into applause. "And Mom, Matt, and Nathan. I love you guys, but not as much as I love you, Mary Jane. And sweetheart, I'm coming home soon," I said in English. "I love you all, and thank you."

The cold night air raised the hairs on my arms while the stars sparkled in the cloudless sky. It was a beautiful winter night, but lurking somewhere on this small island was my enemy. I had tracked him through the woods and to his house, but that's where the tracks ended. It's not easy tracking a ninjutsu master.

Crouching behind a tree, I glanced around. The double doors to the front of the house were cracked open.

Quickly and without a sound, I walked to the porch and knelt before it. Again, I looked around, listening carefully. The door was a trap, so I climbed onto the deck and through a window.

Cautiously, I crept from room to room, but Master Yusokagi was nowhere to be found. Slowly opening the door to the backyard, I threw a rock into some bushes out by some trees.

A glint of steel flashed in the moonlight as a shuriken ripped into the tree where my rock had landed.

A moment later, Master Yusokagi jumped down from the roof and made his way toward the bushes. I crept up on him, weaving in and around the jungle gym and training equipment.

Spinning around, Master Yusokagi hurled a knife at me, which stuck into an oaken beam only inches from my throat. He charged me with his staff in hand.

Drawing both nun chucks, I deflected his staff with one and struck him in the leg from around a wooden beam with the other.

Dancing around the oaken pillars, Master Yusokagi stabbed at me, but again, I slapped away his attack with my nun chucks. He raced towards more open ground and waited for me.

Sheathing my weapons, I drew my kusarigama and began to spin the ball around my head. MasterYusokagi smiled. With one arcing swing, I hurled the one-pound steel ball towards his legs, but he stopped it with his staff. Unfortunately for him, his staff got tangled in the chain.

With a violent jerk, I yanked his staff out of his hands, but before I could get the ball spinning again, he drew his katana and rushed me.

Raising the sickle of my kusarigama, I blocked his downward slice at my collarbone. Sparks of steel lit up the night. I then entangled his wrist with the chain, jerked him forward, and hooked his ankle with the sickle, tripping him.

Rolling out from beneath me, my sickle slicing into the ground, Master Yusokagi jumped to his feet. He then ran up a wooden plank to the first level of the jungle gym. His black ghee fluttered in the wind.

Dropping my kusarigama and drawing my katana, I joined him on the walkway. With a flick of my wrist, I deflected his attack and slapped his leg with the flat of my blade while kicking him in the chest.

After regaining his footing, master Yusokagi rushed me, slashing at me relentlessly. Our blades must have clashed nearly a dozen times, but he failed to strike me even once.

Continuing his bladed onslaught, he threw several kicks and hand strikes. Again, I blocked and slapped his attacks away.

Jumping onto a narrow beam several feet to my right, I pulled out a black egg from my belt, crushed it, and threw the powdered glass at his eyes, but he raised his arm and blocked the glass with the sleeve of his ghee.

I slashed at his chest, which he deflected, and retreated to a wider board.

Following me, Master Yusokagi slashed at my head, and as our steel blades clashed, I grabbed his wrist and jerked him forward while kicking his legs out from beneath him.

Landing hard on his side, Master Yusokagi rolled off the board onto the ground as my blade chopped into the wood.

Jumping to the ground below, my adrenaline pumping, I attacked him with everything I had. It was one form after the other, but he deflected each of my attacks. Stepping into me, he put me on my back with an excellent hip and arm toss, but it was just what I wanted.

Rolling out of the way of his slashing blade, I entangled his legs with mine and tripped him to the ground while striking his weapon out of his hands. I put the edge of my blade to his neck. After standing up, I helped him to his feet.

"You fought well, Scott." He patted my shoulder. "Very well."

"Thank you, Master."

"Now go and pack your bags. Your training is complete." He brushed himself off. "There is nothing more that I can teach you."

I sighed heavily and lowered my head. "I understand."

I knew my time here was running out, and a part of me didn't want to leave. I had grown quite fond of Master Yusokagi and the peaceful tranquility of this small island. But the more I thought about it, the more I couldn't wait to return to Janestown and start my life with Mary Jane.

After packing my belongings, I went out back and sat near the edge of a stream. I can't believe that it's all over. Two and a half years.

Pulling out my picture of Mary Jane, the moonlight illuminating it, I kissed it. She is so beautiful, my little honeybee, and I can't wait to hold her in my arms.

"You miss her dearly, I know," Master Yusokagi said. "She is a good woman for remaining faithful to you."

"She is, and I feel horrible for leaving her."

"Sometimes it is best to face your fears than run away from them," he said. "And if not for yourself, then for those whom you love."

"Yeah."

Master Yusokagi held out a black-sheathed katana. "Now rise and claim your sword."

Standing up, I took the katana from Master Yusokagi. Grabbing the black silk-laced handle, I pulled the razor-sharp blade out of its sheath. An odd sensation flooded my senses. Scarlet. Strange golden symbols were engraved on the blade just above the hilt. Empress.

I collected myself. "You're giving me this sword?!"

"No," he said. "I am returning it."

I gave him a puzzled look. "I am very honored to have trained under you, Master Yusokagi, and I am very thankful for everything you have taught me." I bowed at the waist. "Thank you, Master."

"If there is one lesson I wish you to remember, one to truly master, then let it be this," he sighed and bowed slightly. "There are none who can stand before you and live," he said. "None, not even yourself."

The morning of the fifteenth of February 1997 came early and marked the end of my ninjutsu training. After saying goodbye, I again, and for the last time, took the short boat ride and flight to Tokyo. Twelve hours later, I arrived at the town I called home, Janestown.

CHAPTER ELEVEN

It was dark and windy outside, with black clouds threatening to rain. House after house, including Jessica's, was vacant and boarded up. The neighborhood was utterly lifeless except for a group of forest green fatigue-clad teenagers who I passed along the street. This is not the loving town I grew up in; it wasn't the town I remembered.

"Scott, oh, sweetie! You're home!" Mom cried out, hugging me tightly.

I hugged her back. "Hi, Mom."

"Oh, you look so much more handsome in person than on TV!" she said. Come inside, and let me make you something to eat."

"Thank you, Mom, and I missed you." After closing the front door behind me, I hung my brown leather jacket in the closet. "And I love you, Mom."

She hugged me again. "Oh honey, I missed you too. Have a seat and tell me how you've been doing."

I sat down on the couch. "It was really wonderful down there. Calm and peaceful."

Mom sat next to me. "I can't believe it's been nearly three years since I last held you." Tears were swelling in her eyes. "You'll never really know how much you miss someone until they're gone."

I fought to keep from crying. She was right. I missed Mary to no end and desperately wanted to see her. "Can you call Mary and tell her to come over?" I wanted to surprise her with the day that every girl dreams of.

"Sure, honey."

Ten minutes later, there was a knock on the door, and like a kid in a candy store, I jumped off the couch and raced to open it. And there she was, standing before me as gorgeous as ever. Her bright blue eyes sparkled under the porch light, and her long brown hair hung across her delicate shoulders. She was so beautiful, my Mary Jane.

"Scott?!" she said.

I took a deep breath and choked back my tears. "I never should have left you, Mary Jane, and-" I wiped my eyes. "And I am terribly sorry for lying to you." Dropping to my knees, I pulled out a small felt-covered box and opened it. "But tonight, I swear to you that I will always and forever be by your side."

Mary covered her mouth with her hands and gasped.

"Mary Jane, will you marry me?"

Trembling, with tears streaming down her face, she dropped to her knees and embraced me in her arms. "I love you so much! So very much!" she said. "And yes, I'll marry you!" I put the diamond-studded silver engagement ring on her finger and hugged her closely. "But don't you ever leave me again, you big dummy. Now kiss me!"

After spending a few hours at my Mom's house, we left for my hotel room downtown, where we spent the rest of the night holding each other in love's embrace.

I woke up to sunrise the next morning, put on my clothes, opened the curtains, and let the early rays of dawn flood the room.

Sitting next to her, I ran my fingers through her soft brown hair and watched her slowly come to.

Stretching her arms above her head, Mary opened her eyes and smiled lovingly at me. "How long have you been watching me?"

I kissed her gently on her forehead. "Only a few minutes, my love. And you looked so peaceful."

Mary opened her silver heart locket and showed me the pictures of us inside. "I never took it off, not even once while you were gone." She kissed me, got out of bed, and put on her clothes.

"Do you have to go to school today?" I said.

"I do, but I'm not," she said. "I want to spend my day with you instead."

I wrapped my arms around her slender waist and nuzzled her neck. "I was hoping you would say that."

That day, Mary and I walked the streets of Janestown, reminiscing about our days in high school together. By the time the sun had begun to set, we were strolling the beach of Lake Caldell, holding hands.

"This is where we first met. Do you remember?" Mary said.

"It is, and you were the most beautiful thing I had ever seen," I said. "And so aggressive."

Laughing, Mary faced me and took hold of my other hand. "I was not. I just knew what I wanted and went after it. Besides, you kissed me first."

I looked up at the sky, pretending to ignore her. "I'm sorry you believe that."

"Ugh," she muttered, shaking her head.

I leaned forward and tried to kiss her, but she pulled away. Laughing, I tried again, but the result was the same. She was teasing me. "So where do you want to live my love, and it can be anywhere you want."

"How about Cancun?"

"Anywhere you want, sweetheart."

"Can I have a horse and twenty pairs of shoes?" she said. "Or a Porche and a dresser drawer full of jewelry?" She planted her lips on mine.

"Anything to make you happy."

She laid down on the sand and pulled me on top of her. "Can I have your heart?"

My smile faded. "I'm sorry I lied to you." She squeezed me tighter. "I will give you my heart, Mary."

"Thank you, Scott. That's all I've ever wanted. Truth and honesty." I took in the scent of her body. "And I've been thinking about something."

"Oh yeah, and what would that be?" I ran my fingers through her soft hair.

"I've been thinking that maybe after I graduate and we find a place to live-" Biting her lower lip, she pulled me closer. "That we could make little brownies together," she whispered in my ear.

I could feel my face getting warmer. I've never thought about having kids, but there is nothing I would deny her. "You're such a lovely woman, Mary Jane, and I'll see to it that our wedding day, and all the ones that follow, will be the happiest of your life."

"I'll take that as a yes then."

"How could I ever say no to you?"

The following day, Matt and Nathan came up from Phoenix to visit us for the weekend. The sun was high in the cloudless sky, and a gentle breeze blew at our backs. We walked aimlessly through the neighborhood streets, just talking away the day. It almost felt like summer break all over again.

"You never told us, Browny, what camp Xavier took you to train in," Matt said. "And no one seems to know, so what's up?"

"What's up with the tux and red tie?" I said. Matt just winked at me.

"Yeah, Browny, you've been real quiet about all that," Nathan said.

"I just learned a little judo, that's all," I said.

"No, that's not just judo, man," Nathan said. "And some of those holds and strikes aren't jujitsu either."

"Spill it, man," Matt said.

"Alright, alright. I guess I can tell you."

"What? Is it like a secret or something?" Matt said. "We just want to know what camp you trained with."

"You guys promise you won't laugh?" I said.

Matt gave me a funny look. "What is there to laugh at? You're the Pride middle-weight champion of the world."

"I promise," Mary said.

"Alright," I said. I knew they would laugh at me just like I did when Xavier told me, but that's what friends are for, right? "I was training under a man who I'll call Master for this conversation."

Both Matt and Nathan burst into laughter. "Master?!" Nathan said.

"Master?" Matt said. "Are you serious?! Master?!"

"Quiet, you guys. I want to hear this," Mary said.

"He never told you either, uh," Nathan said.

"Anyways, he was a ninjutsu master who taught me-"

"A ninja?!" Nathan said.

"Oh shit! Come on, man!" Matt said, barely containing his laughter. "The way of the ninja?!"

"No, that's not what-" I said.

"Oh yeah. I have to act this out." Running out before us, Matt balanced himself on one leg and began to flail his arms around. "I am master Splinter, and I will defeat you, Shredder!" he yelled. Nathan burst into laughter while Mary let out a short chuckle.

I sighed. "That's right, guys, laugh it up. Laugh it up."

Mary kissed me on the cheek. "It's okay, honey."

"You're serious, aren't you, man?" Matt said. "Ninjutsu?"

"Yeah, and I'll even show you my katana."

"What did you learn?" Nathan said.

"I learned to kill."

Everyone traded looks.

Rounding the last block, we continued down the street. The Dark Woods loomed into view.

"Did you kill someone?" Matt said.

"No, but I learned how to," I said. "So what's been going on down here? I've heard that some pretty bad things have happened here since I left." Four more girls in the past two years had been murdered. There was no end to his depravity.

Matt and Nathan glanced at each other.

"Oh, nothing, really, sweetheart," Mary said.

"It's still the same old town you remember," Nathan said.

"Is it?" I said. "Because if it's anything like I remember, two of my friends were murdered during our senior year."

An awkward silence fell over the four of us. "Three of our friends were murdered, Scott," Nathan said. "My department ruled his kidnapping a homicide last year."

"We even attended his funeral," Matt said.

Stopping at the curb, I sighed and stared off at the Dark Woods that lay just beyond the grassy field ahead of us. I was tired of running from the secrets that I held within. I had to tell them even if they wouldn't believe me. Besides, I promised Mary my heart.

"He wasn't murdered."

"What do you mean?" Matt said.

"Johnathan murdered Jessica."

Mary gasped.

"What?!" Matt said.

"I know this because you remember that day when I came to school all messed up like I'd been in a fight?" I said.

"Yeah, I remember that," Matt said.

"I told everyone that I fell in the woods, and I did. Next to the chasm. That's when Johnathan appeared out of nowhere."

Matt sighed and started to tap the curb with his foot.

"You're telling us that you saw Johnathan and that you know he killed Jessica?" Nathan said.

"He was wearing his Halloween costume and Jessica's necklace. You know the silver chain and ruby pendant he gave her for her birthday?" I said. "She was wearing it the day she died, but when I found her, it was gone."

Mary looked down at the ground.

"He told me that we all have our price and that he was going to kill everyone I hold dear to my heart. That's how I know he also murdered Karen."

No one said a word. They all looked shocked and dumbfounded. "Do you guys remember the last day of the state wrestling championships?" I said.

"Yeah," Matt said. Nathan nodded.

"So do I because that night I couldn't sleep. And I know how this is going to sound, but all throughout the night, Jessica plagued my dreams, calling to me. I don't know what was wrong with me, but for hours, I wandered around the neighborhood until I came across her house," I said. "I found her inside her room, floating next to her bed in the same dress that she was murdered in. She told me not to cry and to be strong, and then she flew off down the street." The dead and burnt trees of the Dark Woods swayed in the gentle breeze. "I tried to follow her but lost sight of her in the woods. That's when I saw a swirling shadow staring at me, so I ran, and then I tripped."

Mary shook her head slowly, her hand covering her mouth. Matt was grinding a pebble into the pavement with his foot while Nathan stared at me. His face said it all.

"I came to school all messed up that day because I fought him in the desert. There was no way that I was going to let him live for what he did to Jessica," I said. "But he was different, faster and stronger-inhuman. I just couldn't beat him." I looked at the ground and shook my head. Even now, I couldn't understand how he beat me that day. It just seemed so surreal.

"Come on, Scott, let's go home." Matt put his hand on my shoulder. I brushed it off.

"I'm sorry for not telling you guys sooner, especially you, Mary, but this is why I didn't. Not one of you believes me. But that's okay. I know what I saw, and I know that I'm not crazy." At least, I hoped I wasn't.

The next day, the four of us went swimming at Lake Caldell. It was great to hang out like we used to, but we were adults now, and along with that came responsibility. Matt and Nathan both had to work while Mary Jane had school. This left me all alone and with nothing to do during the week but to stay in shape for my upcoming title defense. Honestly, alone time was what I needed. I could finally focus on what I've neglected for so many years. My life with Mary.

"Hello, sweetheart, I'm home." Mary walked through the front door of my hotel room.

"Oh, Mary, you're so pleasing to my eyes and soothing to my heart," I said.

Getting off the bed, I walked across the room, wrapped my arms around her, and kissed her. The smell of her lavender hair reminded me of the first day we met and the taste of her strawberry lips, the first time we kissed.

"I'm so in love with you, Scott," she whispered in my ear.

"And I'm so in love with you, Mary Jane, my sweet little honeybee."

I put on some soft music, and for the rest of the night, we slowly danced until we fell asleep in each other's arms.

I woke up early the next morning, shivering from the cold. The window across the room was wide open, and the thin white curtains were fluttering from a steady breeze.

After getting up and putting on a clean pair of blue jeans and a black T-shirt, I put Mary's clothes in the laundry bin and stood by the window. The rising sun was beginning to peek above the mountains and fill the blue sky with its orange light.

It was going to be another beautiful day, and then I saw her, my sweet Mary Jane, sprawled out on the pavement two stories below. My heart stopped while time itself froze. Tears swelled in my eyes, and a feeling of anguish tore through my soul. She was lying there in her white nightgown, staring at me with her dulled blue eyes.

Slinging my leather jacket over my shoulder, I grabbed my katana and left the hotel.

Kneeling next to Mary, tears streaming down my face, I kissed her softly on the lips. Her silver heart locket was missing.

CHAPTER TWELVE

For five long minutes, I pressed through the untamed wilderness surrounding downtown Janestown and through the Dark Woods until I stood before a small desert expanse by the plateau near the chasm.

"Johnathan, you fucking coward!" I screamed. "Where are you now?! Where?!"

I dropped to my knees and began to cry uncontrollably. I cried and cried for longer than I could remember. The pain. I just couldn't take it. He could have killed her when I was so far away, but instead, he killed her when she couldn't have been any closer. I was such a fool. I should have stayed in Japan. At least then, she'd still be alive. My heart burned with hatred. The love of my life was dead, and now so was I.

I cried for hours.

"I understand the pain that you are going through, and I am terribly sorry for your loss."

Quickly, I jumped to my feet and drew my katana. The strange glyphs on the blade glistened in the early rays of dawn. I was ready to kill whoever had just crept up on me, but it was an elderly man around fifty or so. He had long white hair, a matching beard, soft, wrinkly features, and brown eyes. He was dressed in a sky-blue robe with a hood, and in his right hand was some sort of glass or crystal wand with a five-point star on its end.

I wanted to laugh. I mean, who dresses like this?! But I maintained my composure. He could be an enemy. I glanced around.

"What?!" I said.

"Your anger towards the one who murdered them is justified, but you know that you cannot kill him," he said. "For he is no longer human."

"How do you know this, and who are you, old man?" I said with my sword ready.

"I can help you, Scott. Unfortunately, I must shatter whatever reality of this world that you have left."

I lowered my katana and gave him a funny look. "What are you talking about?" I said. "How do you know me?"

He smiled at me. "My name is Merlin, and I know many things Browny. Things that would cause most to lose the sanity of their mind."

Appearing out of thin air, a small orb of fire began to hover over his left hand. With flames licking his fingers, he pointed at the plateau, and like a blazing comet, the orb of fire shot from his hand and exploded upon impact with the plateau. Shattered rock flew everywhere as dust and smoke enveloped the area.

A moment later, when the dust had settled, the damage to the plateau became evident. A small crater several feet in diameter had been blown into the rock. The stone surrounding the crater was cracked and scorched black.

I stared at him with a blank expression and utter shock. I didn't know what to say. I didn't even know what to think. I mean, he just shot fire from his hand, I think.

"I can assure you, Browny, that what you have seen is real and not a figment of your imagination. You are not crazy, nor are you dreaming, but you already know this, for you have already seen the beast's shadow."

As if I wasn't dumbfounded enough, the Dark Woods, plateau, and desert began to distort and swirl together into a blur of colors. My limp body was then sucked into the swirling vortex, and that's when my vision went black.

Merlin's voice filled my mind as the images he described appeared before my eyes.

"Many, many millennia ago, in an age that has been forgotten, there was a vast and great kingdom that ruled the known world."

I was flying high above the clouds over a rolling green landscape dotted with hundreds of simple villages and great cities of stone.

An enormous castle with many spires, thick walls, and a wide moat loomed in the distance. Peasants, chickens, and livestock roamed the streets while chain mail-clad soldiers stood guard at their posts.

"This kingdom was ruled by a wise and gracious king who had a son, a prince, by the name of Johnathan. He was a righteous prince, as the king did well to raise him. But when his betrothed and beautiful Ariel fell sick with a mysterious illness, Johnathan went mad. He called upon every doctor, sorcerer, and magician to save her, but none could."

I could see inside a large room with many dresser drawers, small elegant tables, a fireplace, and a large royal bed with silken drapes. A beautiful young woman with long, flowing blonde hair was lying still on the bed. She was wearing a fine white dress and a silver necklace with a ruby pendant.

Men in black robes surrounded her bed while a young man with sharp features and short brown hair knelt beside her. He was screaming at the heavens with his fists in the air.

"With the love of his life dead, the mad prince gathered all the ancient writings on the dark arts and studied them, looking for a way to bring her back to life. I tried to console him, but he would not listen. For years, he locked himself away in his study, begging the gods for her life. I attended to his every need, and under his command, I had built an altar surrounded by five pillars of varying but precise heights to his exact specifications. For weeks and then months, he prayed and sacrificed animals upon this altar, but still, he could not bring her back."

The stone altar was in the middle of a large grassy field several hundred yards beyond the castle walls. A dense forest nearby swayed in the strong wind, and black clouds loomed overhead. It was dark and stormy, with rain coming down in sheets, pounding the earth.

Johnathan was standing by the altar, wearing black robes and raising a knife above his head. Clenched tightly in his other hand was Ariel's necklace.

Lying before him on the stone altar was a girl no older than sixteen. She was bound hand and foot, begging him to be spared, but her cries of protest were drowned out by the crackling thunder.

Lightning lit up the sky as the prince's blade slid across her throat, spilling her precious life onto the rain-soaked earth.

"I secretly watched from the woods as my master cut out her still-beating heart and held it up to the sky. An offering to the gods. For his sake, I prayed that his beloved would be brought back from the dead, but it was not to be. The dark arts were wrong."

The sky burned a dark red as unnatural flames devoured the clouds and enveloped the five pillars. A tremendous creature standing over thirty feet tall on two powerful legs emerged through the smoke by the altar. It had ram-like horns and veins bulging from its red muscular body. A cold chill raced down my spine.

Placing a cloven foot on the altar and cracking it, the creature leaned down and stared at the prince with its piercing black eyes, its long and thin spade-tipped tail whipping around.

Reaching down with a five-clawed hand, the creature picked up the girl's lifeless body and sunk its wicked teeth into her. She was consumed with two bites.

Spreading its arms and huge black bat-like wings, the creature tilted its head back and roared a roar that could be heard for miles. Drops of fire, like rain, began to fall from the sky.

"It was a creature whose name had never been whispered until now. A daemon from hell itself. A Balrog. I was too afraid to keep watching, so I hid among the trees, praying that the evil would not see me. It was there on that very night that Johnathan was forever immortalized by the great evil he invoked."

My vision went black.

"For years, the good king searched the earth for his son, but to no avail. And though I was questioned by the king himself, I told not a soul what I had seen. Thirty years had passed since the prince had disappeared, and within that time, so did the good king. I was still serving the royal family when a messenger rode through the gates on that fateful day. The message was for the king and his counselors only, but I eavesdropped. Our kingdom has been at peace for over a hundred years, but this would be no ordinary war. Devils rained fire from the sky while creatures of the dark roamed the earth, devouring all within their path. Unseen spirits sucked the souls out of men, and the dead walked. It was as if the very gates of Hades had been opened and all inside released.

"'This evil marches from the South and will soon be at our gates.' proclaimed the messenger. However, our new king was not wise and disregarded what the messenger had said as nonsense. He had him seized and taken to the dungeon, where I asked him one question in secret. Is Johnathan, our late prince, with them? The messenger thought long and hard with terror gripping him.

'With my own eyes, I have seen it. A hideous creature of the dark. An undead, they say. It can shape and crack the earth at will.

Fire rains from the heavens at its command, and the dead rise before it. It feeds on men's souls and possesses the keys to hell itself. In a black robe, it walks the earth, and a swath of death trails in its wake. A silver necklace and ruby pendant hangs from its neck, and all who do not bow before it die a thousand deaths. Its name is never spoken in the light, only whispered in the shadows-Calignosity. Is Johnathan with them? I pray not.'

Upon hearing those words, I headed to my study and pulled out all the prince's dark arts manuscripts from a secret compartment in the wall. For twelve long days and nights, I intensely studied what my master had compiled. I fought every day to maintain my sanity, and the knowledge nearly corrupted my soul, but I remained true. On the thirteenth night, I stood before the altar, but I had found another way. A way my prince had overlooked."

I saw Merlin in a sky-blue robe standing before the altar, placing five crystals on it. After opening a thick black book and raising his staff above his head, he began to chat.

The cloudless, starry night was shattered by the sound of lightning continuously striking each of the pillars. The crystals then began to hover and spin rapidly in a large circular pattern above the altar, and with lightning crackling everywhere, a blue and greenish field appeared between the spinning crystals.

Merlin climbed onto the altar and stepped through the field, disappearing into the unknown.

My vision went black.

"I will not allow you to see what was on the other side. Instead, I will tell you that the portal led from this world to another, a realm of the spirits. A world known as Ethereal. The following day, the kingdom I called home for fifty-two years, the kingdom which had stood for over a thousand years, had been burned to the ground. Not a single soul had survived."

Images of the destroyed kingdom flashed before me. Buildings were burning and rapidly crumbling by unnatural means. Women and children ran from unimaginable beasts while brave soldiers fought demons. But all was in vain. They were slaughtered by the tens of thousands. The sky was black, and the rivers ran red with blood.

Powerful explosions shook the earth, and green coils of death flew from the bony fingers of the evil perched on the highest tower of the destroyed castle. Its tattered robe fluttered in the wind while its hood covered its face in darkness. Only its piercing red eyes were visible.

Raising its human spine staff, it cried out in victory as devils flew overhead.

"It fell short of power to only one other denizen of the deep. The Balrog. A Lich is what Johnathan had become, bound in soul to the very creature he invoked.

For over a hundred years, the remaining men of the world and I, the Dragon Masters, waged war against Calignosity and his undead army. The planet in its entirety was ravaged. Whole continents were destroyed while others were made. Thousands fled our world to live in peace elsewhere, for mankind was on the verge of extinction. But with help from the great Batlords, we, the Dragon Masters, pushed the remnants of evil hordes back to where they had come from, but Calignosity was not among the ones we slew."

A charred and barren landscape appeared before me. Smoke billowed from deep fissures in the earth, and volcanoes in the distance spewed out ash into the already-blackened sky. Rippling fire gripped the black clouds while light gray ash fell steadily. It truly was an apocalyptic scene.

The undead army to the east numbered in the millions and stretched to the horizon. Hideous beasts sharpened their teeth with human remains while spirits of the nether world hovered silently as they have for all eternity, patiently waiting to feed on the souls of men.

Sitting high on a jewel-encrusted golden throne was Calignosity. The undead kings of the world who refused to bow before him now carried him on their backs. Balrog Lords, his personal guards, walked beside him. Always watching. Always listening.

To the west, across from the demon horde, stood the brave knights of the Dragon Masters. They were dressed in dull, mud-covered plate armor with shields and halberds ready. Archers in the rear wearing mail stood at the ready with barbed arrows. Catapults and heavy ballistas were loaded and ready to fire while soaring overhead were dozens of dragons that Merlin had enchanted.

Death was a mere hundred yards away, but with a steel resolve, the Dragon Masters stood their ground, waiting for Merlin's call to charge.

The two sides then clashed in warfare that had never before been seen. Soldiers were torn to pieces and eaten alive, while the lucky ones had their souls drained of life. Monsters were slaughtered, and zombies were hacked to bits. Devils had to be pierced with ten thousand arrows before they plummeted to the ground below.

For days, Merlin and Calignosity were locked in magical combat as the battle raged around them. The numbers were ten to one in favor of the horde, but the Dragon Masters steadily marched forward, killing ten monsters for every knight lost.

By the fifteenth day, Merlin declared victory and destroyed the last portal. Millions of dead littered the ground, and out of one hundred thousand brave soldiers, only seven survived.

The bright sun nearly blinded me when my vision returned to reality. Rubbing and blinking my eyes, I sat on the sandy ground, shaking my head in disbelief. I couldn't wrap my head around what I had just seen or what was happening. Mary was dead, and now magic and monsters exist?! What the hell was going on?!

"I know you are still grieving, and I am sorry I did not get to you sooner," he said. "I also know that you are greatly confused like I was when I first read the manuscripts, but give me an hour of your time, and I promise that you will be able to see again. For this world is not what it seems." He extended his hand to help me up.

I sighed and slowly shook my head. "How do I know that you aren't Calignosity?"

"Because you are still alive."

"Alright, Merlin, alright." I nodded my head, took his hand, and stood up. "I'll give you an hour, but only because I can't explain what I've seen. Because I can't explain seeing Jessica's ghost or what you've shown me or Johnathan and his, his..."

"His inhumanity. I know."

"Or how you know so much about me. I can't explain any of it, and I guess I'm hoping that you can because she meant the world to me, Merlin, and now she's gone." I took a moment to gather myself. Tears streaked down my cheeks. "She didn't deserve this. None of them did. So tell me that what I've been seeing is real, and tell me what all this means. Tell me everything."

Smiling, Merlin put a hand on my shoulder and led me into the desert. "I will, Scott. Now, come along. There is much that I must teach you."

"Then start with Johnathan. Did he kill them? And why," I said. "Why can't I kill him?"

"Because he is faster, stronger, and tougher. Because he has spells to protect and spells to harm," Merlin said. "He is an initiate of magic and has been for years now. That is why you can not kill him. At least not as you are."

"A gun will take care of him."

Merlin smirked at me. "Your desire for revenge is strong, Browny, but certainly, you now know that you are no longer involved in a personal battle with Johnathan but in a war against evil itself for this very earth. And believe me when I say that Calignosity will not stop until it all burns at his feet," he said, facing me. "Join me, and together, we will find those brave enough to venture with us into the very depths of hell and forever slay this evil."

I paced around in small circles, staring at the ground. A war against evil? Where? And why me, and why now? Why not yesterday when she was still alive? And why should I even care? I had so many questions and was so confused that I couldn't even think straight.

Merlin sat down on a large rock. "For many millennia, since the destruction of the last portal, I have tirelessly searched the worlds for Calignosity," he said. "And as of today, I search no more. I have found him and the general of his undead army, Goresavice." Merlin pointed at the chasm. "That is why I come to you now. Because it is now that we must fight."

I looked back at the chasm. I was still lost. "Who's Goresavice?"

Merlin's expression turned solemn. "Johnathan."

A cold chill shot down my spine. I sat down and hung my head. He's the general?! "How?! And when?!"

"You know the day. You know, even the hour."

It was beginning to make sense now, and the reason for my existence became clear. "I'll fight, but you must promise me one thing."

"Anything."

"Promise me that I will be the one to take his life and no one else."

Merlin smiled. "His blood was destined to be spilled by your hands since the day of his resurrection."

"Thank you. Now please explain this magic crap to me because I feel like I'm going crazy. Explain it all."

Merlin laughed. "So did I, but let us not doubt your senses whenever something unexplainable occurs. Was the fire bolt that I cast real or imaginary?"

I looked back at the scorched crater in the plateau wall. "Real, but at the same time, you could have had a grenade launcher up the sleeve of your robe."

Merlin laughed again. "And the vision I showed you?"

"Well, now that I don't know," I said. "I mean, monsters and demons don't really-"

"And Jessica?" he said.

I sighed. "Yeah."

Thin strands of lightning began to crackle between Merlin's fingertips. I took a few steps back and stared at him with a blank expression on my face. I could no longer doubt him. He was right. Magic does exist. But that means-

"Perhaps you would be more convinced if you were to feel the power for yourself." The lightning jumping between his fingers stopped.

My mouth dropped open. "You mean I'll be able to cast spells like that firebolt?"

"Yes, but only if you allow your soul to be opened up to the mana of Ethereal."

"My soul? What do you mean?" I said, frowning. "And what's mana?"

"It is the power, the energy that spells require to be cast," Merlin said. "And at first, you will possess a minor amount of mana, but with each passing day, this amount will steadily increase as your soul is..." He sighed and glanced away.

"What?"

"Never mind, my friend. Just know that from the moment mana enters your body, you will never age another day."

"What?!" I said. "Really?"

"Yes, but do not confuse this with being immortal. You can still die."

I almost couldn't believe what I was hearing. Not only would I be able to cast spells, but I would never grow old. I was going to be twenty until I died! "So I'm never going to die of age. Not even of a heart attack?"

"No."

"Or cancer, or whatever?"

"No."

"Only guns and stuff like that can kill me?"

Merlin smiled at me. "Yes, Scott, only external forces, including diseases, can kill you. Your body will be made perfect by the mana of the Ethereal."

"Is this what Johnathan went through?"

"Yes."

I sighed. "How can I become immortal?"

Merlin smiled. "You ask many questions, Browny, which is wise, but I have spent thousands of years seeking answers to questions like those, and I do not mean to insult your intelligence, but you will not understand," he said. "Perhaps in time, you will. Now, are you ready?"

Thousands of years?! "I guess, but what are you going to do?"

"Prepare yourself, for this is going to hurt." Taking a few steps back, Merlin raised his wand in the air and began to speak in a strange language.

The hair on the back of my neck stood on end, and goose bumps riddled my arms. A brief moment later, my breathing stopped, and so did my heart. I couldn't move, and as my vision faded to black, I slowly floated free of my body and into the air. A blinding flash of light from a rift in the sky pierced my heart, and that's when I blacked out.

When I came to, my head was swimming, and my vision doubled. Strange three-dimensional symbols flashed before my eyes, and my whole body tingled like it had fallen asleep.

Once my senses had returned and the numbness faded, I could feel an energy pulsing through my veins. It felt like my blood was on fire. "Is it over?" I said.

Merlin helped me to my feet. "Yes."

"So, how long was I out for, and what happened?" I said. "And what's this weird feeling in my body? Is it mana?"

"Yes, my friend. It is."

The strange symbols kept running through my mind. "So how do I learn spells, or do I know any already? And these symbols in my head; what are they?"

"Count the symbols in your mind. How many do you see?" Merlin said.

I closed my eyes and thought for a moment. I could see only three. "Three."

"To learn a spell, you must combine all of its symbols in the correct manner, its formula. This will enable your soul to properly channel the mana and cast the spell. Of course, the more powerful the spell, the more complex the formula. The more complex the formula, the longer it will take you to correctly combine the symbols."

I understood exactly what he meant. The 3-D symbols were all different in size and shape. They were like puzzle pieces that could be interlocked in many different ways with other symbols to create countless unique shapes and strings.

"Or I can teach you," Merlin said. With an unseen force, he drew two symbols in the air and then linked them together. Immediately, the two symbols turned green. I knew both of them. "Now, see them in your mind and join them as I have."

Closing my eyes, I pictured the symbols and joined them together. A short burst of energy pulsed throughout my body, and for a brief moment, I felt stronger. The two-symbol formula in my mind turned green. My heart began to race a thousand miles an hour.

"Hey, I just felt something, and they turned green!"

Merlin smiled at me. "Good, you have learned a spell that will increase your strength. A spell that I call ogre's strength," he said. "Now cast it, and feel the power for yourself."

I looked at the symbols in the air and thought about what to do. What was I supposed to do to cast it? "Um, ogre's strength?" I said. Merlin laughed, smiling widely. "What?!"

"You will understand it soon," he said. "Test your strength by lifting this boulder."

"Alright." I approached the large rock and set my feet on either side. I then wrapped my arms around the boulder and began to lift, but it didn't budge. My face started to burn with embarrassment.

I stood all the way up and stared Merlin down. I wasn't in the mood to be played with.

"Visualize the formula in your mind," he said.

I visualized the two symbols in my mind and combined them, and not a split second later, an energy, unlike anything I had ever felt before flooded my muscles. At the same time, I felt the mana in my veins weaken sharply and lessen with each passing second.

Again, I prepared to lift the three-hundred-pound boulder, but as I lifted the rock this time, it came up off the ground with remarkable ease. It felt like it weighed only thirty pounds!

Hoisting it above my head, smiling ear to ear, I hurled the boulder a good ten feet. The ground shook slightly as it landed on the hardened sand. I shook my head and sat down. I couldn't deny it anymore. I just threw a three-hundred-pound boulder!

"It's all real, isn't it? This evil you talk about and Johnathan? It's all real?"

Merlin's smile faded. "Yes, my friend."

I sighed. I felt like throwing up. If this is reality, then what was my life before this? A dream?

"So, what's up with the wand." I could see a bluish-green, black-and-white aura shimmering around it. "I can see some sort of aura around it."

"Ah, now that your soul has been opened, you can see the mana of Ethereal," Merlin said. "My wand is enchanted, an ancient relic from eons past. But never mind that, now come. There are more spells that I must teach you."

By late afternoon, I had learned four more spells: lightning reflexes, giant's toughness, hammer hands, and jump, all of which required combining two or more of the three symbols I already knew. They were all green formula spells from the power category.

It was pretty easy to understand how magic worked. All spells required a certain amount of mana to cast. The more powerful the spell, the more mana, and of course, if you didn't have the mana to cast the spell, then you couldn't. But the great thing was that if you spent any mana, it would slowly replenish itself until you were full again.

Merlin had figured out all the math and crunched the numbers, but it was beyond me. I was happy with what I knew and even more so that I could do it. But the more we talked about it and the more I thought about it, the heavier it weighed upon me. Mary Jane was dead, and magic and monsters existed. My life was never going to be the same again, but when was it ever?

That night, we camped on top of the plateau, but I wanted to be alone. I needed time to grieve and reflect upon what the hell was going on. So after Merlin retired to his tent, I painstakingly climbed the jagged tower of rock that protruded nearly a hundred feet above the plateau's surface and stared out at the unfamiliar world before me under blood-red skies. Tears streaked down my face. I promise you, Mary Jane, that I will kill him. I promise you, my little honeybee.

It was the second of March 1997.

CHAPTER
THIRTEEN

I woke at dawn to find Merlin tending the fire with breakfast ready. I couldn't help but think that what happened yesterday was just a dream, and honestly, I hoped it was. At least then, Mary would still be alive. But when Merlin levitated us to the desert below, I knew it wasn't. I had a strange feeling that this nightmare was just beginning.

"What's on the agenda today? Are you going to teach me some new spells?" I said.

"Not today, my friend," Merlin said. "I need you to bring Matt and Nathan to me."

"You want them to fight too, huh?" I said. "That's good because they're great friends, and I know they'll fight."

"That is good to hear, but their will to fight, your will to fight, is not the true reason." Merlin said.

"Then what is? Why did you choose me?"

Merlin sighed. "You will understand in time my friend."

"Are you going to do to them what you did to me?"

"Yes, and you best go. They are looking for you near the school." They're looking for me? How does he know that?

I chuckled softly and put my hand on his shoulder. "Alright."

"But before you go, there is one thing that I must command of you."

"I'm all ears."

"Under no circumstance are you to use your spells in the presence of the people of his world. You cannot heal them, nor can you harm them. You are their guardian, not their magician," he said. "And as hard as this will be, know that it is for the good of all that you do this. For now, this war we fight must be waged in secret. Do you understand, Scott?"

"Yes, I do."

Throwing on my leather jacket, I headed into the Dark Woods and towards the school. It was fairly cool outside, with only a few clouds sweeping the sky.

Mana was pulsing through my veins, and the 3-D symbols kept flashing in my mind. I was trying to combine them in every way to unlock new spells, but nothing was coming to me.

I visualized the green symbol formula for hammer hands and squared up with a large tree. With power surging through me, I kicked it. Chunks of wood and bark flew everywhere as my leg passed almost effortlessly through the entire tree. A second later, the top half of the tree came crashing down.

Shaking my head, I sighed heavily. This was all so surreal.

Several minutes later, while walking through the neighborhood streets, a police car turned onto my street and pulled up in front of me.

The sheriff has been patrolling the neighborhood ever since the murders began, but it wasn't helping. They were never going to be able to stop him.

Matt stepped out of the squad car. He was wearing a black tuxedo and a red tie. "And what do we have here? It's a Brown Stuffings."

Nathan also got out and stood by his door.

"That's me, and I'm glad I bumped into you guys," I said. "I've got a lot to show and tell."

"And we have a lot to talk to you about," Nathan said. Matt's smile faded.

I already knew what they wanted to talk about. I was the last one with her, and fleeing the scene didn't look good, but I needed to get them to Merlin, and then they'd understand.

"I know, and I know how it looks."

"We know that you wouldn't kill her. You wouldn't hurt any woman," Nathan said. "But still, I have to take you in for questioning."

"I know, and I will, but not right now," I said.

The two of them glanced at each other.

"I have something I need to show you guys, and it will only take five minutes."

"It's going to have to wait, Browny," Nathan said.

"Just five minutes, man," I said.

Matt closed the squad car door. "I don't see how five more minutes can hurt," he said.

Nathan sighed, looked around, and then closed the door. "No, I guess not."

"So what's up, Browny? What do you have to show us?" Matt said.

"Come on, I'll show you," I said.

I then led them back in the same direction I had come from until we were a good fifty feet or so inside the Dark Woods.

"Are we almost there? Because this is starting to feel like a field trip," Nathan said, frowning.

"Yeah, I think we're good," I said. I had to make sure no one could see us. "Now, find me a good-sized rock."

Again, they glanced at each other. "Are you serious, Scott?" Nathan said. "You brought us all the way out here to find you a rock?"

"Yeah."

Nathan shook his head and put his hands on his hips. Rooting around in the underbrush, Matt found a head-sized rock and handed it to me. "Here you go, man."

"Is it cracked or broken in any way?" I said, holding it out for them to examine.

"It's a rock, man," Nathan said.

"Yeah, I know, but you'll see," I said.

"It's a perfectly healthy baby rock," Matt said. Nathan chuckled hesitantly.

"Good, now watch this," I said.

Holding the rock away from my body, I cast hammer hands and jabbed the rock with my finger. It shattered into a thousand pieces and filled the air with dust. Mana drained from my body.

Matt and Nathan's eyes got big. "Yeah, I didn't believe it either when I first saw magic," I said. "But hey, you guys want to see more?" They just stared at me. "Alright, you asked for it."

Crouching down, I cast jump and catapulted myself over thirty feet into the forest's canopy. A brief second later, I landed safely on my feet. My mana was getting low, and I perhaps had enough for only one or two more spells, but I didn't care. I had to convince them.

"So what do you guys think? Am I still crazy?" I said, slapping Matt on the shoulder.

"Yeah, you're crazy," Matt said. "But so am I!"

Nathan was pacing in small circles, running his hands through his short black hair.

"That's what I used to think, but everything you saw was real," I said. "Magic really does exist, and I know how crazy that sounds, but-"

Nathan stopped pacing. "How did you do all that, Browny? How did you shatter a rock by touching it and jump thirty feet in the air?!"

"I know how this sounds, but I can cast spells," I said. "I mean, you saw what I did."

Nathan stared at the ground, looking confused, while Matt sat down on a stump. "This still isn't as crazy as that ninja turtle shit you learned," Matt said.

I laughed. "One of these days, man, one of these days," I said. "Now, come on, guys, I have someone I want you to meet."

"I have to take you in, Browny," Nathan said, frowning and shaking his head.

"It can't wait a little longer?" I said. "The guy I want you to meet will clear my name."

"Come on, man, he just shattered a rock with his finger and broke the standing high jump record by a good twenty feet!" Matt said. "We can wait to take him in."

Nathan sighed and nodded his head.

We then continued walking, but no one said a word. I could tell by their casual glances at me that they were still utterly dumbfounded at what they had seen. It would all make sense to them soon, or at least as much as it could.

It wasn't long until we reached the tapered beginning of the chasm. "It does exist," Nathan said. "And I never would have thought."

"This keeps getting weirder and weirder, man," Matt said.

"Yeah, I know," I said.

Merlin was standing outside the forest edge.

"Come on, guys, he's right over here."

"Please tell me this isn't the dude you want us to meet," Matt said. "I mean, look at him, Browny. He's dressed like a fourteenth-century homeless person!" Nathan snickered. "No offense, man, but I've seen some pretty whacked-out stuff here in the last ten minutes, and you here take the cake!"

"None taken, my friend. I have been called worse." Merlin stroked his beard.

"Who are you?" Nathan said.

"My name is Merlin, and I am an archmage."

Matt smiled and cupped his mouth to contain his laughter.

"Browny says you know some things. What's going on?" Nathan said.

"Wait. Before you answered that, you said you're a mage, right?" Matt said.

"Yes," Merlin said.

"Then magic truly does exist?" Matt said. "And what Browny showed us wasn't fake, was it?"

"Yes, magic is real, and if you allow me, I will show you what I must and give you the same choice that I gave Browny," Merlin said.

"How do we know that we can trust you?" Nathan said.

"Because it was Gorsavice, Johnathan, who murdered Jessica and your friends and because I fight against him and his lord-Calignosity," Merlin said.

"So you're a witness. That still doesn't explain what the hell's been going on," Nathan said. "Or even how I can trust you."

"Time is what I need, Nathan, to help you understand," Merlin said.

Nathan shot me a look. "You told him about me?"

"He told me nothing I did not already know about you," Merlin said.

"Uh-huh," Nathan said.

"I know what it was that you saw that Halloween night. The thing you still refuse to believe you saw," Merlin said. "Browny has seen it too. The beast's shadow."

Nathan brushed his hands through his hair and shook his head. He looked so confused.

"Well, um, I don't have anything better to do," Matt said. "I've got time."

"I know how strange this all seems, guys. magic and all, but it really does exist." I said. "It will all make sense soon."

For the remainder of the day, I watched Merlin show them everything he showed me. My poor friends. They were just as blown away by all this as I was, if not worse.

It wasn't until Merlin empowered them and they began to cast spells that they finally snapped out of their stupor. I think they understood that our tranquil world no longer existed. Instead, living in its shadow lay a world of demons and magic, and we were chosen to fight it.

"Hey Merlin, have you ever fought a Balrog?" Matt said.

"Once, but only briefly," Merlin said.

"Did you kill it?" Matt said.

"No, I teleported."

We all looked at each other. By now, night had fallen, and we were sitting around a campfire atop the plateau. The sky was partly cloudy, and the temperature was near freezing.

"Why? You're thousands of years old and super powerful," Matt said.

"There are some things you will pray to never see," Merlin said. "But you will understand this in time."

"So what's the first thing on the agenda?" I said.

"As we speak, Calignosity is building his undead army, and Goresavice his, but his consists of men, not creatures," Merlin said.

"There are two armies?" Nathan said.

"Yes."

"Sweet, bring 'em on," Matt said.

"Do not take lightly the path that you have chosen, my friends. You are the defenders of this world fighting not for peace, land, or prosperity but for the very souls of the innocent," Merlin said.

"Who are we fighting, and where are they?" Nathan said. "And what are we to do when we find them? Kill them?!"

"They will be men like you, and yes, when the time comes, they must all die," Merlin said.

Nathan looked perplexed, almost troubled.

"I will explain all of this to you in a few day's time, but before the night escapes us, there is one more matter that I wish to discuss with you," Merlin said.

"What's up?" Matt said.

"When you were first born, your parents gave you names. It seems fitting that I, seeing how you have all been reborn into the realm of Ethereal, give you new names as well," Merlin said. He was smiling through his white beard.

"Are you serious?" Nathan said.

"Yes, and from now on, you will be known as Police." Merlin put a hand on his shoulder.

Nathan shot Merlin a hard look, but Merlin stared back. "Come on now. Police?!" Nathan said.

"Yes, that will be your name."

"It's bad enough that I get called pig or fuzz, but Police?!" Nathan threw his arms out in protest, but Merlin maintained his stare. "Alright, whatever."

Matt and I snickered quietly. "Hey Merlin, Nathan- I mean Police, just got stuck with a pretty horrendous name here, so I was thinking mine could be like Master Splinter or something," Matt said.

I punched him on the shoulder. "One of these days, man. One of these days."

"You, Matt, will be known as Doubles," Merlin said.

Matt nodded. "That's cool. I can live with that."

"And you, Scott, your name will remain the same, Browny,"
Merlin said. "Now get some rest. War is on the horizon, and there is
much that you must prepare for."

The following days were rather hectic for the three of us, especially
me. After being questioned relentlessly by a few detectives, I was
eventually cleared as a suspect in Mary Jane's death. It was ruled a
suicide even though the coroner couldn't determine how she died.
There were no physical injuries from the fall or any for that matter;
however, her veins were black.

Later in the week, we attended Mary's funeral. Only a few people
were in attendance, and once they had all left, I sat beside her. I told
her about all the places that I wanted to take her and all the things I
wanted to do with her. I talked about how many children we would
have and what we'd name them, where they would grow up, and
where we'd spend the last of our days. She was so beautiful, my Mary
Jane, even in death.

After kissing her goodbye, I took off and found a place to grieve.
In just a few days, my life had changed so dramatically. Mary had
been murdered, and I was an initiate of magic chosen to fight in an
apocalyptic war against an undead evil, and against my old friend.

It was hard for me to comprehend the reality of all this. After all,
I could crush rocks with my bare hands, jump three stories, and fall
over a hundred feet without breaking a bone. It would be hard for
anyone, really, but at least I had Merlin. And even though I didn't
know him for more than a few days, I trusted him unquestionably
like I did Master Yusokagi.

Mary Jane was buried next to Jessica and Karen.

CHAPTER FOURTEEN

"Remember to squeeze the trigger straight back. Don't jerk it," Police said.

I took aim and fired at the target.

Doubles and I cleared our background checks early this morning, and ever since then, the two of us have been taking target practice in the desert behind the plateau.

We had bought a plethora of shotguns, rifles, pistols, Kevlar vests, and a whole assortment of tactical gear. Not to mention thousands of rounds of ammunition. We were all geared up like a special forces team and ready for anything.

Merlin appeared out of thin air. "Good afternoon, my friends," he said.

"Hello, Merlin," I said.

"Enjoying your ability to teleport, eh?" Police said.

"Yeah, that's a pretty awesome spell," Doubles said. "When are you going to teach it to us?"

"None of you have acquired the symbols necessary to learn the formula yet," Merlin said. "Therefore, none of you can learn the spell."

"Thanks for reminding me that I still don't know anything about magic," Doubles said.

Merlin smiled.

Over time, new symbols will form in your mind, and when they do, new spells will also become available to you if you can figure out their formulas. But that's not the only way to learn symbols. There's a technique that allows you to steal mana from other spell casters, which can dramatically increase the number of symbols you know. It was quite simple, actually. The more mana you possessed, the more symbols you knew. But that technique was way beyond any of us. It was slow and steady until then.

"So what's up, Merlin?" I said. "It's been a few days since we last saw you."

"And it will be a few more days before you see me again," Merlin said.

"What are you doing now?" I said.

"I must resurrect some ancient brothers of mine who will help us in this war," he said. "This will take me a few days, so be sure to make this desert a regular stop."

Police glanced at me. "Resurrect?!" he said. "You can bring the dead back to life?"

My heart started pounding in my chest. "Mary, Jessica, and Karen, you can raise them?!" I said.

Merlin looked at me and smiled half heartedly. "I can resurrect any who have been dead for whatever length of time, but I cannot raise one whose soul is corrupted," he said.

"What do you mean, corrupted?! Mary Jane, Karen, and Jessica are the sweetest people I know!"

"I am sorry, but this corruption in which I speak of is not of the heart. I can not raise them; none can."

"What corruption? What did he do to them?" I said.

Merlin glanced at me and paused. "Your heart still bleeds, my friend. Let it heal, and let the memories of who they once were strengthen your resolve."

My heart sank back into the pit of my gut where it had grown so fond. I don't know why I allowed myself to get so excited. She was dead, and I could do nothing about it.

Police patted me on the back. "I'm sorry, man. I didn't know."
Doubles kicked a rock.

"Let us not dwell on that for now," Merlin said. "Instead, go to 195th Avenue, the abandoned warehouse at the end, and slay the men you find there."

"Consider it done, Merlin," I said.

Both Doubles and Police stared at me with a shocked expression. I knew full well what Merlin was asking of us, and honestly, it was about time. I didn't care about my Pride career, the law, or even my life. I just wanted to kill Goresavice and all who stood by him.

"You're asking us to break the law and commit murder?!" Police said, his face creased in concern.

Doubles laughed hesitantly. "Yeah, man, I don't know if I want to do that."

"The law does not apply to any of you," Merlin said.

"It does when it comes to murder. I won't do it," Police said. "I'm not murdering anyone, and even for asking us to do this, you're breaking the law."

Doubles started grinding his foot into the loose sand. "Yeah, I can't. I can't do it either, Merlin. I just don't know that much about magic or what's going on or even about you," he said. "I just don't feel right about this."

I shot both of them a look. "Are you serious?! What's wrong with you guys?" I said with a slightly raised voice. "Goresavice murdered all of our friends, and if we don't stop him-"

"The world will burn, I know," Police said. "But we don't know that. We don't know anything." Police played with his badge as he paced. "I took an oath to uphold the law, and now I'm being asked to break it? Aren't we supposed to be the defenders of good?"

Doubles sighed heavily. "I'm with Nathan on this one, Scott. I'm sorry, guys."

A long silence filled the air.

The sun was high in the sky and warmed my skin. A gentle breeze swept the desert, pushing the fluffy white clouds across the blue expanse. It was a beautiful day.

"My friends, I know what I ask of you is difficult, and our purpose nearly incomprehensible. I know that you are still confused about magic and that I have not given you much reason to trust me," Merlin said. "But of all the men in the world, I have chosen you because it is only you who are capable of bringing about its salvation. Now, please do not waiver in your dedication to protecting this world, and please trust me. For in time, you will understand and see everything for what it is, but only in time."

Doubles kicked a rock and nodded his head. "All right, Merlin. I'm all in. So how many of these badguys are we looking for, and how do we spot them?"

Merlin looked at the ground and sighed. "As to how many there are, I do not know. Calignosity's ability to conceal his activities is far greater than my ability to uncover them. And as for the badguys, you will know them when you see them."

"Well then, it's time to go hunting, eh?" Doubles said, strapping on his Kevlar vest. "We didn't buy all this crap for nothing, eh?"

Merlin vanished into thin air. "That's as real as it gets, and we-we..." Sitting down, Police threw his badge onto the ground and began to take apart his gun.

I put my hand on his shoulder. "Our friends are dead. Nothing is ever going to be the same for us again. Nothing."

Around six 'o'clock that night, we pulled into a small dirt field facing an abandoned three-story building. Shrubbery engulfed the decrepit structure, and trees surrounded it on all sides. We were at the end of a dead-end street off 195th with no one in sight.

"This is the place," I said.

"Let's do this," Doubles said.

"Wait-" Police said.

Doubles, and I looked back at him in the back seat.

"You follow my lead, and we only fire if fired upon," Police said. "I need to be able to cover our asses, so this needs to look like self-defense like I saw some suspicious activity and-"

"We know," Doubles and I said in unison.

"So, can we do this now?" Doubles said.

Police nodded his head. He was wearing his police uniform, badge, gun, and gear.

Once out of my car, we crept through the dense shrubbery until we found a rusty steel door. I heard a man talking on the other side. My adrenaline was pumping, and excitement was building in my chest.

After a silent count to three, Police kicked open the door, and we rushed inside. The entire ground level floor was wide open with evenly spaced steel I-beams here and there that supported the second and third level floors, or what was left of them, at least.

In the far corner, to my right, was a metal staircase leading up to the second and third floors. To my left were over a dozen men sitting on the floor. A man with four grenades strapped to his chest and an assault rifle over his shoulder was standing behind a wooden podium. They were all dressed in forest green fatigues and black boots with short black hair. Merlin was right. I did recognize them.

"Everyone get down on the ground now!" Police yelled, pointing his 9mm at the crowd. "On the ground!"

Taking cover behind a steel beam, I leveled my shotgun at the man behind the podium and squeezed the trigger. Buckshot peppered his chest and knocked him down. One down. Fifteen to go.

"Browny?!" Police yelled.

In a blur of motion, the grenade guy crawled out from behind the podium, jumped to his feet, and fired round after round at us with his assault rifle. Luckily, the steel beams that we were hiding behind were thick and stopped the bullets cold.

I visualized the formula for lightning reflexes and cast the spell. Lightning raced throughout my body, and it seemed like everyone had slowed by a factor of ten, all except for the grenade guy. He was reacting just as fast as we were. He was an initiate of magic.

Stepping out from behind the beam, I planted the butt of my shotgun in between the eyes of a charging bad guy. He was knocked out cold.

Swinging my gun low, I cracked another one in his kneecap, which dropped him. To my left, a third man threw a heavy right for my chin, but he was too slow.

Whipping my shotgun back, I slammed the butt across his temple. A sickening crack echoed throughout the building as blood splattered everywhere. My shotgun was busted, so I dropped it next to his unconscious body. Apparently, guns weren't made for beating people. Well, at least not this one.

Several gunshots rang out as Police shot back at the grenade guy who was running towards the stairwell.

Racing beside me with unnatural reflexes, Doubles threw a hard right hook that connected cleanly with the chin of a badguy, knocking him out. He then threw a left inside leg kick that broke the leg of another. The man fell to the ground screaming, holding the mangled mess that was once his leg.

In one second, we had dropped five bad guys, but there were still ten left, and they had us surrounded.

Casting giant's toughness, my body hardened; I swerved to the right to avoid the knife stabbing at my throat. Slapping the knife out of the hand of my attacker, I chopped him in the throat and delivered a hard left into his chin. He collapsed to the ground, choking.

Ducking under a flurry of fists from yet another bad guy, I struck him in the groin and followed with a left hook to his jaw as he doubled over. He was out before he hit the ground.

Blocking his opponent's high kick, Doubles stepped into his slower foe and delivered a brutal uppercut, which snapped his head back and shattered his teeth. It was obvious by the power with which Doubles was striking his opponents that his strength was enhanced.

I was tempted to do the same, but lightning reflexes, giant's toughness, and ogre's strength were all sustained spells. They drained your mana little by little every second for as long as you kept the spell active or until you ran out of mana, and I wanted to conserve as much mana as I could.

Through the corner of my eye, I could see Police hunkered behind a steel beam near the stairwell. He was dumping rounds at the grenade guy, who apparently was on the second floor firing rounds back at him.

A kick to the back of the head caught me by surprise. Normally, a kick like that would have knocked me out or, at the very least, down, but with giant's toughness, I barely felt a thing. Spinning around, I quickly finished my opponent with a barrage of well-placed fists. A few seconds later, all but two of the bad guys were either unconscious or seriously injured. I looked over at Doubles. "You got those two?"

"All day," Doubles said.

Drawing my Berretta 9mm, I ran towards the nearest gap in the ceiling and catapulted myself through it by a casting jump. Flying high above the second-story floor, I spotted the grenade guy crouching by the top of the stairwell. He was pinning Police down with a hail of bullets.

Raising my gun, I emptied the entire magazine at the grenade guy before landing safely on my feet.

Stumbling sideways, blood spurting out of his neck, the grenade guy collapsed to the ground.

"Where the heck did you come from?!" Police said, hobbling up the stairs. He was holding his left hip.

"How bad is it?" I said.

"I'll be fine." He kneeled next to the grenade guy and checked his pulse. "How's Doubles?" Police said.

"He should be mopping up now."

After checking the grenade guy for personal information, we took his assault rifle and grenades and headed down the stairs.

On the far side of the room, Doubles had every conscious bad guy up against the wall with their hands on top of their head.

"Do you guys even know who we are? Well, do ya?" Doubles said, waving his pistol around. "I didn't think so."

"What do they know?" I said.

"I haven't got that far yet." Doubles said.

"We should probably think about getting out of here soon," Police said. His breathing was becoming labored. "I'm going to need medical attention."

"You're hurt?" Doubles said. "Weren't you sustaining giant's toughness?"

"I've been shot, you idiot." Police glared at him.

"Oh." Doubles said. "I guess we now know that giant's toughness doesn't protect you from bullets!" I shook my head. Now was not the time for jokes.

"We'll leave here in a minute, but for now, we need information," I said. "Who are you guys?" No one answered. Reloading my 9mm, I put the barrel to a bad guy's forehead.

"What are you doing, Browny?" Police said.

"Who are you guys?" I said.

He smiled at me and said nothing. I squeezed the trigger and watched him slump to the floor. Blood ran down the wall.

"Holy shit, Scott!" Police cried out, throwing his hands on top of his head.

Doubles adjusted his vest and stared at the ground. "Browny, man."

Ignoring them, I moved to the next bad guy and put the gun to his head. "Who are you guys?"

"We are the meek who will inherit the world," a man's voice said from behind us.

The three of us quickly turned around.

Standing near the bottom of the stairwell was the grenade guy. His clothes were drenched in blood, but the hole in his neck was completely healed.

Raising my pistol, I took aim and fired two rounds at his head. The bullets struck him in the face but pancaked and fell to the floor. I let out a deep sigh. This initiate was far more powerful than we were. I holstered my pistol.

"You've got to be shitting me!" Doubles said.

Raising the assault rifle, Police unloaded a barrage of lead into the grenade guy, and this time, the bullets managed to tear up his fatigues before scattering across the floor, but still, he remained unscathed.

"All right." Police dropped the gun. "What now?"

"The three of us can take him, right?" Doubles said.

"You two are on your own." Police leaned up against a steel beam, grimacing. Blood soaked his left pant leg and was dripping on the floor.

Cautiously, I approached from the left of the badguy while Doubles came from the right. I could tell by this man's stance that he had skill. "Let me handle him, Doubles."

"No way, man. I'm not letting you fight alone," he said.

Feinting to his right, Doubles threw a looping right for the bad guy's chin. Slapping it down, the grenade guy chopped Doubles in the throat while drawing a knife with his left. He then stabbed

Doubles in his exposed right side, and as he keeled over, the badguy pushed him to the ground.

He could have killed him with a strike to the back of his neck, but for some reason, he didn't. Doubles rolled to his back, holding his side while coughing up blood, gasping for air.

"You are a brave man but foolish," the badguy said.

Ducking away from his slashing knife, I countered with a sharp blow to his kidneys with the spell of hammer hands, but whatever spell he was sustaining absorbed my attack and left him uninjured. If hammer hands and bullets couldn't hurt him, then neither could my katana, so I wondered if leverage pressure would work.

Swerving backward to avoid an uppercut, I kicked the inside of his right leg to unbalance him, but he didn't budge.

Lunging forward, he stabbed at my stomach. Grabbing his wrist, I twisted his hand inward and disarmed him. I then continued with the twisting motion and tried to force him to the ground, but he resisted me with incredible strength.

Taking hold of the front of my Kevlar vest, he jerked his arm free of my grip and hurled me to the ground a good ten feet away. His strength was definitely enhanced.

Jumping to my feet, I squared up with my opponent and cast ogre's strength to balance our strengths. More mana drained from my veins.

After throwing a few jabs to distract me, all of which I slapped away, he kicked high at my head. Catching his leg, I effortlessly picked him up, and using his momentum, I slammed him into a steel beam. His body didn't even make a noise as it struck, nor did he.

Jumping on top of him, I tried to mount him, but he wrapped his legs around my waist in guard. Throwing his right leg over my shoulder, I threw myself backward, wrapped it up with my legs, and grabbed his ankle. He tried to roll out of my heel hook, but it was deep. Twisting violently, I heard it pop and him cry out.

Without hesitation, I repositioned my grip and applied pressure to his knee. A brief second later, it popped as well. I should have been able to tear off his leg with my enhanced strength, but I just couldn't. He had to have been sustaining giant's toughness, too. I was beginning to see the usefulness of these spells.

Spinning around, I swept past his broken leg and lay on top of his chest in side control. With his right arm over my back, I slipped my left arm under it and locked my hands around his neck. I then scurried clockwise around his head, choking him. He clawed at my face and ripped at my arms.

Cinching my lock even tighter, I jerked on his neck violently. It popped but didn't break. I let go of his head, and with one smooth motion, I grabbed his left arm and fell back with it in between my legs in a tight arm bar. I snapped it near the elbow.

Releasing his limp arm, I jumped to my feet. Everything around me slowed, and I felt weaker and frailer. All of my spells had failed. I had no more mana to sustain them. Not even a drop.

Climbing to his knees and then to his feet, he threw a stiff right into my face. My head snapped back from the impact, and my nose broke. He was just too quick; it was all just a blur of motion, like the first time I fought Goresavice.

The grenade guy delivered a straight kick into my stomach, which knocked me down and sent me sliding several feet into a steel beam. He had kicked me with his broken leg, but like his arm, it was now completely healed.

With the wind knocked out of me, I jumped to my feet and kicked out in front of myself in anticipation that he would charge me. My timing must have been perfect because my foot caught him in the lower stomach, which stopped him dead in his tracks and caused him to stumble backward.

He stumbled?! Quickly drawing my katana, I thrust it into his belly. He gasped in pain, his eyes wide. Twisting and ripping the blade out, I spun around him and brought the blade down on the back of his neck. He slumped to the floor, his head hanging on by a sinew.

"Regenerate that," I said.

I ran over to Doubles and knelt beside him.

"Y-You really did l-learn that crap, didn't ya?" Doubles said, wheezing.

"You know I wouldn't lie to you," I said. "Now, let's see that wound."

Police removed his vest and cut open his tux.

"I'll be fine. It's only a flesh wound, really," Doubles said. "I've been stabbed worse at the bar."

"If anything, his ribs are broken; there's not much penetration," Police said.

"Thank you giant's toughness. Yeah!" Doubles voice was weak.

"But we still need to get him to a hospital, and me too, and quickly," Police said.

I looked up at Police, my nose still bleeding. "You two can't hang in there until tomorrow?" I said. Police looked at me like I was crazy. "Going to the hospital is only going to draw unwanted attention, and I really think we should lay low until this is all figured out."

Doubles sat up, groaning all the way. "Yeah, man up, dude," he said.

"Merlin will heal us tomorrow; now, come on, let's get out of here," I said.

By the time we left, only two bad guys remained, the two I had killed. They were my first, and honestly, it felt good. It felt like I had delivered a small piece of justice to those so cruelly taken from me. And I know how that sounds, but for the first time in my life, I had a reason to fight, a reason to kill, and I'm not going to stop until Goresavice is lying dead at my feet.

CHAPTER FIFTEEN

Doubles crawled out of his tent and made his way to me. It was just past eight in the morning, and for the last two hours, I had been practicing my forms. My mana had completely refreshed and surged through my veins like fire. I was again ready for anything.

"You really kicked that initiate's ass, man," he said.

"Yeah, thanks," I said.

"You do this every day?"

"Every day for two hours beginning at sunrise."

He picked up my kusarigana. "With all these weapons?"

"Yeah, sure do."

Doubles stared at me for a long moment. "I'm sorry I didn't believe you about all this."

I put my hand on his shoulder. "That's all right."

"No, I really mean it. I'm sorry."

"It's ok my brother."

Doubles smiled. "But you know, I really did think that you were crazy."

I chuckled lightly. "So did I, man. So did I."

Police limped over. "What's going on over here?" he said.

"Nothing much. Browny's showing off for the snakes and lizards," Doubles said.

"How's your leg, Police?" I said, trying to hold back my laughter.

"How's your face?!" he said.

Doubles snickered. "I've never looked better, man," I said.

"I can't tell," Police said. "It looks like you cut yourself shaving."

"Really?" I felt my neck and face. I did just shave this morning. "Where?"

"Ahh, my bad, Browny, that's where his fist collided with your face," Police said.

We all busted up laughing, and for a moment afterward, we stood in silence. Police patted me on the shoulder. "You fought valiantly, Scott."

"And you saved our asses back there," Doubles said.

"Thanks, guys, but we all fought hard last night, including you," I said.

"I don't know what you were seeing, but all I did last night was get shot," Police said.

"Yeah, that's true," I said.

"It was definitely a fight to remember," Doubles said.

"That's for sure," Police said.

"So what does this mean for us?" Doubles said. "Where do we go from here?"

Police sighed. "I don't know. Maybe we'll wake up one day, or maybe..."

"It means we're fighting in a war that we can't even begin to comprehend," I said. "And as to where we go from here. We go to hell."

For the remainder of the morning and part of the afternoon, I took target practice until Merlin appeared out of nowhere, along with seven others.

"Merlin!" Doubles cried out. He doubled over, cringing in pain. "Ow-oh."

"It is good to see you again, my friends," Merlin said.

"You too, now can you heal me, please?" Police said. "Browny thought it would be a good idea to let an ounce of lead fester in my leg."

In the blink of an eye, the bullet in his leg plopped to the ground; his flesh mended, and my broken nose corrected itself. All the cuts and bruises on our bodies were healed instantly.

I don't think the miracles of magic will ever cease to amaze me. "Thank you, Merlin," I said.

"Thank you. I can finally breathe again," Doubles said.

Police just stood there examining his leg with a dumbfounded expression.

"You are welcome; now let me introduce you to a few good brothers of mine," Merlin said.

Standing on both sides of him were seven large and scruffy men. Four were dressed in medieval-styled clothing from like the fourteenth century, while the others were dressed as pirates. It was difficult for me to contain my laughter, especially with the snickering of Doubles and Police. But I kept my composure and remained courteous.

"This is Hook, the captain of my fleet," Merlin said, pointing to each of them as he introduced them. "Pirate, my trusted scout, and Buccaneer, a swashbuckler."

Hook had a thick black beard, mustache, and long black hair. His arms were spotted with tattoos, and he had numerous piercings above his left eyebrow and in his ears. On the other hand, Pirate had a well-trimmed and short red beard, mustache, and red bandana wrapped around his head. Buccaneer, however, was clean-shaven except for his brown mustache and wore a shiny steel helm and breastplate. He almost looked like a Spanish Conquistador from my history textbooks.

"Howdy, partners!" Pirate said with a Western accent. "It lookin' like we have some good 'ol city slickers here."

The three of us stared at him with wide eyes. "All righty then. Moving on now," Doubles said. "Who's this big fella?"

"That is Batlord, the king of the Batlords, and his general Basil. They were my only allies in the war against Calignosity, and for being such, I am grateful."

The two of them were the largest of the seven, and they both had short black hair and sharp, chiseled faces. Their black tabards swayed in the cooling breeze and featured an embroidered black bat in the center of their chest. An unrealistically massive black spiked mace was hanging from the Batlord's leather belt. It looked like it must weigh about fifty pounds.

"And here is Guard, a foot soldier of the Dragon Masters, and beside him is the valiant and honorable general of my army, Bestguard," Merlin said.

Aside from Guards at attention stance, the one thing that stood out the most was how badly his face and bald head were scarred. He must have seen some pretty harsh battles in his time.

Bestguard was almost as large as Basil, around two hundred and thirty pounds, with somewhat curly red hair and a well-trimmed red mustache and beard. He had a huge silver claymore strapped to his back, and like the Batlords, the two wore tabards. They were light red in color with yellow trimming and featured an intricately embroidered green dragon with black wings breathing fire across the front. I smiled and slowly shook my head. Both Xavier and Master Yusokagi had this tattoo. My mind raced with questions.

"It art an honor to fight alongside thee," Bestguard said, nodding at us.

"Likewise," Police said, glancing at me through the corners of his eyes.

"These are the seven men who survived the last battle, aren't they, Merlin?" I said.

Merlin smiled. "Yes, they are," he said.

"Well, I can definitely tell they're ancient," Doubles said. Police snickered.

"Why did you have to resurrect them?" I said. "Why weren't they alive with you this whole time?"

Merlin raised an eyebrow. "That is a good question, my friend. You see, back in those dark days, I knew of no magic to open another's soul to the mana of Ethereal as I have done to you. After all, it is what makes you ageless. And many years after the war, once my spells to preserve their youth and extend their life had worn off, one by one, they died," Merlin said. "Centuries passed before I learned the technique of opening, and now that another great war is upon us, it is time for my brothers to fulfill their oath and once again pick up the sword."

For a moment or two, I stood in awe of the seven before me. These are the men who have been to hell and, without hesitation, are risking their souls to go back. And all for a cause that I was just beginning to understand. These men are the true heroes.

"So what's next on the agenda?" I said. "We only killed two of the sixteen badguys we encountered; the rest escaped."

"He means he killed two. We just got shot and stabbed," Police said.

"Yeah, including one that was damn near invincible," Doubles said. "If it wasn't for Browny, I'm sure we wouldn't be here right now."

"I know you wanted them all dead, Merlin. I won't fail you again," I said.

Merlin placed his hand on my shoulder. "You did well, Browny; you killed the one that mattered."

"The initiate?" I said. Merlin nodded. "But why was he more important than the others?"

"Because few are the ones who wield magic."

"Huh, makes sense, I guess," Doubles said.

"And you were right. I did recognize them," I said.

"What do you mean, Browny?" Police said.

"I've been seeing guys dressed like that, like Goresavice was during Halloween, for years now."

"Where?" Doubles said.

"Phoenix, Japan-everywhere," I said.

"That can't be good," Police said.

"No, not at all," Doubles said.

"What of thee monsters that lieth in the Dark Zone?" Guard said. "Should not we destroyeth them as welleth?"

Doubles exhaled deeply and tried to cover the smirk on his face with his hand. "Oh boy, these guys are hard-core medieval."

Police and I snickered. These guys were just too much.

"What's the Dark Zone?" Police said.

Merlin pointed at the chasm under the plateau. "As worried as I am over their existence, they are not what we must be concerned about. It is Goresavice's army of men that we must concentrate on."

"Wait, wait, wait," Doubles said, putting his hands up. "There's monsters down there?!"

"Yes, my friend," Merlin said.

Doubles sighed heavily and pretended to silently count to ten. "So you're telling me there are creatures down there in that abyss, and we're going to let 'em chill?" He scratched his head. "I mean, don't get me wrong, I'm not all that excited to face the monsters in the closet, but shouldn't we do something about that?"

"Normally, I would agree with you, but Calignosity's minions from hell are where I can see them and doing nothing. Goresavice army of men, however, walk-in secret amongst the nations of the world, and what they do, I do not know," Merlin said. "It will be your responsibility to find these evil men and kill them where they stand."

Police started to pace in circles.

"With pleasure, my liege," Batlord said. His voice was deep.

"But you must not be reckless, for the people of this world are not our enemies, and we must not be seen as their enemy either," Merlin said.

"There's monsters down there?!" Police said. Merlin nodded.

Sitting down, and then in a fit of laughter, Police laid on the sandy desert ground. "That's why, guys. That's why no one has ever returned alive to confirm the chasm's existence."

Doubles shrugged his shoulders. I wasn't the least bit surprised. Not with everything that's been going on as of recently.

"What about my job?" Police said. "I can't be an officer of the law and do this simultaneously."

"Don't worry about me. I quit yesterday," Doubles said.

"For now, your job takes precedence, and for the rest of you, there are more that I must call to our cause, so stay close by," Merlin said. "Browny, Doubles, perhaps you can show your new friends the modern world. I think they will like that."

"So, just do my job like I'm not casting unbelievable spells or getting in shootouts every night?" Police said. "Alright, got it." He sighed heavily, shaking his head.

"No problem, man, but before we go anywhere with these guys, they'll need some new clothes because I'm not walking around the streets of Phoenix with Sir Lancelot and Black Beard," Doubles said. "It's not happening."

"Thy taketh offense at thine's remark," Basil said.

Doubles patted him on the chest. "Sure ya do, big fella. Sure ya do," he said. "And another thing, these guys are going to need to know how to fight twentieth-century style, not just Conan the Barbarian style."

"Then teach them," Merlin said.

"You can't just cast a spell on them?" Doubles said.

"I have done what is necessary to enlighten them on the modern world; however, the rest is up to you."

"Have you listened to them speak?!" Doubles said. Merlin disappeared. "Oh, okay, I see how it is."

"How did you know that there are creatures down there?" Police said. "Do you know what else is down there?"

"Monsters have lieth down there ever since thee was alive ages ago," Guard said. "Thee desert here was art a great battle site ages ago."

"You mean back during the great war?" I said.

"Yay," Guard said. "Thy Lich War." I looked over at the plateau and the chasm beneath it. A chill raced up my spine.

"What else is down there?" Police said.

"Thy not knoweth," he said.

Doubles glanced at me. "I want to get this straight, and I don't doubt Merlin or anything, but you guys really fought in that last battle, didn't you?" he said.

"In every battle," Hook said. "We witnessed the laying of waste of this world and, argh, seen thy great evil with thine own eyes."

"So Merlin is telling the truth then about Calignosity?" Doubles said.

"You guessed 'er right, partner," Pirate said.

"This is really happening right now, isn't it?!" Police mumbled.

Doubles chuckled.

"What about Ethereal? Have you seen it?" I said.

"Merlin hath permitted none to cross," Bestguard said.

"Me stomach rumbling," Buccaneer said.

"Why not?" Doubles said.

"It art a place of dreams and nightmares. A place of incredible power where nay a mortal dare step," Bestguard said. I caught his eyes staring at the great tower of rock that jutted from the plateau's surface.

"Is Ethereal an evil place?" I said.

"Nay, but it art dangerous," Bestguard said. "Though thou heard it hath notteth always been such."

"Is that where all portals lead?" I said.

"Nay," he said.

I sighed. There was so much that I wanted to know but so little time. "Well then, let's get you guys something to eat," I said.

The first place we took them to was a steakhouse and, afterward, an ice cream and donut shop. We spared no expense when it came to their taste buds, and once they had their fill, we took them shopping. They were in desperate need of some new clothes, but they hated everything they tried on. They wouldn't even get new shoes to replace their worn-out leather boots. In the end, and much to Double's embarrassment, they decided to keep their ancient trousers and woolen shirts.

Overall, I had a great time watching them enjoy the wonders of the modern world for the first time, despite the snickers of passers-byes. After several days of acclimating them to our culture, we took them back to the desert behind the plateau and introduced them to twentieth-century firepower, though the concept of firearms wasn't new to them. Especially the pirates.

Unfortunately, because they didn't legally exist, they couldn't own a gun or anything else for that matter, but I wasn't too concerned about that. They'd just have to lay low until we got the problem fixed.

"How old is Merlin? Does anyone know?" Police said.

"Nay," Batlord said.

"Can you speak English, please?" Doubles said.

"He was fifty-two when the Lich War began," Pirate said. He was taking careful aim at a target with his rifle.

"Why doth thee wish to knoweth?" Bestguard said.

"Because I'm curious," Police said.

"His age can answer a ton of questions about history. Heck, you all can," Doubles said.

"The Lich War lasted one hundred and six years, two months and a fortnight. I art the last of thine's warriors to die twenty-five years later," Bestguard said.

"That would make him about one hundred and eighty-three years old, but how many years passed between then and now!?" Police said.

"Let's start a pool. The first person to guess his age wins," Doubles said.

"Count thee in, but what art thee buy-in? Hook said.

"A hundred," Doubles said. "And as soon as Merlin gathers everyone, we'll get this pool started."

"It soundeth good," Buccaneer said.

"Lich War? Why is it called that?" I said.

"Before thy Lich War, none existed. Calignosity was thee first, but not thee last," Bestguard said.

"And what's a Lich, and why is it so feared?" I said.

"Twisted souls fusethed together by a sick magic, anchored to some object. For no created denizen of Ethereal canneth match them in power or evil," Bestguard said.

"Ethereal is notteth as wonderful as it soundeths," Batlord said.

With the sun sinking below the horizon, we decided to give up target practice and set up camp for the night.

"This art a well-crafted blade," Bestguard said. He was holding my katana and inspecting the symbols on the blade closely. He glanced at Batlord.

"Thanks, my Master gave it to me," I said.

"Thy sees thee practicing forms. You art well trained," Bestguard said.

"Doubles say thee art a ninja," Guard said.

I shot Doubles a grin. "What else does he say?"

"That thy slayethed an initiate of great power," Guard said.

I laughed. "Yeah."

"That art good. Creatures do not killeth from afar," Basil said.

"And how do they kill?" Police said.

"Up close, with tooth and claw, liketh real men," Basil said.

"Yeah, well, try saying that when your head gets blown off from a mile away," Police said.

Basil glared at him. "It must have been terrifying fighting monsters without magic," I said.

"Or guns," Police muttered.

"Merlin casteth what thou could on all before battle," Bestguard said.

"Merlin's pretty powerful, isn't he? I said.

"Yay, thou art," Bestguard said. "And in time, so shall we."

Doubles opened a bag of marshmallows, grabbed a few, and passed it around. "So what spells do you know?"

"All thou knoweths. We art like thee in power," Buccaneer said.

"So what was it like living in your time before the Lich War, aside from not having a public school system to teach you proper English?" Doubles said.

"Have thy wipeth thine arse with corn husk?" Guard said.

Doubles looked puzzled. "No, but your points are well taken."

"Merlin's back," Police said.

He appeared along with a dozen others.

"Merlin, my man, it's so nice of you to drop by," Doubles said. "So, who are our new friends?"

"I will let them introduce themselves, but what I will say is, like you, they are all great men," Merlin said. "Now, for the last time, stay close. There are still eight more that I must call to our cause." He vanished.

"Man, I can't wait until I can do that," Doubles said.

"Argh, come join we round the fire," Hook said. "We be having some getting to knoweth each other to do."

"Oh fuck no! I didn't sign up for this shit!" A young, clean-shaven, bald guy said. "And where the hell are we?"

"We sure ain't in Kansas no more." another said.

"You're in Janestown, Arizona, which is located about twenty miles northwest of Williams, and my name is Browny."

There were a total of twelve men who were all dressed in normal, everyday street clothes except for three who stood out the most to me. One was a rather fat man wearing oil-stained white coveralls named Pudgy. He was an auto mechanic who knew everything about every type of vehicle. He even used to be a NASCAR pit crew leader.

Another one that stood out was a baby-faced eighteen-year-old named Kid. He was a professional thief who could break into any physical security system in the world and has never been caught, so he claims. He's even robbed blind a few high-security bank vaults.

The last one was a Polynesian man with long black hair named Islander. He was strange to me because he was dressed as if he was still vacationing in the tropics. He had no shirt, wore flip-flops, and, of course, had on the tropical shorts. He was a wilderness survival expert.

The other guys joining our ranks included two firefighters, Fire and Chief. Chief, as his name suggests, was the current chief of the Los Angeles Fire Department and has a wife named Carol and a son named Mike. Fire was an ex-firefighter for the New York Fire Department and has a daughter named Amber.

There was an ex-army helicopter pilot named Octane with ten years of experience flying the Apache. He took part in the Gulf War and racked up over thirty vehicle kills, including ten tanks.

We had an electronics engineer named Whiteguy because of his white jeans and t-shirt. A navy diver of twelve years named Aqua. A black construction engineer named Big Blue because of his blue coveralls, and a gifted computer hacker named Big Red. We even had a top-notch lawyer named after his multi-striped turtleneck shirt-Striper.

And finally, there was the bald-headed Aqua Shark. A hardened Navy SEAL of eleven years.

For the remainder of the night and the next few days, we all hung out around the desert, getting to know one another, and to help pass the time, we showed off our spells; however, we all knew the same four spells and three symbols, took target practice, and even swam in the nearby lake across the desert. It almost felt like summer break again, minus the girls, of course.

I love you, Mary Jane, and I will find a way to save you. I promise.

CHAPTER SIXTEEN

"You're Browny, right? The first one Merlin initiated?" Fire said. He had wavy brown hair like me and was clean-shaven except for a mustache. "I'm Fire if you don't remember."

"Yeah, I was," I said.

"I heard about what happened to your fiancé, and I'm sorry for your loss."

"Thanks."

"It looks like you have more reason to fight than any of us."

"It would seem that way, but really, we all fight for the same reason," I said. "Goresavice has just taken more from me than anyone else, at least for now."

"That's true, but why her, if you don't mind me asking."

"To get to me."

Fire shook his head. "And this was your friend?"

"Yeah."

"That's twisted."

"So, what's your daughter's name again?" I said. "There are just so many new names that it's hard to keep track of them all."

I knew her name and age. I just wanted to change the conversation before I got too depressed.

"Yep, I know how that goes. Her name is Amber, and she's eight," Fire said. "I don't know how I'll manage all this and raising her by myself, but I'll find a way."

"I'm sure Merlin has a plan for guys like you and Chief, who have families to raise."

"You're probably right, but it makes me wonder why he chose me. I'm just a simple firefighter, you know. Did he ever tell you?"

"Not really," I said. "He doesn't tell us much, but I suppose if he did, it might be too much for any of us to handle at one time. I mean, magic, you know."

Fire took a swig from his beer and turned to face the sun. "It sure is something out here, isn't it?"

"Yes, it is."

"So, what's going on over here?" Kid said.

"Not a lot," Fire said.

"Did you know that you're standing in the presence of the Pride middleweight champion of the world?" Kid said.

"Who-you?" Fire said. "I thought you were a professional thief."

Kid wrinkled his brow. "No. I quit stealing a long time ago."

"And how long ago was that?" Fire said. "Yesterday?"

Kid held out a wallet. Fire quickly snatched it from Kid's hand and shook his head. Kid was slick. "And no, Browny's the champion," Kid said.

"Really? You're a professional fighter," Fire said.

"He's like a superstar over there in Japan," Kid said. "He kicks everyone's ass."

"And initiates too with a fucking Katana," Whiteguy said, strolling up behind me. He was wearing his usual white jeans with a white tank top.

"Now that I heard about," Fire said.

Whiteguy threw his arm around my shoulders and hugged me close. "Browny! Ya little killer you."

"What martial arts do you study?" Kid said.

"I'm a wrestler with a black belt in Muay Thai, jujitsu, judo, and ninjutsu," I said.

"Shit, what don't you know?" Whiteguy said.

"Wow, that's pretty impressive," Fire said. "What's your record?"

"Thirty and oh," I said. "My first title defense is the sixteenth of next month."

The kid grabbed a beer from the cooler. "You wanted to be a fighter your whole life, huh?" he said.

"Put it back. You're under the legal age to drink," Fire said.

"Are you serious, dude?" Whiteguy said. "He's old enough to kill and with unbelievable magical powers, of course, but he's not old enough to drink?! Give the kid a beer."

Fire glanced at Whiteguy and then at Kid. "No. Now put it back."

"The laws don't apply to us, man; those were Merlin's words," Whiteguy said.

"It's alright, buddy, and as a show of respect for my elders, I'll put it back and grab a soda instead," Kid said. Putting the beer back, he grabbed a soda and joined the others.

By three o'clock in the afternoon, Merlin had arrived with the final eight, and they were absolutely massive in stature, not to mention beyond unbelievable. They were all seven to nine feet tall and incredibly well built, like professional bodybuilders with veins bulging everywhere. By my estimate, they each probably weighed close to five hundred pounds.

They were all wearing black boots, slacks, a tight black shirt with white sleeves, and a small blue and white planet on the left side of their chest.

"My friends, I have searched the galaxies for those brave enough to fight in this unholy war, and these are-" Merlin said.

"Oh, hell no!" Aqua Shark cried out. He was jumping up and down and pointing frantically at one of the eight. "Did you see his eyes? He-he blinked but never closed his eyes!"

The eight new guys traded looks, and then I saw it. They had cat eyes, which ranged in every color, and every so often, a clear eyelid-like thing would slide over their eyes while their eyelids stayed open.

"Did you see that, Browny?" Doubles said.

"Yeah, that's not normal," I said.

Everyone was whispering to each other. "I studied biology in high school, and these guys are definitely not human," Whiteguy said.

"Nice to know, expert," Big Blue said. Whiteguy shot him a look

"Good afternoon, men. I am Lord Iceman, and this is Lord Inspector," Iceman said. His eyes were bone white, as was his short spiked hair, well-trimmed mustache, and short-cut goatee. Inspector, however, was clean-shaven with bright red wavy hair and emerald green cat eyes.

"With us are our two generals, Bazooka and Ice 8, and our four elite Sentinels, Greyguy, Space Police, Moonwalker, and Smartguy," Iceman said. More whispering filled our ranks.

"We are Icemen; homo sapiens type 1096 from planet 412A, the empire of Iceplanet, which is located in the Lystrene galaxy," Inspector said. "We are here to fight along your side until this planet, this universe, is rid of the evil that plagues it."

No one said a word for the longest time, and if I had to guess by the looks on their faces, I'd say they were just as shocked as I was. You'd think that with everything we've seen so far, we wouldn't be, but this was like finding out that magic exists all over again.

"You know Merlin, I really like you, but you can't keep doing this to us," Doubles said. "I mean, first, you brought into our ranks the Knights of the Round Table, and okay, we can survive that, but Star Trek?!"

Everyone burst into laughter. "I enjoy your sense of humor, Doubles, and I hope it never fades," Merlin said.

"My name is Browny," I said. "Welcome to our group." I shook Iceman's hand. It was cold to the touch and dwarfed mine.

"It is a pleasure to join forces. Now let's kill some badguys," he said.

I grinned ear to ear. It's about time someone shared my sentiment. "Yes, let's do that."

"Dudes, I kept telling everyone that aliens existed!" Kid cried out. "And now here they are, and damn they're huge!"

Running up to Ice 8, the largest of the Icemen, Kid began to inspect him by poking and pinching his skin. He even lifted up his arms and played with his fingers. It was kind of funny to watch.

"I never would have believed you, Smartguy, but you were right. Aliens do exist, and they're so tiny," Ice 8 said.

A few of the Icemen chuckled. "Let me get this straight. You guys are another species of human from another planet?!" Whiteguy said.

"That would be correct," Space Police said.

"What the hell is up with your eyes? They're so freaky," Aqua Shark said.

"They are highly specialized nictitating membranes," Greyguy said.

"Nict-what branes?!" Whiteguy said.

Aqua Shark was just staring at the Icemen. "Wow," he said.

"How advanced are you guys? Do you have spaceships?" Octane said.

"We are very advanced, and yes, we have spaceships," Space Police said.

"Is that how you got here?" Big Blue said. Iceman smiled.

"Alright, Kid, that's enough," I said. "Leave the big guy alone."

By now, he had turned his attention to Ice 8's legs. He had both arms wrapped around them, but just barely, and was trying with all his might to lift him, but couldn't.

"Dudes, this guy is frickin' heavy!" Kid said.

"I weigh only three hundred and sixty-seven kilos," Ice 8 said.

"How much?" Aqua said.

"Eight hundred and ten pounds or so," Big Red said.

"Holy shit!" Whiteguy said. "You guys won't be hearing me complain about Pudgy's weight anymore! We've got some heavy worlders here!"

For the remainder of the night, and as expected, everyone bombarded the Icemen with every question imaginable. But they kept a pretty tight lid on everything and only let us in on a few details of who they were. They are a genetically engineered species created by a civilization Merlin had started during the Lich War. Now I knew what he meant when he said thousands fled our world to live elsewhere.

The following day, our group decided to elect a leader, and surprisingly enough, they chose me. My Pride fighting career, the murder of my fiancé, and my killing of the invincible badguy were the talk of the group.

And while I respected the admiration of my new friends, I had to refuse. There were others far more qualified to lead than I was, so everyone re-voted and chose Iceman and Inspector, the supreme lords of two Ice Planets. And it didn't take them long to demonstrate their leadership.

By late afternoon, they had broken our group into three specialized squads, assigning everyone to a squad based on their occupation and abilities. There was a search and destroy squad, a tactical support squad, and a logistical support squad.

The SD squad was the largest, with sixteen men divided into four teams. Their job was simple: find the enemy and kill them. Naturally, because of my fighting skills, I was assigned as the leader of SDS One. Doubles was assigned to SDS four.

The TS squad was the second largest, with two teams of four. Their task was to gather intelligence on the enemy and their whereabouts so the SD squads could do their job. Police was assigned to TS squad one because of his job and how valuable an intelligence source it was.

Finally, with one team of six men, the LS Squad's responsibility was to procure and transport weapons, gear, and teams to where they needed to go. It was all pretty incredible, but frankly, it was still a shock.

"Alright, men, now that you have all been assigned to a squad, I'm going to explain how we will train and equip you," Iceman said. "Normally, the LS squad would be responsible for procuring equipment. Unfortunately, the squad is not yet active. So during the duration of your training, the Icemen and I, along with Merlin, are going to be working overtime to get this group the military hardware and equipment it needs."

"Um, where are you guys going to get all this gear from?" Police said.

"US armories and intelligence headquarters," Iceman said.

"So we're stealing it?" he said.

"Our primary method of obtaining the necessary gear, once the LS squad is up and running, will be through the use of forged physical and electronic currency," Inspector said. Police sighed and shook his head. "This means the LS squad will create several dummy corporations to funnel money and purchase any equipment necessary. They will also have a large shop in Phoenix for special R&D projects such as creating false identities and mil-spec equipment."

"Can my new identity be Blackbeard?" Kid said.

Some of the guys laughed. "This sounds like a pretty sophisticated criminal operation," Octane said. "Is this really necessary?"

"Currently, our intelligence on the badguy's organization is limited and unreliable," Iceman said. "But we know that to win any war, you must have the latest in firepower and cutting-edge technology, as well as information. These dummy corps and false identities will give us just that."

"Where are we getting this information, and how will we get it?" Octane said.

"Aside from the old school methods of prisoner interrogation and electronic surveillance, certain TS squad members will be hacking various government and civilian databases across the world," Inspector said.

"That's what I'm talking about." Kid said.

"How are we going to do this from prison?" Chief said.

A few of us laughed. "I can assure you that the hacking skills of Big Red, Space Police, and Bazooka are more than sufficient to hack any database on this planet and get away with it cleanly," Iceman said. "This group's security and secrecy is of the utmost priority. We cannot and will not be seen by this world as criminals. Still, at the same time, you must remember that we must do absolutely everything necessary to prevent this evil from laying waste to your world, our world."

People started whispering. "When will all this be up and running?" Big Red said.

"Our gear will be procured as soon as possible; however, everything else will be established within a few months after your training," Iceman said.

"What do you mean 'your' training?" Aqua Shark said.

"Beginning tomorrow, the Icemen and I will put all of you through a rigorous sixteen hours-a-day, one-hundred-and-twenty-day combat training program," Iceman said. "This program will consist of hand-to-hand combat training, POW training, wilderness and apocalyptic survival techniques, surveillance and counterintelligence methods, and basic and advanced combat tactics."

"These guys know their shit, don't they?" Doubles said.

"Yeah, it sure sounds like it," I said.

"What about Pudgy's lard ass? He can't even do a single push-up!" Whiteguy said. "How's he going to survive a four-month-long alien boot camp?!"

Laughter erupted from our ranks. "He'll do just fine. Even if he has to use his spells to push himself through the physical stuff," Inspector said.

"So wait, his fat ass gets to cheat?!" Kid said. Iceman shot Kid a look. "Whatever. Your call."

"I have enough training. Why don't I help you guys instruct?" Aqua Shark said.

"You can still benefit from our training," Iceman said. "Now get a good night's sleep, men, because it's going to be the last one you get."

"Can I just use my magic to sleep through your training?" Aqua Shark said. Some guys laughed.

"It seems like these guys have it all figured out, uh?" Fire said.

"Yeah," I said.

"I think it's good. At least I don't have to do much of the thinking," Striper said.

"Argh, shut yar mouth ya belly bloat!" Hook said. "Nobody be a listening' to ya anyway."

Striper took a few steps back, looking puzzled.

I snickered. "Well, I'm not too convinced their training is any better than mine," Aqua Shark said. "You can bet I'm going to question everything, even how they run this group."

"We're a civilization that has only mastered warp travel, so I wouldn't trust their instruction either." Bazooka said.

Aqua Shark glared at him. "Bug off, ogre."

"What do you know about these badguys, Browny?" Bazooka said, "You seem more familiar with them than anyone else."

"Nothing much, but what I can tell you is that the grenade guy that I fought was more powerful than any of us," I said.

"But you killed him, right?" Striper said.

I let out a short laugh and shook my head with amusement. Striper's full-bodied brown hair, mustache, gray khakis, and striped turtleneck were just too much to look at. "Yeah, but only after his protection spell failed. Not even bullets could penetrate it, at least not what we were firing."

"It's a good thing that there was only one of them, eh," Aqua Shark said.

"Were they trained?" Bazooka said.

"The grenade guy, yeah, but the others, not really," I said. "He definitely knew how to use an assault rifle and a knife, and he was certainly a skilled martial artist."

"It sounds like these badguys have been busy," Bazooka said. "I like a good fight."

The sun was beginning to rise when the Icemen woke us up the next day. They wasted no time and quickly broke us into seven teams of three. Each team was assigned an Iceman who would be our instructor for the duration of our training. Their reasoning for small teams was that more one-on-one instructor time translates into more information learned. I agreed.

After a quick crash course on general safety, our training began. It was then go, study, and go some more for sixteen hours a day, every day, just like Iceman had said.

One week, we'd be in the Amazon learning how to survive, what's edible, how to make herbal medicines, and how to cover your tracks. The next, we'd be in a mock city learning the basics of urban warfare, how to spot an ambush, plan assaults and breach buildings, and even set mines.

We learned everything from how to fire pistols to rocket launchers to stalking and sniping to evasive vehicle maneuvering tactics. It was very technical training, more mentally draining than physically exhausting, though some, like Pudgy and Big Blue, saw it otherwise.

I don't know how the Icemen knew so much about our world's weaponry and military tactics, or even our planet, for that matter. But they did, and well enough to shut up Aqua Shark. And if one thing was clear, these Icemen knew war inside and out. It was like they lived for it, breathed it.

We had only been training for a month when it came time for me to defend my title. So on the fifteenth of April 1997 I flew to Tokyo to prepare myself for the fight ahead. I was really excited to fight in front of my new friends and show them what I could do, even though they'd only be watching on pay-per-view. But nothing could compare to the feeling I got from being in Japan again. I felt alive, like my life was normal, back when Mary Jane was still by my side.

The following night at seven O'clock, I entered the ring to my theme song of Metalica's 'Wherever I May Roam' and the chanting of my name. And once the fight had begun, I again proved to the world why I was the best. I knocked my opponent out in just over a minute in the first round. I was now the defending Pride middleweight champion of the world. I felt empty.

Afterward, I hung around Tokyo for the next couple of days, touching base with my fans. I signed hundreds of autographs, gave a few interviews, and even did a commercial for one of my sponsors.

I then traveled to the island where I had spent many years of my life training. However, Master Yusokagi wasn't there. His house was vacant, and it appeared to have been vacant for quite some time. Run down. It was depressing to reminisce about all the lessons that I had been taught there, but wherever he was, I'm sure that he watched me fight.

Three long and rigorous months later, our training with the Icemen had ended.

"Congratulations, men, you have all successfully completed basic combat training," Iceman said. "And as promised and on time, your own personal weapons and tactical gear."

To Iceman's left lay dozens of crates and stacked boxes. Both Space Police and Greyguy were opening them while the other Icemen passed the gear out.

I was quite amazed at how easy it was for them to steal the equipment. First, they hacked the base's armory inventory at headquarters and made all the necessary number and date changes. They even hacked the DOD to cover the stolen 'special hardware.' Merlin would then teleport them inside the armory, cameras looped or fried if necessary, and back out again with the goods. Or sometimes Merlin would just teleport the equipment out by himself. It was that easy, and nothing has ever been reported missing or stolen, at least not yet.

"This kind of makes you feel like a true professional, doesn't it?" Whiteguy said, slapping a mag into his .45 automatic.

"It sure does," I said.

"I was born a professional just like I was born dead sexy," Doubles said. He was still wearing the same old black tuxedo and red tie.

Whiteguy laughed. "You're too much, man. Too much, but I like ya," he said.

"Finally, me get good boomstick," Buccaneer said.

"Too bad our training didn't include English lessons," Doubles said.

Buccaneer shot Doubles a look.

"Alright, men, I need your attention, please." Iceman raised his hands in the air. "Merlin has something to say," he said.

Merlin flew several meters above us. A moment had passed before everyone quieted down.

"My good friends, it is wonderful to see you so well-trained and eager to fight. But I must warn, have no illusions amongst yourselves, for this war will not be easily fought, nor will it end quickly. We are vastly outnumbered, and our enemy powerful. There are things you have not yet seen and powers you could never have imagined. There are things of such horror that they are best left undisturbed. Things you will pray never to see." Merlin looked around at us and sighed. "Do not waiver in your dedication to defending this world and fight the good fight until the very end. You are all selfless, brave, and honorable men, and from this moment forward you will all be called the Goodguys."

Hooting and cheering erupted from our group and lasted a good minute before dying down.

"Now prepare yourselves, for tomorrow we wage war against Goresavice and his army of men," he said.

More whistling and applause filled the air, but I remained quiet and emotionless. These past few months had been so hectic. It was like I was slowly going mad. Magic, monsters, knights, and aliens, and the murder of my love.

I wanted everything to be normal again like the time we soaked the soccer girls or the night we camped by the Lake. I wanted to wake up from this horrible nightmare, but the truth of the matter was that this was reality. Everything in my life before this was just a beautiful dream.

CHAPTER
SEVENTEEN

"Can I have a coke, please?" I said, taking a seat on a stool with my back against the bar counter.

"Sure thing," the bartender said.

Walking up and sitting next to me, wearing a tight white halter top and a short red skirt, was a beautiful blonde-haired woman. "What's a handsome man like yourself doing in a bar all alone?" she said.

"Waiting for a phone call," I said.

"Who's calling lovely, if you don't mind me prying?"

Glancing around the bar, I noticed a Hispanic man watching us intently. "Just a friend."

She put her hand on my leg. "Would you like to have a little fun while you wait?"

Smiling, I gently removed her hand. "Sorry. I'm engaged."

"Oh." She then walked out of the bar. The man who was watching us left with her.

A few minutes later, my cell phone rang. "This is Browny. What's up?"

"Howdy, partner!" Pirate said. "Ya, sure are takin' ya time gettin' to this here sock hop. Now get on over here."

I laughed. I never quite understood how Pirate could speak so well, even like a cowboy, and how the others couldn't or wouldn't.

Either way, I thought he was hilarious. "I'm coming, man. I'm coming."

Hanging up, I motioned to Fire that it was time to go, but before we could make it to our SUV, a group of four guys cut us off in the parking lot. The woman who approached me in the bar and the man who had left with her was with them.

"What's up, hombre?" one of them said. "You don't like women? You gay?"

Fire glanced at me. He looked tense. "No, sir," I said. "I'm engaged."

The man got up in my face. "What you doing touching my girl, then?" he said.

The streets were busy with cars, and people were walking in and out of stores. The sun was setting over the horizon, and a gentle breeze blew while hot mana coursed through my veins. I'll never look at this world the same again.

"I'm sorry. I must have misinterpreted the whole situation," I said. "Now, if you please excuse us, we have business to attend to."

I tried to walk around him, but he put his hand on my chest and stepped back in front of me. "I don't think you understand me, hombre. You touch, you pay."

Moonwalker got out of the SUV. "Is there a problem, gentleman?" he said.

The gangsters glanced behind themselves and moved out of our way. I heard a few of them utter something in Spanish. "You best hope he's around the next time we meet."

"You're engaged already?" Fire said.

"Yeah, you know, Mary," I said.

"What art that about?" Guard said.

"A hooker, I guess," I said.

"You handled that well. Now is it time to rock' roll?" Moonwalker said.

"It certainly is. Now, let's gear up," I said.

Thirty minutes later, we pulled into a large but empty parking lot two blocks from our target warehouse. We were in an industrial zone on the outskirts of Phoenix, where the streets were quiet and dimly lit. Warehouses and other large buildings surrounded us.

It was a little past nine, and the moon shone brightly in the cloudless sky. This was our first operation since completing our training one week ago, and our objective was simple: kill or capture all badguys.

"Moonwalker," I said.

"Sir," he said.

"I'm relinquishing tactical command to you." I wouldn't say that I was nervous, just uncomfortable about leading the squad.

"Yes, sir," Moonwalker said.

"You're relinquishing command? Why?" Fire said. "Aren't you a ninja?"

I rolled my eyes. Fricking Doubles. "That's the problem," I said.

"Thou art able to recognize thee's and thou's strengths and weaknesses, which art a great trait," Guard said.

Fire reached for Guard's face. "You've got some brown stuff on your nose. Let me get it for you."

Slapping his hand away, Guard opened the SUV door and stepped out. We were all geared up and ready to roll: black Kevlar vests and helmets, ski masks, earpiece transceivers, and a variety of weapons.

"Weapons hot," Moonwalker said.

"Weapons hot," we all repeated.

For several tense minutes, we crept in between and around nearby buildings until we reached the back of our target warehouse. It stood adjacent to another concrete building across from a small dirt clearing.

With a few hand gestures, Moonwalker ordered Fire and Guard to post up by the corner of the building to our left and cover us. Once they were in position, Moonwalker and I hurried across the clearing towards the back door of the wooden warehouse.

"My old friend, how good it is to see you again," a familiar voice said.

It was Goresavice. He just appeared out of nowhere, standing on the roof of the building next to our target warehouse.

Without hesitation, Moonwalker raised his M-60 and put a dozen rounds into his head.

Reeling back with his arms covering his face, Goresavice groaned loudly. Blood trickled from small puncture wounds where the rounds had impacted, but he was still alive.

"It's an ambush!" Pirate yelled over my transceiver.

The backdoor of the warehouse swung open, and countless men in green fatigues came rushing out with knives, staffs, and axes. "Four teams of four are closing in all around your position!"

"Take them out," Moonwalker said into his transceiver. He then sprayed a short burst into the onrushing crowd, which killed and maimed several. Dropping his gun, Moonwalker drew his bowie knife and charged the badguys. There were too many, and they were too close to gun down.

Gunfire erupted from behind us and tore into the badguys, which dropped several more.

Instinctively, I cast lightning reflexes, giant's toughness, ogre's strength, and a new one that I had just learned, stone skin. It was another green spell that made my skin as tough as steel, well, kinda. I now knew four symbols, and a fifth has been slowly forming in my mind for weeks.

Slinging my shotgun over my shoulder, I drew my katana and slashed at the throat of a charging badguy. He fell to the ground never to get back up. Dancing to my right to avoid a slashing knife, I deflected another's staff and lay open his belly with one clean stroke.

Were these guys suicidal?! Not one of them was as blazing fast as we were, and they certainly weren't as skilled, but there sure were a lot of them.

More automatic and heavy gunfire filled the air. Fire and Guard were being pinned down by a group of badguys taking cover behind some crates beside a building forty meters ahead. That must be one of the teams that Pirate was speaking about. I now saw the genius behind their foolhardy charge. Engage as many of us in melee combat and gun us down while we're too busy fighting hand-to-hand. They didn't care about friendly fire.

Unfortunately for them, Bazooka of TSS two, Pirate's crew, anticipated an ambush like this and set up the TSS for a counter-ambush. All four were in separate locations a few hundred meters away, killing badguys with well-placed shots.

Dropping his gun, Guard drew his broadsword and, just in time, deflected a badguys bo staff. Pushing him back, Guard thrust the point of the sword into the man's stomach, but it somehow glanced off. The badguy was lightning quick and sustaining protection.

Twirling around, the initiate slammed his metal staff into Guard's head, which knocked him to the dirt.

Scrambling to his feet, his helmet cracked, and on the ground, Guard again deflected the initiate's attack, but in doing so, he was stabbed in the back by another badguy. Stumbling forward and grimacing in pain, Guard took hold of his sword with both hands and cleaved the badguy who had stabbed him in the back in half with a mighty backhand stroke.

With a quick twirl of his staff, the initiate swung for Guard's head, but Moonwalker entangled his arms with the initiate and slammed him face-first into the hard ground. It was a strange takedown that I had never seen before. Taking his back, Moonwalker snapped his neck.

"All outer perimeter threats eliminated," Pirate said over the transceiver.

That was quick. I guess speed does kill. Several more gunshots filled the air, and collapsing to the ground was Guard. Stepping over him, Goresavice unloaded the rest of his magazine into his chest and smiled at me.

Throughout the swirling chaos, I had lost sight of him. There were too many badguys, and they all looked the same.

Like a tiger rushing in for the kill, I raised my katana above my head and charged. Holstering his pistol, Goresavice raised a hand towards me. A shimmering, nearly invisible bolt of energy flew and struck me in the chest. Excruciating pain, like a searing fire, radiated throughout my body.

Temporarily paralyzed, I fell to the ground. I tried to stand, but my legs wouldn't cooperate, and I fell back down. Blood was gushing from my nose and trickling from my ears.

Four badguys rushed to attack me, and with my katana just out of reach, I pulled out my 9 mm and shot them all dead. With the barrel still smoking, I holstered my Beretta and clambered to my feet while coughing up blood.

Despite my deafened hearing, I could still hear the cries of dying men and rifles firing from a distance. Pirates' TS squad was dropping badguys like flies, and by now, only a few remained standing.

With a swagger in his step, Goresavice attacked me with a few lazy jabs, which I partially slapped away and followed with a hard looping right hook.

I should have taken him down, but his loose right was too tempting. Fighting through the intense pain, I grabbed his arm, twisted my hips, and violently slammed him to the ground. Stepping on his shoulder, I wrenched his arm until it popped at the shoulder.

I then tried to jump onto his back, but he ripped his arm free and rolled onto his back, wrapping me in his guard.

Without hesitation, I fell backward with his right leg between mine in a knee bar, but I was too messed up to lock it in tightly.

Sitting up, Goresavice broke my grip on his leg and stabbed his K-bar into my left leg. Thanks to my stone skin, it penetrated less than an inch, but it still hurt like hell. Pulling it out, he tried to stab me in the stomach, but I deflected it. I now had him wrapped up in my guard.

With a frenzied fervor, he stabbed at me repeatedly but failed to find his mark. Pulling his head down, I threw my left leg over his neck and locked my foot under my right knee. Rolling him onto his back, I pinned down his knife hand, and with my free hand, I began to gouge out his left eye. That's when his whole body burst into flames.

The searing fire was too much for me to bear, despite my spells, so I reluctantly let go of my triangle choke and jumped to my feet. The power that Goresavice was displaying was incredible, yet frustrating. I had him dead in my triangle. I had him dead several times.

Gasping for air, blood running down his face, Goresavice stood up. His broken arm had already healed. Ducking under Moonwalker's swinging staff, Goresavice blasted him with the same shimmering bolt he struck me with. Stumbling back, Moonwalker doubled over, blood seeping from his pores.

Slashing at me with his k-bar, I stepped into him, grabbed his arm, and threw him to the ground. I wanted to finish my technique, but my fire-retardant armor and clothes were starting to melt. I was suffocating from the intense heat, and my skin was starting to burn, even at this distance.

My stone skin failed. I only had perhaps another twenty seconds until all my spells failed. Luckily for me, Goresavice was the only badguy standing.

Intense pain raced up my left leg. I never saw him kick me because the fire and smoke concealed him. I collapsed to the ground. My leg was shattered. He must have struck me with hammer hands. His fire aura ceased.

Clambering on top of me, Goresavice pressed his left forearm onto my throat and pinned down my right arm with his. "You should have seen the look on Jessica's face as she begged for her pathetic life," he whispered. "And I can't begin to explain how wonderful it felt to watch the life drain from her pretty green eyes." I groaned and tried with all my might to get him off. "You will watch them all die. You will know suffering."

Jumping to his feet, he vanished.

Pirate ran up and kneeled beside me. "You alright, Browny?"

I coughed up some blood, which ran down my chin. "Yeah, I'm good," I said. "I'm just in a lot of pain, that's all."

"By the looks of it, I can tell," he said. "Don't worry. Help is on the way." Pain wracked my body as I tried to sit up, but I fought through it. I had to kill Goresavice. "You just lie here. Merlin's on his way."

He laid me back down. "H-How's Guard doing?" I muttered.

"Alright, his vest stopped most of the rounds; his spells the rest."

"F-Fire and Moon-Moonwalker?" My vision was slowly beginning to fade.

"They're good, man; now, just relax."

Merlin appeared out of thin air, and without so much as saying a word or raising a hand, he healed everyone and caused the dead badguys bodies to rapidly decompose until nothing was left. Even their clothing and gear had rotted away to dust. It was a rather impressive spell but almost too much to watch.

Fully invigorated, I jumped to my feet, picked up my shotgun, and sheathed my katana. "Thanks for healing me, but where's Goresavice?" I said. "He couldn't have got that far."

"He has. Now, let us go before the authorities arrive," Merlin said.

I looked at my watch. Only thirty seconds had passed since the bullets first started flying until now. Thirty seconds. And in that time, we had killed twenty-four badguys and captured three. It was an overwhelming victory, but I had no cause to celebrate. Goresavice had beaten me again and gotten away.

CHAPTER EIGHTEEN

Doubles gave me a brief hug. "Browny, my man. How are you doing?"

"I'm doing great. You?" I said.

"It seems like yesterday since we completed our training, and now here we are again," he said. "I heard about your first op. Goresavice ambushed you guys, eh?"

"Yeah, but we kicked ass," I said. "Only a few of us got injured."

"This magic is a whole other game, man. It flips all convention upside down."

"Yeah, tell me about it," I said. "Goresavice has three years on us and can cast fire aura and mana bolt."

"Yeah," Doubles said. "He's gotten very powerful."

There was a long pause. "So, what have you guys been up to?" I said.

"We shot up an eighteen-wheeler."

"Really?!"

"We only killed two, though. It was just an arms shipment," he said. "So, how's your mom been doing?"

I laughed to myself. Here we were, talking about killing people like it was just another day at work. "Doing well and enjoying her early retirement."

"Yeah, I bet," he said. "Aren't you like a millionaire now?"

"Close."

It was just past noon, and the temperature was nearing forty degrees Celsius, and like always, we were waiting in the desert for Merlin to show up to get things rolling. "Um, can I have everyone's attention please?" Striper said. "I have a few things that need to be addressed." Everyone quieted down.

"Spit it out, Stripper!" Aqua shark yelled. "We don't have all day, ya know."

Striper frantically began to set up his laptop, fumbling with cords until he accidentally knocked it onto the ground. Everyone laughed at him. Poor guy.

"It's okay, you can calm down," Aqua Shark said. "We've got all day, man. You just take your time."

"You'd think four months of live fire drills would have sharpened his wit, but I think it made him worse," Police whispered.

"Uh, I have some legal issues to discuss with the TSS members. Um, if you aren't active Police, then at some point in the near future, you'll be given another identity with the legal authority of a private investigator."

"Another ID, Stripper?" Pirate said. "We already have two."

Striper wiped the palms of his hands on his striped turtleneck. "I'm sorry, but it's necessary. The powers of being such are many, including the right to request certain sensitive information from the Police, which should expand your ability to gather intel on the badguys activities," he said, adjusting his glasses. "Once your IDs are ready and if you have any questions, please feel free to ask Space Police or Big Red. Thank you."

"Why not you?" Kid said.

"Or-or me." Striper hurried to sit down.

It wasn't long after Striper's informative speech that Merlin came walking out of his tent and stood by Iceman and Inspector.

"Welcome, Goodguys, to our first monthly meeting since operations began," Inspector said. "Today is Tuesday, August 1, 1997, and without further delay, here's Smartguy for a quick tech update."

"Good afternoon," Smartguy stood next to Inspector. "As some of you already know, the LS squad and I are re-engineering your firearms from the frame up. These new weapons will be exact replicas of what you possess now, except they can fire both caseless ammunition and standard ammunition for their type. These firearms will also be outfitted with the latest and greatest imaging and targeting systems available to your world," Smartguy said. "I am estimating, according to our current production rate, that the last of your firearms will be completed on the twenty-fourth of this month, and once they are in your hands, take extreme care not to lose them. They are not easy to replicate."

"On a tactical note, from this point forward, all squads, when on an SD-type op, must use caseless ammo," Iceman said. "We must leave absolutely no evidence of our presence anywhere."

"But doesn't Merlin wipe the scenes for us?" Big Blue said. He was stretching the suspenders of his blue coveralls.

"Yes, but we must do our part to minimize exposure," Space Police said.

"Also, your new body armor will be completed and issued by next month's end," Smartguy said.

Pirate raised his hand. He was sprawled out on a lawn chair with his red bandanna covering his eyes. "Some of us haven't received ceramic plate inserts for our current armor yet. When are we getting those?" he said.

"Last month," Smart guy said.

Pirate sat up. "What?!"

"Did you read the memo postdated on July 10? Your LS squad representative, Greyguy, sent it to you."

Pirate began typing away on his laptop. A moment later, he gave the thumbs up. "Got it."

"Continuing, at the end of this meeting and everyone hereafter, I will be giving all of you a thorough medical exam," Smartguy said. Groans and mumbles swept through our ranks. "From this day forward, I will be monitoring your health, so stay active and eat your fruits and vegetables."

"Whoa, you're going to give us physicals?" Big Blue said, holding his beer gut.

"Yes, and monitoring your diets," Smartguy said.

"Boo!" the crowd yelled.

"Argh, ya be gettin' a physical with me. I be gettin' a physical with yar face!" Hook said.

"I don't think I'm very comfortable with that," Pudgy said.

"The physical or the vegetables?" Aqua Shark said.

"Both!" Kid shouted over the laughing crowd.

"Thank you, Smartguy," Inspector said. "To date, we have killed sixty-five badguys, seized two shipments of illegal firearms, and shut down two training facilities. Through the diligent work of the TS squads, we have also confirmed that the badguys are operating internationally. Their organization is far more expansive than we had thought."

"How is this affecting the TS squads?" Big Red said.

"Their presence in the field, greatly; after all, we have only two TS squads, and they can't be everywhere at once. That is why we prioritize our intelligence and the targets we strike," Inspector said.

"Speaking of that, how will our strikes affect Calignosity's ability to attack this world?" Aqua Shark said.

"Presumably, they should greatly impact his ability to wage war," Iceman said. "But bear in mind that we lack sufficient intelligence to know much of anything on that matter for now."

"It makes sense, though; if we defeat Goresavice's army, it would be rather pointless for Calignosity to attack, right?" Whiteguy said. "All the armies of the world plus us, we'd crush him."

"Not pointless, futile," Octane said, smiling.

"Again, we can only speculate as to what impact the loss of Goresavice's army will have on him," Iceman said. "However, I can say that the defeat of Goresavice and his army is vital to our success."

"Smartguy will be compiling bi-monthly and yearly progress reports to help address these questions, amongst others," Inspector said. "You can get them from your squad leaders, and I strongly suggest you all read them."

"Out of curiosity, if the TS squads are stretched as it is, why not recruit more Goodguys?" Chief said.

"That would be a question for Merlin," Inspector said.

Everyone turned their attention to Merlin. "The number of our ranks is sufficient."

Chief looked puzzled. "Okay."

"What about the Dark Zone? What's our plan for that?" I said.

"That's funny that you ask about that. Merlin will be speaking on that issue later tonight," Iceman said. "But in other news, Merlin has suggested that we start a Goodguys charity organization, and we agree. So with help from Striper and Big Red, we'll be doing just that."

"A charity organization?" Whiteguy said, raising an eyebrow.

"Yes, and this will be a legitimate non-profit company whose goals will be to alleviate the pains and misfortunes of the less fortunate," Inspector said. "After all, we are the Goodguys. It's not just our job to protect them, but also help them."

"That's a great idea," Chief said.

"This would be the first good thing we've done," Police said.

A few laughs rose up from our ranks.

"Argh, why it be not-profit?" Hook said. "We be a needin' as much booty as we be a gettin' our grimy hands upon."

"I found our treasurer," Double said, slinging his arm around Hook's shoulders.

A few Goodguys laughed. "To minimize the chances of exposing our criminal activities, only certain Goodguys will be elected as board members to be known by the public," Iceman said, "They'll be the face of the company, which is a huge responsibility."

"Who art in thou's mind?" Basil said.

Doubles snickered. "Not you," he mumbled.

Basil stared Doubles down while grinding his fist into his open palm.

"Right now, we are looking at Browny, Police, Chief, and a few others," Iceman said.

"They're already well-known and respected in the community, which will give our charity the credence it needs."

"Art thou considereth thee?" Basil said.

"No, mon, ya too ugly," Islander said.

"Art thou?!" Basil said.

Iceman laughed pretentiously. "I'm sorry, but-"

"Argh!" Basil cried out. Picking up a large rock, he slammed his head into it, shattering it into dust.

"Someone needs some anger management therapy!" Doubles said. Some Goodguys backed away from Basil and started to laugh.

"Alright, men, Merlin has the floor," Inspector said, trying hard to contain a grin.

Merlin floated several meters above us. "My good friends, you have all tasted combat in the fight against Goresavice and his army of men. Now it is time for you to taste another kind of combat against creatures." Merlin pulled his hood over his head and pointed towards the Dark Zone with his wand. "The black abyss and the monsters that reside there, I have not taken my eyes off. Now it is time for you to see the evil that is Calignosity's army, the evil that will haunt your dreams for the rest of your life. Now, once again, prepare yourselves. For tonight, you will all be baptized in the flames of hell."

"Oh, how encouraging," Big Red said.

"Ahh, it be 'bout time," Buccaneer said.

"We're going down there? Striper said, pulling down the collar of his turtleneck.

"Do all of us need to go?" Pudgy said.

"You heard Merlin ladies, now listen up," Iceman said. "You will all maintain your original squad designations; however, the primary responsibility of the SD squads will be to engage all targets in melee combat unless otherwise directed."

Laughter slowly started to rise from our ranks. Kid was pretending to fight an imaginary beast with a flimsy shrub branch.

Iceman scowled. "This means you better have a close-quarters weapon other than a stick to fight with Kid."

More laughter broke out. "Some of us don't have swords and maces just lying around, not to mention most of us don't know how to use weapons like that," Whiteguy said. "So what are we to do?"

"Yeah, I can probably use a mace pretty well because it's like a baton, but why don't we just use guns?" Police said.

"Thou shall see," Batlord said.

"I don't want to," Pudgy said.

"Actually, most of us do know how to use martial weapons, Whiteguy. There are just a few city slickers like you who forgot their training already," Iceman said.

"I didn't forget. I'm just not using a knife," Whiteguy mumbled.

"TS members, your primary responsibility will be to supply covering fire for the SD squads. LS members, you are to engage with either melee or fire support for all squads as ordered," Iceman said. "And remember, all orders to move come from Inspector and me or Browny and Merlin. You have twenty minutes to gear up. Any questions?"

Why was I in charge? I don't want to be responsible for leading people to their deaths. I had enough of that on my shoulders already.

Kid was waving his arm around frantically. "I have one! I have one!" he cried out.

Iceman sighed, flickering both sets of eyelids. "Yes, what is it?"

"I just want to say that no matter what happens down there, I love you guys!" Kid said with a whiny voice like he was going to cry.

Again, the crowd laughed. It was one of the many things he was good at. No matter how serious the situation was.

Twenty minutes later, we were all geared up and standing near the edge of the Dark Zone. My heart was pounding.

"I can't believe he's having us climb down," Pudgy said, his brow sweating. "Why can't he just teleport us down?" Peeling off the wrapper of a chocolate bar, he shoved the whole thing into his mouth and chased it with a swig from a two-liter Pepsi. He then wiped his chocolate-covered fingers on his grease-stained coveralls.

"Unbelievable, Pudgy," Smartguy said, taking the pop from his hands. "This is poison, and you wonder why you have an unhealthy body weight amidst other health issues."

"What?! I Can't enjoy my last meal before I die?" Pudgy said.

"You are not going to die, and even if you do, Merlin will resurrect you," Smartguy said.

"That's great; I get to feel the pain of death at least twice in my life," Pudgy said.

"And the fate of the world rests on his shoulders," Pirate whispered to me.

Our descent into the Dark Zone was difficult, to say the least. The walls were vertical, but the further we descended, the more inverted our climb became. Six hours and three thousand meters later, we finally reached the bottom. I was exhausted, and by the looks of it, so was everyone else, well, except for the eight Icemen, even though they were the ones who led the way, anchoring the ropes and retrieving them behind us. They were incredible climbers for their size. Incredible at everything, really.

I took the last swig of water from my canteen and put it back into my backpack.

"What the hell are we walking on?" Police said, fighting to maintain his balance. "Can I get some more light over here or what?"

"Silence, friend, thou'll attract them," Basil whispered.

Chief turned his lantern on and held a small whitish object to the light. "I don't know, guys. I think this is some sort of bone," he said.

Raising his wand, Merlin illuminated the large bottle-shaped cavern with soft white light. We were standing on bones. Piles and piles of bones. Some monstrous and huge, others human. A cold chill raced up my spine.

Three man-sized tunnels were branching from the cavern leading to who knows where, but most impressively was a hallway lined with enormous granite blocks some thirteen meters tall and seven meters wide.

"Holy shit! What the hell is this place, Merlin?" Police said.

"You know as much as I know," Merlin said.

"Man, I can't believe this is what has been down here all this time," Doubles said, his eyes wide.

"And how is it that no one's ever found this place?" Police said.

Octane held up a miner's helmet. It was still attached to a person's head. "Here's your answer," he said.

"Can you imagine if we would have found this place as kids?" Doubles said.

I picked up a human femur bone. I was struggling to reconcile my old life with what was now my reality. Our reality.

"Guard behind you!" Space Police shouted.

With unnatural reflexes, Guard spun around with his broad sword slashing through the air. Whatever it was, I didn't see it until its orange guts covered the bleach-white bones littering the floor.

"We'd probably be dead!" Police said. He was shaking, M-16 in hand.

"Yeah," Doubles said, frantically turning around. His eyes were wide, and he was breathing heavily. I didn't realize it at first, but I was shaking ever so slightly.

"What is it?" I said, kneeling next to the creature's body. It was still twitching.

"It art a Shadow Stalker, and where therith be one, there art a thousand," Guard said.

The creature's body was a thin and articulated exoskeleton nearly three meters long with a sharp, bony tail that was just as long and ended in a needle-sharp point. It had two clawed hind legs and two unusually long arms with three-fingered claws, and its head was narrow and streamlined with two black eyes and a gaping mouth filled with serrated teeth.

"It's aptly named," Ice 8 said. The creature's skin color and texture flawlessly mimicked the bones that it was lying on. Islander was breathing heavily and making his way behind Space Police.

"Sharpen your senses, boys. These walls are alive," Iceman said. "SDS one, take up a position by the hallway. Two, three, and four, watch those tunnels. All others look up."

Drawing my kusarigama, I posted along the wall by the hallway entrance. My team quickly followed.

"I think I'm going to be sick, you guys," Pudgy said. He was resting against the rocky wall with his head hung low in his arms.

"What's wrong with Pudgy?" Big Blue said.

"It is likely he has too much epinephrine in his system," Smartguy said.

Pudgy began to blow chunks. "Ahh." a few Goodguys said, backing away from him.

Islander offered Pudgy a napkin.

"That's what your fat ass gets," Whiteguy said.

Pudgy moaned and then farted loudly, which sounded like a chainsaw echoing throughout the cavern. "I feel better now," He said.

A rotten egg smell hit my senses. My eyes started to water.

More Goodguys mumbled. "Do you, because my nose is fucking bleeding from the fecal particles you just polluted the air with!" Bazooka said, covering his nose.

"Gosh damn you stink!" Aqua Shark said.

"Sorry, guys," Pudgy said, lowering his head.

"It's alright," Iceman said. "Move out SDS one."

With the go-ahead, I led my team through the thirty-meter-long hallway, looking for traps or hidden surprises until we reached the enormous wooden doors at the end. "There's light on the other side of these doors," I said into my transceiver.

"And movement," Moonwalker said.

I shrugged my shoulders at him. I couldn't hear anything, but if he could, then I'd take his word for it.

"Prepare to breach SDS one. Merlin will clear the obstacle," Iceman said.

With a flick of his hand, the large double doors slowly creaked open to reveal a spacious room the size of a football field. Twelve giant pillars spanned the room's length in two rows of six and supported a vaulted ceiling nearly forty meters high. There were five double doors. Two are on the left and right sidewalls, and one is at the far end. They were all closed. Dozens of illuminated crystalline chandeliers hung from the ceiling, and hundreds of lit torches lined the walls and pillars. The size and grandeur of this room was amazing.

I rushed inside with my team, but Fire remained frozen by the doors.

A gigantic ten-meter-tall humanoid skeleton stood next to a pillar on the far side of the room. Its bones were thick and heavily scarred from battle, and its fingers and teeth were filed down to sharp points. A massive, gem-encrusted golden crown rested atop its head.

Turning to face me, with saliva dripping from their thirty-centimeter-long canines, were three bull-sized dogs like beasts with red scales covering their muscular bodies.

Near the first double doors, to my left, were two humanoid monsters that stood nearly three meters tall with pale white flesh. They were muscular with large potbellies and bony faces that were sunken inwards. Both were armed with an enormous meat cleaver-like weapon.

I'm not going to lie, but I'm scared shitless. Part of me hoped Merlin was full of it, but again, and like always, he was right because here they were, as real as you and me, just waiting to kill. I cast all of my enhancement spells and ran towards the two white monsters.

"Do not fear these creatures!" Merlin yelled, flying past me.

Pointing his wand at the skeleton, a thick, continuous stream of molten rock, mud, and steam splashed across its chest. Stumbling, the skeleton fell to the ground in a thunderous crash. Its ribcage had melted away, and its spine had been crushed into a fine dust.

Merlin then washed the molten rock over the hounds but only managed to strike one, killing it instantly. The other two charged us, nimbly avoiding the pyroclastic blast, which tore up the ground with deafening power. Hot smoke and fiery embers filled the air.

The two white creatures were slow and clumsy, and once I was within range, I hurled the spiked ball of my kusarigama into the face of one of them. Blood splattered everywhere, and with a quick yank on the chain, I jerked the ball, along with bits of flesh and bone, out of its face.

Grunting, the white-fleshed beast swung at me with its cleaver, but I easily avoided it. With a quick twirl around my body, I launched the sickle end of my weapon into its neck. Ripping it out proved to be the killing blow.

Rushing past me, Bestguard lopped off the weapon-wielding arm of the other beast with his silver sword. One mighty swing later, and it was dead.

All that remained now were the two red beast dogs. They were incredibly fast and vicious animals, and one of them had already drawn blood on Batlord, but he, too, was a ferocious animal. With one powerful blow from his oversized black spiked mace, he crushed the dog's skull into pulp.

Side-stepping the other lunging hound beast, Basil cleaved open its exposed and unarmored underbelly with an upward swing from his two-handed great ax. Sliding across the floor, the dog tried to find its footing but kept slipping on its blood. A split second later, Basil put it down for good.

"Art that it?!" Basil cried out. His voice was booming. "Art that all of them?!"

"It art feel great to once again slay the beasts of hellith!" Bestguard cried out giving Guard a high-five.

"Calm down, big fellas. At least you got to kill one of them," Greyguy said, twirling his long knife.

"Area secure. Now let's move out, men." Iceman said. "SDS one, lead the way and secure the far-end doors."

Pudgy was leaning up against the wall again, throwing up.

"Hold on, Pudgy's sick again," Octane said.

"Tell him to let one rip and keep it pushing," Iceman said.

I don't think he was sick this time. I think he was scared like all the other city slickers. I could see the tense expressions on their faces.

The pirates and knights have been through this many times before. And the Icemen, well, they were born and bred for war, so it came as no surprise when they rushed into battle with fervor. Their fearlessness gave me courage.

"What the hell are you doing, Pirate?" Inspector said. Pirate was prying and pocketing the gems out of the skeleton king's crown.

"Hey, man, this is the spoils of war," he said. "You got a problem with that cowboy?"

Inspector sighed. "Yeah, you're ever-changing accent."

"See, I'm not the only one that thinks it's weird!" Doubles said.

Merlin opened the large double wooden doors at the far end, and we rushed inside.

The room was identical to the last, except there were only two doors, one on the left and one on the right. However, at the far end stood a giant throne made of marble. Other than that, the vast room was empty.

"Area secure," Iceman said. "SDS one, protect Merlin and look sharp. Two, cover the left door. Three, the right door. Four, watch our rear. All others fan out and keep your eyes peeled."

As I got closer to the throne, I could see that the armrests were laced with thousands of gems of every sort, and across the headrest were dozens of ethereal symbols written in gold.

"What spell is that?" I said.

"Not every combination of symbols is the formula for a spell," Merlin said. "This is the language of Ethereal, something you will learn in time."

"What does it say?" I said.

"Born of the Shadows," he said, raising his wand. "But never mind that now. It comes."

Slowly materializing and floating above the throne was a nearly formless shadow with piercing black eyes. A young girl was balancing on the throne armrests with her arms out wide. She had long, flowing blonde hair and sparkling blue eyes. She was barefoot and was wearing only a plain white nightgown.

My blood turned to ice. I had seen this shadow once before in the Dark Woods.

"Flee from here, my friends, and help the others!" Merlin said. Behind us, the door we had come through closed while the other two creaked open. "These two are beyond you."

"Lock and load men! We've got company!" Iceman shouted.

Automatic gunfire filled the air. My squad ran for the right-side hallway.

"Merlin," the shadow whispered in a raspy voice. Its formless black body seemed to flutter in the dim light.

"Ghost, the Eyes of the One Who is Nameless," Merlin said. The girl jumped off the armrest, landed gracefully on the floor, and walked towards me smiling.

"Do not let her get near to you, Browny! She is not who she appears to be!" Merlin shouted.

I dropped my kusarigama and drew my katana. He was right; she was probably a demon in child's skin, but there was something about her. It was like I had seen her before, but I couldn't put a name to her face. And her eyes, they were so...

My vision faded to black.

I was kneeling at the end of a small coffee table in the middle of a living room. There was a plush cushioned couch to my right and an entertainment center with TV, Nintendo, and movies to my left.

Sitting across from me was a girl about eight years old with long blonde hair and blue eyes. She was wearing a pink shirt, blue jeans, and white sneakers.

"Do you like it?" She said, holding up the picture she'd just drawn.

"It's beautiful, Chandler. I really like the colors," I said.

"Really?"

"Of course, and I was thinking-" I pulled out the picture she drew for me last week from my binder. "That you could draw me in this picture with you."

"I'd love to."

She took the picture and began coloring on it.

"Would you like a snack?"

"Yes, please."

A few moments later, I returned with a glass of milk and a chocolate cupcake. "Don't let it ruin your dinner, okay?"

"I like it when you watch me." She took a bite of the cupcake. "You spoil me, and I like that."

I smiled at her. "You deserve to be spoiled."

She licked the chocolate off her fingers and smiled back. "Do you have a girlfriend?"

"No, not yet."

"Why not? You're a super nice guy and cute," she said.

I chuckled. "Well, Chandler." She raised an eyebrow at me. "Alright, there is this one girl, but I'm too afraid to ask her out."

"Why?"

"Well, because I really like her, and I'm afraid asking her out will ruin our friendship."

"Who is it?"

"I don't know if I can trust you, sweetheart. I haven't even told my best friends."

"You can trust me. I promise I won't tell."

"Pinky promise?"

She interlocked her pinky with mine. "I promise."

"It's Jessica."

"Ooo, she's pretty."

"Yeah, she sure is."

It wasn't, but a few minutes later, her stepdad came home.

Chandler hugged me tight. "Please don't leave me. We can play in my backyard."

"I'm sorry, but I have to, sweetie," I said. "But I'll see you next week, and perhaps we can go to the park, okay?"

She squeezed me one last time. "Okay."

Again, my vision went black.

I saw Chandler walking through the woods. She was a little older now, like ten, and behind her was Goresavice. He was pushing her along with his K-bar and jerking her around by her hair. She was crying and begging him to let her go, but her cries of protest fell upon deaf ears.

For over a minute, I watched him shove her around until they were standing knee-deep in a shallow pond. I tried to look away and close my eyes but couldn't. The image of her thrashing around as he held her under the water will forever be seared in my mind.

The water turned red, and that's when my vision returned to normal.

"Browny!" someone yelled, shaking me.

"Huh?" I muttered

Blinking my eyes, I looked around. Dozens of creatures, some I had seen and many that I hadn't, were pouring through the hallways into the room. The TS squads were unloading a storm of bullets while the SD squads battled it out, sword and claw. The fighting was intense, but the bullets were tearing the monsters down.

Laughing, Chandler attacked Merlin with multiple streaks of electricity from her fingertips and several swirling green energy coils. The hair on my arms stood on end from the mana-charged air.

Absorbing the energies with his wand, Merlin blasted her with a continuous blazing column of Fire, but the bluish-green field that surrounded her held strong.

Meanwhile, the shadow was engulfing Merlin with a black aura, but the bluish-white haze emanating from Merlin's body seemed to be protecting him. The spectacle of power was amazing, to say the least.

"Browny, snap the fuck out of it!" Octane yelled. "We need you up here!"

Aqua and Hook were slashing at a muscular humanoid beast twice their size, but its thick, gray, callous skin was proving difficult to cut through. It attacked back with two four-fingered claws and a huge horn that protruded from the middle of its forehead. It was an ugly beast.

Running, I cast jump and flew nearly fifteen meters in the air, and with one swing of my katana, I cut deep into its throat. Landing smoothly on my feet, the creature fell to its knees and then its face. Blood was gushing from its neck.

Ice 8 was backing up from a dozen or so black and brown-skinned worms. They were nearly a meter long and crawled forward like inchworms. Several leaped up at him, but he cut them all in half in the blink of an eye with his serrated claymore, except for one which latched onto his shoulder with its sucker-like mouth.

Wiggling violently, the worm tore off a chunk of his flesh and fell to the ground. Automatic gunfire and rifle shots were a constant noise, and so were the screams of the Goodguys. The dozens of creatures that once filled the room were now beginning to thin out.

A gigantic twelve-meter-long worm slithered out of the right hallway on its soft underbelly. Hard and thick articulated scales covered its entire body, and row after row of razor-sharp teeth filled its gaping mouth. Its brownish-black body was slimy and reeked of rotting flesh, and with every lunge forward, baby worms wiggled their way out from in-between its scales and plopped to the ground.

"What the hell?!" Fire said, backing away. He was holding his left side tenderly and trembling slightly.

A pink-skinned, beach ball-sized creature with a mouth nearly the size of its body lept at Buccaneer. With a slash from his cutlass, he cleaved it in two. Buccaneer wasn't wearing his plate carrier or Kevlar. Instead, he was wearing his usual plate cuirass which was proving quite effective at protecting him from slashing claws.

"Aqua Shark, cover thee!" Buccaneer said.

"Come on, guys, we can't fight this!" Aqua Shark shouted. He was rushing towards the door we had come through with Pudgy and Chief. "We need to get out of here!"

"Merlin, healing!" Kid yelled. He was pressing down on Big Red's stomach with both hands, trying to keep his innards in.

Space Police was rolling on the ground, groaning and holding his right leg while Guard coughed up blood beside him.

Everywhere I looked, there were Goodguys scattered about. Some fought whatever monsters remained, while others ran for their lives or cowered in the corners.

"Hold your ground!" Iceman yelled. He then leaped through the air a good twenty meters and brought his great ax crashing down on the worm's scaly head. A small trickle of brown blood oozed from its cracked scale.

If that was all the damage that a superhuman enhanced with ogre's strength could do, then certainly, there was nothing any of the rest of us could do. We had to attack its soft underbelly.

Ear-ringing machinegun fire from Big Blue's M-240b riddled the worm's body but couldn't penetrate through its tough scales. Hot shell casings clinked across the stone floor.

Reeling upwards, the giant worm opened its gaping mouth to engulf Moonwalker, but just as it struck, he leaped out of the way. With its underside exposed, Ice 8 ran forward and slashed at the belly of the monster, but he failed to draw blood.

Taking a knee, Bazooka took aim with his AT-4 missile launcher. "Clear!" he yelled, checking his six.

A split second later, the rocket exploded upon impact with the worm's head. Chunks of flesh and bits of scale flew everywhere as a deafening boom echoed through the room. Brown blood gushed from the large wound in its head, but still, the worm refused to die.

"Son of a bitch!" Bazooka said as he reloaded.

Climbing onto the worm's back, Inspector stood up and plunged his great sword deep between its scales. Writhing around, the worm rose and attempted to shake him off, but he maintained his balance with amazing athleticism.

Casting jump, I quickly closed the distance and landed on the worm's back. I then plunged my katana a good half meter in between its scales and watched as brown blood squirted out.

I gagged while pulling my blade out. The sickening stench was almost too much to bear.

With a violent shudder, the worm's guts erupted from its mouth. It then fell motionless, dead.

Merlin was flying in the air, not too far from us. Chandler and Ghost were gone, and all the creatures were dead. It suddenly got very quiet, except for the moans and groans of injured Goodguys.

"We're going to need some healing over here!" Fire shouted.

Whiteguy was lying on the ground, bleeding from his chest. "S-Scratch that, M-Merlin," he muttered. "I-I'll just w-walk it off."

I jumped off the worm's back. "You alright, man?" I said. Moonwalker was bleeding from his arm.

He looked at it. "Just a flesh wound."

"Way to kick some ass, Browny!" Inspector said, patting me on the back.

"Yeah, you too."

Suddenly, we were back in the desert, and everyone injured was miraculously healed. It was jarring to be teleported so suddenly.

A calm silence filled the air. The moon shined brightly in the cloudless sky, and a gentle breeze cooled my skin.

I sheathed my katana and sat on the ground. I was so confused. We were just fighting monsters and a girl that I used to babysit. "Chandler, that was Chandler you were fighting."

"Ya knew that girl?" Islander said.

"I used to watch her when she was younger," I said.

Aqua Shark laughed. "That little hellion?! Fuck no! You couldn't pay me all the money in the world to watch her!"

"No way, mon," Islander said.

"But she was murdered," I said.

"That art not possible," Bestguard said.

"She was murdered two years ago," Police said. "She was found floating face down in a pond with her throat cut. I know because I was one of the first officers to arrive at the scene."

I glance at him. I wondered what else he knew.

"How art this be?" Bestguard said.

"Do you all remember when I told you I had found another way? A way that Calignosity had overlooked? All of you, including myself, are of this way," Merlin said. "But Chandler, a queen of the damned, is of Calignosity's way."

"And let me guess, his way makes you vastly more powerful?" Doubles said.

Merlin sighed. "Yes."

"Sweet, sign me the fuck up!" Doubles said.

"But she is no longer who she used to be," Merlin said. "Through her death, her soul was forever joined with another. A demons."

"Sweet, a demon child," Doubles said. "A fucking demon child!"

Aqua Shark shot Doubles a look. "And it is through this unholy joining of souls, it becoming her in her own sacrificial body that overnight one can become," Merlin said. "Like a god."

Bestguard lowered his head and shook it. "Art thereth no endeth to thee depths of evil?"

"Well, what are you waiting for?" Doubles said. "Hook me the fuck up!"

"Shut up, Doubles. Just shut up," Aqua Shark said.

"No, you shut up, ya coward," Whiteguy said. "He's right; if you can't beat 'em, join 'em."

Aqua Shark got in Whiteguy's face. "What did you say?"

Bazooka stepped in between them.

"I made a tactical retreat. It's what you do when being overrun," Aqua Shark said.

"More like a tactical coward," Kid mumbled.

Police was pacing in circles, and Doubles was sitting on the ground playing with his knife. The look on almost everyone's face was somber.

"A god?" Chief said. "How do we fight that?!"

"We don't," Big Blue said. "I can't."

"None of us can," Octane said.

"Cause you're a coward, too!" Whiteguy said.

Octane flipped him off. "Yar pissed thee panties too, ya belly bloat!" Hook said.

"That was hell down there, Whiteguy, and I almost died!" Big Red said. "We all almost died. I know I don't want to fight that anymore."

"Yeah, I'm not fighting this anymore. Not with these guys." Chief said. "I've got a wife and son who need me." He then picked up his gear and started to walk away. "I didn't know we'd be fighting gods."

"If ya leave, you're giving up on your family." Kid said.

"Who said that?" Chief said, looking around.

"Fuck this, nobody here can fight," Aqua Shark said. "And certainly not against gods."

Merlin glanced at me.

"We know you can't fight," Big Red said.

"Screw you, man," Aqua Shark said.

Big Blue started to walk off. "I need time to think. I didn't know that this is what I was getting into," he said.

"Yeah, this cause is lost," Whiteguy said.

"Just like-" Kid said.

"Alright, guys, sit down and shut up!" Iceman shouted. "You were all scared shitless. So what?! We're fighting monsters, demons, and gods that are vastly more powerful than we are. So fucking what?! You're all going to die one day, but the question is are you going to die a fucking coward, or are you going to die a Goodguy?"

Everyone quieted down.

Iceman sighed and held his hand out in front of himself. Slowly, a misty ice ball began to form and float above his hand. Big Blue stopped walking, as did Chief. "Look at what we can do, men, just look." Silence overcame our group. "We have powers that no one can comprehend, and I know that it is not easy coming to terms with this new reality, but we have to. We must hold it together because if we don't, who will? Who will fight if we don't? Who can fight if we don't?" The night air was cold, and a gentle breeze was blowing. "That's right. Now take a good look at yourselves because what you see is man's last hope, but only if we don't lose it ourselves."

For the first time since our group came together, no one said anything for the rest of the night. Not even Kid, who normally has a joke to cheer us up, had anything to say.

We had no idea about the depth of this evil. Not a clue.

CHAPTER NINETEEN

I didn't get much sleep last night, and for obvious reasons. Chandler plagued my dreams. The cute little eight-year-old that I used to watch was dead, just another victim of Goresavice.

After cleaning up at the lake in the desert and practicing my forms, I headed to Merlin's big blue tent. By this time, the sun was just beginning to rise, and only a few Goodguys were awake.

"Morning, Bestguard. Is Merlin awake?" I said. He was standing guard.

"Morning, he art."

He pulled aside the heavy cloth curtains to allow me inside. Merlin was sitting on an old wooden stool at the far end of the tent. There was a small wooden table before him that had a large black leather-bound book and a burning candle on top of it. To my left and up against the tent was a huge wrought iron chest, and to my right was a well-made bed with blue covers. A greenish-blue, black, and white aura emanated from around the black book.

"Good morning, Browny." Merlin motioned for me to come closer. "What is it that I can do for you?"

"I know four symbols now but can't seem to learn new spells."

"And you want me to teach you?"

"Yes."

"And be charged with favoritism by the others?"

"Teach all of us."

"I cannot."

"Why?" I said. "Calignosity is teaching Goresavice."

"And you are certain of this?" I sighed. With his finger, he drew three symbols hovering in the air. He joined two but left the third one floating alone.

"You never told us about that shadow thing you fought, the one Born of the Shadows."

"Ahh, yes. Ghost, as I have come to call it, a wraith," he said. "It has been here since the beginning."

"The beginning? Doing what?"

"Watching."

"I've seen it in the Dark Woods before I met you, and so has Police."

"Ahh." Merlin nodded. "I would not venture into those woods at night."

"How come?"

"There are some places best left to the dead."

I sighed and turned around to leave. I was tired of one-word answers. I wanted to know more.

"Browny?" Merlin said.

"What?"

"Do not let their deaths consume you, my friend."

For a good portion of the day, we all sat around and discussed a new attack strategy. With the badguys operating internationally in Japan, Russia, France, and who knew where else, we needed to focus our attacks on critical aspects of their organization.

It was easier said than done. The badguys ran a tight ship, and gathering any intelligence on their activities, let alone determining who was a badguy or not, was nearly impossible for the TS squad.

However, they did discover that all initiates of the badguys had a balrog tattoo on their chest.

"How art thou, Browny?" Bestguard said.

Just ahead of us was a scraggly dressed man. He was sitting along the sidewalk with his back against a large rock, holding a sign that read 'need money and food.'

"I'm just looking at this homeless guy, that's all," I said, and thinking of Mary. She was all that I thought about. "Pull-over Doubles," I said.

"No problem," he said, pulling the SUV to the curb, to the honking of several cars.

Getting out of the car, I pulled out a few hundred dollars and handed it to the man. "Spend it wisely, old man."

With wide eyes, he gazed at me. "Thank you, stranger. Thank you so much."

"Yeah." I climbed back into the car.

"That was very generous of you," Inspector said. "But not to be a downer, Debbie, but he's most likely to spend it all on drugs."

"And art knows this cause?" Buccaneer said.

"I can smell the cocaine on him."

I sighed and gritted my teeth.

Not long afterward, we pulled up to a restaurant and went inside. Both Guard and Bestguard, heck, all of the pirates and knights, were still dressed in their traditional medieval clothes, tabards and all.

It was so embarrassing to be seen in public with a bunch of guys who looked like they belonged on some Star Trek or Brave Heart movie set, but they were my friends, and I'll always stick by them, no matter how horrendous they looked. The whole restaurant went quiet, and everyone was staring at us.

"Not it!" Doubles said as he raced for a table near the wall.

"Notteth thee." Bestguard said.

Soon, everyone said 'Not it' until Inspector was the last one who didn't.

We all laughed at him as he strolled up to the counter and ordered for the eight of us. The woman at the register couldn't stop gawking at him.

Moonwalker sat on the bench beside Doubles, squishing him against the wall.

"Are you kidding me, man?" Doubles said. "Are you going to eat up the entire seat with your fat ass?!"

"Those dinky chairs can't handle my weight," Moonwalker said as the bench groaned.

"I forgot you guys eat like pigs." Fire said. "It's a good thing that we're creating money out of thin air, eh?"

"Only because your foods are so poor in the nutrients we require," Moonwalker said as he popped four pills into his mouth. "We even have to supplement our diet with your crappy multivitamins."

"Well, ya shoulda packed a lunch then, huh, big fella?" Doubles said.

Moonwalker glared at him. "We couldn't risk even the slightest of our technology falling into Earth's hands."

"But even you will have to admit that the most significant technology you could have brought was yourselves," I said. "If you are indeed engineered from the DNA up."

Moonwalker looked over at Inspector and nodded. "How very keen of you, Browny."

An hour later, our food arrived on four carts. "We're sorry for the delay, and we hope everything is to your liking," a waiter said.

"It art no problem, just keep me ale a flowing," Buccaneer said.

Not a moment after the waiters had left with their carts, a little boy wandered up to Moonwalker and tugged on his sleeve. "Are you a giant, mister," he said.

"Some would say so, but believe it or not, I was once your size," Moonwalker said.

"Why is your hair gray like an old man's? You don't look old," the kid said.

"You're right. I was created this way," he said.

"We're sorry that he's bothering you. He likes to run around a lot, and sometimes we lose track of him." a man said, taking hold of the kid's hand. His wife stood by him.

"It's fine. I wasn't offended." Moonwalker said.

"You guys have a good night," the woman said, following her family out of the restaurant.

"You know, for a moment there, I was really beginning to fear for that kid's safety," Doubles said.

"You're going to be fearing for yours in a minute," Moonwalker said.

"What?! I'm just saying you looked at that kid with hungry eyes," Doubles said, singing, hungry eyes.

We all laughed. "And didn't you mean born, not created?" Fire said.

"No, I meant what I said," Moonwalker said. "The first two thousand of us were created in laboratories. The generations that followed were born."

Doubles creased his eyebrows. "So you're test-tube babies?" he said.

"More or less," Inspector said. A few of us laughed.

"I'm curious here, Inspector. So you really are the lord of a planet called Iceplanet." Fire said.

"Yes, but the planet is called 412A. My empire is Ice Planet."

"Okay?" Double said.

"So you and Iceman rule an empire like dictators?" Fire said.

"Art thou Kings?" Bestguard said.

Inspector chuckled. "No. Iceman and I share supreme lordship over our planets. He commands all of Storm, while I command all of Ariel. The structure of our government is a democratic lordship."

"Wow, and you two came all this way to help us fight, two lords of some planets?" Doubles said.

"Yes," Inspector said.

"That's like our president going to the front lines and fighting, it just doesn't happen? So come on with this lord bullshit. Who are you guys really?" Doubles said.

"They are our lords, Doubles," Moonwalker said.

"Huh." Doubles said.

"There will always be those with the position of lord, king, or president, but there won't always be great men, and great men are great because of what they do whether they sit behind a desk and lead or lead on the field of battle. We choose to lead on the field of battle," Inspector said.

"Have thee children?" Guard said.

"No, none of us do, except for Iceman," Inspector said. "He has two daughters, Jessica and Tiffany."

"I'd hate to see what they look like." Doubles mumbled. Inspector smiled and shook his head.

"Does not thee have a daughter, Fire?" Guard said.

Fire pulled out a picture and handed it to him. "Yeah, Amber, and she's a beautiful thing too."

"She art lovely," Guard said. "She reminded me of thine own girl."

"You have a daughter?" Doubles said.

"Yay, after the war, thy settled and sired two sons and a daughter."

"She must have been blind." Doubles said. A few of us chuckled while Guard glared at him.

"The total came to six hundred and eighty-four dollars. Now, who's paying?" Inspector said.

We all laughed at him.

After eating our fill, Moonwalker, Guard, Fire, and I climbed into our armored SUV while the others got into their vehicle. We then began to head out, and though Pudgy had completely remodeled our SUV fleet to accommodate their massive size, there still wasn't enough room. Moonwalker was slightly hunched over with his knees to the chest. It was nine o'clock on a warm August night.

I looked at my watch. It was nine-thirty. Pirate should be giving us a call here any minute.

"Me never have a children untileth Calignosity is deadeth," Buccaneer said over our earpieces.

"Looking like that, you'll never have children," Doubles muttered over his.

"Hey, pull over, Doubles," I said, motioning for Fire to pull us over as well.

The woman who approached me in the bar a few months ago was walking down the street. Walking next to her with one of his hands pulling her hair was a well-built man wearing black jeans and a black t-shirt.

After coming to a stop, we all jumped out. Wrapping his arm around her neck, the guy spun her around and held her close like a shield.

"Let the woman go, sir," I said.

"You would risk your life over this one whore?" he said.

"Her status in society is not our concern. It is her life that is important." Inspector said. "Now, release her."

"Hey, I know you from-" the woman said. Her eye shadow was running down her cheeks.

"Shut up, whore!" the man said, cupping her mouth with his hand.

We had him cut off and partially surrounded. His only escape was the alleyway behind him.

"You're outnumbered and outmatched. Now give her to us and go home," Inspector said.

"You're right, but do you risk exposing your secrets by fighting me?" he said. "After all, the only way you can beat me will be to use-"

A red hole appeared in the middle of his forehead as blood splattered the wall behind him. "A forty-five automatic-silenced," Doubles said, stepping out from behind the car. The barrel of his pistol was smoking.

"Nice shot." Fire said.

Trembling, the woman wrapped her arms around me and started crying. "They killed him! They killed everyone!"

Buccaneer and Guard started to load the dead badguy into the SUV. "Bestguard, get on the phone with TSS one and tell them we need a cleanup on 32nd Ave," Inspector said.

"Who'd they kill? The guys with you at the bar?" I said.

"Our whole clic. They just came in shooting!" she said.

"Men in forest green fatigues?" Inspector said.

"Uh huh, and how'd you know?" she wiped her eyes. "Who are you guys?"

I looked at Inspector. I felt terrible for her, but there was nothing that I could do for her. Reaching into my pocket, I pulled out a few hundred dollars and gave it to her. "Take this money and get out of this city," I said. "Better yet, get out of this state and do something good with your life that you can be proud of."

"They're taking over everything. That's what they said," she said. "They're taking over everything."

"I know, sweetheart. I know," I said. "Now, just go and get out of this state."

We climbed into our SUV, leaving her on the sidewalk. "That was a good call, Browny," Inspector said.

"Yeah." My cell phone rang. "What's up?" I said.

"Howdy, Alex, it's me, Jordan," Pirate said.

"How's it going, buddy?"

"Great. Do you think you could stop by?"

"Sure thing."

"See you shortly," Pirate said. He hung up.

"Suit up, men; we've got business to handle," I said.

Two weeks ago, the Biomed Corporations CEO died of 'natural causes' and was replaced by a guy named Michael Windsor. We knew he was a badguy, but that was about it, and we were going to kidnap him. We needed the intel.

Opening my duffle bag, I pulled out my black two-piece Kevlar body suit and began to put it on. After slipping in the ceramic thigh, chest, back, and side plates, I strapped on my helmet and gas mask. A few minutes later, we were all dressed and ready to rock and roll except for Fire who was driving us.

"Um, we've got problems, dudes!" Doubles said over his transceiver. A cop was trailing and blaring his siren at him.

"Go ahead and pull over, and get out before he gets here," Inspector said. "We don't want him looking in here."

"Pull over Fire," I said.

"Cops totally hate that, but alright," Doubles said, pulling his SUV over to the curb of the main drag.

Doubles got out of the SUV and readjusted his black tuxedo and red tie, leaving the door open. "Good evening, officer. What seems to be the problem?" he said.

"Now let's hope that he doesn't say anything about our black windows and want to look inside," Inspector said.

"Yeah." Fire said.

"Nothing too serious. One of your tail lights is out." the cop said. "Now, can you get back in your vehicle, please?"

"Nay," Guard said. A few of us chuckled.

Doubles walked around back the car and looked around. "You're right. One is out," he said. "I'll have that fixed ASAP, and thanks for pointing that out."

"Now go away," I said, tightening the grip on my shotgun.

"No problem, and you're welcome," the cop said. "And can I ask you where you were headed?'

"Well, I just left my office at Sky Corp Industries. We had a late meeting, and now I'm headed

home, officer," Doubles said. At least he looked like the part of an office executive, but then again, when did he not? He's just too cool to wear anything else.

"Really-you work for Sky Corp?" he said. "But you look so familiar. I know I've seen you from somewhere."

"You have got to be kidding me!" I whispered. "Out of all the cops in Phoenix, we had to get pulled over by the one who just happens to know Doubles."

"Shit happens, man," Moonwalker said.

"We call it the x-factor," Inspector said over his mic. "It's the great pie in the sky or when pigs fly type of shit that just ruins your entire op."

"You're Matt, from the Double Duece bar. The bouncer who always calls us up when the trash needs to be taken out," the officer said. "And you work for Sky Corp?!"

"Bingo! We have ourselves a winner, folks!" I said. Everyone snickered quietly.

"Yes, sir, I do."

"Well then, you have a good night and drive safely."

"I will, and thank you," Doubles said, getting back in the car.

"We dodged a bullet there." Fire said.

Again, the cop flashed his lights at us. I saw Doubles grip the steering wheel and slump into his seat.

"It looks like Doubles or nothing tonight, fellas!" Moonwalker said. We all chuckled.

"You know, guys, I can't be two fucking dudes at one time. And if this car was tied to my original name, you know, me-Matt, like I had originally suggested, then we wouldn't be in this fucking mess!" Doubles said. "Instead, he's running the plates and finding out that this car is owned by Jeremy Stomburn, a Sky Corp employee. Who, by the way, is not Matt, the bouncer." He opened the car door. "I hope you guys are ready 'cause the shits about to hit the fan." Stepping out, he slammed the door.

"You go get 'em, tiger!" Fire said.

"Can I please see some identification Matt? It seems that your vehicle is registered and owned by a Jeremy Stromburn," the cop said.

Doubles pulled out his wallet and handed it to him. "Here you go, officer."

"Can I have you stand by the front of my car, and do you mind if I take a look inside your vehicle?"

"Not at all, officer. Feel free," Doubles said, covering the grin on his face with his hand.

"Is there anything in the car I should be aware of, sir?" he said, opening the driver's side back door. His hand was on his pistol.

"Good evening, officer," Inspector said. His voice was muffled by the gas mask, which only added to the humor. "What can we do for you?"

"Holy shit!" the cop said, jumping back.

"Not unless you're talking about them!" Doubles said. With incredible speed, Doubles laid into the officer with a hard kick to the face. The officer fell to the pavement with his arms stiff by his side. He was out cold. "Now, someone clean this crap up and make it quick."

A car drove past us.

Five minutes later, and with no more incidents, we pulled up along the TS squad's white van on the second level of the parking garage. The place was virtually empty, with no one in sight.

"How are you guys doing?" I said.

"What's up, buddy guts?" Pirate said.

Doubles pulled up next to us in the cop car and got out. Pirate looked confused. "Don't ask," Doubles said. His face was tense.

Bazooka leaned closer to Pirate. "What crawled up his ass?" he whispered.

"The cop in the trunk," Inspector said. "We'll need Merlin to wipe his memory before we let him go."

"Got it." Big Red said.

"So what do you have for us?" I said.

"Michael Windsor, top floor, and there's nearly a dozen with him," Pirate said.

"What's their relationship to him?" Inspector said.

"Unconfirmed," Bazooka said. "We believe that they're board members."

"Great, break down the security for us, Big Red," Inspector said.

Opening the two rear double doors of the van, Big Red jumped in and began to type away on his laptop. The entire interior of the van was loaded with electronic equipment. "I've tapped into the network and looped all the security cams. With a push of the button, this entire building will be whited out. Other than that, there are only two security guards, and they're both on the lobby floor."

"Well done. Now be ready to push that button on mine or Browny's command," Inspector said. "Buccaneer, Guard, get the climbing gear. Pirate, we'll meet you at the rendezvous point; however, be ready to pick us up anywhere if things go wrong," Inspector said.

"Sure thing," Pirate said.

Doubles was all suited and geared up now. "So how much time are we looking at for this?" he said.

"At least twenty," Striper said.

"And with the cop?" Doubles said.

"Life."

"Nice."

"You have anything to add, Browny?" Inspector said. I shook my head. "Alright, men, let's make this quick and efficient."

We headed towards the elevators. "Ahh, how convenient. The elevator says no lard asses allowed," Doubles said.

"Two thousand pound load capacity?! That's ridiculous!" Moonwalker said.

"SDS eleven, you take your squad and the rest of mine up this elevator and clear the lobby," Inspector said. "We'll take the emergency stairwell and meet you there."

"Roger that," I said.

Once everyone was inside the elevators, the doors closed, and we went up. Soft classical music filled the elevator. Guard bobbed his head and tapped his leg to the beat.

I glanced at Doubles through the corner of my eyes. "Weapons hot," I said, flicking off the safety of my shotgun.

"Weapons hot," everyone said.

"White them out, LS thirteen," I said into the transceiver.

"Roger that SD eleven. All communications are-" There was a pause on the other end. "Down," Big Red said.

The elevator came to a stop, and the doors opened. I rushed into the lobby and scanned for targets. Two guards were sitting behind a crescent-shaped desk at the room's far end, just like Big Red said. One was eating a candy bar while the other was reclining in his seat with his feet propped up on the desk, reading a magazine.

"Get your hands in the air!" I yelled. "Get them in the air now!" With my shotgun leveled at the one eating the candy bar, he dropped it and raised his hands high in the air.

"No sudden movements," Doubles said, leveling his shotgun at the other.

Inspector and Moonwalker entered the lobby from the stairwell entrance. "Good work, guys," Inspector said.

Fire and Guard then bound and gagged the two officers and laid them under the desk. "SD thirteen and forty-two, stay here and cover our retread. SD eleven split up your squad, and take both elevators. Me and SD fourteen, we'll take a stairwell a piece and meet you at the top."

"Roger that SD forty-one," I said, motioning for Doubles to come with me. Once inside the elevator, I pressed the thirtieth-floor button and sat down with my back against the wall.

"You okay, man?" Doubles said.

I sighed. "It only seems like yesterday since we were sitting in class, doesn't it?"

"It sure does, man, and now here we are kicking ass and taking names."

"Do you remember the first day of our senior year, after football practice, when we were soaking the soccer girls?"

Doubles chuckled. "Yeah, and we were getting 'em good, even Jessica."

"Did you see the look on her face? She was hating life!"

"She sure was, but that was so fun," he said. "The best times of my life."

"Same here, Matt. Same here."

He looked at me, nodding his head. "I really do miss those days, and I wish that I could go back. Things weren't so complicated, you know."

"Yeah," I said, standing up. "I do, too."

The elevator doors opened with a bang. Directly ahead was a long corridor, while to our left and right were two hallways that ended at the emergency stairwells.

Inspector and Moonwalker were already posted up along the wall on either side of the corridor ahead of us, peeking down it. How the two of them managed to run up thirty flights of stairs in about thirty seconds was beyond me.

I took up a position behind Moonwalker. Doubles followed me while Bestguard and Guard posted up behind Inspector.

"There's two down the first hallway to the right and ten inside the room they're guarding," Inspector said. "Now let's get to work."

Without a sound, Inspector and Moonwalker hurried down the hallway. We followed closely behind. Raising his suppressed .40 automatic Inspector rounded the corner and fired two shots. Two men in forest green fatigues lay dead, each with a single bullet hole in their head.

A moment later, we had the boardroom door surrounded. After a silent countdown from three, Inspector kicked the door open, and we rushed inside.

"Get down on the ground!" Inspector yelled, pointing his pistol at the man on the far side of the room. "Get down on the ground now!"

Grabbing a man in a suit and tie, I forced him to the ground and put my knee on his neck. I then motioned with my shotgun at another suit to get down.

Guard opened the coat closet. "Clear."

"This is impressive-Goodguys," Michael Windsor said. His hands were raised to chest level, and he was smiling.

Walking around the elongated table, Inspector lowered his pistol and slammed his left fist into Michael's chin, knocking him down.

Spitting blood on the white carpet, the badguy slowly shook his head. "You cannot stop us. We are everywhere."

Inspector shot him once in the knee and then once in the shoulder. Michael didn't even groan. He just kept smiling. Kneeling on him, Inspector hog-tied him with three pairs of handcuffs. "Are the execs secured?" he said.

"All secure," Bestguard said.

"Good. Now let's move out," Inspector said as he was slinging Michael over his shoulder. "TS twenty-one, this is SD forty-one. Do you read me?"

"Loud and clear, forty-one," Pirate said.

"The package is secure. We are proceeding out the northwest fire escape." Inspector said.

"Roger that forty-one, you are clear and covered."

Running down the main corridor, we took a right at the elevators and headed down the emergency fire escape. Two minutes later, we were piling into our SUV and heading back to base. The long night was finally over.

Our successful kidnapping of the Biomed CEO was breaking news the following morning and a cause for us to celebrate. It was our first significant blow to the badguys, and the treasure trove of information Merlin extracted from Michael ensured it wouldn't be our last. The badguys, with knowledge from Calignosity, were dabbling in cybernetics.

CHAPTER TWENTY

It has been three years since we first organized as the Goodguys, and since then, we've accomplished a lot. We've liberated several cities in Arizona from the scourge of badguy gangs, police chiefs, and mayors, but no matter how many weapons caches we seized, corporate offices we broke into, or soldiers of theirs we killed, they just kept spreading like the black plague. It was depressing, but it had to be done.

"Welcome Goodguys. It is the eighteenth of March, 2000, our third year anniversary," Iceman said.

"Ahh, who the hell just shit themselves?" Pirate said, covering his nose.

"Whoa, that does stink," Chief said, stepping away from Pudgy.

"And that's Pudgy, gentlemen," Iceman said, gesturing towards him. I could hear some chuckles.

Whiteguy smelled the air behind Pudgy. "Hello! Someone needs their diaper changed!" he said.

Pudgy hung his head low with his hands in his pockets. "Sorry, guys."

"It's alright, Pudgy. We still love you," Iceman said.

"No, we don't!" Kid yelled.

More laughter erupted from our ranks. "Alright, guys, we have several topics up for discussion today, so without delay, here's Smartguy for a quick tech update," Iceman said.

Everyone moaned and groaned. "Good evening, Goodguys," Smartguy said. "Currently, I am developing a new body armor that will be far more resistant to bullets and other forms of damage, such as fire and conductivity. However, it is a long way in coming."

"Then why ya be tellin' us ya belly bloat?!" Hook cried out.

Smartguy glanced at Hook with just one eye while keeping the other one straight. "In other news, I have noticed that a few of you, namely Pudgy and Big Blue, are rising in your cortisol levels, which will continue to have a negative impact on your body's ability to process glucose. I cannot stress enough the-"

"Ahh, come on, Smartguy, spare us the health crap, man!" Aqua yelled. "We're infused with the mana of Ethereal and will live forever!"

"Ya mon, they know they fat," Islander said.

Smartguy sighed and glanced at Iceman. "I cannot stress enough how important it is for some of you to stick with my diet. That is all," he said, frowning and blinking both eyelids.

"Thank goodness that's over with," Octane said.

"Yeah, but for a moment there, I really thought he was going to go on for another hour-long spiel like he did last month," Police said.

"Don't even remind me," Octane said.

"He sounds like my mom," Kid said.

"As all of you know, last week's fundraiser blitz was a big hit, but what you didn't know was that we raised over a million dollars in proceeds," Inspector said. Everyone clapped. "How much have we donated to date Big Red?"

"Thirty-two million and some change," Big Red said.

Again, everyone clapped and cheered. "But that's not all. With all the money that we've been creating and through the hard work of Striper, come this May, we will have our very own charity organization and a thirty-story office building," Inspector said. He was grinning proudly. "And our charity organization will be called 'The Goodguys.'"

For the third time, everyone erupted into a thunderous rip-roar of hooting and hollering. Finally, we were doing something that could be considered helping the people of this world, but truthfully, I didn't think any of it really mattered. It's been three years since we have stepped foot in the Dark Zone, and I know that no one has forgotten what lies down there. I mean, how could they? We've been camping by it at least once a month for three years now.

We should be focusing on the Dark Zone, not Goresavice's army, but I guess everyone's too afraid to go back down and do what needs to be done. But I couldn't really blame them.

"Thank you, Inspector, for the heartwarming news. Now, let's move on to something more serious," Iceman said. "Space Police and his TS squad have been following up on some leads overseas, but what they've confirmed isn't pretty. The badguys have opened a private militia training camp in the hills about forty kilometers north of Leon, Spain. What's worse is that they have the full support of the Spanish government to include financing and instructors."

"This militia is to Spain what the French Foreign Legion is to France," Inspector said.

"So what's so bad about that?" Whiteguy said. "Let's assemble a few teams and take 'em out."

"This means that they have legitimate government support ya moron." Doubles said.

"I saw this coming from a mile away," Police said. "It was just a matter of time."

"So what does this say about our progress in this war?" Octane said.

"It says that we've got our shit cut out for us. That's what it says," Aqua said.

"Ya, mon. Ya," Islander said.

"So we're like going to be killing government soldiers?!" Chief said.

"If they serve Goresavice, then they die," Greyguy said. "Simple as that."

"When more intelligence becomes available to us, we'll assemble a few teams and do what we do best; kick some badguy ass," Iceman said.

"We killeth them whereth they standeth!" Basil yelled.

"That's right! Let's let them know who we are!" Bazooka shouted as he threw a fist into the air.

"Hell ya!" Doubles yelled, slapping Kid with a high five.

"Excuse me, Goodguys, can I have your attention, please?" Smartguy shouted over the ruckus.

"Ah, man, not you again," Whiteguy said.

"Boo!" Kid hollered.

"Can I have your attention, please?" Everyone quieted down. "Thank you. My annual report has been sent to each of your laptops. Make sure you read it. You will find that our progress against Goresavice and his army has been quite impactful. We are far from losing this war, but our fight from here on out will not be easy."

"Will your report contain any intel on the Spanish government and who's pulling the strings behind the scenes?" Big Red said. "Will there be anything new that me or my team can work with?"

"Not at the moment, but we are working on that," Smartguy said. "The problem is that these Badguys are far more entrenched in the affairs of world governments than we had anticipated, and monitoring all the different government agencies is not easy."

"And what about the FBI?" Octane said. "Have they made any connection to the assassination of Senator Thompson and us?"

"Not yet. They're still chasing ghosts," Smartguy said.

"You done yet, 'cause I got a party to attend," Kid said.

Smartguy glared at Kid and set his laptop down. Kid ran. "You're going to feel the pain this time, Kiddy!" Smartguy yelled as he chased after him.

"How are you doing, Browny?" Iceman said, tossing me an orange juice.

"Just fine," I said.

"Do you really think that attacking a military base with eight or even sixteen of us is a wise idea?" Aqua Shark said.

"Ahh, ye of little faith." Iceman put a hand on Aqua Shark's shoulder. He was like the size of a child compared to Iceman. "How many times do we need to prove to you our wisdom in the field of tactics?"

"If I had a squad of well-trained SEALs and the right equipment, then I wouldn't be so concerned, now would I?" Aqua Shark said. "But these guys aren't professionals. They're good and even better with their killer spells, but I have more years of training than they have combat experience."

"And I have more combat experience than a thousand years of training," Iceman said.

Aqua Shark gave him a funny look. "It's your call, boss," he said

I headed to the grill to grab a burger, but Big Blue approached me before I could get there. His bald black head glistened with beads of sweat. It was still warm out even though the sun was beginning to set. "Hey, Browny. You got a moment?" he said.

"Sure. What's up?"

"Do you know this symbol?" He drew a three-dimensional symbol in the air with his fingers.

"That's cool. Where did you learn that spell?""

"A few years ago. It's for drawing schematics and such," Big Blue said. "Is this symbol used in the spell cold bolt?" The 3D symbol continued to hover and slowly rotate in the air.

"I don't know cold bolt, but Iceman does," I said. "I just know that it's used in the spell protection."

"The Icemen seem to know everything, but alright, thanks."

"No problem."

"How's everything been going with you?" he said.

"I'm doing alright," I said. "You?"

"Actually, pretty well," he said. "I'm going on a date tonight."

"Wow, good to hear, brother," I said playfully, punching him in the arm. Big Blue chuckled.

"Browny, come speak with me," Merlin's voice said in my mind.

Walking over to Merlin's tent, I pushed aside the heavy cloth curtains and went inside. "You wanted to see me?"

"Yes, my friend. Please sit down." I sat on the large iron chest. "You are growing in power and quickly."

"Yeah, a little bit."

"And you have proven yourself to be a good leader."

I nodded. "Yeah, I guess."

"And you believe that we should focus on the Abyss-Calignosity."

I sighed, staring at the ground. You'd figure that your thoughts are your best-kept secrets, but I guess not with Merlin around. "Yeah, but we're not ready."

"You are right, but do not think I have taken my eyes off what lies below."

"I know."

"Soon, I will send you all to be hardened by the things of the dark Zone in preparation for the end."

I gave him a puzzled look. "What do you mean?"

Smiling, Merlin stood up and walked over to me. "You have not changed since the first day I met you, Browny, and that is good." He put a hand on my shoulder. "In time, you will understand these things that I say to you. In time. Now go and enjoy the rest of the evening with your friends."

And that's what I did. I took Doubles, Police, and a few others to a club in Phoenix, where we partied all night long. Actually, they were the only ones partying, dancing, and enjoying the company of women. I just sat at the bar drinking pop and watched everyone having a good time. They had no idea of the war that raged around them, the power of magic that permeated everything, just like I had no idea what Merlin meant. I let a tiny spark of lightning jump between my fingers and shook my head. No idea at all.

"You look like you could use some company," a beautiful blonde said, walking up to me. "My name's Nicole, what's yours?"

"Scott, but everyone calls me Browny."

"That's cool. So, would you like to meet some of my girlfriends?" she said.

I glanced at a table that had four women sitting around it. "Are those your girlfriends?" They were eyeing me intently like I was a piece of candy.

Nicole laughed and looked back at her friends. "Those are my girls."

I envied their blissful ignorance. "I'd love to keep you girl's company, but that's as far as I can take it." The bouncers ran towards the front entrance. "I'm engaged already, and I love her dearly."

She looked at my hand with her smile fading. "Oh."

The dancing crowd slowly began to part, and then the music stopped. Standing in the middle of the dance floor with four other badguys behind him was Goresavice. Anger filled my heart.

"Browny, my old friend. How good it is to see you enjoying the last of your days," he said.

Nichole backed away from me. "Excuse me, dude, but you and your wanna-be soldier posse need to bounce, and now!" a large, muscle-bound bouncer said. He had three others with him, but they had no idea who they were talking to.

A sly smile crept across Goresavice's face. "Do you even know who I am?" he said.

Kid and Buccaneer pushed their way to the front of the crowd. "I don't care who you are. You have three seconds to split or be split!"

A blur of motion and blood squirting across the floor was all I saw. The bouncer was dead before he even hit the floor. His head was nearly severed. Screams erupted from the crowd."How dare you disrespect your prince, you fool." Sheathing his k-bar, Goresavice turned full circle before the retreating crowd. "You will all do well to remember my face and, even more so, my name, Goresavice." The club went silent. "Now, let me introduce you to my captains."

Jessica's silver necklace and ruby pendant sparkled under the strobe lights. My adrenaline began to flow and mix with the mana coursing through my veins.

"Gorgan and Tangier."

The two men were about my size. Gorgan had a metal bo staff in his hands and straight black hair draped over his head like a mushroom cut. Tangier had a pistol on his hip, short, parted black hair, and sharp facial features. He looked like the military type.

"And Kilroc and Dracor."

Kilroc had eight pineapple grenades strapped to his green camouflage fatigues and short spiked hair like Goresavice. The other, Dracor, was a giant man standing nearly seven feet tall and was exceptionally well built, but what was most disturbing about him was his oversized right hand. It was twice the size of his left.

"Let me introduce you to my captains," I said. Doubles, Police, Kid, and Buccaneer stepped onto the dance floor and encircled the badguys. By now, most people in the club were trying to get out.

"Do not do this, Browny. You know that you cannot win." Chuckling quietly, Goresavice and his captains headed for the door.

I shook my head, and Doubles and Buccaneer let them go. "Just like you know, this war is in vain."

We left the club and headed back to Janestown.

"Hey, Browny, wake up, man," someone said, shaking me. "Wake up."

I looked around. Octane was kneeling beside me, and a few others were standing around. I was sweating and breathing heavily. "You were really going through it. Are you going to be okay?" Octane said.

Putting on my brown boots, I stood and grabbed my katana. I felt like crap.

"You were rolling around and talking in your sleep, saying something like, 'come back to bed,'" Big Blue said.

"I'll be fine," I said. I don't know why what Big Blue said bothered me, but it did. I don't remember hearing or seeing anything that night, and I hated myself for it.

"You looked like you were having a nightmare, man," Whiteuy said.

"Yeah, I've been having a lot of those myself," Octane said. "Ever since the Dark Zone, things haven't been the same for me. I'm afraid to turn the lights off, but I know that won't help."

"It's the weird noises at night, isn't it?" Big Blue said.

Octane ran his hands through his thin brown hair. "In my closet and downstairs. Anything that sounds unnatural. I'm scared shitless now, and of everything."

"Aren't we all?" Whiteguy said.

"And what's worse is that we're virtually helpless," Big Blue said. "I can't help but think that if a Shadow Demon, or a Ghost, or whatever comes through my walls at night, I'm dead. That there's nothing that I can do to stop it."

"Yeah, man, this is one fucked up reality," Whiteguy said. "I have to take trazodone to sleep."

I picked up my katana and headed deeper into the desert.

"What ya off to do, Browny?" Kid said, tailing me.

"Practice my forms."

"I told everyone what happened last night," Kid said, adjusting his red bandana.

"Isn't that Pirates?"

"No, not until he takes it back," Kid said. "So we came up with some new names for Goresavice's captains. You want to hear them?"

The bright orange sun was beginning to peak over the mountains while a gentle wind swept over the desert. "Sure."

"The one with the pistol everyone named Gunguy, and the one with the grenades we named Grenadeguy. Those names aren't that original, I don't think. The other two are better," Kid said. "I named the one with the staff and mushroom haircut Mopguy. Do you get that one? He carries around a mop, but the mop is on-"

"Yeah, I get it. It's pretty funny."

Kids smile faded. "The other one, Basil, named Hamhand. I'll let you be." Kid ran off to join the others.

Early that same morning, after Merlin agreed that we needed a vacation, I and a few other Goodguys flew to California to enjoy the beaches for a week or so. It was just what I needed.

"What the heck are you doing, Kid?" Police said.

Kid was dressed in tropical shorts like Islander and was holding a surfboard. "Islander is going to teach me how to surf," he said.

It was warm outside, nearly twenty-five degrees Celsius, and there was not a cloud to be seen. Beach umbrellas dotted the beach, and people were sunbathing and splashing in the water. I wish I could be like them. Ignorant.

"Ya, mon. He goin' surfing for the first time," Islander said. "Ya should join us." He waved us over.

"Smartguy, how about you? You want to surf with us?" Kid said. Smartguy shot him a look. "Ooo, that's right, my bad. These boards don't come in size, fat ass!"

Dropping his board, Kid ran towards the water. Kipping up with incredible athleticism for such a huge and muscular guy, Smartguy gave chase, and a moment later, he had Kid pinned to the ground. He then began to tickle Kid until he began to scream and cry.

"Ahh!" Kid yelled. "Get this gorilla off me!"

"Heck, why na?" Islander said, shrugging his shoulders and dropping his board. He then bull-rushed Smartguy but bounced off and fell onto his back. Smartguy may be the smallest of the Icemen, but he was still a barrel-chested, three-hundred-kilogram beast. That's what they all were. Superhumans on steroids, and truthfully, I wouldn't doubt it if they did have a little gorilla in their DNA.

A moment later, Smartguy was sitting on top of both of them, tickling them.

"Why don't you shed those ancient clothes and catch some sun?" I said. Guard was sitting next to me, wearing his light red Dragon embroidered tabard with his black cotton trousers rolled up to his knees.

"Thee rather notteth," he said.

"Could you perhaps change for me?" Doubles said.

"Nay."

"Chief, what are you doing here," I said, running over to him. He was walking along the beach with his wife while his thirteen-year-old son ran around nearby.

"Wow, what a coincidence," Chief said. "It's nice to see you guys."

"Good afternoon, Carol. How have you been?" I said.

"Just wonderful, Scott. And you?" She said. "Hi, Nathan."

"Hey, Carol, Chief." Police said.

"How about you, Mike?" I said.

"I'm fine," Mike said. "It's been a while since the last time you visited."

"Yeah, it has, and I'm sorry. I've just been so busy." I said.

"That's okay," Mike said.

"We saw your last fight, and I must say you are an incredible fighter. You really are," Carol said.

"You kicked butt!" Mike said, giving me a high five.

"What are you now forty-five and zero with six title defenses?" Chief said.

"Yeah. It's something like that," I said.

"It's too bad that Pride isn't more popular over here," Chief said.

"That's a good thing. For me, at least," I said.

"So, how are you doing, Nathan?" Carol said. "Are you still working for the Phoenix PD?"

"I sure am, and I'm SWAT now," Police said. "I've moved up the food chain and pay scale."

"Yeah, I bet. Congratulations," Carol said. "Michaels moving up the ladder, too. We held a re-election fundraiser for LA Mayor Emmanuel Santos last month. It was wonderful." Carol hugged Chief close.

He and Police were the only two in our group who worked a full-time job in the normal sense. Their contributions to the group came in the form of information and what valuable sources they turned out to be. To date, we've acted on more intel from them than all the other TS squad members. All thanks to their government contacts.

"Oh my! Would you look at the size of that man?" Carol said.

"That's another one of my friends. His name is Smartguy," Chief said. "Come on, I'll introduce you two."

"Smartguy uh, did he dye his hair bright red on purpose?" Carol said. "And his name should be Buff Guy, not Smartguy."

"No, honey. It's natural. Now come on, he won't bite."

"Do you want to play catch, Mike?" I said

"Yeah, I'd love to," he said.

I gave him a high five. "Alright, let's play keep away from the big bad police officer."

"Yeah, he'll never get the ball from us!" Mike ran down the beach for a pass.

Police looked at me and smiled.

For the rest of our vacation, we stayed with Chief and his family at his summerhouse along Malibu Beach. We spent the days surfing and the nights around a campfire roasting marshmallows and listening to the waves crashing upon the beach. It was one of the best times that I had in a long time. I'm sorry that I wasn't more vigilant, Mary. I am so sorry, my love.

CHAPTER TWENTY-ONE

It was noon, and the rain had been coming down in steady sheets for the past week with no end in sight. We were in central Brazil, pushing through the thick rainforest en route to a Brazilian military base. Like the Spanish, they were also holding hands with the badguys, but who could blame them? The badguys paid extravagantly well to become a government-sponsored mercenary group, and Brazil needed the money. Too bad for Brazil because our objective is to slaughter them all. Just like SDS two and four did to the militia training base in Spain two months ago. They killed two hundred and eighty-five soldiers; all confirmed badguys. They then burnt the entire base to the ground.

It was the worst act of terrorism to ever strike Spain. The government vowed to track down and bring to justice those responsible, but despite the hyped media coverage and all the efforts of the world's finest, we still alluded capture. We were good and getting better with each new spell. We could conquer the world if we wanted.

"Alright, men, let's move out," Iceman said. "We've got four ki's to go until showtime!"

Picking up my rucksack, I followed in line after Batlord.

"Man, this really brings me back," Aqua Shark said. Rain streaked down his face.

We were all dressed in armored ghillie suits and looked like walking bushes, but none of us could match the camouflage skill of Iceman or Moonwalker. Even at five meters away and moving, I couldn't distinguish between his head and the leaves or his arms and the branches sticking out from his suit. Even their weapons looked like branches.

"Where did you serve?" Fire said.

"Grenada, Panama, and as of late Iraq," Aqua Shark said. "I've served the United States for eighteen years. Eleven of them as a SEAL."

"Eighteen years, uh?" Iceman said. "I've been serving Storm since I was sixteen."

"I've been serving Storm since I was sixteen," Aqua Shark said in a mocking tone. "And you're what, like forty years old?"

"Six hundred and sixty-eight," Iceman said.

We all stopped marching. "Wha?" Islander said.

"Six hundred and..." Fire said.

"Well, that's in A-years," Iceman said.

"Which is like maybe a hundred of our years?" Aqua Shark said.

"No, two thousand nine hundred and sixty-seven years and some change," Iceman said.

For a moment, everyone got quiet. "You can say that we've seen some things in our lifetime," Moonwalker said.

"So let me get this straight. You two have been alive for nearly three thousand years?!" Aqua Shark said.

"Yes," Iceman said.

"Naturally? No magic, clones, or whatever?" Aqua Shark said.

"We are the first and only human species to be completely engineered from the amino acids up. We are perfect in our DNA," Moonwalker said.

"I smell bullshit," Aqua Shark said.

"Wow, mon. Ya learn somethin' new every day," Islander said.

"That makes Merlin at least three thousand years old," I said.

"At least." Fire said.

"What art thee pool up to?" Guard said.

"Thirty-two fifty," I said.

"But I don't get it; who would make you like this?" Aqua Shark said. "You're an athletic monster with bone-white hair and white cat eyes for crying out loud!"

Iceman and Moonwalker glanced at each other. "Come on, men, let's move out," Iceman said, motioning to us.

I don't know how much further we had traveled, but it couldn't have been that far when bullets started to tear up the undergrowth around us. Dropping to the ground, I scanned the jungle for the enemy.

"They're shooting blind; one hundred and fifty meters at two o'clock!" Iceman yelled, taking cover behind a tree. "Set up that sixty mil thirty-three!"

"How'd we end up on the receiving end of an ambush?!" Aqua Shark shouted over the gunfire.

More bullets flew toward us. Taking a knee, Aqua Shark unslung the mortar launcher off his back, pulled out a shell, and dropped it down the tube. With a loud thank noise, the shell exited the barrel, and a second later, the trees and bushes off in the distance exploded. My heart was beating out of control.

"Good hit thirty-three, now keep 'em coming!" Iceman fired a short burst from his .50 caliber machine gun. I don't know how Smartguy did it, but he modified an M2 .50 cal to be hip-carried and fired from the waist.

It was a rather simple setup consisting of an articulated pneumatic arm, which supported the gun and was attached to a heavily padded rotating belt worn around the waist. The system was so flexible and stable that it allowed the user to lie prone and fire the weapon without a folding bi-pod, though it did have one for added support when firing prone. And that's why they call him Smartguy. He was a genius.

Looking through the optics of my M-4, I saw a soldier peek around a tree. I let off a few rounds and watched him drop.

Another explosion rocked the enemy's position. We were hitting them good and hard, but now the enemy's fire was zeroing in on us, and it was coming in heavy. I couldn't tell how many there were.

"Incoming!" Moonwalker yelled as he dropped to the ground.

A loud explosion tore apart the foliage dangerously close to us. "Is this your idea of superior tactics?!" Aqua Shark shouted.

Iceman continued to unload short bursts from his .50 cal. "Their comms are down!" Moonwalker yelled.

"Good, now pour it on!" Iceman yelled.

Batlord screamed and collapsed to the muddy ground. Blood was seeping from his pores like beads of sweat and trickling from his eyes like tears.

"Thirty-four hit! He hit!" Islander shouted.

No, he wasn't shot. Something else was wrong with him. Batlord was still screaming, but now his whole body was beginning to twist and contort unnaturally until his bones broke and ripped through his flesh. It was too much to watch.

"Thirteen, we have a priority!" I shouted.

"Where's it coming from?" Iceman said, shooting a good twenty rounds at the enemy.

"Two-thirty at thirty degrees elevation!" Aqua Shark shouted, dumping an entire magazine at the target with his M-16.

A round embedded itself into my helmet. "Holy shit!" I rolled behind a tree. More rounds tore up the ground nearby. I was done taking chances. I cast stone skin and giant's toughness.

After adjusting my helmet so it wasn't in my eyes, I looked up where Aqua Shark was firing. Flying above the treetops was a black-robed man with a staff in his hand.

"Rounds ineffective!" Aqua Shark shouted.

"Roger that. Permission granted for open spell casting," Iceman said, pointing towards the mage. A small orb of ice and snow shot from his hand, leaving behind a thin blue trail in its wake.

With a wave of its staff, the mage caused Iceman's cold bolt to dissipate into nothing.

"Spell ineffective!" Iceman said. "Thirteen, what's the status on thirty-four?"

Turning his attention to the bloodied mess that was Batlord, Fire miraculously healed him with not so much as even speaking a word or waving a hand. Whatever that spell was, it was designed to kill slowly and painfully. "Combat ready!" Fire said.

Climbing to a knee, Batlord cast a fire-bolt at the mage, but it too dissipated into nothing. Batlord then fell to the ground and screamed in agony. More blood was seeping from his pores while his bones twisted and contorted. He was cursed, and none of us had the power to break it.

I cast regeneration on Batlord. It was a white formula life spell and very mana-draining. The effects of the curse ceased, but he wasn't healing. The two spells canceled each other, but he was at least stable now.

The heavy gunfire that once filled the air was now only sporadic. There was no one left to shoot at except the mage, but nothing seemed to hurt him. He was invincible, just like the first badguy I fought.

The mage spread his arms like he was conducting an orchestra. The ground beneath us began to shake and rumble. Trees began to splinter, sending lethal shards of wood in every direction, while the underbrush was slowly being ripped from the ground and tossed high into the air.

"What the hell is going on?!" Fire screamed. He was curled up in a ball, holding onto his helmet as exploding trees showered him with debris.

Iceman stood and pointed at the mage. "Target that mage soldiers and give him everything you've got!" he yelled.

With dirt, wood, and plant debris flying everywhere, Iceman cast cold bolt after cold bolt while unleashing a barrage of hot lead at the mage. Flames spewed out the end of his gun and turned the rain into vapor. It was like a scene straight out of a Rambo movie; there was no fear in Iceman's eyes.

It wasn't but a moment later that the trees began to uproot from the ground, leaving gaping holes in the muddy earth where the roots used to be. Everything within a hundred meters, from trees to bushes, was uprooted and flung far away. The crashing of the falling trees was deafening and drowned out the crackling thunderstorm above.

Without an ounce of cover, the rain struck me full force and drenched me more completely. Scrambling for the nearest crater, I rolled inside and searched the black sky for the mage. My adrenaline was pumping out of control.

As if things couldn't get worse, huge shards of ice twice the size of footballs began to fall from the sky with incredible velocity.

Guard was immediately struck in the back. The icicle and his ceramic plate exploded into a thousand pieces. Another shard shattered upon striking his helmet, which punched a hole through it and knocked him out.

The Batlord cast another firebolt and fired a continuous stream of heavy lead at the mage with his M-60, but nothing could hurt him.

Islander was then struck in the leg by an icicle, which violently spun him to the ground. Groaning loudly, he crawled towards the nearest pit, dragging his mangled leg behind him.

A dozen or so cracking rays of electricity raced toward Iceman from the fingers of the mage. Iceman tried to doge, but he couldn't. The continuous tendrils of lightning pulsed through his body, which caused him to collapse to the ground in a convulsive fit. Several shards of ice then struck him. The mud turned red.

Taking a deep breath to calm myself, I focused my mana into my M-4 and cast fire enchantment on it. It was a blue formula elemental spell that allowed me to imbue almost anything, preferably weapons, with intense fire. I could even cast it on my fists if I wanted.

I held the trigger and watched as my flaming rounds tore into the mage. His robe immediately caught fire, and his skin burned, but the bullets failed to pierce him.

The mage flailed his arms about frantically, trying to put out his robe. The electrifying spell shocking Iceman stopped. The dark mage was finally getting a taste of his own medicine.

A shard of ice slammed into the ground mere inches from my face, splashing me with mud.

After reloading a fresh box of one hundred rounds, I cast fire enchantment on Batlord and Aqua Shark's weapons and unloaded another barrage of fiery hell at the mage. "Hit him twelve and thirty-two; you've got fire!" I yelled into my transceiver.

Without hesitation, they dumped every round in their weapons at him, burning him alive.

I don't know if he was distracted by the pain or had run out of mana or what, but Iceman's cold bolt found its mark. The mage was killed instantly, torn to unrecognizable pieces by the sheer force of the spell.

The blizzard of ice suddenly stopped, and a calm filled the air. It was over.

"Gi' me a health check," Iceman mumbled loudly. He was staggering around, coughing, and spitting up blood, well beyond injury that any normal person could sustain. Three football-sized shards of ice were embedded in his body: one in his right shoulder, one in his lower back, and the other in his left leg. Blood was streaking down his face.

"Eleven clear," I said, rolling onto my back. Closing my eyes, I rested in my crater and let the rain wash the mud off my face. I laughed out loud.

"What art so funny?" Batlord said.

I smiled at him and shook my head. I missed the days of lying on the beach with Mary, soaking up the sun.

After Fire had healed anyone injured, we all checked in the clear. "Check your ammo and gear, and let's move out, men," Iceman said.

I climbed out of the crater and fell in line. "So, who the hell was that guy?" Fire said.

"He certainly wasn't an initiate," Aqua Shark said.

"That entire engagement lasted ninety-four seconds, and within that time, the mage demonstrated an incredible array of power," Iceman said. "So that's a good question."

"He art a mage as guessed, and in ten years, we too will possesseth such power," Guard said.

"So mon, what a mage doin' out here?" Islander said. "TSS ain't said nothin' 'bout na mage."

"Thee either protecteth something important or doth not want another Spain," Batlord said.

A few of us laughed.

Twenty minutes later, we were at the jungle's edge, one hundred meters from the base's perimeter.

Five wooden barracks were arranged perpendicular to the main gravel road, with a hospital and a chow hall across from them. The armory was to the west of the hospital, while north of it was the communications center and the headquarters building.

The base was secured with a triple coil of concertina wire around the perimeter and four wooden towers at the corners, with sand bunkers and trenches interspersed throughout. Between the base's perimeter and the tree line was a minefield.

"I've got four teams of three patrolling the perimeter and what has all the makings of a scouting party assembling near barrack one," Moonwalker said. "They're on high alert."

"Alright, what's the plan?" Fire said.

"Fire and Batlord, you'll post right here at the six o'clock position. This will give you a perfect killing field along the front of all the barracks and the main road. You're team white," Iceman said. "Guard and Islander, you'll take the nine o'clock position from here and, on my orders, drop white phos on those barracks. You're team blue."

Aqua Shark handed Guard his mortar launcher and a rucksack full of shells. "You sure you know how to aim this thing 'cause it's not a catapult?" he said.

"Better than thou," Guard said.

"Browny, Aqua Shark, you must breach the perimeter and infiltrate the comm center. Once inside, kill all quickly and quietly. Afterward, cut off their communications and await further orders. You're team red," Iceman said. "Moonwalker and I will strike the HQ in a similar fashion. However, our strikes must be simultaneous, so we wait for my signal to attack. We're team black."

"A passive alert on a base with over three hundred personnel behind some decent fortifications. Piece of cake," Aqua Shark said.

"At least they don't have armor or air support," Moonwalker said.

Aqua Shark smiled hesitantly.

"On my mark, teams blue and white take out those towers but do so quietly. One shot, one kill," Iceman said. "And remember men, we are not leaving until they are all dead. Any questions?"

"Doth thee have thy permission for open magic?" Guard said.

"No, only enhancements," Iceman said. "Anyone else?"

We all shook our heads. "Alright, teams white and blue, take your positions and get ready to cover us. Now move out, men."

Gathering their gear, Guard and Islander headed off for their position while Fire and Batlord set up a few meters from us. "Team red, your best angle of attack will be to creep behind the armory and the surrounding buildings here and enter the comm center from this window." Iceman drew our attack plan in the mud. "Our target is closest to the northern perimeter, so we will breach from here and take this route to the HQ."

"And watch out for those mines," Moonwalker said.

"That's right, and remember, if any team is compromised, then it's all teams go," Iceman said. "We are going to eat this place alive from the inside out."

"I hate fucking minefields," Aqua Shark said.

"Rely on your training; we'll rely on our noses," Moonwalker said.

"You'll what?" Aqua Shark said, frowning.

I raised an eyebrow. "What? You didn't know?" Moonwalker said. "We can smell your dirty ass a kilometer away."

"You didn't have to put it like that, man," Aqua Shark said, grinning.

A moment of silence passed. "You guys will do fine. We'll see you when it's over." Iceman patted me on the shoulder.

After thirty minutes or so to fix and alter the camouflage on our ghillie suits, we began the painstaking crawl through the minefield toward the base's perimeter.

Two hours later, we had traversed the tall grass field and cut our way through the concertina wire undetected.

"White-this is red. Are we clear to cross?" I whispered into my transceiver. There was a gravel road ahead of us with no cover.

"You're clear to cross," Fire said.

Jumping to our feet, we sprinted across the main gravel road and in between two warehouse-like structures. With my back up against the wall, I pulled out my Beretta 9mm and screwed on a LSS custom suppressor. It was specifically designed by Smartguy and constructed by Greyguy. It quite literally made my 9mm silent.

"Cover me," Aqua Shark whispered. He then raced across fifteen meters of open ground and disappeared behind a building. Peeking around the corner, he gave me the all-clear sign.

A few seconds later, I joined him. My heart was racing, and I couldn't help but feel excited. There were nearly three hundred badguys here, and as far as I was concerned, they all had the blood of my beloved on their hands, and for that, they were going to die.

I wiped the rain from my brow. It was coming down sideways in heavy sheets. Lightning lit up the sky, and thunder roared. It was a beautiful day.

We proceeded to our next checkpoint a dozen meters northwest of the armory. "Red, you've got a straggler approaching your six; he's coming along the building," Fire said.

I glanced at Aqua Shark, who nodded at me. Holstering my pistol, I drew my K-bar. I snuck along the building and posted up near the corner.

A split second later, a man in jungle fatigues walked past me. Throwing my arm over his neck, I covered his mouth and plunged my blade to the hilt in between his ribs under his armpit. I then quickly withdrew my knife, slid it across his throat, and lowered him to the ground quietly.

After wiping the blood off my k-bar, I sheathed it and pulled out my pistol.

"Clean kill. Good job," Aqua Shark whispered.

"Team black is in position. What's your status red?" Iceman said.

"Roger that black, we're moving into position," Aqua Shark said.

"Another scouting party is on the move and heading southeast," Fire said. "All teams, be advised that we now have sixteen hostiles outside the perimeter."

"Roger that, Blue," Iceman said.

"Ten meters. Cover me," Aqua Shark whispered.

Once he was in position, I ran to join him behind the comm center, my grenades bouncing on my chest. "Red is in position black," I said.

"Roger that red. Mission is go," Iceman said. "White and blue, take out those towers on my mark."

"Roger that black." Fire said.

"Roger," Guard said.

Aqua Shark pulled out a small mirror and held it to the window. "There are blinders, but I can see a single target with his back to us," he said. "Can you take him out?"

Nodding my head, I walked around him and knocked on the window. Aqua Shark's eyes got big. A second later, a hand split a few blinders, and two eyes peered through. I fired two silenced shots.

"He's down," I said. Sometimes, the best tactic is to pretend you're doing nothing wrong.

I used my K-bar to lift the window as quietly as possible. We then crawled inside the small office and took positions on either side of the door. I could hear numerous people talking on the other side.

Aqua Shark opened the door, and we rushed inside. I cast lightning reflexes to match Aqua Shark's speed. Everything slowed down.

Nine badguys were sitting behind some desks loaded with electronic equipment, and one was walking towards us with a clipboard in his hands. The look on his face was priceless.

A single round blew through his head as Aqua Shark squeezed the trigger. Four more silenced rounds of his found their mark into the chests of two more badguys, killing them instantly.

With only thirteen rounds left in my Beretta before reloading, I had to make them count. I put a single round into the head of the nearest comm specialist and two rounds into the one behind him. Blood splattered everywhere.

The office door to my left swung open, and a badguy came walking out. Turning, I put a bullet in his head and watched him slump to the ground. I then put two rounds into the two remaining specialists.

Everything got quiet. In less than two seconds, we had shot dead eleven badguys, twelve altogether. It was a good start.

"Red clear," I said into my transceiver.

"Black clear. White and blue, take out those towers and phos those barracks," Iceman said.

Smiling at Aqua Shark, I holstered my Beretta and put a few rounds into each computer with my M-4. The bullet-riddled equipment crackled with electricity.

"Towers three and four are down." Fire said.

"Towers one and two art down. All towers art downeth," Guard said. "Here cometh thy rain!"

The front double doors swung open, and two soldiers rushed inside. With a short burst from my M-4, I dropped both of them.

A loud explosion rattled the windows. To my right, I could see dozens of men rushing out of a burning barrack.

Breaking out a window, I knelt behind it and unleashed a hail of lead. I dropped five in a matter of seconds, and whoever I didn't, Fire and Batlord did it with their machine guns. They were mowing down everyone.

With so many soldiers running around, it was difficult to select an opportune target. Aqua Shark, however, wasn't and was firing round after round at whatever moved. He hit and killed nearly every target that he shot at. I was impressed with his skill.

Pulling out a fresh mag of armor-piercing rounds, I slapped it in and fired a short burst into the hip of a soldier. He fell to the ground and crawled behind the hospital.

A badguy peppered the wall I was kneeling behind. I fired back at him before he could duck behind the hospital's corner, but I missed.

More rounds ripped into the wall before me. We were taking fire from the armory, too. "Let's move out!" I yelled.

Another explosion rattled the windows as a shell blew apart another barrack. "Roger," Aqua Shark said.

We ran back into the office and climbed out the window. I cast another power spell, haste on the both of us. We could now run twice as fast.

Sporadic gunfire, both light and heavy, filled the air. My ears were starting to ring.

I ran behind a building and posted up along its corner. Seventy meters across the base and near the chow hall was a jeep. Three soldiers were climbing into it while a fourth readied the .50 cal.

I pulled the trigger of my under-barrel M203 grenade launcher and watched as the grenade struck the side of the jeep and exploded. The four men were killed instantly, and falling from the sky were chunks of metal and body parts.

Bullets began to punch into the building next to me, one of which grazed my shoulder. Kneeling behind a sandbag bunker were two soldiers armed with AKs. With a ten-round burst, I blew off both of their heads. Their bloody helmets were left spinning in the mud. Everything was a blur of motion, like the movie Matrix. I felt invincible.

Another mortar exploded in the near distance. "Let's move eleven, follow me," Aqua Shark said as he motioned for me to follow him.

We raced across some open ground toward a small two-story concrete building that, oddly enough, had no windows. Aqua Shark posted up next to the door. "Two just went inside. We're going in after them," he said.

Nodding my head, I cast ogre's strength, walked around him, and kicked in the heavy steel door. Aqua Shark rushed inside and fired two shots. I quickly followed,

There was a simple wooden desk near the end of the hallway that turned right and a steel door just behind the desk to the left. A soldier lay dead on the floor with two bullet holes in his back.

Stopping at the end of the hallway, I looked around the corner. Five meters away was a wooden door on the right and a steel door above that one with a metal staircase leading to it. "Hold," Aqua Shark said. He was training his gun on the door to our left.

The first-floor door down the hallway opened, and a soldier peeked through the doorway. I riddled his chest and shoulder with a short burst that dropped him.

Rushing towards the door, I peered inside and saw two badguys. One was standing behind a desk, and the other was raising his gun at me. Pulling a frag grenade off my chest, I tossed it inside the windowless room and slammed the door shut.

It seemed like an eternity while I waited for the grenade to go off, and once it did, I stormed inside while reloading a fresh mag.

Thin smoke enveloped the room, and debris was scattered across the bloody floor. One badguy was dead, and the other was severely maimed. Walking behind the shredded desk, I put a single round into the maimed badguy's chest, finishing him off. "Clear!" I shouted.

"I can't get these other doors open. They're locked."

After searching for the badguy I had shot, I found a large bronze key. "This might help," I said, tossing him the key.

"You ready?"

"Ready."

Aqua Shark unlocked and opened the first-floor metal door. I rushed inside but quickly stopped dead in my tracks. My fiery hate for Gorasavice and his army burned a little hotter.

Over a dozen young girls were huddling together on thin blankets.

"Holy-" Aqua Shark said.

"Go check the other room," I said. The girls stared at me; some were sobbing. Slinging my M-4 over my shoulder, I removed my helmet and set it down. "United States Special Forces, everything is going to be okay," I said. "We're here to take you home."

Still, no one said a word. They just continued to stare at me. "We have ten more upstairs," Aqua Shark said over the transceiver.

"Thirty-one, this is eleven," I said. "We've got twenty-three children in a concrete structure about fifty meters due east of the comm center. What are your orders?"

"Leave them put, there's still resistance out here, and we need your guns," Iceman said. "Team white will cover the building."

"Roger that thirty-one. We're moving out," I said. "Let's get all the kids in this room."

"You got it," Aqua Shark said.

Thirty long and precious seconds later, we had herded the other kids inside the room. "You ready?" Aqua Shark said.

"One moment." I motioned for the oldest girl to come to me. "What's your name?"

Cautiously, the long, brown-haired girl walked over to me. "Alencia," she said with a thick Hispanic accent while staring at the ground.

"That's a very lovely name, Alencia," I said, taking a knee. She half-smiled. "My name is Scott, though my friends call me Browny. You know, like the Brownie Scout." She snickered softly, as did some of the others. "How old are you, Alencia?"

"Sixteen," she said.

"Sixteen, holy cow!" I said. "You're older than me!" She and the other girls laughed. I un-holstered my pistol and held it in front of her. Everyone got quiet again. "Do you know what this is?" I said. Alencia nodded. "Now listen very, very carefully, okay? You are going to be these girls' protector. If anyone opens that door without knocking twice, twice, you aim this at them and pull back on the trigger. Understand, Alencia?"

"Yes," she whispered. I handed her the gun. "Please don't leave."

I put my hand on her shoulder. "I promise I'll be back, Alencia. I promise." Picking up and strapping on my helmet, I left the room and locked the door.

We then moved down the hallway and took positions on either side of the front doorway. To my three o'clock, about thirty-five meters were four soldiers. They were being pinned down behind a jeep by some pretty heavy gunfire. It had to be Fire and Batlord.

Reloading my grenade launcher, I aimed at the jeep and fired. With a loud boom, the grenade exploded and wrecked the jeep beyond repair. The four soldiers lay dead in the mud.

Several rounds tore into the doorway. Aqua Shark fell to the ground. "Aqua Shark!" I shouted, ducking out of the doorway.

"I'm good!" he said, giving me thumbs up.

I poked my head around the doorway as more rounds impacted the wall. A badguy was crouching behind a window inside a building. Four others were spraying our position with bullets from around the building's corner.

I fired a short burst at the man behind the window, but my rounds impacted low. Aqua Sharks, however, were not. The badguy disappeared from view. Blood splattered the windowpane.

Aqua Shark fired one rapid burst after another at the other four, dropping three. I shot the last one twice in the chest.

"Let's move," Aqua Shark said.

The pouring rain splashed across my face as we sprinted from cover to cover towards the southern end of the base. Machine gun fire was a constant noise while black smoke from burning buildings filled the air.

Slowly, we crept in between two buildings, checking windows and our surroundings for any hostiles. Twenty meters up ahead and a little to our left was another clearing and a building.

Several rounds tore across Aqua Shark's chest. He stumbled against the wall as more rounds impacted him.

Squeezing the trigger of my M-4, I fired over a dozen rounds into the window of the building ahead where the gunfire was coming from.

Falling to the ground, Aqua Shark rolled up against the building to our left. I continued to unload at the window until my mag ran dry. "Talk to me!" I yelled.

I felt the hard impact of bullets striking my body, and I collapsed. Sitting back up, I pressed my back against the wall and pulled a grenade off my chest. Leaning forward, I tossed the grenade at the window, but it landed a good seven meters shy. My right arm was bleeding.

Crawling around me, Aqua Shark fired a few short bursts at the enemy. The grenade then blew, showering us with mud. "Target is down," he said, standing up. "You going to be alright?" He helped me to my feet.

"Yeah."

"Congratulations. You just earned yourself a purple heart."

I had been shot in my right shoulder, but it was more than that. My breathing was labored.

A jeep packed with five badguys screeched to a skidding halt about forty meters ahead.

The man behind the .50 cal cranked it towards us while the others jumped out and took cover behind their jeep. We were virtually sitting ducks in between these two buildings.

"Shit!" Aqua Shark said. He then fired a dozen rounds at the gunner, but they ricocheted off the gun shield. "Run!"

We sprinted towards the building up ahead, where the one who had shot at us was hiding. Reloading on the run, I strafed the jeep, hitting one in the shoulder.

Bullets whizzed behind us and ripped into the ground at our feet. We crossed twenty meters of open ground in just over a second and slid prone behind the building. The .50 cal then roared to life. Massive bullets punched through the building's thin wooden walls and showered us with splinters.

I cast giant's toughness and stone skin and felt, even more, mana drain from my body. I was running dangerously low.

Terrified, I lay down in the fetal position behind Aqua Shark while the fifty tore up our position. Mud and wood splinters covered us. All I could hear was my heart beating in my ears.

On the other hand, Aqua Shark was just lying there chewing on some gum calmly. Everything went quiet. Climbing to a knee, Aqua Shark posted up behind what remained of the corner of the building. "You good buddy?" he said, brushing himself off.

I stood up and looked myself over. "Y-Yeah, I th-think so," I said.

"It's clear," Aqua Shark said. He walked towards the jeep.

Iceman stood beside it with his modified Barret M207 .50 sniper rifle in hand. His M2 .50 cal. was gone. "It looked like you guys could use some help," he said. All the badguys were dead.

My breathing was becoming more labored, and I was starting to wheeze. "Th-Thanks."

"You've been hit in the lung. We'll get thirteen to heal you up here." Iceman said.

"Really? I thought you were shot in the shoulder?" Aqua Shark said.

With caution, Iceman lifted my right arm. There was a small hole in my Kevlar below my armpit. "And this is why Smartguy needs to hurry it up on that armor of his," he said.

"Ooo, that is serious," Aqua Shark said. "Why didn't you tell me?"

"Eh, it's j-just a flesh wound," I said.

Iceman chuckled. "Come on, there's only a few stragglers left," he said, slapping a new mag into his gun.

Two minutes later, the base, or whatever was left of it, was secure. Nearly every building had been burned to the ground, and every vehicle was destroyed. Dead bodies lay everywhere while streams of blood ran through the mud. We had killed every last soldier, three hundred and fifteen total, all in less than four minutes. Only three of us had been injured, including myself, but Fire healed us to perfect health. It was a flawless mission.

Iceman slammed a kilo of cocaine on the hood of a wrecked jeep. "Based on everything we have gathered so far, I'd say these Badguys are involved in the drug trade," he said.

Fire dumped out a bag of cell phones next to the cocaine. "And Brazil."

"Well, there is a demand for children, and even more so for drugs, and if the Badguys are taking out everyone, then someone has to supply the demand," Moonwalker said.

"You're right, and it's smart," Iceman said. "These Badguys do know what they're doing."

"Calignosity-he art wise beyond any mere mortal," Guard said. Inspector nodded.

"Do you guys ever think that the TSS will ever get their shit straight and supply us with some accurate Intel?" Aqua Shark said.

Islander chuckled. "No way, mon," he said.

The rain was still coming down in sheets. "I'm going to get the girls," I said.

"Someone clear these bodies. We've got little ones who don't need to see this," Iceman said.

After sprinting to the concrete building and walking down his hallway, I knocked twice on the steel door. I then unlocked and opened the door and stepped inside.

Alencia dropped my gun and rushed to embrace me in her arms. "Browny, you came back!" she cried out.

Several other girls swarmed and hugged me. "Are we going home now?" a girl said as she looked up at me with her blue eyes.

I rested my hand on her head and held Alencia tight. "You're going home now," I said. "You're going home."

We had plans to have Merlin teleport us out of there, but with twenty-three kids, we decided upon a more conventional evacuation. We called LS squad one, who then called in some pretty heavy favors with their military contacts to get us out of there, the same ones who supplied us with the Intel on the base. Of course, the LSS had to hack the necessary United States bases to complete the electronic trail and authorization, but that was the easy part for them.

Four hours later, a US army Chinook helicopter escorted by two attack Cobras picked us up and dropped us off at a Brazilian airbase nearby. The brass at the airbase didn't even check our authorization or IDs once they saw the kids. They decided to chalk up the militia base as a loss and sweep the program under the rug for obvious political reasons.

I don't know how Smartguy and company managed to pull all this off, but I guess that's why they were assigned to the logistical squad. They were good at pulling strings.

Once back in the States, the LSS worked around the clock for two weeks to find the missing kids' parents. If that wasn't possible, or they were orphans, they'd send them to a well-established adoption agency in their home country.

It was a good and clean op, and rescuing those kids was reward enough. But I couldn't

help to think that Gorasavice and the badguys had a more sinister motive behind the girls kidnapping other than exploitation.

CHAPTER TWENTY-TWO

"**Y**ou know, I think this is the most rewarding part of our job," Fire said.

"It sure is, and today is your time to shine," Big Blue said.

"Yeah, and I can't believe you shine every day in those disgusting blue coveralls," I said.

"Ouch, good one, buddy guts," Octane said.

Big Blue stared out the window and nodded. "Alright, I got ya number."

We all laughed. "We're almost there, sirs," our driver said.

We were heading to St. Jude Children's Hospital in Seattle, Washington, to donate a check for ten million dollars. Usually, the LSS handled the publicity stunts, but occasionally, guys like Fire would show up to help. I had to tag along because I was the president of the Goodguys charity organization, and this was our first major public donation. I didn't mind being the face of our group, but it wasn't me.

The cameras started flashing once we pulled into the parking lot and exited the limo. Photographers and news reporters were everywhere. "Welcome to St. Judes, Scott. I am Dr. Jenkins, CEO," he said, shaking my hand. "This is such a big day for us, so please, let me lead you inside."

For the next twenty long minutes, Dr. Jenkins led the reporters and us around the hospital, telling us what the money would be used for. I wasn't very entertained. Perhaps because I just wasn't in the mood for publicity today. He then led us into a large chow hall decorated with banners and pictures drawn by the kids. The room was packed full of hospital staff, reporters, and children, all there to thank us.

After a brief handing over of the check ceremony, Dr. Jenkins gave a short speech and invited the press to ask us some questions. "What's the Goodguys mission statement, if you have one?" a woman said.

"To protect the world," I said.

The woman looked confused. My friends smiled.

"But you're a charity organization," a reporter said. "What are you protecting the world from?"

I grinned widely and tried to contain my laughter. "Diseases, poverty, and the monsters in the closet." Chuckles filled the room.

"You have a great sense of humor, Scott, but can you tell us what spurned you to found the Goodguys Charity Organization; after all, you are the Pride middle-weight champion of the world?"

"I needed something to do with all the money I'm earning." More people chuckled.

"Do you donate to hospitals only?" a man said.

"No, we donate to any organization that helps others," I said. "And once we become more established, we'll expand our outreach programs."

"Who are your major sponsors or donors?" a woman said.

I looked at Octane. "The Los Angeles and New York fire departments, Phoenix PD, Boeing, Chrysler, and a host of others," Octane said. "Our website has an exhaustive list of all who donate unless they wish to remain anonymous, of course."

"What other projects does your charity wish to accomplish?" a woman said.

"We plan on starting a cash-for-cures sports camp in Phoenix this October, and in the following months, we'll be opening a Goodguys club right here in Seattle," Octane said.

"This question is directed at you, Scott, and I do apologize in advance if it seems out of place," another reporter said. "How have you been coping with the loss of your late fiance? Do you blame yourself for her death?"

I sighed. There's not a day that goes by I don't think about her.

"Wow, that's really something, Goodguys," Dr. Jenkins said. "And to further show our appreciation-" he gestured to three children. "We at St. Judes present you this."

A boy handed me a plaque. The cameras began to flash. "This is from all of us. Thank you, mister," he said.

"Does this mean we'll get better now," a bald girl said.

Fire picked her up. "Do you believe in miracles," he whispered in her ear.

"Uh-huh."

"Then, yes, it does."

Mana charged the air.

"So what art this about, Browny?" Hook said. The steel ring in his left eyebrow glistened in the early rays of dawn.

"Space Police and his tactical squad believe they've stumbled across a badguy HQ," Big Red said.

"Thank ya, Browny," Hook said.

Big Red patted Hook on the back. "Yup."

"So, who are we waiting for? Merlin?" Big Blue said.

"And SDS three," Big Red said. "Merlin went to get them. They'll be here any minute now." Merlin and the four SDS three members appeared out of thin air. "And speaking of."

"Goodguys, can I have your attention, please," Inspector said. Everyone quieted down. "Today is August 20, 2000. This is an emergency meeting, and without further delay, here's Space Police."

"Morning, fellas; how are all of you doing?" Space Police said.

"Get to it, sucker!" Whiteguy yelled.

Some of us chuckled. "Alright, dude! Chill!" Space Police said. "Three days ago, my TS squad and I followed a semi-truck to a well-camouflaged blast door built on some mountains' side. Those mountains." He pointed to the mountains that encircled us. "So far as we know, there is only one way in and one way out, aside from a few inaccessible ventilation shafts."

"Is this like a badguy headquarters or something?" Whiteguy said.

"We don't know," Space Police said.

"And all this time, they've been right under our noses, and no one noticed until now, eh?" Aqua said.

"According to Merlin, this facility is warded against clairvoyant spells," Ice 8 said. His voice was deep. "It's a miracle we even found the road leading to it."

"Art there any higheth value targets or captains within?" Bestguard said.

Space Police shook his head. "We don't know."

"Then what the hell do you know?!" Doubles said

"That's the problem, we don't," Iceman said. "So in one hour from now, we'll be striking that place. Now gear up, men."

"We're all going?" Pudgy said, his eyes widening.

"Yes, Pudgy, you finally get to kill some Badguys," Iceman said.

"Instead of stinking up the shop all day," Greyguy said.

"All squad leaders, please meet in Merlin's tent," Inspector said.

Everyone began scrambling for their gear.

"Hey, Browny," Pudgy said, looking around. "Can I have a moment?"

"Yeah, what's up?"

"Do you think I could hang around you when we get inside?" he said.

All the leaders had already walked inside Merlin's tent. "Sure, Pudgy."

"Thanks." He looked around some more. "I just can't fight well with my hands, and I don't-"

I patted him on the shoulder. "I'll be right by your side, don't worry."

He smiled. "Thanks."

I headed inside Merlin's tent.

"How nice of thee to show up, buddy guts," Pirate said.

"Goodguys," I said, nodding.

"This is what we were thinking, Browny. Greyguy will sneak along the mountainside, loop the only camera that overlooks the road, and blast door. We'll then pull up to the door in a semi-truck and storm inside after Greyguy hot wires the blast door open," Iceman said. "What do you think?"

"What about the magical methods of detecting us?" I said.

"Merlin's got that covered," Ice 8 said. "And if we can't bypass the security of the door, he'll open the door the old-fashioned way."

"If the shit hits the fan, your squad will be our breakwater, the last in line," Iceman said.

"And Merlin?" I said.

"Watching our six at all times," Iceman said.

"Then that sounds like a plan," I said.

"All righty then. Let's go kill some Badguys," Inspector said.

Riding in the back of a semi-trailer with no seats, lighting, or air-conditioning with twenty-seven other heavily armed guys for over an hour was not very comfortable. I should have pulled rank and sat in the cab with Pudgy.

"Camera looped," Greyguy said over my transceiver.

"Roger that," Iceman said. "Lock and load men, ETA thirty seconds."

"Hoo-rah, let's get 'em boys!" Aqua Shark yelled.

"Hell yeah!" Octane shouted.

A few seconds later, the semi-truck rolled to a stop. The large double doors swung open, filling the trailer with sunlight.

"Let's move out, boys!" Iceman shouted, jumping out of the trailer.

I followed behind him and ran towards the opening blast door with my squad. I cast lightning reflexes, stone skin, and giant's toughness and rushed into the tunnel.

It was a twenty-five meter long, two-lane road and was well-lit. Two men dressed in forest green fatigues with plate carriers stood near the end. Two suppressed gunshots rang out behind me as the two guards reached for their guns. Both of their heads exploded in a red mist. Ice 8 and Space Police ran past me, the barrel of their Barret M107 .50 cals still smoking.

The tunnel led to a very large, two-story receiving bay packed with crates and boxes lining the walls on high shelves. There were three ground-level, oversized hallways, one in the far left and right corners and one in the lower right corner of the bay. The second story mirrored the first in every way, except there were numerous doors here and there, and a wide balcony ran around the entire perimeter. A stairway led to the second floor, and a few elevators near the far-right hallway.

Surprisingly, only a dozen or so badguys were walking around. Some were driving forklifts while others carried boxes of whatever. We had caught them with their pants down.

"SDS one, hold the bay. SDS two and four, and TSS one take a hallway a piece on the second floor," Iceman said over the transceiver. "TSS two take the lower right hall. LSS one, the upper right."

The badguys in the bay began to drop as automatic gunfire filled the air. Goodguys dressed in full tactical gear raced towards their objectives with precise movements. I was proud of what we had become, a well-tuned spec ops platoon, but torn over what we were accomplishing. I hope Gorasavice is here.

Jumping, Inspector grabbed a hold of the balcony and quickly climbed over the railing.

Ice 8 and Space Police followed suit. The rest of their squad members had to use the stairway, except for Basil, who cast jump.

I motioned to my squad members to take cover and scan the second-floor doors for any hostiles. "LS eleven, please send me LS fourteen," I said. "SD twelve is replacing him."

"Roger that SD eleven. LS fourteen is on his way," Smartguy said.

I nodded at Guard, who then took off towards the upper right hall to join LSS.

Kicking open a door, Inspector fired several shots from his .50 cal sniper rifle. "Clear!" he yelled.

A door several meters to Inspectors right opened, and a badguy stuck his pistol out. Fire wasted no time and riddled the metal door with depleted uranium rounds. The badguy slumped to the ground. Inspector gave Fire a thumbs up.

Pudgy ran up to me and saluted. "LS fourteen reporting for duty, sir," he said.

I smiled and patted his shoulder. "Watch the doors and elevators," I said.

A minute later, SDS two and four and TSS one had cleared all twelve rooms on the second floor and had gone down their separate halls. Automatic gunfire was now a constant noise in all directions.

"This is SD twenty-one; we're encountering heavy magical resistance!" Ice 8 yelled over the transceiver. "We're requesting immediate backup!"

A massive explosion rocked the hallway that Ice 8's squad had run down. Smoke billowed from out the hall and began to fill the bay.

"Roger that SD twenty-one, I'm sending two your way," I said. "SD thirteen and fourteen move out."

Moonwalker and Fire ran up the stairs and down the hall. "This is SD forty-one. We're encountering heavy resistance!" Inspector shouted. "We're heading your way, SDS one!"

Bullets ricocheted off the balcony railing in my direction. Buccaneer hobbled out of the second-story lower right hallway and fell. Crawling around the corner, he sat against the wall. A moment later, Doubles and Bestguard limped out of the hall and took cover around the corner.

This op was not going according to our previous ops. Something wasn't right.

"Roger that SD forty-one. I'm heading your way." I said. "Stay here and watch our flank LS fourteen."

"Yes, sir," Pudgy said.

Running towards the balcony, I cast jump and flew over the railing. I landed smoothly on the second-floor balcony and immediately began to spray lead down the hallway. I could see countless heavily armed and armored badguys ducking and weaving behind desks and cabinets in the large room at the end of the hall. They were well-trained and just as fast as we were. They were all initiates.

Pulling a grenade off his chest, Inspector hurled it down the hall and into the room. He then pulled off another and tossed it, too.

Buccaneer, Bestguard, and Double's wounds were instantly healed.

Opening a door to my right, I stepped into a small room and took cover behind the doorway. Bullets punched through the steel door behind me, dangerously close to hitting my head.

Taking aim through my scope, I fired a short burst of depleted uranium rounds into the chest of a badguy who was taking cover behind a desk. His ceramic-plated Kevlar exploded, and he fell to the ground. The grenades that Inspector had thrown then exploded, tearing up everything in the room.

"Cover us, SD eleven!" Inspector yelled.

I held down the trigger of my M-4 and sprayed everything in the room that I could see with hot lead. Inspector and his squad sprinted down the hall and took a left inside the room. Heavy gunfire mixed with screams echoed down the hall.

"This is S-SD t-twenty-one! We've encountered G-Ghost!" Ice 8 yelled. "We're h-heading your way SDS one."

Ice 8 emerged from the hall across from me. He was carrying Hook on his shoulder and unleashing lightning bolt after lightning bolt down the hallway. Following right behind him was Moonwalker. He was carrying Aqua and Fire while Basil supplied covering fire with his M249b machine gun.

"This is LS eleven; we've encountered Goresavice and his captains!" Smartguy said. "We're heading your way, SDS one!"

The knot in my stomach tightened while the hatred within me stirred to life. A smile crept across my face.

"This is SD thirty-one ordering a full retreat! I repeat, full retreat!" Iceman yelled over the transceiver. "SDS one, cover our asses!"

Smartguy and his squad came running out of the hallway. Goresavice and his captains were walking after them.

Steadying his stance, Pudgy raised his M-16A4 and emptied his entire magazine into Goresavice and his captains. The rounds cut up their armored fatigues before falling harmlessly to the ground.

Over a dozen heavily armed initiates ran out of the hall and fired at Pudgy and Smartguy's retreating squad. Not one of them had cover from the incoming fire, and all of them should have been killed, but the rounds bounced off them.

It wasn't a protection spell; the rounds would have at least damaged their armor. It was something else. Walking into view out of the tunnel was Merlin. He was dressed in his usual blue robe and was pointing his wand at the badguys. Six of them collapsed to the floor, dead.

Flying out of the hallway across from me was a wispy shadow with piercing black eyes. It shot four crackling rays of dark energy at Merlin. Absorbing two of the rays with his wand, Merlin reflected the other two back at it, but Ghost absorbed them as well.

Casting fire enchantment on my M-4, I emptied the rest of my mag into the shadow. Glowing embers appeared within its body where my rounds had passed through, but it appeared unharmed.

An initiate drew a knife and charged Pudgy. Scrambling to reload his weapon, Pudgy dropped his magazine.

Running out from behind the doorway, I cast a jump and flew over the railing towards the initiate. He saw me out of the corner of his eye and went to raise his knife, but he was too late.

Drawing my katana, I cleanly severed his head and landed on my feet. The soldier's body slid to a stop at Pudgy's feet, spraying him with blood.

More initiates poured into the loading bay from the halls. Four of them attached bayonets to their assault rifles and charged me.

Several bullets ripped into my right leg and up my body, but I didn't even stumble. My armor and spells protected me, but only partially. I could feel a warm liquid trickling down my leg. "Run Pudgy!" I yelled.

Pudgy ran.

The first initiate stabbed at me, but I deflected his blow and stepped into him. My elbow slammed into his chin, but it didn't have the desired effect that I was looking for. He must have been sustaining giant's toughness.

I visualized the formula for ogre's strength and felt even more raw power flood my body.

Spinning around the first initiate, I chopped at the back of his neck with my sword, severing his head. Following through with my motion, I kicked the second initiate in the side with hammer hands while I deflected his knife attack. The spell's power blew his ceramic-plated Kevlar and most of his body to pieces. Blood splashed everywhere as his guts splattered on the floor.

Twisting to my left to avoid another attack, I slipped my blade past an initiate's defenses and pierced him through the stomach.

Withdrawing my blade, I quickly spun around and opened the neck of the initiate behind me. He collapsed to the ground in a pool of blood.

Our spells effectively canceled each other out, and clearly, my ninjutsu training was superior. I felt the impact of more bullets riddling my body.

Goresavice smiled at me.

Mopguy charged me with his metal bo staff in hand.

I cast fire enchantment on my katana and deflected his downward attack at my head. I then slashed at his left leg, but he deflected my sword and countered with the opposite end of his staff, but he was too close to me. I caught his staff under my arm and tossed him over my hip and onto the ground. I then stabbed him in the chest and held my blade in him.

Mopguy groaned loudly through gritted teeth as the fire from my blade consumed his body. His Kevlar armored fatigues were starting to melt, and his skin was bubbling.

"Let's go, Browny!" Moonwalker shouted, waving for me to come.

Doubles jumped off the balcony and raced over to me. He had a knife in his hand while his assault rifle was slung over his back. Gunguy casually walked toward him.

Readying himself in his traditional Muay Tai stance, Doubles closed with Gunguy and threw a few jabs to back him off. Unphased, Gunguy absorbed Double's jabs with his arms and threw an inside leg kick that connected with Double's right leg.

Doubles slashed at Gunguys neck, but he was too close, and being overextended, Gunguy countered by wrapping Doubles knife-wielding arm in his and threw him to the ground. The knife skittered across the ground.

Kipping to his feet, Doubles checked Gunguys leg kick and threw one of his own. It landed almost cleanly with Gunguys temple, which caused him to stumble off-balance. Doubles pressed forward with a barrage of fists, most of which landed on Gunguys face, who reeled from the attack.

"Browny!" Aqua yelled, spraying bullets everywhere.

By now, most of the Goodguys were running down the tunnel. Only a few stayed back to suppress the Badguys with gunfire.

Breaking off his magical combat with Ghost, Merlin ran down the tunnel.

Ripping my katana out of Mopguy, I pointed it at Goresavice and charged him. There were dozens upon dozens of flattened slugs at Doubles and my feet. Thank you, Merlin.

Several initiates charged me with knives and bayonets in hand. More bullets pancaked on my body and scattered across the floor.

Drawing a throwing knife, I threw it into the neck of an initiate while deflecting another badguys upward thrust at my belly.

Spinning around my attacker, I hurled another knife into the neck of yet another initiate. I then slashed at the hamstrings of my attacker. Both collapsed to the ground, squirting blood.

More initiates swarmed me as Goresavice and his other captains walked down the hall and disappeared from my view.

There were too many, and my window of escape was narrowing.

Blocking an initiate's bayonet attack, I slashed at his inner thigh, severing his femoral artery. Doubles and I ran for the tunnel. Bullets flattened against my body and skittered across the floor at my feet.

Popping around the tunnel's corner, Striper waved me over and fired one round from his modified AE Desert Eagle. The ice-enchanted bullet streaked blue through the air and tore through Ghost's head.

With a loud, ear-piercing shriek, the shadow blinked in and out of existence as a black gas spewed from its wound. As more and more black gas leaked into the air, Ghost got smaller and smaller until it disappeared into nothingness.

Glancing around with wide eyes like he had done something wrong, Striper ran down the tunnel. I followed behind him, and once the last of my squad had exited the tunnel, we were teleported back to the desert by the plateau.

"Striper shot Ghost!" Moonwalker shouted. "It's dead!"

"He shot him in the head!" Pudgy said.

"He wha?!" Islander said.

"Heck, ya Striper! Way to go, man!" Kid said, jumping on Striper's back.

Pirate and Guard high-fived. "Cannot it not get bettereth?" Guard shouted.

"So tell us, Striper, how did you do it?" Doubles said, sticking an imaginary mic in his face. "How does it feel to be a hero?"

"Well, I-" Striper said.

"And don't forget Browny; he kicked the crap out of countless initiates and a captain," Iceman said, patting me on the back. "And Doubles, good job, man!" Doubles smiled at me.

"And his textbook suppressive fire," Inspector said.

"Thou certainly did. Thou art saveth our booties," Buccaneer said.

I wiped the blood off my katana and sheathed it.

"So, how many did we kill? Because I know that I got three," Whiteguy said.

"I killed sixteen and maimed one," Greyguy said.

"I'd say close to a hundred dead and about half that number injured," Iceman said. "But the important thing is that Striper killed Ghost."

"Uh-huh, that's right!" Big Blue said. Sweat was beading off his bald black head.

"And judging by today's victory and Smartguys reports, I'm more than convinced that we are dealing crushing blows to Goresavice army," Octane said.

"At least someone reads my reports," Smartguy said.

"No, I'd say we are winning this war hands down," Greyguy said.

"Absolutely, man," Police said, throwing an arm around my shoulders.

"Arrg, dar ship be a sinkin' matey!" Hook shouted.

I slinked out from under Police's arm and began to remove my gear. Everyone was in an uproar over what we accomplished, and what that was, I don't know. Sure, Striper killed Ghost, maybe, but we left Goresavice and his captains alive, not to mention countless initiates. And for the life of me, I couldn't figure out why we retreated. We could have finished it right there. I could have killed Goresavice.

But maybe we let them live because we were taking so many casualties. After all, Hook, Fire, Aqua, and Islander were all killed in action, but I doubt anyone noticed. I'm sure they didn't even notice themselves. I guess that's why everyone is so excited. We're playing a video game with unlimited lives. We're invincible.

"Alright, guys, quiet down," Inspector said. "Merlin has the floor."

It took a few moments, but once everyone had quieted down, Merlin floated above us.

"You have done well, my friends. Yes, you have, but we are far from victory. To edge closer, Bazooka, Big Blue, Islander, and Guard, you will all be journeying with me into the Dark Zone." Merlin said. "Now prepare yourselves for tomorrow; you will be tempered in the flames of hell."

It suddenly got very quiet. "What is the length of time that we should prepare for?" Bazooka said.

"Up to five months," Merlin said.

A few Goodguys gasped. "Ya mon, is this like something that we all goin' to do or can like someone else, ya know-take me place?" Islander glanced at the ground. "It no fun dyin' mon. It ain't no fun."

"Is this something that we all must do?" Striper said.

Merlin glanced at me. "Yes."

It was about time we started to do something.

CHAPTER TWENTY-THREE

"**D**id you guys hear what happened to Fire?" Police said.

"Yeah, he told me all about it," I said.

"I just can't believe that he died," Police said. "Again."

"He'd be the fifth one to die down there since we started going down there," Doubles said. "And really, it's a miracle that any of Fire's group survived."

"It's like a fucking nightmare down there," Police said.

"Exactly what our SD ops are becoming," I said. "Basil was killed last month by an RPG."

"At least he died quickly," Police said. "Big Red was eaten alive, and literally."

"Yeah, I'm not going down. I'm not spending two to five months crawling around in small, cramped tunnels, getting torn up by monsters at every twist and turn," Doubles said, rolling up the car window. "I'm cool."

I chuckled softly.

"You think I'm joking," Doubles said. "Pudgy hasn't gotten a peaceful night's sleep since he went back down there, and that's been nearly two years ago."

We all laughed but quickly quieted down. Janestown loomed into view as we sped down the highway. Thick black clouds blotted out the sun while a steady but light rain fell. "You know, man, there's a little truth in what Big Blue said a while ago. I can't sleep either."

"I know how you feel." Police said, staring out the window.

"They can just come right through your walls or vents or just appear out of thin air," Doubles said. "I'm talking about ghosts or, worse yet, demons. I mean, where do these things come from?! I know they come from Ethereal, but where or even how do they cross into our world? I'm just stressed out, man. Every little noise I hear, I jump up and cast my spells, but I know that even with them, I'm as good as dead. I even get jumpy to weird noises in broad daylight. This shit is fucking me up, man. It's fucking me up. That's why I can't go down there. Not again."

Police nodded his head.

"Yeah, I know, but I understand Merlin's reasoning," I said. "It's something that we all must go through."

"That's great, but I'm with Doubles on this one," Police said.

"Oh yeah, well, I'm betting you two are next," I said.

Doubles and Police glanced at each other. "We probably are." Doubles said.

Once we pulled into my mom's driveway, I jumped out of the SUV and headed for the front door. But before I could knock, my Mom opened it and wrapped her arms around me. "Scott!" she cried out. "Oh, honey, it's been such a long time since you've visited!"

"I'm sorry. I've just been so busy lately," I said.

"Don't apologize, Mr. President. You have so much on your shoulders, " Mom said, kissing me. And you haven't changed a bit."

I was wearing blue jeans, a black T-shirt, and brown boots. My hair was still short and wavy, and I was clean-shaven. She was right; I haven't changed.

"Well, come on in, guys. Dinner is ready to be served, " Mom said, hugging Doubles and Police.

After washing up, we sat at the table and began to eat. "This is pretty good, Mom," Doubles said.

"Thank you, and you know, I think it's so wonderful that the three of you are still friends after all these years," she said.

"We're more like brothers now," Police said.

"So honey, are they going to put anyone worth his salt up against you next?"

"We'll see next month," I said.

"He's seventy, and oh, Mom. What do you think?" Doubles said.

"I still think he's my little baby," Mom said, rubbing my back.

"Thanks, Doubles," I said.

"Doubles?" Mom said, giving me a funny look.

"Yeah, that's the nickname we gave him when he started working at the Double Deuce bar," I said.

"That's pretty funny." Mom said.

"But don't worry, I've cleaned up my act since those days," Doubles said. He was trying to cover the grin on his face with his napkin.

The kitchen window rattled loudly. Police glanced at me.

"Oh, it's just the wind and rain, boys," Mom said.

"Yeah," Doubles said, clenching his teeth.

"And the Goodguys was a much better career choice," Mom said. "So, how's that going for you?"

"Great, and we just opened up two more cash-for-cures camps, one in Paris and the other in London," Doubles said.

"Wow, that's wonderful." Mom said.

"And we'll open a Goodguys club in Chicago next week. It's our seventh across the states," Police said.

Mom smiled, continuing to rub my back. "I'm so proud of you guys for starting this company. It's done so well and done great things for the communities it touched," Mom said.

"We do what we can," Police said.

Mom smiled at him. "How have you been, Nathan?"

"Between SWAT and the Goodguys, I'm doing alright, I guess," he said. "One moment, I'll be volunteering my time with the Goodguys; the next, I'll prepare to breach a door in a hostage situation."

"That has to be pretty rough, being SWAT," Mom said.

"Not as rough as working for the Goodguys." Police said.

Mom laughed. "I bet. Kids can be quite a handful, can't they?"

The three of us looked at each other. If only she knew. "They sure can," I said.

"How are your parents, Nathan?" Mom said.

"They're in the Bahamas right now, enjoying their early retirement," Police said.

"I want to go to the Bahamas," Mom said, nudging me with her elbow.

"You know I can't afford that with my measly six-figure contract, Mom," I said. "Not even with the tens of thousands I get from my sponsors."

Mom smiled warmly at me.

An hour later, we were saying our goodbyes and preparing to leave. "You are the greatest fighter in the world and the President of the most generous charity organization. If only your father could see what you've become, he'd be so proud of you. I'm proud of you." Mom kissed me on the cheek and zipped my brown leather jacket. "I love you, sweetheart. Now take care, alright?"

I've always wanted to make her proud of me and give her something to hold onto while I was away. I can only imagine how difficult it is for her without my father around, and I can only hope that whatever I've accomplished gives her something to cherish.

I promised to visit her more often if time permitted, but it was always go-go-go with the Goodguys: one SD op after another, followed by yet another.

I couldn't help but think we were wasting our time with the badguys, even though we continued to score major victories against them. It was almost as if we were fighting this war in vain.

"I love you Mom."

"SD eleven, we have the target in sight. He just left the building," Pirate said over my earbud transceiver.

"Roger that TS twenty-one. Let us know when he arrives at his destination," I said.

"Roger," Pirate said. "Wait, we have a problem. It appears that he has an escort."

"An escort?" I said.

"Yeah, he's got an escort. Four agents in two vehicles, " Pirate said. "What are your orders?"

I looked over at Moonwalker, who was sitting in the driver's seat of our black SUV. Fire and Guard were in the back seat. We were all dressed in black suits and realistic prosthetic masks and wigs, waiting in a Safeway parking lot in Pierre, South Dakota. It was a bright and sunny day, with not a cloud to be seen. It was the eighth of June 2002. "It's your call," Moonwalker said.

Yesterday, Senator Douglas had no security detail, but now he does, and on the very day that we are poised to kidnap him, the badguys are onto us. I sighed. This could get messy. "LS twenty-one, keep your eyes on him and update me on his position," I said. We're going after him, boys."

"Good call," Moonwalker said.

"That art what thee talking 'bout," Guard said. We all looked at him. "What?"

"Don't try to be cool, man," Fire said.

"What art thou saying? I not cool?" Guard said.

I sighed and slowly shook my head. "He doesn't even look like an agent. I mean, look at his face, for crying out loud," I said.

Guard touched his face. "What? Art thy mask ok?"

Moonwalker and Fire chuckled. "Yeah, and Guard, when we do this, try not to speak. You'll just blow our cover." Moonwalker said.

"At least thee no have to stayeth in car for op like thou," Guard said.

"Ooo, he got you on that one, Moonwalker," Fire said.

"Yeah, that's because I'm an ogre and will stick out like a sore thumb. My handicap is my size. Guard's handicap is his stupidity," Moonwalker said. We all laughed, including Guard.

"Yeah, and let's hope Smartguy's prosthetic masks do the trick," I said. "Our entire organization will collapse if I'm made out, not to mention my life."

"And mine." Fire said.

"Ah, you all look fine. No one will ever notice," Moonwalker said.

I pulled out my fake FBI badge. "None of us are cut out for this, well, except for you, Moonwalker. Hell, we're just a bunch of normal guys trying to save the world, that's all," I said. "I sure hope everything works."

"SD eleven, the senator's convoy just turned onto the freeway. I think they're heading for the airport," Pirate said.

"Roger, that TS twenty-one. Keep your eyes on the target and provide overwatch. We're moving in to intercept," I said.

"Roger that SD eleven. We've got ya back," Pirate said.

I reached into the glove box, pulled out a magnetic red light, and placed it on top of the roof. Moonwalker then turned on the rear window emergency lights. "Let's do this, men," I said.

With a screeching of the tires, Moonwalker sped out of the parking lot right into the middle of oncoming traffic. Cars slammed on their brakes and swerved out of our way while honking their horns.

"Holy shit, Moonwalker! This isn't a spaceship, man!" Fire said. He was gripping the handhold above the door for dear life.

"No, but it sure does drive like one!" Moonwalker said. Putting the petal to the metal, with our siren blaring, Moonwalker blazed past car after car down the main thoroughway.

"So how are we going to arrest this guy when he's on the move?! I mean, if I remember correctly, the executive protection protocol states that you're not supposed to stop for anything or anyone," Fire said.

Guard started to dig around in his large black duffle bag. "That art why we haveth this," he said, pulling out a spear-gun-shaped weapon with a two-pronged electrical spearhead loaded.

"We'll take him at the airport. We don't want a fight," I said.

Guard sighed and put away the electrical spear gun. "That makes me feel a little better," Fire said.

With the engine roaring, we raced towards Pierre Regional Airport. "The target has just arrived at his destination," Pirate said.

"Copy that," I said, glancing at Moonwalker.

"ETA two minutes," Moonwalker said.

"ETA two minutes, TS twenty-one," I said. "Will we make it?"

"Possibly, but you'll be cutting it close."

"Shit."

Moonwalker pushed the gas pedal down further while weaving in and around traffic. "I have a team ready. We can cause a diversion." Pirate said.

"Stand by TS twenty-one. We'll make it."

"Copy that SD eleven. Standing by."

Ninety seconds later, we skidded to a halt in front of the main entrance to Pierre Regional Airport. Throwing the car door open, I jumped out and raced inside the airport lobby. Guard and Fire followed right behind me. People scattered in all directions away from us.

"Sirs!" a police officer yelled at us, reaching for his pistol. "Stop right there!"

I pulled out my FBI badge and held it out for the cop to see. "FBI, sir. We're on a matter of national security," I said. We need to find Senator Douglas, and now."

The cop looked over my badge. "Well, um, he's getting ready to board his flight," he said. "He's at gate three."

More officers were making their way towards us. "Thank you, sir," I said, putting away my badge. With a nod of my head, the three of us hurried towards gate three. People were staring at us intently with looks of bewilderment. I could only hope that our prosthetic masks and wigs weren't falling apart. Up ahead, walking towards the boarding area, were Senator Douglas and his four FBI bodyguards.

"Senator Douglas!" I said with a raised voice. He stopped and turned to face me.

"I'm sorry, but I'm very-" he said.

"Sir, I'm special agent in charge, Sylvanas, of the Phoenix field office," I said, pulling out my badge and holding it out for him to see. "You need to come with us, and now."

Senator Douglas smiled and let out a soft chuckle. His agents surrounded him and rested their hands atop their pistols. "Agents, call for backup and arrest these men. They are not who they say they are," he said.

The agents all glanced at each other. "What's going on here?" an agent said.

I pulled out a warrant for Senator Douglas' arrest and handed it to the agent. My adrenaline was overflowing in my veins. "Senator Douglas needs to come with us, and now," I said.

"I'm Markus, sir. Special agent Markus," he said, looking over the warrant. The cops in the background were escorting everyone out of the lobby.

"What's going on? Why haven't you arrested these men?" Senator Douglas said.

Special Agent Markus continued to look over the warrant. After another moment, he handed it back to me and holstered his weapon. "I'm sorry, senator, but you have to go with Mr. Sylvanas," he said.

"Backup is on the way if you want to wait for further authorization, Markus," an agent said.

Markus shook his head. "No," he said. "Senator Douglas, please go with Mr. Sylvanas."

Senator Douglas smiled and nodded his head. He then brushed his shoulder against mine while walking past me. "Your cause is lost, Browny," he whispered.

Fire and Guard led Senator Douglas through the lobby. "Do you need our escort, Mr. Sylvanas?" Markus said.

"No thanks, Markus," I said. "And you have a nice day."

It was a good op. Clean and efficient, and no one was the wiser. Not even the news caught on to our 'arrest,' well, except when he never returned to the office or public life. We executed Senator Douglas after Merlin extracted everything he knew, and since then, every government agency in the United States has been looking for the fake FBI agents who arrested him. However, our kidnapping of Senator Douglas only proved that the badguys were far more embedded in the government than we had originally thought. We can't stop them.

CHAPTER TWENTY-FOUR

"My good friends, I am pleased to see that you all have arrived safely," Merlin said. "It is now your turn to accompany me in the Dark Zone, and there is much that we must explore."

"Hell ya! It's about time, Merlin," Whiteguy said. "And I was beginning to think that you had forgotten about me."

"Are you crazy, Whiteguy?" Striper said.

"Some would say so," Whiteguy said.

"You are the last to venture into the abyss, and by now, I am sure you have all heard the stories. What lies down there is not to be taken lightly. Be on your guard at all times, for there will be things that you will wish to have never seen. But these are the things that you must see in order to become who you must become, for their sake," Merlin said. "Now, who will join me?"

Whiteguy scratched his bald head. "Really? Like you needed to ask me?"

"I'm with you until the end," Aqua said.

I smiled at Merlin. "I'll protect you, old man."

Merlin turned towards Striper. He was just standing there, staring at the ground. "I'm a Goodguy, right?" he said.

"Of course you are," I said.

"Then hell, yes, I'm in," Striper said, trying his best not to look concerned. I think that was the first time Striper had ever sworn.

"Good, my friends. Now gather your gear and enough of it to last you several months. Food and water, I will supply," Merlin said.

The setting sun was the last thing I saw before climbing down into the darkness. It was eighth of November 2003.

"Come this way," Merlin said, illuminating the cavern with a light spell centered on his five-pointed star wand.

Drawing my katana, I followed Merlin down the giant hallway and into the first enormous room we explored as Goodguys. There were skeletons of monsters everywhere, and dried bloodstains splattered across the floor.

"Holy cow," Aqua said. "There weren't this many bodies the last time we were here."

"The first group that followed me cleared all the rooms and halls of monsters," Merlin said. "It was not an easy task."

"And that was three years ago," I said.

"Is this where Islander was killed?" Striper said.

"No," Merlin said.

We followed Merlin into the throne room and down the hallway to our left until we came to another large set of double doors at the end. With a wave of his wand, the doors creaked open, revealing another room littered with skeletons. "This is where we will be headed," Merlin said, pointing to a small, crudely carved tunnel thirteen meters high up the wall opposite us.

"We're going in there?" Striper said.

"Yes," Merlin said. "Browny, please lead the way."

Aqua tossed me a grappling hook. "Thanks, but I don't need this," I said. Attaching the rope to my harness, I cast a new green formula power spell named gecko crawl and began to climb up the sheer granite wall with minimal effort. Most of the spells I knew were power spells, but as I was figuring out, each category of spells had subcategories. Gecko crawl and many other of my spells belonged to the body subcategory. It was complicated, but I was learning.

Peeking into the tunnel, my sword ready to strike, I secured a camming device to a small crevice within the tunnel's rock face. "Clear," I said, climbing into the tunnel.

"Showoff," Aqua said. After tugging on the rope to test its hold, he climbed.

Once Aqua was in the tunnel, everyone else began to climb one after the other, except Merlin. He just levitated.

We then began to head down the tunnel, which never seemed to end. There was always another tunnel, crevice, or hole to follow or climb. Some went up, and some went down. Some we could only crawl through, while others were so large that we could all walk side by side with room to spare. The Dark Zone was just like everyone said: a labyrinth of tunnels.

"Oh, my goodness. It's hot down here," Striper said, wiping his brow.

"Yeah. It's like a sauna," I said.

"Shh," Whiteguy whispered. We all paused. "Do you hear that?"

I could hear a faint scraping noise. "Something's ahead of us," I whispered. I tightened the grip on my katana. Coldness crept up my spine.

"No, it's behind us," Striper said. "I can hear something behind us."

My eyes strained to see into the darkness. "We need more light, Merlin," I whispered. Merlin's wand was glowing with the intensity of a candle.

"With more light will come more creatures," Merlin said.

"What?!" Striper said.

Aqua stepped behind me with his serrated machete in hand. "You're the ninja. You hold the front line," he whispered.

"Where's it coming from, guys? Where's it coming from?" Whiteguy said. He was standing only a few feet from Striper, turning every which direction.

"Are you going-" Something violently slammed Striper against the jagged tunnel wall. I heard some of his bones break.

Rushing towards Whiteguy was a large, white-skinned humanoid beast with a potbelly and thick, callous hands. It was a Butcher.

With a downward chop, Whiteguy buried his battle ax deep into the Butcher's arm. He then struck it two more times with incredible speed before it slapped him in the head with its four-clawed hand. Whiteguy collapsed to the ground, blood running down his face.

Appearing around the bend ahead of me, lumbered two more Butchers. I cast lightning reflexes and ogre's strength and sprinted towards them.

The closest Butcher to me swung at me, but it was much too slow. Ducking under its arm, I spun around and slashed at its back. It collapsed to the ground and stopped moving. I had severed its spine.

After completing my spin, I lunged forward, thrusting my katana up and through the other Butcher's jaw. The point of my sword was sticking out the top of its head. I then pulled my blade out and watched the Butcher fall to the ground in a pool of blood.

Running past Aqua and Merlin, I jump-kicked the injured Butcher with hammer hands. Chunks of flesh and bone flew everywhere as its chest exploded from the spell. Whatever was left of it fell to the ground.

Whiteguy stood up and wiped the blood off his face. "I 'ink it brak my 'ose," he said.

I knelt next to Striper. "At least you aren't messed up like Striper," I said. He was rolling around, holding his chest, and groaning loudly.

"Mer' in, can I het some he' in please?" Whiteguy said.

"Conserve your mana, my friends, for our journey is young," Merlin said, waving his wand. In an instant, Striper was completely healed, and Whiteguy's nose corrected itself and stopped bleeding. I'm going to have to learn that spell one day.

I walked past Aqua and continued down the tunnel. "I froze, sorry," Aqua said.

"Thanks for saving my hoop back there, Browny," Whiteguy said.

"You'd do the same for me," I said.

After six grueling hours of spelunking, we stopped for a break. My body was scratched and bruised from the narrow and jagged tunnels.

"I believe we've explored quite a lot, Merlin. What do you say we head on home?" Striper said, peering into a large smooth tunnel in the cavern wall.

"I agree; we've had enough action for the day," Aqua said, setting his pack down.

Merlin pulled a thin red cloth from a small leather satchel and laid it across the ground. He then pulled out five sets of fine silverware, china plates, cups, and a pitcher. I glanced at the other three.

"What else are you packing in there, Merlin?" Whiteguy said. "I mean damn, man!"

Merlin smiled.

"What's for dinner?" Striper said.

"K-rations," Aqua said, pulling out an MRE.

"Suit yourself," Merlin said.

Five large steaks, asparagus, and sliced bakery-style bread with melted cheese appeared on the plates. Sauces of all sorts and ice-cold water filled the cups. The aroma was more than enough to get my mouth watering.

"Okay, who didn't give me the memo?" Aqua said, dropping his MRE.

Striper took a bite of steak. "Mmm, this is good, Merlin," he said. "Thanks."

"Stay vigilant, guys. We don't want to be caught off guard," I said, taking a knee to eat. "So, what other types of creatures can we expect down here?"

"You are always focused on the task at hand, Browny. That is good," Merlin said.

"You've got some brown stuff on your nose, Merlin," Whiteguy said, pointing to his nose.

"To answer your question, there are many: Tentacles, Rippers, Night Crawlers," Merlin said. "I can only hope we do not encounter any of those things."

"I hope we do because the more we kill, the less there will be in Calignosity's army," Whiteguy said.

"And the less in my nightmares," Striper said.

"There is a difference between bravery and foolishness. I hope the distinction has not eluded you," Merlin said.

"Come on, man. You chose me to kick ass with you, right?" Whiteguy said.

"More like get your ass kicked!" Agua said.

"Whatever, dude," Whiteguy said, flipping him off. I chuckled.

Once we were done eating, we set up a night watch order and went to sleep. I tossed and turned all night long. Dreams about Karen plagued me.

"So these creatures come from Ethereal through a portal, right?" Aqua said. "So what if we were to run into one? How would we destroy it."

I used the narrow walls for support and carefully climbed down the steep tunnel.

"You could not," Merlin said.

"Not even with some good 'ol C-4, eh?" Aqua said.

"No. Portals consist of pure mana, which cannot be destroyed by any physical means," Merlin said.

"Then how do you destroy it?" Striper said.

"It is a complicated ritual that requires several techniques, including the one used to open it, but they are well beyond you," Merlin said.

I stopped and looked back at Merlin. "But that was the first thing you learned. Explain that to us," I said.

"How keen of you to remember such a small detail, but there is much I have not told you."

"I know," I mumbled.

The tunnel suddenly veered straight down. All I could see was darkness. Merlin's pathetic candle wand was a poor excuse for a light. "I can't see anything, guys. It just goes straight down," I said.

"Then climb down there and check it out for us, Spiderman," Whiteguy said.

Casting gecko crawl, I climbed down the tunnel. About ten meters later, my feet touched solid ground. I waved my hand out in front of me and felt nothing. I must be in a cavern or a wide tunnel, so I drew my katana.

"Light, Merlin," I whispered.

Something like a rock skittered across the floor. Something was down here with me, and I couldn't see a thing. My heart began to race.

I gripped my katana with both hands. "Merlin," I whispered.

A dim light illuminated the cavern as Merlin floated down to the ground. I breathed a sigh of relief. There was nothing with me in the cavern. "It's about time," I said.

Aqua, followed by everyone else, rappelled to the cavern floor. "Miss us?" Aqua said.

I laughed hesitantly.

The following day, which was really only eight hours later, we continued through the endless tunnels.

"All righty guys, I've figured it out," Aqua said. "You're forty-one hundred years old." Merlin shook his head. "Damn."

"That's a hundred," Striper said.

"Can you at least give us a hint, ya old geezer?" Aqua said, handing Striper the cash.

Again, Merlin smiled. "What was it like living back then?" Whiteguy said. "Did you meet Alexander the Great, George Washington, or anyone else famous?"

"Yeah. Tell us about it, Merlin. Are the history books right or what?" Aqua said.

"The history books are fairly accurate, and yes, I have met many influential people in my time," Merlin said.

Whiteguy gave Merlin a look of discontent. "Thanks for the wealth of knowledge, Merlin."

"Tell us about Ethereal," I said.

Merlin stopped and turned towards Aqua and Whiteguy. "Now, that is a question that will bring about true wisdom," he said.

"Shh!" Striper said.

Everyone froze in place. "What is it?" Aqua whispered.

Striper pulled out his battle ax. He was trembling ever so slightly. "Something's coming," he whispered.

One minute passed, and then two and three, but nothing came. We continued walking.

"You need to get your ears checked, man," Whiteguy said.

"Yeah, you're fired," Aqua said.

"But I know I heard something," Striper said.

"You're still fired," Aqua said.

Twelve hours later, we found a large cavern with only two branching tunnels to fall asleep.

———— ✦ ————

"Guys, wake up!" Someone said. "Wake up, guys, something's coming!"

I kipped to my feet and drew my katana. The cavern was dimly lit, but I saw absolutely nothing.

Whiteguy and Striper crawled to their feet. "It was coming from that tunnel," Aqua pointed to it. Whiteguy and Striper peeked down the tunnel. "There's nothing down here, dude," Whiteguy said. He walked a good five meters down the tunnel. See, there's nothing here."

"Who's fired now?" Striper said.

Aqua stared Striper down. "You hungry?" he said.

"Am I hungry?!" Striper said.

"Yeah, 'cause I've got a knuckle sandwich for you sucka!" Aqua said.

I chuckled. "It's your watch, Whiteguy," I said.

"Whiteguy?" Striper said, looking back into the tunnel.

"Merlin!" I shouted. I cracked a glow stick and took off as fast as possible down the winding tunnel.

"Shit!" Aqua said, running after me.

After a short run, the tunnel led to a spacious cavern where I stopped. I tossed the glow stick towards the middle of the cavern and gripped my katana tight.

Whiteguy was hanging limply from the enormous claw of a monstrous white-skinned creature clinging to the ceiling eight meters above. My body shivered as fear gripped me.

Staring at me with its beady yellow eyes, the humanoid monster growled. Its jaw then unhinged from its face like a rattlesnake and split into two parts down the middle. Each part had a long fang and dozens of razor-sharp teeth. A long, needle-sharp proboscis-like tongue shot in and out of its mouth.

Suddenly, the creature's body began to pop and bulge at the joints while its limbs dislocated and grew to twice their original length. In mere seconds, the monster had gone from the size of a bear to that of an elephant. I was adrenaline-sick and felt like throwing up. Now, this was a monster.

Two more walked into the cavern from the tunnels across from me. "Holy hell!" Aqua said. "What the fuck are those things?!"

"I don't know, but I'm not waiting to find out!" Striper said, slinking back into the tunnel behind me.

"Come on, Whiteguy's gone," Aqua said. "There's nothing we can do for him now."

Merlin's light filled the cavern. "It is a White Macashi, and they have been following us for days now," he said. The creatures continued to stare at us.

"Days, uh?" Aqua said.

I cast lightning reflexes, giant's toughness, and stone skin and raised my hand towards one of the Macashis.

A shimmering, nearly invisible bolt of energy, a mana bolt, flew from my hand and struck the monster in the chest. Blood dripped from its split mouth and oozed from its eyes and ears, but still it stood.

The two creatures across the cavern charged me. Casting jump, I flew high in the air over them and towards the Macashi on the ceiling.

With incredible speed, speed that surpassed mine, the Macashi lashed out at me with its enormous claw and raked me across the chest. I was sent hurtling into the wall from the impact and fell to the ground below. My Kevlar was ripped, and my ceramic plates shattered.

Rifle and automatic gunfire echoed loudly throughout the cavern. Bullets tore into the two charging Macashi's, but they had little effect.

I staggered to my feet. Despite my spells, the creature's claw had sliced me open pretty well and broke several of my ribs. I don't know what these creatures were, but they were too fast and strong to engage directly. I had to find their weakness and exploit it quickly.

Sheathing my katana, I unslung my M-4 and aimed at the back of one of the monster's heads.

The Macashi on the ceiling slinked towards one of the far tunnels while the other two took turns clawing at my friends who were taking refuge inside a tunnel. The beasts were much too large to fit inside the tunnels now.

I cast fire enchantment on my gun and fired a single shot into the back of the Macashi's head. Bits of flesh and bone flew everywhere as the depleted uranium slug tore into its skull. The skin around the hole caught fire, but the round only pissed the monster off.

Spinning around, the White Macashi charged me. Red bullet holes dotted its body, but it wasn't bleeding. Only the one that I had hit with the mana bolt was.

Holding down the trigger, I unloaded a dozen burning bullets into its chest and cast mana bolt. I then cast jump and hurdled twelve meters to the other side of the cavern before it could get within striking range of me.

Just then, and before I could recover from landing, the White Macashi on the ceiling dropped Whiteguy and jumped down on top of me. Its claw slammed into my chest and pinned me to the ground. More of my ribs shattered as I vomited blood. My organs felt like they were about to burst from my mouth due to the beast's sheer weight. I couldn't breathe.

The monster then flayed open its mouth and sunk its fangs into my exposed right side. I could feel its fangs scraping across the ground beneath and through me and a warm liquid soaking my back. I squirmed in vain to escape.

With whatever strength I had left, I cast ogre's strength, drew my K-bar with my left hand, and stabbed the beast in its massive neck. My blade penetrated less than an inch in its thick hide.

I kipped to my feet and drew my katana. Aqua and Striper were sitting near each other, eating in silence. Merlin was tending to Whiteguy, who was shaking uncontrollably. He then vomited.

"What happened?" I said. "Did I die?" My Kevlar armor was destroyed.

"No, my friend, you merely fell unconscious due to the White Macashi's poison," Merlin said.

"Merlin took them out," Aqua said.

The mood was somber.

CHAPTER TWENTY-FIVE

For days and weeks on end, we crawled and climbed through the maze of tunnels and caverns. We never brought up Whiteguy's death.

"Is there any spell that will make me tougher because these tunnels are tearing me up," Striper said.

"I got a can 'o man," Whiteguy said. Aqua snickered.

"Giant's toughness," I said.

"Giant's toughness, eh? I don't know that spell," Striper said.

"You don't know that spell?!" Whiteguy said.

"No. I have a hard enough time fitting in all my legal work in one day, let alone finding a few hours in the day to solve a spell formula," Striper said. "Especially now with the astronomical growth of our charity organization."

"I hear what you're saying," I said. "I'm still trying to learn protection and have been for six months now."

"Damn, protection eh?!" Whiteguy said.

"Isn't that the spell that makes you bulletproof?" Striper said.

"If you define bulletproof as shallow puncture wounds and bruises," Whiteguy said.

"Is there anything more powerful, Merlin?" Aqua said.

"Yes, there is," Merlin said.

"Well, what is it magic man?" Whiteguy said.

Merlin smiled. "I do not think I should tell you," he said.

"Come on and spit it out," Aqua said.

The tunnel we were walking down was getting smaller. We could no longer walk upright and had to crawl on our hands and knees.

The air of the abyss was hot and humid and smelled like death.

"It is invincibility, and under it, one will become immune to every form of physical damage," Merlin said.

"Wow, that is powerful," Striper said.

"Every form of physical attack?" Aqua said. "Even from, let's say, a nuke?"

"Every form," Merlin said.

"Then damn, Merlin, what are you waiting for? Teach me it." Whiteguy said. Merlin chuckled quietly. "What?"

Aqua shook his head with a look of disappointment. "We don't have the mana to cast it, do we?" he said.

"No, it requires more mana to sustain per minute than you possess," Merlin said. "That aside, it is a three hundred and forty-five symbol formula."

My mouth dropped in astonishment. "It requires that much mana to sustain per minute and that many symbols?!" I said.

The spell of protection was the most complex formula I knew, and it only had nine symbols. I knew twenty-one symbols altogether, meaning it would take over a hundred more years until I knew all the symbols of invincibility. I can only imagine how long it would take to figure out the spell formula.

"Yes, but there are even more powerful spells requiring more mana and even more symbols," Merlin said.

"Like what?" Aqua said.

"Another time, Aqua, another time," Merlin said.

"Agh, it's getting tight down here," Aqua said.

"How could I harm someone under that spell or defeat it?" I said.

"Any and all magic can pierce the spell to its full effect," Merlin said. "The technique of dispelling will cancel it."

"That stinks," Aqua said, frowning.

"Not as much as your ass. Now get it out of my face," Whiteguy said.

I laughed. I'm sure glad I was leading and not following. This tunnel was tight.

"So what can protect you from magic?" Aqua said.

"There is a spell called mana shield that will protect you against most magical damage," Merlin said. "However, the magical technique of shielding will protect you completely and from all spells."

"What is a magic technique?" Striper said.

"Ahh, techniques, they are enhancements upon the very fabric of mana," Merlin said. "They are the true standard of power, but this you will learn in time."

"You know Merlin, this is the most we've heard you say," Aqua said.

"Yeah. You got that right." Whiteguy said.

Merlin sighed.

"Freedom!" I said, squeezing out of the tunnel. Standing up, I drew my katana. Merlin followed behind me and increased the light from his wand. I gave him a look while he just shrugged his shoulders.

We were in another large cavern with stalactites hanging from the ceiling and three other tunnels branching to who knows where on the far side.

"Can we set up camp here because I can't take much more of this squeezing through-tight tunnels crap?" Whiteguy said, sitting up against the wall.

Merlin looked at me. "Browny?" he said.

"Yeah. That sounds good," I said. "And Striper, don't be peeking into tunnels you don't belong to."

He was on the other side of the cavern, running his fingers along the rounded edge of a smooth tunnel bored into the side of the wall.

"This is the second tunnel I've seen that-" Striper said.

An ear-piercing shriek echoed throughout the cavern. I cupped my ears and fell to my knees. Nausea washed over me, and my vision began to blur.

Striper stumbled away from the tunnel, holding his ears while Whiteguy and Aqua doubled over. Their ears were bleeding. Merlin, however, was standing in a tunnel to my far left, just staring at me. He appeared completely unphased by the continuous shrieking.

A gaping mouth filled with row after row of tiny serrated teeth was crawling partially out of the slimy hole. A white liquid dripped from its mouth and fell to the ground. The rock began to dissolve. Four black tentacles with two razor-sharp hooks at the ends shot out of its mouth and gripped the wall.

After pulling its glossy black body even further out of the tunnel with its tentacles, the worm shot one of them towards Striper and hooked him in the back. The razor-sharp hooks had no problem slicing and melting through his Kevlar. Striper collapsed to the ground unconscious.

Another tentacle shot towards Aqua, wrapped around his leg, and yanked him to the ground. The worm dragged him across the floor and into the air towards its mouth.

A bluish-white mist began to emanate from Aqua's body. He had cast frost aura, but the worm seemed quite resistant to the freezing cold. The worm then dug its hooks into Aqua's leg, and he, too, went limp. How many of these fricking creatures are poisonous?!

Fighting through ear-piercing screeching, I stood and cast my usual spells. I then cast jump to close the distance, and while in the air, I swung my katana hard and severed the tentacle that held Aqua. Black blood squirted everywhere, but even before the worm's severed limb could hit the ground, the tentacle had already grown back to its full and original length. I couldn't believe what I had just seen! Aqua fell hard to the ground.

Stumbling, my ears bleeding, I slashed at the other tentacle holding Striper and severed it as well. More black blood gushed out, but in a split second, and like before, the tentacle grew back instantaneously. The hair on my head and arms began to stand on end.

Striper crawled up against the wall and unslung his M-16A4. Holding down the trigger, Striper sprayed the worm's body with bullets. Dozens of small holes opened up, but as quickly as they appeared, they disappeared. Lead chunks squirted from its body and fell to the ground.

A bright flash of light was all I saw. Whiteguy was lying motionless up against the wall. Smoke was rising from his body. I collapsed to my knees, too nauseated to continue fighting. I couldn't hear a thing anymore. Not even my heartbeat. Again, the hairs on my body stood on end. It was charging the air with electricity.

Pointing his wand towards the worm, Merlin shot a continuous and searing hot ray of fire across its body that burned through it like a laser. Its orangish black guts burst across the floor, but the worm was healing so quickly that it appeared as if nothing was happening to it.

More chunks of flesh and fire embers flew everywhere as the scorching ray continued to burn into the worm. The fire was so intense that the air in the cavern was becoming too hot to breathe. My lungs were beginning to burn.

The worm then slipped back into the tunnel, and the shrieking stopped. Merlin waved his hand and miraculously healed us. My vision returned, and I could finally hear again.

Aqua checked his leg. There were two holes in his Kevlar where the hooks had pierced him. "Now, what the hell was that thing?"

he said, scrambling behind Merlin. "And gosh damn, that thing was scary!"

Whiteguy shook his head. His face was pale white, and he was staring at the ground with a blank expression.

Whatever it was, its regenerative ability was ten times that of the first initiate I had fought, and we were powerless to stop it just like we were powerless to stop the White Macashis.

"A Night Crawler," Merlin said.

"Oh, how nice," Whiteguy muttered.

"You will learn to respect it if you have the power to destroy it or fear it if you do not."

No one said a word for the rest of the night.

I checked the two tunnels ahead of us to see if they were clear. "Are we any closer to where we're heading, Merlin?" I said.

"Close, but not yet," Merlin said, pulling out a scroll and unfurling it. "Here is everything we have explored thus far and where we are located."

At first, the parchment was blank, but slowly, an intricately drawn maze of 3D tunnels and caverns began to appear. Seven kilometers to the west of the Dark Zone's entrance was the Breeding Cavern. That's where thousands upon thousands of creatures called home, and many Goodguys have died. To the South, only twelve kilometers from the throne room was the Dragon's Lair. Iceman's crew only lasted four days down there, and three of them died. We were headed east of the entrance and were already well beyond a place called Caverns Forever.

"We've traveled sixty-five kilometers!" Whiteguy said.

"Yes," Merlin said.

"So where are we headed? Any place in particular?" Aqua said.

"Not really," Merlin said.

Whiteguy laughed and buried his head in his arms up against the wall. "So we're headed in this general direction?" Aqua said, waving his finger all across the map. Merlin looked at him. "Are you serious?! We're just wandering around aimlessly?"

"To an extent, my friend. Now let us continue," Merlin said.

"Can we just stop for a minute," Whiteguy said. "These creatures, where do they come from and how? How are they created, and how many of them are there in Calignosity's army?"

Merlin stopped walking. "Millions," he said.

Whiteguy forced a chuckle. "Awesome."

After climbing up the wall and into a tunnel above, we continued on our way.

"Which way, Merlin?" I said. There was a fork in the tunnel up ahead.

"Pick one," Aqua said.

"Never mind." I drew my katana.

A semi-clear, gelatinous blob-like thing was rolling slowly towards us down the right tunnel.

"I take it that this thing won't be harmed by my sword, uh, Merlin?" I said.

Whiteguy took aim with his shotgun and fired a single round into the ooze. The slug managed to penetrate a few inches before coming to a complete stop. A couple of seconds later, the bullet plopped out onto the ground. Whiteguy looked over his shotgun. "Huh, that's funny."

"Though it is not fast, it has other qualities that more than make up for its lack of speed," Merlin said.

"So it's impervious to bullets and swords. What about pure mana?" I said, pointing my sword at it. A mana bolt flew from my sword and slammed into the giant ooze. With a violent quiver, a watery substance began to leak from its skin or membrane. It began to retreat back down the tunnel.

"That is one of the only ways to destroy it," Merlin said.

"It reminds me of the movie 'The Blob,'" Aqua said.

"Yeah, it does," I said.

"And that thing is supposed to be scary?" Whiteguy said.

"Maybe not to us, but to normal people, yes," Striper said. "Your shotgun did nothing to it."

Whiteguy shot Striper a look. "And what can you do it, Stripper?" he said.

"What can you do, Whiteguy?" Aqua said sarcastically.

"The only combat spell I can cast is magic arrow," Whiteguy said. "Besides, at least I can cast giant's toughness."

"Wait, did you just say that the only combat spell you have is magic arrow?!" I said, looking back at him.

Merlin chuckled quietly. "What's up Merlin? You got something to say?" Whiteguy said, puffing his chest up.

"No. I do not," Merlin said. "Magic arrow is," he paused. "a good spell."

"It's been nearly seven years now, and you're telling us that your most powerful attack spell is magic arrow?!" Striper said, his eyes wide. "At least I can cast lightning bolt!"

"That's impressive," I said, giving Striper a nod.

Whiteguy held his arms out in protest. "No! Well, I know other spells," he said.

Aqua was laughing hard and slapping his leg. "Like what, feather bolt?!" he said.

It was hard to stay focused on the tunnel ahead with the roasting of Whiteguy behind me. I stopped and joined in their laughter. Soon enough, even Whiteguy was laughing at himself. It's been a long and stressful journey, and I needed a good laugh.

"So there's really a place down here called the Under Earth Ocean, uh?" Aqua said. "What's it like?"

"It is a place, as the name suggests, an under-earth sea that spans dozens of kilometers," Merlin said.

"Thanks for the elaborate details, buddy," Aqua said. "I guess I'll grab my scuba gear and explore it later."

"We've reached another dead end," I said, running my hands along the rough wall.

"That's the third one today," Striper said. "Maybe we've reached the end of the Dark Zone."

I picked up a rock, rapped it up against the wall, and listened. "No. It's hollow on the other side," I said.

"Dudes, I totally feel like I'm D&D'ing right now," Whiteguy said. "We've got a mage, a ninja rogue, and two fighters. We've even got swords and axes!"

"You played that crap, didn't you?" Aqua said.

"I'm an electronics engineer. I grew up on D&D," Whiteguy said. "So did Big Red and Big Blue. All us geeks did."

"Okay, I just lost all respect for you," Aqua said. "Now, what are we doing?"

"Move aside, my friends," Merlin said. With a wave of his wand, the rock began to shift, and a moment later, a doorway was formed. Bright sunlight flooded the tunnel and blinded me.

"Oh, my gosh," Striper said, partly shielding his eyes with his hands.

"Damn!" Whiteguy said.

Once my eyes adjusted, I couldn't help but be dumbfounded at what I saw. Stretching out for as far as I could see was a grass-covered landscape with gentle hills, small clusters of trees, and several crystal-clear lakes and streams. Above us was a cloudless blue sky and a bright yellow sun in the distance.

"Well, this is rather awesome," Aqua said.

"Stay close, and do not lower your guard," Merlin said. He then levitated us two hundred meters to the ground down below.

Striper sprawled out on the grass and breathed a loud sigh of relief. "I've forgotten how good grass feels!" he said.

"And it's so much cooler," Aqua said.

Merlin turned full circle, looking around intently. "This place is not what it seems my friends," he said. "Someone or thing of great power has created this place."

"There's even a gentle breeze!" Aqua said, taking a deep breath.

"Man, this place is so..." Whiteguy said, staring at the sky.

"Come, but stay on your guard," Merlin said.

Aside from its sheer immensity, the rocky cliff spanned from horizon to horizon and beyond the sky. The grass was perfectly cut and edged along every tree and bush without a single weed. The trees and bushes were evenly spaced apart and planted in gardener's soil. There wasn't even a single fallen branch or leaf anywhere, not even an insect. There were just tame deer and white bunnies hopping about. This place is eerily immaculate.

"This place is incredible," Striper said.

"Yeah, now, if I could get my lawn to look like this," Aqua said.

"Who could have made this place, Merlin?" I said.

"Everyone rest; we set up camp here," Merlin said.

Setting down my tattered rucksack, I lay on the soft grass and closed my eyes. The stream behind me trickled ever so quietly. It was all so soothing, like the times Mary and I strolled the beach of Lake Caldell holding hands.

"There are not many who possess the power to create, not many at all," Merlin said. "And those who do, you would be wise to fear, for there are far worse fates than death."

"Create what, rocks and stuff?" Whiteguy said.

"Everything you see here, except life," Merlin said.

"Why not life?" Aqua said.

"Magic has its limits, my friends," Merlin said. Lying down, he covered his eyes with his hood. "Now, get some rest."

"Striper, you've got first watch," I said.

"You got it."

"Browny, it's your watch," someone said, gently shaking me.

I opened my eyes and sat up. I felt wretched inside, like a thousand pounds was crushing my chest. I just wanted all of this to be over with. "Yeah."

Aqua crawled into his sleeping bag. "See you in a few," he said.

I grabbed my shotgun and walked around. The sun's yellow rays warmed my skin while a light breeze blew at my back.

Kneeling next to a huckleberry bush, I picked up a bunny and ran my fingers through its soft fur. Lavender flooded my senses, and I could hear Mary giggling.

Pulling her picture from my back pocket, I kissed it and dried my eyes. I miss you so much, Mary Jane, and I'd give the world to hold you in my arms one last time. I'd give my soul if that's what it took.

"You love her so dearly, Browny, I know," a familiar girl's voice said.

I looked up and couldn't believe my eyes. "K-Karen?"

She was wearing a plain white nightgown with her long brown hair hanging freely down her back. Her neck was scarred deeply. "Merlin cannot save her, Browny," Karen said. "She is beyond life and death, unlike us, but not beyond you. For I have seen it."

I opened my mouth to speak, but no words came out. I just didn't know what to say. I looked down at Mary. Her smile was so beautiful, and her blue eyes were so bright. She couldn't be; she just couldn't.

"I am so sorry," she said.

"Tell me plainly what you mean, Karen," I said. "I don't understand."

"You have no place here in my presence!" Merlin said with a raised voice. "Now leave at once before I destroy you."

Karen sat on her knees before me and placed her hand on mine. "I have always loved you, Browny. Always, but I was just too afraid to ever ask you out," Karen whispered, gently squeezing my hand. "And I will never forget that night after homecoming when you walked me home. You were so sweet to me, Scott, and the best friend that I ever had." A tear rolled down her cheek. "I love you." Karen slowly faded into thin air.

I struggled to hold back my tears. The anguish of losing Mary forever was almost too much to bear. "Why didn't you tell me?!" I said.

"I did not know, but that is not of importance right now," Merlin said. "You must remain strong."

I looked up at him in shock. "Not of importance?!" I said. "She meant the world to me, Merlin. She meant everything to me, everything! And now she's one of them or something worse?!"

"I know she did, but you must remain strong for your friends," Merlin said. "They need you, and now more than ever."

"Why?" I said. "They have Iceman and Inspector."

"Because they first chose you, as I have. For your goodness, your courage, and your heart," Merlin said. "You are what they need; what the world needs."

I stood up and stared at Mary's picture. "Then why do you keep secrets from me? And why don't you answer my questions?"

"Why did it take Master Yusokagi so many years to train you?"

Because some things take time to learn, but what did that have to do with anything? "And what happens when we run out of time, Merlin? What then?"

Merlin sighed and looked at the ground. "Some things are best kept to oneself for the sake of hope, but this, too, you will learn in time."

It was the twelfth of February 2004 when Merlin teleported us back to the desert.

CHAPTER TWENTY-SIX

"Hey, it's great seeing you again, Browny," Moonwalker said as I walked into the Logistical Support Squad's R&D facility. High-tech, automated machinery and computers were everywhere. "How are you doing?"

"Much better now," I said. Actually, I was still depressed from this morning, but there was no reason to worry them with my feelings.

Guard gave me a quick hug. "It art great to see thee Brown Stuffings."

I looked at everyone with a half-cocked smile and shook my head. "I can see that Doubles has you saying that, too," I said.

"Everyone knows you as Brown Stuffings," Fire said, patting me on the back. "So, how was it? Where did you guys go?"

"It was hell. That's all I know," I said.

"Uh huh, it sure was." Big Blue said. "Especially them big 'ins"

"Yeah, like the White Macashi and Nightcrawler," I said. "And speaking of, I'm going to need a bigger gun."

"You haven't said anything!" Big Blue said.

"I believe I have what you are looking for," Smartguy said. He was sitting at a workbench across from me with body armor and rifles before him. It looked like some pretty sophisticated stuff. "This is your new Kevlar armored titanium scaled body armor, or KATS for short, and your new M4 assault rifle and Beretta ten gauge automatic shotgun."

"It's some damn tough armor, man," Fire said. "No rifle round can penetrate it. Not even a fifty firing AP rounds."

"Really?" I said.

"Na, a fifty will fuck you up," he said.

"Aside from the most obvious features, it can resist fifty thousand volts and mask your thermal signature for up to an hour. It will also protect you from nuclear fallout, Sarin, VX, and even weaponized anthrax." Smartguy said. "Though without the helmet and an oxygen supply, all these protective capabilities will be severely hampered."

"Wow, that's pretty impressive, Smartguy," I said.

"Your weapons, which possess an internal ballistics computer, automatically compute for wind, altitude, temperature, grain, distance to target, and other ballistic data. This data is then sent from the grip of your gun through a palm induction system to the HUD in your helmet." Smartguy said. "Your weapons also come equipped with a thermal day/night camera and optics system, a laser sight, and an infrared flashlight."

Everyone was standing around, nodding their head or smiling. I couldn't help but crack a smile, too. I was proud to be a Goodguys, not just because of what we fought for but because we were professionals. Professionals with the best equipment and firepower forged money could buy and alien intelligence could create. "So, what's been going on up here? Any good news?" I said.

"The Cardinals failed to make the playoffs again," Fire said.

"Typical," I said.

"It's the same old, same old," Big Blue said.

"We're still kicking ass and taking names, my man," Greyguy said.

"Good, where's our next SD op destination?" I said.

"Great Britain," Moonwalker said.

"Alright, alright, get this, guys," Whiteguy said. "So the entire LS squad is in the shop just doing what they do, right, when halfway across the shop, Pudgy rips some gnarly ass." He took a drink of red wine. "I mean, that shit was loud, but it gets worse."

"Yar just one big land lubbin' gas bag, aintcha?" Hook said, nudging Pudgy in the side.

"Is everything alright, Goodguys? Can I get you anything?" a waitress said with a thick British accent.

"Na ma' am, we be fine," Islander said. "Thank ya."

The waitress smiled and walked off.

"Alright, anyways, so Pudgy's over there stinking it up when Octane walks in the door, and unbeknownst to him, he just walked into a category-five shitstorm." We all laughed. "But it hasn't hit him yet, and to make matters worse, he's eating a hotdog with the works." Some people were glancing over at our table, shaking their heads. "The stink then hits him, and he just blows chunks everywhere."

Again, we busted up laughing. "I didn't know that Octane was-" Pudgy said.

"No need to defend yourself, Pudgy. You're alright in my book even though you suck at fighting," Bazooka said.

"Here ye here ye!" Hook said, raising his tattered black captain's hat.

"Excuse me, sirs, are you the Goodguys? A man in a tuxedo said. Standing beside him was a fair-skinned woman and a teenage boy. All of them were well dressed, unlike us. We were wearing casual clothes in a very upscale restaurant in London.

Our table got quiet. "Yes, we are, sir," I said. "I'm Scott. This is Islander, Hook, Whiteguy, Pudgy, and Bazooka."

"You're the president and that fighter, aren't you?" the woman said. She was smiling happily, but her eyes were glued to Bazooka.

"Yes, ma'am," I said.

"We see you and commercials for the Goodguys all the time, but it's really something to meet you in person," the man said. "Our son attended your cash-for-cures soccer camp a few months ago. We're grateful for what your organization has done for our community."

"Thank you," I said.

"It's amazing how many lives you've touched across the world and how much good you've done," the woman said.

"It is, and well, we're bothering you because we'd like to get a picture of you and us together if that's not too much to ask," he said. "It's our son's birthday today, and it would mean a lot to him and us."

"Of course, we'd be happy too," I said. Standing up, I stood before the couple while Bazooka readied the camera.

"This means so much to us, Goodguys," she said. "Thank you."

Taking out a wad of cash, Islander counted a thousand pounds and handed it to the kid. "Buy y' self some presents, 'cause it's all ya's mon," he said.

Bazooka snapped a few pictures. "Thank you," the kid said. He was smiling ear to ear.

"Wow, that's an awful lot; thank you, Goodguys," the man said.

After taking a few more pictures with them, they said goodbye, and we sat down.

"Did you enjoy your meal? Because we enjoyed having you," the waitress said.

"It be a fine meal, miss, now what be thee cost in pieces of eight?" Hook said.

The waitress laughed politely, handing him the bill. "Eleven hundred and fifty pounds," she whispered.

"I'll pay, guys," Pudgy said. "Put everyone else tab on our bill, too, please."

"You're paying for everyone's bill?!" she said with astonishment.

"Yes, ma'am," Pudgy said.

"Wait one moment, I have to get my manager," she said.

It took a good twenty minutes to settle everyone's bill and another thirty to accept everyone's thank you's before we could return to our six-room suite. Once there, we kicked back and relaxed in the living room.

"Well, dudes, we head back to the States tomorrow," Whiteguy said. He was leaning back in a recliner. "Did you all have a good time or what?"

"Me have a greateth time," Hook said.

"Ya mon, and I think we accomplished quite a lot, ya know," Islander said.

"Eighteen dead badguys, a warehouse full of mil-spec equipment seized, and intel linking some prominent universities to supplying the Badguys with medical R&D. It's been a good week," Bazooka said.

"Now, if Merlin would get to killin' Calignosity, we can end this war," Islander said.

"Definitely, because at the rate we're inflicting casualties upon Goresavice's army, he'll be out of commission in no time," Whiteguy said.

"What if he can't be killed?" I said.

"Who?" Bazooka said.

"Calignosity," I said.

Everyone got quiet and turned their attention towards me. "What do you mean?" Whiteguy said.

"Merlin couldn't destroy him the first time," I said. "Can he destroy him now?"

"Arg! Calignosity art a coward who fled thee battle," Hook said. "He's a dead bloat when Merlin layeth ahold of him."

"Besides, there's thirty more of us to kick his ass," Whiteguy said.

"Merlin knows what he's doing. Once we're finished with Goresavice, we'll be unleashed to destroy Calignosity and his army," Bazooka said. "It's one step at a time."

"Is it really?" I said. "Because everywhere we turn, it seems like the badguys know us; are onto us."

"I have noticed that as well, but there is much about magic that we do not know," Bazooka said.

"And much we don't know about Calignosity, either," I said.

Everyone got quiet again.

"I think our behavior at the restaurant was inappropriate," Pudgy said.

"I think so too, Pudgy," I said.

A few weeks after our return to the States, Merlin gave us a one-week vacation, so I headed to the beaches of Orlando, Florida, where I was renting a small house on the beach. I needed to be alone.

My cell phone rang. "This is Scott, what's up?"

"Chief has been arrested," Space Police said.

I stopped walking along the street. The sun was beginning to set. "For what, and by whom?"

"We don't know, but we suspect it's the FBI."

"Call Striper and alert the others," I said.

"It's being done as we speak," Space Police said.

"Thanks for the heads up."

"No problem. Now stay sharp."

I hung up and took a look around. Eight black SUVs rounded the corner and pulled up in front of me while two SWAT trucks and four cop cars blocked the street behind me. Two helicopters with snipers flew overhead. It was going to be a long night.

Getting out of their vehicles, ten men in full tactical gear approached me with their SMGs trained on me while the other officers took positions behind their cars.

"Alex Summer, this is the NSA," an officer said. "Keep your hands where we can see them. You're coming with us."

I sighed and shook my head with a cocky smile. After handcuffing and searching me, they put me in the back of an SUV and threw a black bag over my head.

"Can I ask what this is all about, gentlemen?" I said.

No one answered me.

After a short car ride somewhere and then a several-hour-long helicopter flight, I was led inside another building and chained to a metal seat. My black hood was then removed.

I was sitting in a large concrete room with gray walls and a steel door at the far end. Two agents were sitting across the table from me, and two soldiers were standing behind me. Both were armed with pistols.

"We have quite a file on you, Alex Summer, and your charity," an agent said. "But of course, you're not Alex Summer, and your charity is anything but."

"You are Scott, born on July 2nd, 1976, in the Children's Hospital in Phoenix. You grew up in Janestown and graduated from Janestown High in '94. A short while later, on January 1995, you signed a contract to fight for Pride, and as of recently, May 20th, 2000, you started a charity organization named the Goodguys, of which you are the President." the other agent said. "Are we missing anything?"

"Just one small detail," I said. "When do I get my phone call?"

They both traded looks. "I don't believe you understand the severity of the situation you're in right now," one said.

"Then please enlighten me, gentlemen," I said. I had a feeling in the pit of my stomach that everything we had worked so hard to accomplish for the good of the world was about to come crashing down.

"You are being investigated as the leader of a terrorist organization in the United States and abroad," the other said. "The

NSA, with help from the CIA and Interpol, has been gathering intelligence on you and your terrorist group for many years now."

This was starting to get very interesting. Either the badguys were more deeply involved in the government than we had originally thought, or we slipped, and big time.

"But we'll get to that later, Scott," he said. "For now, we're going to ask you some questions, and you're going to answer them." I sighed. "Are you the leader of the terrorist group 'The Goodguys?"

"I am the president of the Goodguys Charity organization, not a terrorist group," I said.

An agent pulled out a recorder and pressed play.

"Breech on my mark," I said.

"Copy that SD eleven," Ice 8 said.

"Go! Go! Go!" I said.

I heard the sound of a door being kicked in, followed by silenced gunshots. The agent stopped the tape. "You and seven others murdered eight people that night. Eight innocent office employees, and you're telling me you're not a terrorist?"

"We have audio and video surveillance of this attack, along with over two dozen others in the US, the UK, Germany, France, and Japan," he said. "We even have strong evidence linking your terrorist group to the massacre on a Spanish base in April of 2000. So before you pretend that you don't know what's going on, consider our evidence against you, SD eleven."

There was no way these guys had active surveillance on us during our ops. The LS squads were always thorough in their post-op sweeps for Intel. Sometimes, even Merlin swept up for us. Something wasn't right.

I hung my head low and slowly shook it. The badguys have been busy, very busy, and we never saw it coming. "Look, gentlemen. It's quite apparent that you know more than you should about us, so before you waste any more of your time, there's something you should know," I said. I was done playing with these guys. I had to get back and see Merlin. The badguys were finally on the offensive, and if we don't regroup quickly, Merlin will be resurrecting a lot of us. "I am a Goodguys, and despite what you think you see on the surface, I fight a war against a hidden evil that you can't even begin to comprehend. So please, for the sake of the world, release me."

The agent to my right chuckled. "Does your war include assassinating the president of the United States?" he said.

What?!

"No," I said.

Again, the agents traded looks. "Like I first said, Scott, we are going to ask you some questions, and you are going to answer them," one said. "Now, if you want to continue playing hardball, we can increase the intensity of this interrogation."

The other agent stood up and opened the cell door. Four uniformed soldiers walked in, pushing a modified gurney. There were several large buckets, a garden hose, a black hood, and duct tape on top of it. The agent then closed and locked the door.

"Oh really, I didn't know that you guys are allowed to torture?" I said.

"You're the leader of the most well-trained, armed, and technologically equipped international terrorist group in the world who's plotting to assassinate the president of the United States and steal Pakistani nukes," the agent to my left said. "We can do whatever we want to those who threaten the national security of the United States."

"You guys don't want to do this. You really don't," I said, shaking my head. The situation was serious and was getting even more serious by the minute. I could feel the mana pulsing through my veins.

"Where are your other cells, and when are they planning to assassinate the President?" an agent said.

"You guys really believe that we're out to kill the president, don't you?" I said.

The agent to my right pulled some pictures from a file and spread them across the table. "Integrated full protection body armor, firearms of all types, caseless depleted uranium rounds, RDX rounds, grenades, AT-4 CS and Javelin missile launchers that you have somehow modified to fire standard missiles of their type and Hellfire missiles of which you had dozens of. Complete and accurate blueprints for the Whitehouse, Andrews Air Force Base, and Air Force One," he said. "You also possess the highly sensitive and classified security procedures of the Secret Service, which are current as of this morning." He pulled out some more pictures and documents. "And this is your assault plan against Air Force One at Andrews Air Force Base."

I almost couldn't believe what I was seeing. The pictures showed us training when our group was beginning. They showed us in action on actual SD ops we did, and even when we were on vacation. They showed the LSS shop and the equipment in it, as well as our latest firearms. They had pictures of everything.

"Your terrorist organization is so clandestine and sophisticated that we had to store our counter intel on you offline in a secure physical database lest your hackers retrieve it. So yes, with your training, intelligence, and firepower, we strongly believe that you have every intention of assassinating the President," he said.

"And this plot pales in comparison with what you are planning to do in Pakistan," the other agent said, pulling out another file. "Do you want to see the file on that too?"

"So again, where are your other cells, and when are they planning to assassinate the President?"

One of the soldiers pulled out a syringe and began to fill it with some liquid from a small vial. Another soldier was attaching the hose to a spigot in the wall.

By this time, I didn't even know what to think. The badguys have been watching us since day one, and we didn't have a clue. They knew what we were going to attack and when. They were letting us win. It was as if we were their puppets in their little game, but what game? And was Merlin a part of it? Is he really using us to save the world from evil, or is he Calignosity himself? Or maybe it was all Ghost; after all, he was the Eyes of The One Who is Nameless. It didn't make sense, not a single bit of it.

I had to get out of here, but there were eight highly trained men in this room with me. Even if I wasn't handcuffed to the waist and shackled to the chair, there was no way that I could take them all out and escape, at least not without using my magic, something Merlin vehemently warned us never to do, but what choice did I have and what did it matter? If I were to escape, I'd have to use magic; if I used my magic, I'd have to kill all of them. There could be no witnesses. Our cause is lost.

"I must apologize for my behavior, gentlemen. I have been very disrespectful to you as authority figures, and I sincerely apologize for that," I sighed heavily. What did it matter? "But as sorry as I am, I must offend you one last time."

The agent to my left shook his head. "You really enjoy being a smart ass, don't you, Scott?" he said. "Dope and rack him, men."

I wanted to be able to go back and tell my buddies that I didn't say a word, but that would have been a lie. After eighteen straight hours of waterboarding and strange drug injections, all they got out of me was a bunch of profanities. I was then electrocuted and waterboarded some more, but still, I said nothing. Merlin would never have forgiven me for killing them. I never would have forgiven myself. The burden of Mary Janes's death was heavy enough.

The shackles around my wrists and ankles were bone-crushingly tight. My head was swimming from the cocktail of drugs, and I was shivering uncontrollably. I was lying half-naked on the floor of a small concrete cell that had no windows or toilet when Merlin appeared in the room with me.

"I am very proud of you, Scott, for it is never easy to restrain the use of your magic against those who do you harm," Merlin said. My restraints opened, and fell to the floor. My head stopped swimming, and I felt fully invigorated. He then handed me my clothes from out of his leather satchel. "Now come, there are things that you must see and things that you must know."

Not a moment after I was fully clothed, we were both standing near the edge of the southern rim of the Grand Canyon.

"Tell me, what do you see before you?" Merlin said.

The early rays of dawn caused the reddish-orange rocks to glisten while a gentle breeze swept over me. The canyon's grandeur was breathtaking and a sight that calmed my nerves. I guess that's why I've always loved nature. It was a place of peace where I could reflect and enjoy the only beauty left.

"Serenity," I said.

"And beauty."

"Yes."

"But it will not remain this way for much longer."

I sighed. "What are we to tell the world when it burns?"

Merlin's robe fluttered in the wind. "It was never my intention for you to stop the destruction of this world, for you cannot," he said. "It was my intention to prepare you to survive it and do what I could not."

"Why can't you destroy him?"

Merlin smiled at me. "Oh, Scott, the one whose knowledge can never be sated. Now see what I have seen and know what I have known."

With a wave of his wand, my vision faded.

Black clouds engulfed in flames covered the sky and stretched from horizon to horizon. The ground was scorched black and dotted with craters of bubbling magma. Everything was death.

Thousands upon tens of thousands of men, women, and children lay prostrate before a figure dressed in a tattered black robe. Twelve red-skinned balrogs, each adorned with a golden spiked crown, with their black bat-like wings folded stood behind it. Flying high above them, Calignosity raised his twisted human spine staff and cried an ear-piercing shriek.

Screams of agony filled the air as the souls of those below were drawn from their bodies and distorted into thin black threads into Calignositys mouth. Silence overcame the land.

My vision returned.

"I have lived for seven millennia, Scott, but not a day longer," Merlin said. "For you see, he is immortal. I am not."

I stared out across the canyon. The pit in my stomach was growing. Reaching behind his neck, Merlin unclasped a dull gray chain and pulled out an amulet beneath his robe.

"I want you to have this, for you will need it," he said, putting it in my hand.

The platinum amulet was about the size of a silver dollar and had the language of Ethereal written in gold around its edge. An extremely large diamond was in the center, with twelve sparkling black opals surrounding it. It was heavy and unnaturally cold. "It is the Amulet of the Kings; with it, your soul will forever remain yours."

"I can't take this Merlin. It's yours," I said, trying to give it back to him.

He closed my hand around the amulet. "Not a day longer." He then pulled out my katana from his all-holding satchel and handed it to me, but it was different. The blade was nearly translucent, black, and whispy. Power surged through me as memories of Scarlet and the

Empress flashed before my eyes. "And not a day longer can I conceal what will be revealed to you, for my power is waning."

"I've had dreams, Merlin," I said, twisting and turning the blade. "Dreams that I can't explain. And this sword..."

"I know my friend. I know."

"Are my dreams from Ethereal? And are they real?" I said. "Tell me if you know. What does it all mean?"

Merlin stared out across the canyon. "My good friend," he paused, placing his hand on my shoulder. "I know not of your past, nor of the path you will choose, for it is concealed from me by time itself," he sighed, glancing down at my sword. "I can only hope that I have given you the strength to carry the light of the ones whom you love through the darkness ahead." I took a deep breath and let it out slowly. "Now do what I could not. Fight the good fight, and discover the way to destroy him." Merlin said.

I clasped the chain around my neck and tucked the amulet beneath my black t-shirt. It all made sense now. Everything that we had fought so hard for and shed so much blood and sweat for was just to prepare us to survive the inevitable apocalypse.

Our war against the badguys, the trips into the Dark Zone, it was all just training. The end of the world is coming, and quickly, and all we can do is watch it burn.

CHAPTER TWENTY-SEVEN

"**B**rowny, my man, we missed you!" Doubles shouted, embracing me in a tight hug. "You should see it, man! Every single news channel is talking about how we conned everyone and are like the most dangerous terrorist group in the entire world."

"We've been non-stop news for the past twenty-four hours now," Big Blue said.

"They've even increased the terror level to red," Kid said.

"It's pretty bad though," Doubles said. "They arrested Police, Chief, and Striper too."

I hugged Police. "So they got you, too, uh?"

"They sure did, but SDS three was onto them," Police said. "Iceman and company took out the entire escort convoy in the heart of Phoenix during rush hour using non-lethal dart rounds and AP rounds for the vehicles. It was all done and over with in less than thirty seconds."

"LSS one, however, secured Chief's rescue by storming the Federal building in LA," Inspector said. "Eighty-six dart rounds, four destroyed vehicles, some minor holes in some walls, and a teleport later, and here we are."

"And Striper, well, he escaped all on his own," Police said. "Well, with Merlin's help, of course."

"LSS one stormed a federal building?!" I said with a dumbfounded look on my face.

"Yeah, I know," Octane said.

"With Pudgy?!" I said.

"Yeah, I cannoteth believe it toeth," Buccaneer said. "It appeareth as though Pudgy doth have a little fight in thee."

Inspector wrapped Pudgy in a loose headlock and rubbed his brown hair with his fist. "And he performed admirably, too," he said.

"We took no casualties and inflicted no casualties, but we sure did destroy a lot of shit," Iceman said.

"The news is going crazy right now, and people are panicking. They think it's another 911." Octane said.

"Unfortunately," Bestguard said.

"So what's the plan?" I said.

"Continue doing what we have been doing, though our public relations plan is shot to hell," Iceman said.

"There's no easy way to put it; the badguys hit us well," Inspector said. "The NSA has seized everything of ours except what we have here. Our intel links, dummy corps, everything has been shut down."

I looked around our camp and noticed everyone's KATS armor and SOTA weaponry were by or in their tents. Dozens of crates and boxes were stacked everywhere.

"Really?" I said with a half-cocked grin on my face.

"Well, except for what each squad rolled around with," Inspector said. "Merlin has your gear in his tent."

"My interrogators made mention of a plot to assassinate the President while he takes off from Andrews Air Force Base. Any news on that?" I said.

"Hence, why the terrorist level is at red," Kid said.

"Not a thing, aside from the scant details the news channels are spitting out," Big Red said. "We're deaf, dumb, and blind."

"Are the threats credible?" Big Blue said.

"With what the badguys just pulled, absolutely," Iceman said.

"Who art could surveil us like this?" Bestguard said.

"Not a clue," Ice 8 said. "We first suspected Ghost, but Striper put it down, so Calignosity?"

"Come to my tent, Scott," Merlin's voice said in my head.

"Excuse me, guys." I pushed aside the heavy cloth curtains at Merlin's tent and walked inside. He was standing near the back, holding a scroll, and dressed in his usual sky-blue robes. His long white hair and beard were neatly combed, and his soft features had grown harder over the years.

Oddly enough, the only thing in his tent was my gear. All of his furniture and bedding were gone. "Yes, Merlin?"

"I have one more thing to give to you." He handed me a scroll. "When all hope is lost, use this to find the golden key, and you will find me."

I gave him a confused look. "What do you mean?" Merlin smiled and rested his hand on my shoulder. "I'll learn in time, won't I?"

Merlin embraced me in his arms. "You are the light of many worlds, Scott; now lead them, my brother." He turned and led me out of his tent.

"Welcome, Badguys. Today is the 21st of April 2004, and as you are all aware, we are the most wanted terrorists in all of the world," Iceman said.

"Whoa, yeah!" Whiteguy shouted. "We're a terrorist group, baby!"

Everyone cheered and hollered. Kid held his hand up to his ear in the shape of a pretend phone. "Hello, this is the Badguys Terrorist Organization. How may we be of terror to you?!" Kid said.

Everyone laughed. "Alright, Badguys, all right," Iceman said. "On a more serious note, the damage to our group is significant. Our multi-million dollar equipment from the LSS shop has been seized, and our dummy corps and personal accounts have been shut down. Our names are soiled, and our faces are plastered on every news channel, internet site, and bulletin board for every government agency worldwide. Simply put, the badguys hit us hard."

Kid held up a yellow credit card. "Does this mean my Kids 'R Us gift card is no good now?" he said.

I could hear some chuckles in the crowd. "Unfortunately, yes," Inspector said.

"Screw this crap man!" Kid said, throwing his card to the ground. "These badguys are going to frickin' pay!"

"It's all right, Kid. I'll buy you a new one," Bazooka said.

Kid ground the card into the sand with his foot. "Thanks," he muttered.

"We now know why Kid fights," Fire said.

"Hey! Merlin said I could have all the toys I wanted if I joined!" Kid said.

Merlin shook his head, smiling while everyone laughed up a storm.

"How does this affect our combat effectiveness?" Aqua Shark said.

"We're all still here, right? With most of our gear, right?" Greyguy said, pointing around to it. "So we'll continue to lay waste!"

"That be the spirit!" Buccaneer said.

"We'll rebuild the LS squad's capabilities to manufacture war and the TS squad's ability to gather Intel and keep doing what we do best: kill badguys," Iceman said.

"Death art a cometh to thee badguys!" Basil yelled.

"Hell ya, mon!" Islander shouted.

Again, everyone erupted into an uproar, and why everyone was so ecstatic was beyond me. We were the most wanted men in the world, but I guess they didn't know that it was all over. We failed.

"What are we going to do to protect the President?" Octane said.

"Truthfully, there's nothing that we can do, especially if the badguys use their magic," Inspector said.

"Which they are sure to do," Iceman said. "For now, all TS and LS squad members capable of hacking will do so. Everyone else will be providing over-watch."

Merlin looked over at me. He was smiling softly, but I could tell he was forcing it.

"What about our families?" Chief said. "How are we going to arrange to see them? I mean, my wife is in custody, and my son, I don't know where he is."

"That's going to be a tough one. I would advise all of you who have girlfriends and families to talk with Merlin." Iceman said. "I have a family as well back on Ice Planet, and you know my position on this. You all knew what you were signing up for."

"How possible is it that we tell our family who we are and what we do and relocate them?" Fire said.

"That is one of the many courses of action we will be taking in our X-plan, but we are far from needing to implement it, which is something only Merlin can authorize," Inspector said. "Besides, your daughter is smart. It's not like she's going to believe you anyhow."

Some Goodguys chuckled.

"Hey, Fire?" Doubles said. Fire glanced at him. "Do you have health insurance 'cause you're on fire, man!" More Goodguys laughed.

"What's the X-plan?" Octane said.

Iceman ran his hand across his short white goatee. "It's a plan that if the shit hits the fan, we'll walk away with minimal splatter," he said.

Goresavice and his four captains and over a hundred badguys behind them appeared out of thin air. They all had an assault rifle slung over their shoulder and a knife, staff, sword, or club in their hand. Dozens more badguys were lying or kneeling atop the plateau with rifles trained on us.

"Ahh, the Goodguys," Goresavice said. "The last bastion of hope."

"Hey, it's Grenadeguy, Gunguy, Mopguy, and Hamhand in person," Kids said, flicking open his butterfly knife.

"Would you take a look at that hand!" Octane said. "He is a freak of nature!"

"Damn, and I thought I had big hands!" Ice 8 said.

"And I bet he's just as stupid as he looks," Doubles said.

"Me, no stupid," Hamhand said in a whiny, nasally voice. "Me smash you face in!"

"We've got a winner, folks!" Doubles shouted.

We all burst into laughter. Hamhand was retarded.

"He's not as stupid as the one with the atrocious mop on his head!" Space Police said. "What type of hairstyle is that?!"

"So where did you find Hamhand? In Chernobyl?!" Aqua Shark said. "And Mopguy, the gutter?!"

"Argh! I'll be a scrubbin' my arse with yar head!" Hook said pointing his cutlass at Mopguy.

Again, we all burst into laughter. The badguys, however, maintained their composure and stood at the ready in silence.

"You know, Goresavice, it's pretty hard to take you seriously when you have half-retarded SOBs as your captains," Doubles said.

"Do you hear that?" Octane said.

"I hear it loud and clear," Space Police said. "It's coming from the abyss."

I could hear a faint sucking, popping, and slurping noise coming from the Dark Zone.

"We've got something coming, men," Greyguy said. He was standing about ten meters from the abyss, two broadswords in hand.

"Do you remember what you told me back in high school, Browny, when I said, 'I wish I could be king for a day?'" Goresavice said.

"You'll have your moment; we all do," I said.

"Not in this lifetime," Goresavice said. "And how true were both of our words?" His sick smile grew wider. "The end of days is drawing near, Goodguys, and when fire sweeps across this earth, you will all be consumed, and I will take my rightful place as its prince by my master's side."

"You will have your moment, Johnathan, but on the souls of the ones I love, I swear it will not last long." I drew my katana and, cast all my spells, including protection and charged Goresavice.

Pointing at me, Goresavice disappeared, and the badguys rushed us.

I slashed at the nearest one, who lowered his blade to deflect my attack. Our swords should have clashed with sparks, but mine passed through his with no resistance and cleanly severed it, and he at the waist in half, spilling his guts everywhere. He screamed in agony as his veins began to visibly blacken. He died almost instantly as more power flooded my body, but it wasn't a power that I could comprehend. It was darker.

The blade of my katana was a wispy black shadow and virtually weightless.

Following through with my slashing motion, I spun around and brought my blade down on a badguys left shoulder. He raised his metal bo staff to block, but my blade sliced through it and cut him in two from shoulder to right hip. He, too, died instantly, his mouth twisted open and veins black. An aura of darkness followed in the wake of my blade.

A badguy to my left swung a spiked mace at my head. Ducking away from it, I plunged the ethereal blade of my sword into his heart.

Screaming loudly, he grabbed my sword, but it severed his hand. His chest caved in while his blood boiled away.

With a frenzied bloodlust, I hacked and slashed at everyone within reach. Three seconds later, twelve Badguys lay dead at my feet. Halved metal weapons and severed body parts lay everywhere. Whatever my sword had become, it was utterly devastating. The brown sand was turning red as more and more power filled me.

Crawling and slithering out of the Dark Zone were waves upon waves of human organs. Lungs flopped on the ground towards us. Stomachs snaked along the ground using their esophagus; brains hopped along on their stems, while hearts walked using their many arteries. They were truly disgusting, and I could only imagine how they killed.

Not a moment later, sedan-sized monstrous spiders, scorpions, and beetles crawled out of the abyss and raced toward us. Behind them, flying overhead, were man-eating dragonflies the length of limos and June bugs the size of semi-trucks. This was a full-scale attack designed to kill us all. The apocalypse was nearing.

Looking around, I saw Goresavice perched on the narrow ledge of the jagged rock tower that protruded high above and over the plateau's edge. Gunshots echoed throughout the desert.

Sheathing my katana, I ran towards the plateau, cast jump, and gecko crawl. Flying over twenty meters in the air, I stuck to the sheer face of the plateau and cast haste. Six seconds and one hundred meters later, I stood on the tower's ledge facing Goresavice. He smiled at me.

"Do you know what Karen's last words to me were before I watered the ground with her blood?" he said.

Those were the last words that I was going to let him speak. I drew my katana and charged him.

A shimmering bolt of energy flew from Goresavice's hand and slammed into me. Fiery pain spread throughout my body as I fell face-first onto the rocky surface. My katana skittered across the ground and disappeared over the edge.

"Please, Johnathan, please. I'll do anything. Please, anything!" Goresavice said. "And she did, to include giving me her soul."

Slowly, I climbed to my knees and then my feet. My vision was blurry, and blood was pouring from out my nose and ears. I'd be dead had I not been sustaining giant's toughness, but I needed better protection from magic. He could easily kill me with one or two more mana bolts.

"Today, you will die by my hands," I said, wiping some blood off my chin.

Goresavice chuckled through his sly smile. "You've killed me once already, yet here I am," he said. "So tell me, what is it that I die again?"

I cast mana bolt and watched as the bolt slammed into him, but the energy washed over him, leaving him unscathed. He knew mana shield.

Goresavice chuckled. "I've grown so much more powerful since the last time we've met. So much more."

So have I. However, the spell was so mana-draining that I didn't want to cast it this early in the fight, but I was too injured not to. I cast regeneration.

Drawing his k-bar, Goresavice slashed at my throat. With a single fluid motion and as fast as you could blink your eyes, I grabbed his arm and twisted it up and behind his back while disarming him and forcing him to his knees. With his knife in my hand, I stepped behind him and cut his throat, but the blade didn't even scratch him.

More fiery pain spread throughout my body. He had struck me with another mana bolt. Stumbling backward, vomiting blood, I collapsed to my knees. My vision faded to black while feelings of nausea gripped me.

"Why don't you run like you always do, Browny?" Goresavice said. "Like the day you left Mary Jane."

I stood up. "W-Why d-don't you b-burn in hell you, you sick son of a bitch."

Goresavice lunged forward and kicked low at my left knee. Raising my leg, I checked his kick and chopped him in the throat with hammer hands, but again, I couldn't hurt him. He swung his fist for my chin, but he was too close. Grabbing and holding his arm to my chest, I slammed him onto his back on the ledge and stepped over his arm. Jerking his arm back, I broke it over my knee. Goresavice groaned.

Releasing his arm, I reached to wrap up his head and neck in my arms, but before I could, he tripped me with his legs and stood up.

Kipping to my feet, I cautiously walked towards Goresavice. His arm was healing right before my eyes. "It's quite an amazing spectacle of power, isn't it?" he said.

Two mages were flying in the air, casting spell after spell at Merlin, but no matter what they cast, Merlin reflected it at another badguy or insect, killing them instantly. With a wave of his wand, dozens more would just drop dead.

With another wave, any Goodguys who were injured were healed, while several pyroclastic blasts, scorching rays, and swirling green death coils would strike badguys and insects wherever they stood. A black aura of energy emanated from Merlin's body, and anything that touched it died instantly and rapidly decayed. Even the sandy ground that he walked on was crumbling to dust.

"Like a dying star in its death throes, the end is drawing near," Goresavice said. "And soon, a new era will dawn."

Appearing out of nowhere, another mana bolt ripped into me, knocking me down. A feeling of weightlessness overcame me. Goresavice walked over to the edge and looked down at me. I blacked out.

Blinking the blood out of my eyes. I stared up at the blue sky above. Pain coursed throughout my body, though I could still feel myself regenerating.

Slowly, I stood. Dead badguys and insects were everywhere, and all that remained was Goresavice. Several Goodguys were lying unconscious on the ground beside him.

Sidestepping Pirate's clumsy take-down attempt, Goresavice used Pirate's momentum against him and hurled him a good eight meters through the air. Landing hard on his back, Pirate rolled to a stop. Jumping to his feet, Pirate drew his cutlass and charged. Raising his hand, Goresavice sent a mana bolt into Pirate's chest. He collapsed to the ground, skidding to a halt face first, barely conscious.

With his massive, black spiked mace in hand, Batlord swung it at Goresavice's head, but he nimbly ducked under it and stabbed Batlord in the gut. Ripping his blade out, Goresavice quickly spun around, stabbing him in the back. Batlord collapsed to the ground, coughing up blood. Two lightning bolts and a cold bolt struck Goresavice, but his mana shield spell completely absorbed the energy.

Squaring up with Goresavice, Police attacked with his baton, but Goresavice countered with a slash to Police's throat with his k-bar. Blocking his attack, Police disarmed him and threw him to the ground. Entangling his legs with Police's, Goresavice tripped him, picked up his knife, and stabbed Police in the left leg. Kipping to his feet, Goresavice cast a mana bolt, which struck Aqua and knocked him to the ground, unconscious.

"Before this world burns at my feet, I will kill each and every last one of you, one by one," Goresavice calmly said.

"Then you can start with me," I said. Goresavice smiled.

Feinting to my left, I kicked low at the inside of his right knee with hammer hands, and because he flinched, my kick found its mark. His leg buckled, and he grimaced in pain. With his balance off,

I stepped into him, grabbed his right arm, and tossed him over my hip. I then twisted his arm until it popped. His protection spell had failed, and so had mine and my regeneration. My mana was getting dangerously low.

Jumping onto his back, I quickly wrapped my legs around him in a tight figure-four body lock and attempted to choke him out, but his defense was good. Releasing my hold from around his neck, I under-hooked his left arm, prying it away from his body, and dislocated it at the shoulder. The back of his head slammed into my face with hammer hands, breaking my nose.

Releasing my body lock, I staggered to my feet. My head was swimming, and blood was pouring down my face. Scrambling to his feet, Goresavice went to kick at me, but as he raised his right foot off the ground, I threw a straight kick into his left knee. Goresavice's knee buckled, which surprised me. This meant that his other protection spells had failed, too.

Closing the distance between us, I chopped down with a closed fist on Goresavice's right clavicle, snapping it like a twig. Groaning loudly, Goresavice stumbled back on his blown-out knee. Drawing another concealed k-bar, he slashed at me, cutting me along my ribs.

The only spells I was sustaining were giant's toughness, ogre's strength, and lightning reflexes. All my others had failed. He slashed at me again, but I grabbed his knife hand and chopped him in the throat while disarming him at the same time. I then struck him in the nose with an open palm that, caused his head to snap back. Following through with a sharp blow to his liver, Goresavice doubled over, staggered. I then deliver a hard knee to his face. Blood splattered everywhere as he fell onto his back. He was now more than incapacitated, but I wasn't ready to kill him yet. I wanted him to suffer for everything he's done.

Climbing to his feet, blood dripping down his face, Goresavice looked back at the abyss behind him and smiled. Feinting to my left, followed by a few jabs, I jumped high in the air and spun around with my right leg fully extended. Blood and chips of teeth flew out of his mouth as my jumping roundhouse kick slammed into his chin. Spinning violently and stumbling backward, Gorsavice disappeared into the black abyss.

Behind me, the Goodguys erupted into cheers.

Wrapping his massive arms around me, Moonwalker hoisted me atop his shoulders. "You're my man, Browny!" he cried out. "Way to kick his ass!"

"Hell, ya buddy guts!" Whiteguy shouted. "You're my hero!"

"Ghost is dead, and now so is Goresavice!" Octane yelled. "Goodguys forever!"

"Oh yeah!" Big Red said.

Moonwalker set me down. "That's another win for the Goodguys, baby!" Chief said, patting me on the back.

Doubles handed me my sword, but he hesitated. It was like he was entranced by it. "Way to kill him, man."

"Thanks," I said. But deep inside, I knew that he wasn't dead. I should have killed him when I had the chance.

"It's going to be quite the mess to clean up, eh guys?" Police said. Dead badguys and insects littered the desert.

"Yay, it art," Batlord said.

I pushed my way through a huddled mass of Goodguys. They were looking down at something with a solemn expression on their faces. "So what's going on buddies? What are we looking at?" Doubles said.

A sudden silence overcame our group as everyone cleared away from me.

"What do you command, Browny?" Inspector said.

"Thine followeth thee wherever thou goeth, brother," Bestguard said.

Doubles nodded. "To the gates of hell, I won't back down," he said.

"Thy wish is thine command," Batlord said.

"Merlin told us that we're to follow you now," Police said.

Merlin was lying on the ground. His eyes were closed, and his arms were by his sides. Not a day longer.

"Browny, what are your orders?" Iceman said.

I closed my eyes and sighed. My heart was heavy. With my katana still in hand, I headed for the small lake in the distance. I needed time to think.

"What dideth Merlin telleth you in the tent?" Bestguard said. Everyone was watching me. The atmosphere caliginous.

I stopped walking and looked at my katana. The darkness enveloping the blade beckoned me.

Scarlet skipped alongside me, giggling. Her long and elegant blood dress cast drops of blood on the Noir Belge marble floor. A smokey haze filled the circular throne room while black flames danced along the walls. There were thirteen golden thrones, six on each side of a central one, and a grand pentagram covering the entire floor. Blood flowed from the base of the central throne and into the northern point of the pentagram, filling the lines.

"Behold, your kingdom, father," Scarlet said, twirling about with her arms out wide.

I looked up at the intricate vaulted ceiling. The Earth was engulfed in flames. I heard people screaming. I saw people dying. I felt nothingness.

"Browny," Bestguard said. "Merlin art dead. What art we to doeth?"

My body shivered. Everyone was staring at me. "Prepare yourselves, for the end is nigh," I said in a near whisper. "We have failed. The world will burn."

CHAPTER TWENTY-EIGHT

The following day, I ordered Iceman and Inspector to implement their X plan. It was hard for everyone to believe that Merlin's intentions for us were to only survive and even harder still to believe that the end was near, but the facts were undeniable. Merlin was dead. Nothing could stop Calignosity now.

Everyone was gearing up, getting ready for Iceman to teleport each squad to their respective country around the world.

"I'm going to see you again, right?" Doubles said.

"I'll see you again, brother," I said.

Police wrapped his arms around both of us. "We'll all see each other again over the dead bodies of our enemies."

"You're damn straight, dude." Doubles said.

"But on a more serious note, this has been one hell of a ride," Police said.

"I double that," Doubles said. "I love you guys."

We all embraced each other.

"I'm going to miss you, Browny," Kid said, shaking my hand. "It's been a real honor fighting with you."

"Same here, Kid," I said. "And take care of yourself."

"Yeah, you too," Kid said.

"Don't do anything that I wouldn't do, man," Octane said, patting me on the back.

"Sure, I'll keep that in mind," I said, giving him a brief hug.

"You be careful with that sword, man. You can really hurt someone with that thing," Aqua Shark said.

I snickered and nodded my head, and raised my hand.

"For the sake of the world, I hope you're wrong," Iceman whispered to me.

"So do I." Everyone quieted down and gave me their full attention. "My good friends, never in all of my natural life would I have thought that hell exists, but now I do, and we fight against it as brothers," I said. "Now fight the good fight, but do not be careless with your lives because we are the last in line." I sighed, and paused for a good long moment while looking up at the sky. "We are the Goodguys."

With fists raised in the air, everyone shouted with me, "Goodguys!"

A moment later, only my squad was left in the desert. We were assigned to North America. "You guys go on without me," I said.

"You know they're watching your house," Moonwalker said.

"I know," I said.

"Thy cannot fighteth this war aloneth," Guard said.

"Goresavice has hunted me since the beginning, and he won't stop until I'm dead," I said. "I can't let you guys risk your lives by fighting alongside me."

"But you killed him," Fire said.

"Like a Barrow White killed you?" I said. "Now give them hell." I picked up my two black duffle bags and headed into the Dark Woods.

For the next few hours, I walked around the neighborhood, reminiscing of the simple and joyous days of my childhood. I stopped by the high school, sat down in the dugout by the baseball field, and watched myself run around the bases in the last game I ever played. I broke into Jessica's still unsold house, sat on her bed, and cried. I missed her so much.

I strolled along the beach of Lake Caldwell and thought about all the days I went swimming with my friends, and all the water fights we had. It's amazing how quickly things can change for the worse. One moment, I was just a kid living a normal life; the next, I was living anything but, fighting in a war against hell itself. I just wanted, more than anything, to go back to the way things used to be when all my friends were still alive, when I was happy and full of life, and all I cared about was when our next football game was or who I was going to get elected homecoming queen.

With the sun beginning to set, I visited my Mom last. Moonwalker was right; two agents were watching my house, but I knew this neighborhood like the back of my hand and snuck in through an unlocked window around back. I found my mother in the living room, all curled up with a blanket on the couch, watching the news. Newspaper clippings and old photos of me were scattered across the coffee table.

"Mom."

She sat up and looked at me. "Scott?" she said in a near whisper.

I sat down on the couch, put my arm around her, and kissed her on the cheek. "I'm home, Mom, and there's something that I must tell you."

"Oh, Scott, there's nothing you can tell me that will ever cause me to hate you." Mom ran her fingers through my wavy brown hair. "I will always be proud of you, no matter what."

I could see the pain in her eyes, and I wanted to tell her everything: who I was and what was going to happen, but none of it mattered. She is my mother and will always love me, no matter what.

For the rest of the night, I held my Mom in my arms, comforting her until she fell asleep. After kissing her goodbye, I snuck out the back of the house and drove to Phoenix, where I checked into a rundown hotel on the city's outskirts.

I awoke early the next morning to the sound of my door opening. Jumping out of bed, I drew my pistol.

"You're too easy to track, Browny," Moonwalker said, walking in and setting his two black duffle bags on the spare bed. "I'm surprised you haven't been arrested yet-again."

"Did you really think we'd let you fight all by yourself?" Fire said.

"You guys scared me there for a minute," I said.

Fire sat down on the spare bed and turned on the television. "You scared yourself, buddy guts," he said.

"We must notteth stayeth here. It art a likely place for thine's portal," Guard said.

"I know, but I'm a sucker for hard-fought battles," I said.

Moonwalker chuckled. "Calignosity art not shy about thine's power. Thou'll want thy whole world to see it," Guard said.

"Good, then let the whole world see us fighting it," I said. "That might do wonders for our public image."

"This is our public image," Fire said.

CNN had my picture on the screen alongside Police, Chief, and Striper's. They were talking about how unbelievable it was that eight heavily armed and armored 'Goodguy' terrorists destroyed twelve vehicles and shot down twenty-four FBI agents and fourteen officers with dart rounds to rescue Police in broad daylight. The successful rescue of Chief from the FBI headquarters was even more harrowing. The FBI had no comment on that or how Striper and I escaped. They just said that whatever our terrorist organization is, "it is far more capable than we had anticipated." Every news agency across the world was showing video clips of the 'terrorists' gun battle in downtown Phoenix. We were headline news everywhere.

"They both strike us well," Guard said.

"They certainly did," Moonwalker said.

"Oh wait, we've got breaking news," Fire said, turning up the volume.

"I've got money that it's about us," Moonwalker said.

"Let's hope that no one's been captured."

"We have some, uh, disturbing news-" the anchorwoman said. She sounded distraught and looked it. "I can't believe this just happened."

"Some tragic news is developing in Washington DC," the anchorman said. He looked down at his papers. "The president's convoy has just been attacked."

"How much did you pay the desk clerk?" Moonwalker said.

"He didn't recognize me," I said.

"He will now, so we must prepare to move out."

"I'm staying," I said.

"If you're staying, then I'm staying," Fire said, lying down on the bed.

"You're the boss," Moonwalker said. "But if we're made, just know that none of us have the spell teleport or resurrection."

"I know, and I have no intention of going quietly this time," I said.

Later that day, more details of the attack came to light. A shoulder-fired missile blew up the President's limo, and all inside were killed instantly, including the President. A heavy gun battle that involved eight well-armed terrorists and the convoy's security agents then ensued for two hours in the streets of DC, which resulted in the deaths of all the terrorists. However, twenty-six Secret Service members and fifteen officers were killed. Another twenty were injured. The missiles used in the attack were Hellfire anti-tank missiles fired from modified Javelin missile launchers. The same ones that were seized from the LSS shop. We were now the most wanted terrorist organization in the world, and I was their feared leader.

That night, we slept in shifts, in full kit.

"So who's getting breakfast?" I said.

"What doth thee wisheth to eat?" Guard said. "McDonald's, Burger King, or Wendy's?"

"None of that garbage. Go to the store and get us some foods high in carbs, protein, and fat, but none of that processed crap," Moonwalker said.

"Why don't we go out to eat?" Fire said. Moonwalker shot Fire a dumbfounded look. "I know. Browny can stay here and eat MREs."

"Really Fire?" I said.

Fire snickered. "So, what's the bounty on your head now, Browny?"

"One hundred million," I said.

Fire looked astonished. "Wow, that's a lot of cheddar. I'm tempted."

"I can't lie, same here," Moonwalker said.

The window of our room rattled violently as the ground shook. "What art thee hell?" Guard said.

"Nine hundred kilo UGBU. Six of them," Moonwalker said, slapping a mag into his .50 cal sniper rifle.

"A UG what?" Fire said.

Peeking through the curtains, I saw a huge plume of gray smoke rising several kilometers away. Two more plumes were rising off in the distance.

"Perhaps we moveth out noweth?" Guard said.

"Oh, come on, Guard. Things are just beginning to heat up, buddy," I said, lying on the bed and folding my hands behind my head.

"Now would be the time to get out, Browny, before the city is crawling with cops," Fire said.

"It's your call," Moonwalker said.

"I understand the risk, guys, but I'm staying," I said.

Fire sat on the bed. "And there it is."

"It looks like we're all having MREs," Moonwalker said.

Six hours later, the National Guard had the entire city of Phoenix under martial law. The governor's building was completely leveled by several two thousand-pound bombs, as was the Phoenix PD and Children' hospital. The blasts also destroyed numerous other buildings.

Later estimates put the death toll above one thousand to include the governor, but Phoenix wasn't the only city to be bombed that morning. Regina in Saskatchewan, Canada; Prague in the Czech Republic; Tokyo in Japan; and six other capitols across the world were also bombed similarly.

Soon after the attacks, a live video circulated on the internet. It featured several heavily armed and masked 'Goodguys' and me. I promised to bring the world to its knees and usher in the apocalypse unless every tongue confessed me as lord and every knee bowed. The world had twenty-four hours to respond, and the countdown would begin at midnight tonight, eastern time.

"I think you presented a strong case as to why the world should submit to you, Browny," Moonwalker said.

"Yes, I have to agree with you, Moonwalker. However, I think his complexion was rather poor," Fire said, trying to sound sophisticated. They were both sitting on the spare bed, analyzing every frame of the video on Moonwalker's laptop.

"It's Goresavice," I said.

"How do you know?" Moonwalker said.

"That's Jessica's pendant around his neck," I said.

"You were right then. Calignosity did raise him for a second time," Fire said. "We're fucked."

"Or I never killed him," I said.

"That's some pretty powerful magic to transform yourself into someone else," Moonwalker said.

"It art thee spell of transmogrify," Guard said. "It transforms thee into anything liveth thou can imagineth."

I unsheathed my katana and held it to the light. "What can you tell me about my sword Guard?" I said. "Merlin could not conceal it from me any longer." The blade, though nearly transparent, absorbed the light and the golden Ethereal symbols on the blade above the hilt seemed to dance.

"It possesseth power beyond what thy knoweth. Powerfully dark," Guard said. "And even in its presence, I shivereth."

"That sword is brutal. I saw what it did to those badguys," Fire said.

"And steel," Moonwalker said.

"Relics, they art powerful," Guard said, eyeing my katana's wispy blackness. "But this art nothing I have ever heard of. It art not right."

"I understand what you mean," I said, closing my eyes. Fire and brimstone, blood, and ash flooded my senses. "And that's why it will never leave my side," I said.

"Yeah, I wouldn't let that sword fall into the wrong hands either," Fire said. He was looking at me through the corner of his eyes. It was like he couldn't look at the blade. I sheathed it.

"Doth, thy now knoweth why Merlin was so careful in choosing thee?" Guard said. "It taketh only one to bring about thy world's end."

"And you were right, Browny. The world is going to burn," Fire said. "But at least you don't have to worry, Moonwalker. Your planet is light years away and safe."

"For now," Moonwalker said.

Fire sighed and pulled out a picture of his daughter. "I hate this magic; end of days shit. I should be with my daughter."

I put my hand on Fire's shoulder. "If we had more time, bud, we would have taken care of her," I said.

"I know."

Sarah was taken into foster care when Fire was arrested.

CHAPTER TWENTY-NINE

"**B**rowny, time to get up, buddy guts," Fire whispered.

Rolling over, I glanced at the clock. It was almost nine-thirty in the morning. I slept in by more than three hours! After getting up, I took a long, hot shower, shaved, and dressed in my KATS body armor. I then sat on my bed, turned on the TV, and opened an MRE.

It was the twenty-fifth of April, and Congress was having an emergency session. The newly sworn president was addressing them, saying that the United States will not be intimidated and that they will use every available resource to bring the terrorists to justice.

"Would you take a look at you, sitting all comfy in your KATS suit?" Moonwalker said. "You're ready to rock 'n roll, aren't you?"

"Fourteen hours and counting," I said.

"So, what's on the news today?" Fire said.

"Nothing yet," I said.

"Just give it time," Moonwalker said.

"Yeah, isn't that true?" I said.

"What art thy possibility of thee National Guard searching building to art building?" Guard said.

"It's pretty slim, though standard procedure requires them to search high-value, potential targets with bomb-sniffing dogs and equipment," Moonwalker said. "Putting an entire city like Phoenix and the surrounding areas under martial law is no small order. Not even New York City was put under total martial law when the Twin Towers fell."

"Don't you find that a bit odd?" I said.

"Absolutely. It takes a significant threat to lock a city down, and yesterday's attack certainly wouldn't qualify," Moonwalker said.

"How do you know all this," Fire said. "And how do you know how to speak English?" Moonwalker chuckled. "You can tell us your deep, dark secrets now. There won't be a world left to care even if we do tell."

"If we make it out of the apocalypse alive, I'll tell you everything about my planet," Moonwalker said. "I'll even take you there if you like."

Fire smiled. "I'm going to hold you to that," he said.

"Do you think the badguys had something to do with authorizing martial law?" I said.

"I wouldn't put it past them," Moonwalker said.

"Calignosity, remember what thou had sayeth. He art not shy about his power," Guard said.

"He's going to open a portal here, isn't he?" Moonwalker said.

"Thy believeth so," Guard said.

Fire ran his hand through his brown hair. "Here, huh?" he said. "Did I say that we're fucked already?"

"Well, if you're right, we only have twelve hours left, so let's pack up and move out, guys," I said.

"You got it, but I recommend that we wait until nightfall and take the service tunnels out of the city," Moonwalker said.

"Then we head out at nine tonight. That will give us one hour to put some distance between us and the city," I said.

"And if we encountereth anyone?" Guard said.

"Then we'll deal with them appropriately," I said.

"CNN has just lost contact with their reporter in DC," Fire said. He was flipping through the channels.

"And?" Moonwalker said.

"And so has Fox and MSNBC," Fire said. "All stations have lost contact with DC."

I looked over at Guard. "Leave it on CNN," I said.

Several minutes later, some live video from CNN's affiliates came streaming in. An enormous mushroom cloud was rising over the heart of Washington, DC. The hairs on the back of my neck stood on end.

Fire hung his head and let out a heavy sigh. "So this is how the world dies, eh?" he said. "And we're holed up like rats."

"This art not thee first time that thee world hath died," Guard said. "Our timeth for vengeance will cometh soon."

"If we survive," I said.

Later on that day, government officials confirmed that a fifty-megaton hydrogen bomb had been detonated. The District of Columbia was obliterated, as was most of everything within thirty-five kilometers. The United States was again leaderless and without a central government. Millions were estimated to have died instantly, and millions more were sure to in the following days. A few minutes after the explosion, another live web video surfaced. The world had only twelve hours left to submit to my lordship.

"Weapons hot," I said, flicking off the safety of my M-4.

"Weapons hot." everyone said.

It was now nine o'clock, and we were all geared up and ready to move out. The streets were empty, and the curfew was in full effect. "Lead the way, SD fourteen," I said.

"Alright, we have one kilometer and one hour, so let's take our time and check our six. No mistakes," Moonwalker said, opening the bedroom window. "Cover me." He climbed out the window and ran between two buildings across the street. Once Moonwalker gave us the all-clear sign, we ran across the street to join him. We darted in and out of alleyways and across streets for several minutes, avoiding roving patrols until we reached a service tunnel entrance.

Taking a knee behind the corner of a store, I scanned the streets for any hostiles. The infrared vision system of the HUD in my helmet lit up the night like it was day, and wherever I pointed my gun, a small crosshair would follow it in my field of vision along with the range to target, bullet trajectory, wind, and other ballistic data. It was a very impressive system.

"Why do I feel dirty right now?" Fire whispered.

"Thy belongeth to thee most wanted terrorist group in thy world," Guard said.

"You're an international terrorist. Fire, deal with it," Moonwalker said.

"Are you almost done yet, space cowboy?" Fire said.

Thirty seconds later, Moonwalker removed the lid of the service tunnel, and we climbed down. "Keep your eyes peeled, men. They may have soldiers with dogs down here," he said.

I turned on the side-mounted, tactical infrared flashlight on the side of my gun. "Shoot to kill," I said. "No witnesses."

"Roger that," Guard said.

"Man, I can't believe what's going on," Fire said. "Three major terrorist attacks in three days, and a nuclear bomb wipes out twenty-five square miles of Washington DC?!"

"Stay focused, SD thirteen," Moonwalker said.

A short while later, we emerged from a storm drainpipe in the middle of nowhere. We kneeled in the ditch for cover. We were about a kilometer southwest outside of Phoenix. I glanced at my watch. Eleven fifty-five, Eastern Time.

"So, where are we headed?" Fire said.

"You're on a need-to-know basis only, SD thirteen," Moonwalker said.

Guard and I chuckled. "Casa Grande, our original destination," I said.

"Oh hell, and we're traveling by foot?!" Fire said.

"Bingo," I said.

"Your feet hurting will be the last thing on your mind; come here soon," Guard said.

We all exchanged glances. "Wait," Fire said. "What did you just say?"

"Yeah, your whole voice changed," I said.

"I figure I'd let the cat out of the bag," Guard said.

"So you can speak, like English?!" Fire shook his head, smiling.

"Surprise?!" Guard said. "Us pirates and knights had a running bet to see how long we could keep up the rouse. Pirate was the only clue we wanted to give ya."

Everyone laughed, but we quickly quieted down. The wind was beginning to pick up, and the clouds were growing darker by the minute.

Moonwalker nodded at me, so I nodded back. I wish the Icemen weren't so secretive about who they were or where they had come from. I would have liked to know them better.

Fire was stabbing the dirt with his knife. He was a great friend, but this war was taking its toll on him. He should be at home with his daughter. She needs him now.

Guard was kneeling with his back against the storm pipe, and his head hung low. This will be the second time he'd witness the world's end. He was a die-hard warrior and a true hero, though I wonder if he knew that Calignosity was immortal.

The hair on the back of my neck stood on end. Mana permeated the air.

A deep red, rolling fire began to consume the clouds above Phoenix and spread across the sky in all directions. A massive column of fire then shot down from the heavens and pierced the heart of the city. Smoke rose high into the air from the burning buildings. A second or two later, the blazing column of fire emitted a faint black energy that washed over the entire land like a shock wave. In the blink of an eye, the black energy had vaporized everything from trees and people to cars and skyscrapers within one kilometer of the column. The ground shook ever so slightly as the black energy passed over us.

The column began to expand and slowly form an enormous ring of fire that spanned hundreds of meters in diameter around a swirling black vortex of nothingness.

Loud cries and shrill shrieks from the black depths of the portal shattered the silence of the night and turned my blood to ice. In a span of ten fiery minutes, a new era had dawned.

Emerging from the portal in droves of tens of thousands were red-skinned devils with giant black, bat-like wings and enormous dragons over two hundred meters in length with ram-like horns and sharp spikes along their spines.

Following them were countless other flying creatures for whom I had no names. I could only imagine the monstrosities that traveled on foot. Screams from the city began to fill the air.

"Come on, we must hide from their eyes," Guard said, scrambling back into the tunnel.

"I used to think that seeing our mother ship descending through the atmosphere was a display of power, but no, this is true power," Moonwalker said. His eyes were fixated on the portal.

"Yeah," I muttered.

"So this is what the end of the world looks like, huh?" Fire said.

Guard grabbed my shoulder and pulled me towards the pipe. "We must hide now."

I took a deep breath and slowly let it out. The hideous cries of certain death were growing louder.

"Come on, men, into the tunnel," I said, reluctantly taking my eyes off the swarms of creatures and climbing into the sewer pipe.

For what seemed like an eternity, hours, we hid in the drainage pipe until the last of the monstrosities had flown past us. "They're heading west towards California; we'll follow in their wake," I said.

"East is always a great choice," Fire said.

"That was a scouting wave. The second wave is destroying the city as we speak." Guard said. "You cannot hide from them, only run."

Off in the distance, fires were erupting all over the city. The knot in my stomach tightened.

"We'll head for Mesa to gather whatever supplies we can and head west," I said. "We'll figure out what to do from there."

"Supplies are a great idea, but we should also get ourselves a few good vehicles, too," Moonwalker said.

"Let's move out then," I said.

Thirty minutes of fast-paced running later, we were standing in an alley behind a small convenience store on the outskirts of Mesa. I could hear heavy gunfire in the distance. "Take only high energy, non-perishable food items that pertain to survival only," Moonwalker said.

"You've got three minutes, so let's make it quick and quiet," I said.

Once Moonwalker had disabled the back door alarm system and lock, he opened the door, and we walked inside. Fire immediately began to clear shelf after shelf of whatever into his duffle bag, and whatever didn't make it in ended up on the floor with a loud ruckus. "Didn't you hear me, Fire?" Moonwalker whispered.

"Yeah, loud and clear, but if I'm going to be living in a post-apocalyptic era, I'm going to want to remember what a Twinkie tastes like."

"Twinkies are the last thing you need to worry about surviving," I said.

"Then keep it down, buddy. We don't want to draw any unwanted attention," Moonwalker said.

Several minutes later, we each had a duffle bag full of supplies. We then began to prowl the back roads for a suitable vehicle to steal.

"This Land Rover is in good condition," Fire said, peering into the driver's side window.

We were standing out in the middle of a dead-end street, completely exposed. If anyone were to peek out their bedroom window, we'd be busted, but I guess subtlety didn't really matter anymore. The inferno in the sky and the blazing portal were clearly the bigger threat. Devils and dragons and flying monsters were still pouring out from it.

"No. We need a truck," Moonwalker said, continuing down the street.

"Oh, yeah, that's right," Fire said. "You weigh a fucking ton."

"Why is it so quiet here," I said, looking around at all the houses. "Why isn't everyone fleeing this town?!"

"I don't know, man, but it's starting to freak me out," Fire said.

A car turned onto our street, its tires screeching, and sped past us. "Someone just woke up and smelled the coffee!" Moonwalker said.

"We'd be wise to follow. Time is getting short," Guard said.

Fire began turning circles, frantically looking around. "Something big is lighting up my thermal," he said.

"Me too," Guard said.

The trees at the end of the street were rustling. "Lighten your load, men," Moonwalker yelled.

"Run!"

Dropping our duffle bags, we ran toward the heart of Mesa, sprinting across lawns and darting through alleyways. The streets began flooding with cars, and people ran everywhere. They were here.

"Holy shit!" Fire cried out.

Monstrous creatures, the size of small buildings, were picking up and hurling the cars that lined the jammed highway to and fro. Dragons swooped from above and blasted hundreds of cars simultaneously with a single fiery breath. Automatic gunfire and explosions mixed with screams filled the night air. The apocalypse had begun.

"We need to find a secure and defendable place to hide," Moonwalker said.

"A bank vault?" Fire said.

"Whatever it is, let us move quickly!" Guard shouted, pointing to his right.

An armored Hum-V was racing down the street towards us when two bony four, four-clawed feet tore into the roof of the vehicle and hurled it into a nearby storefront. Shattered glass and broken concrete flew everywhere. The poor gunner on the vehicle roof was killed instantly, crushed by the flipped Hummer. The four soldiers inside, however, were unscathed.

Landing on its feet, its bat-like wings folding, the red-skinned Devil turned to face us. It was an enormous, muscular creature standing over seven meters tall with sharp, bony facial features and a long, spade-tipped tail. Saliva was dripping off its oversized canines. A faint black aura, flickering like flames, emanated from its body and caused everything that it touched to rapidly decay and decompose.

Without hesitation, Moonwalker ran across the street and put a single .50 caliber slug between the Devil's red eyes, but the round disintegrated before impact. "Let's move!" he shouted, diving through the glass front of an office building.

Guard followed right behind him, and so did I, but I stopped halfway across the street. Fire was still in the alleyway, sitting on the ground.

The four soldiers were just beginning to crawl out of the wreckage when the Devil turned its attention toward them. The souls of the marines began to separate from their bodies like mirror images of themselves and slowly distort into thin black threads into the creature's mouth. The lifeless marines fell limp to the ground.

I ran back to Fire and knelt beside him. "What's wrong? You going to be all right?" I said. The ground shook under my feet.

"It's over, man; we can't survive this shit," Fire said. Gunshots echoed throughout the streets, and more blood-curdling screams filled the air.

A Scaled-Hound beast was looming at the far end of the alley. Blood covered its red face and was dripping onto the ground. Raising my M-4. I unloaded ten rounds into the bull-sized dog, hitting it in the face and chest. Bone and bits of flesh splattered everywhere as the animal collapsed in a pool of blood. Its thick, scaly hide was no match for my depleted uranium hailstorm.

I went to speak into my transceiver, but all I heard was static. I used hand signals to tell Moonwalker that we'd meet up with them at Casa Grande. I then cast lightning reflexes, giant's toughness, and stone skin. It was going to be a long night.

"We have to get the hell out of here, Fire," I said. "Now, let's move!"

Several people were sprinting down the street while a large, pale-skinned humanoid beast chased them. A brief moment later, the Butcher grabbed two of the people and tore them to pieces with incredible violence. Their dead bodies then began to crawl and slither their way down the street. Their animated guts followed close behind.

After helping Fire to his feet, we ran to the end of the alley. A few creatures were ravaging two cars that had crashed into each other in the middle of the intersection, thirty meters to our right. Brown and slimy, three-foot-long baby maggot worms were devouring the dead inside. There were monsters everywhere I looked.

"There!" Fire said, pointing at the Safeway across the street from us. "We can hide there in the freezers."

We ran across the street and were about halfway across the parking lot when a huge brown tentacle the size of a tree trunk with a razor-sharp tooth-filled mouth at the end whipped across the store's roof and disappeared behind the trees. I stopped running and glanced over at Fire, who had also stopped.

"Shall we go hide somewhere else?" Fire said.

"Yeah, let's go somewhere else," I said, taking a few steps back. The ground shook again.

A gigantic monster that towered above the treetops on four massive legs came crashing through the Safeway as if it was built out of Legos. The creature's brown body was covered in thick, bony plates and had two rows of spines lining its back. Four long and straight horns protruded from its bony skull just above its four yellow eyes while two tentacles on the sides of its mouth flailed around.

"Run!" I yelled, casting haste on both of us.

We ran down the street with amazing speed, and then Fire collapsed violently to the pavement as if something had fallen on him. Pieces of his backpack and armor flew everywhere. My thermal showed a bony white creature clawing and gnawing at him. It was a Shadow Stalker. Raising my M4, I riddled the creature with a good ten rounds or so and watched it slump to the ground.

Fire stood and picked up his M-16A4 and looked at me. His backpack was shredded, and his survival gear was scattered across the street. "I take it we don't have enough time to pick this shit up?" he said. I shook my head. "Didn't think so."

Crawling, hobbling, and running if they could down the street towards us were dozens of zombies animated by pure mana. Already, thousands of people had died, and more were dying by the minute. Fire unloaded an entire magazine into the fast-approaching horde, but not one zombie dropped. I fired one round and struck one square in the forehead, blowing most of its head off, but it still kept running.

"What the hell?" Fire shouted while reloading.

Jets roared overhead, and loud explosions rocked the city. Every light went black. "Come on, let's move!" I yelled.

Again, we ran from street to street, alley to alley. The giant monstrosity that had crashed through the Safeway was now only two blocks behind us, destroying building after building with its monstrous limbs and tentacles.

Crawling out from an alleyway, a man grabbed a hold of Fire's boot. "H-help m-meh-me," he said. The man's intestines were lying on the ground in a pool of blood.

Fire rolled the man onto his back and assessed his injuries. "You're going to be okay, man, just hang in there," he said.

The intestines, like a loaded spring, shot around Fire's neck.

Instinctively, I jumped back, almost tripping over the curb. Drawing my knife, I cut the intestines off Fire's neck and watched in disgust as the other half wiggled its way into a hole in the man's stomach. The man started to convulse violently, with blood gushing from his mouth. A brief moment later, the man stopped moving.

Fire scrambled away from the body while frantically clawing at his neck, trying to remove the intestines that were no longer there. "Fucking hell, man! Fucking hell!" He was breathing heavily through his respirator. "This shits too much, man! Too fucking much!"

"Come on, man," I said, helping him to his feet.

Walking down the alley, we climbed a fence near the end and continued down another back alley. A large fireball lit up the night. A jet had just crashed.

Peeking around the corner of a building, I saw a group of people running through the street. Several hideous monsters were chasing after them and gaining on them quickly. I wanted to help them, but there wasn't anything that I could do.

Four skinny, black, long-bodied creatures with two legs and arms and four incredibly long tentacles with sharp hooks on the ends were trying to claw their way into a car that had crashed into a stop light twenty meters to my left. The woman and two children inside were screaming.

"We have to get the hell out of here!" Fire said. "We have to hide! There's just too many of them!"

Fire was right. There were too many of them. Running down the street with blood dripping from their horns and claws were two gray-skinned Chargers. They had just finished killing off the group of people who were running down the street. A block to my right, slithering through the intersection, was a forty-meter-long Night Crawler followed by a vaguely humanoid black shadow: a Wraith of the Undead.

Blood-curling screams were now a constant background noise amidst the roars of monsters and gunfire. Buildings were burning, and the streets were packed with wrecked cars and debris. The smell of iron was thick in the air.

Casting hammer hands, I smashed a good-sized hole into the building to my left. "Come on, we can hide in here," I said.

Once inside, we quickly and quietly searched the grocery store for someplace to hide. We found a small storage room in the back, so we holed up there and locked the door behind us.

I took a seat on a box and flipped up the visor of my helmet. "You think we'll get hazard pay for this?" I said.

Fire laughed tentatively. "Do you really think that we can stop all this?"

My hands were trembling from adrenaline. "I don't know, Fire. I don't know," I said. " I just know that we're the only ones who can."

"If we don't lose our cool."

I smiled. "Yeah."

"I'm sorry."

"It's alright, man. You're still a Goodguy, and that counts for something."

Chunks of concrete flew into the room like shrapnel as a red, five-clawed hand punched through the wall behind Fire. Jumping back and spinning around, Fire sprayed a short burst through the gaping hole. Another claw punched through the wall, blasting more pieces of concrete into the room, and with one more hit, the shelving fell over along with the wall on top of it.

I cast ogre's strength, grabbed the metal shelving along the wall before me, ripped it from the bolts on the floor, and tossed it aside. A red-skinned and incredibly muscular humanoid creature rushed into the room and raked Fire across the chest with its elongated claws. Several scales from Fire's armor were ripped off, but besides being knocked prone, he looked fine.

The door to the room burst into flames and swung open. A chokingly intense heat filled the air as a large fire entered the room. A Fire Elemental. The metal shelves began to sag and warp while the boxes and crates spontaneously burst into flames. The three-meter-tall hulking Ripper climbed atop Fire, sunk its oversized spiked teeth into his shoulder, and hurled him into the wall with tremendous force. I cast hammer hands and crushed the wall before me to dust, which caught the Ripper's attention.

Standing up, Fire raced through the hole in the wall the Ripper had made while I turned around and ran out mine. Smoke was rising off my smoldering armor.

After rounding a corner and sprinting down an alleyway, something slashed at my back. I fell face-first onto the dirt. I tried to scramble to my feet and draw my katana, but the beast grabbed my left ankle and slammed me into the nearest building. My visor cracked from the impact. My head was swimming.

Again, I reached for my katana, but the Ripper had jumped on top of me, tearing into me in a frenzy. Not only was it faster than me, but it was stronger, even with all my enhancement spells. Pinning me down, it bit into my neck and ripped off my helmet in its relentless assault. I visualized the formula for the spell protection.

The Ripper let out a roar as numerous bullets tore into its overly muscular back. I saw Fire standing in the middle of the street beyond the alley. He was spraying the Ripper with lead one moment and something else down the street the next. The ground trembled.

With five hundred kilos of death sitting on me, I could spare no mana, so I cast electric aura and sent two mana bolts into the Ripper's body. With blood oozing from its nostril slits and ear holes, the Ripper stumbled up and off me.

I kipped to my feet and drew my wispy black katana. Blue lightning was dancing around me and leaping several meters off my body. Charging me, the Ripper clumsily swiped at my head, getting electrocuted in the process. With a gentle but quick swing, my blade passed through its arm before it could strike, and while it convulsed from the electricity, I quickly spun around and decapitated it with a smooth stroke. The Ripper collapsed to the ground while its dark energy flowed into my veins.

A humongous claw the size of a small house crashed through the roof of the building to my right, showering me with debris. Massive tentacles with mouths were swaying above me. I don't think that it could see me in the alley.

Reloading a fresh mag, Fire sprayed the monster above with lead and cast a fireball at it. "Over here, ya big son of a bitch!" Fire yelled, backing up down the street. "Come and get some!" The tree trunk-sized tentacles whipped overhead towards Fire as the gigantic monster's claws crashed through the nearby buildings as though they were built of sand.

The Bracus Slayer stood over fifty meters tall at the shoulders and was covered in bony plates over three meters thick, some of which had deep holes and cracks from missile and artillery strikes. Its massive head was shaped like a flat-faced dog with four reptilian-like yellow eyes. Its mouth was filled with teeth the size of sedans.

What the hell are you doing, Fire? Run! One of the tentacles on the side of the Bracus Slayer's mouth reached towards Fire. Standing his ground, unloading hot lead, Fire cast fireball after fireball at the beast while simultaneously spitting out a continuous flame that soared twenty meters into the air and spread half as high. The skin of its tentacles was bubbling, and the fireballs had blown off chunks of bony plating. Dragon's breath was an impressive spell, but the monster seemed unaffected.

One of the tooth-filled tentacles engulfed Fire's right leg as he tried to jump out of the way. It lifted him in the air towards its mouth. Looking down at me, Fire pulled the pins on two grenades on his chest. My heart sank deep into my stomach.

The monster severed him in half with one bite and then swallowed the rest of him. A brief moment later, smoke billowed from out its nostrils, and huge drops of blood oozed out of its mouth and splashed onto the street below. It continued walking.

CHAPTER THIRTY

Behind me, just down the street, a horde of zombies was quickly approaching, and with them was a huge, five-meter-tall Flesh Golem. It was composed of nothing but human corpses and body parts. Reaching down, it picked up a dead man and compacted it into its own body. It was utterly disgusting.

Slithering out from around a building and through the crowd of zombies was a twenty-five-meter-long Maggot Worm. Trailing it were three Butchers and a monstrous creature with dozens of protruding eyestalks and several elongated limbs with needle-like stingers. I choked back my vomit. The terrors of Ethereal were never-ending.

Walking away from me down the other end of the street was a well-built, bare-chest man wearing only a black execution hood and burlap pants held up by a piece of rope. A swath of faint, swirling black energy followed in his wake, and whatever the energy touched, from the street's pavement to the bodies that littered it, rapidly crumbled and rotted away. He was carrying an immensely large, single-bladed axe in his left hand and the hand of a young girl in his right. The girl was dancing, humming, and skipping alongside him, wearing a plain white nightgown. She was one of Goresavices murder victims and is now a Queen of the Damned.

Ahead of them walked a tall, gaunt, black-skinned creature. A man with a broken leg was crawling on the ground before it, trying desperately to escape it. Opening its toothless mouth, the creature inhaled deeply, drawing in the man's soul. He died with his face frozen in terror.

The young girl laughed and pointed at the sky. Slowly, the fiery black clouds began to swirl while the ground below started to bubble and froth like a thick soup. Everything from the interstate and cars to buildings and bridges was melting into a grayish-brown sludge. Trees folded over like putty while the flesh of those caught within the spells destruction sloughed off. A thick green gas burst from the bubbling ground and rose high in the air, rapidly corroding the helicopters and jets flying above. Soon, they came crashing down or exploded in mid-air. The power of the spell that the girl had cast was insane. In a matter of seconds, kilometer after kilometer of the city had been reduced to a thick gray sludge. I could only imagine how many thousands of people just died.

A cold chill raced up my spine. I was defenseless against such power, helpless against so many. All I can do is survive. That's what I must do. I sprinted across the street behind me and in between two buildings. I then ran through a clearing, hopped over a guardrail, and peeked around the corner of a house.

An enormously fat monster with two huge, squat legs and two human-like arms sat in the middle of the backyard. The creature didn't really have a head, just a gaping, tooth-filled mouth with two yellow eyes above it. Using its long black tongue, the Putrefier picked up a man from out of a black tar-like substance that covered the grass before it and put him in its mouth. I could hear the man's bone breaking as it chewed.

I again struggled to hold back my vomit. The night's bloody carnage was getting too much for me to stomach, and this topped it all. I stepped back and headed down the desolate neighborhood street, and surprisingly enough, nearly every house was intact. There were a few burned-out cars and bloodstains along the sidewalk, but other than that, the neighborhood was in pristine condition. The city, however, was burning.

Despite the flaming clouds overhead, it was getting lighter out, and a calming silence filled the air. Hopping over a fence, I snuck through a backyard and peeked through the window of a house. Nothing was in the living room, so I broke the window and climbed inside. The front door was open and hanging on a single hinge. Blood splatters stained the walls, and bloody drag marks led from the kitchen to the front door, but there were no bodies. Walking down the hallway, I slowly pushed open a door to my right and went inside.

Sitting on the bed with her back against the wall and her knees held tightly to her chest was a little girl no older than five. Tears poured from her pretty blue eyes and streaked down her chin, but she uttered not a noise.

Closing the door, I looked under the bed and checked the closet for anything evil. The girl followed me with her eyes. "Are the monsters all gone?" she whispered.

I sheathed my katana and sat down next to her. Wrapping my arms around her, I held her closely. "They're all gone now," I said. "You're safe. We're safe."

She snuggled closer and looked up at me. "Can I go to sleep now?"

I sighed, "You can go to sleep now. Just don't look into the light."

Far off and above the city of Phoenix, a blinding flash of light lit up the night. I held her tightly, hunkered down below the window, and protected her with every spell I had.

With Lily's hand in mine, we walked down the middle of the street towards a future unknown. The city of my birthplace had been reduced to a smoldering heap of rubble, and in just over eight hours, the whole of the world had been conquered. Not even our most powerful of weapons could stop them.

The clouds were still on fire, and tens of thousands of creatures continued to pour out of the blazing portal. It was now up to us to do what Merlin had called us to do-destroy Calignosity.

The end of the world had come swiftly and suddenly like a thief in the night, but little did I know that the end was just beginning. Now, all I can do is fight it until my dying breath under blood-red skies.

Don't miss out!

Visit the website below and you can sign up to receive emails whenever Thomas Woods publishes a new book. There's no charge and no obligation.

https://books2read.com/r/B-A-QGHLD-RJAEG

BOOKS 2 READ

Connecting independent readers to independent writers.